HAUNTED LEGENDS

EDITED BY

Ellen Datlow and Nick Mamatas

TOR®

A Tom Doherty Associates Book

NEW YORK

HAUNTED LEGENDS

Copyright © 2010 by Ellen Datlow and Nick Mamatas

A Tor Book
Published by Tom Doherty Associates, LLC
175 Fifth Avenue
New York, NY 10010

www.tor-forge.com

Tor® is a registered trademark of Tom Doherty Associates, LLC.

ISBN 978-0-7653-2300-2 (hardcover)
ISBN 978-0-7653-2301-9 (trade paperback)

First Edition: September 2010

Printed in the United States of America

0 9 8 7 6 5 4 3 2 1

Copyright Acknowledgments

To Olivia Flint
—N. M.

To my parents, Nathan and Doris Datlow
—E. D.

Contents

HAUNTED LEGENDS

Saying Boo: Why We Like Ghost Stories

There ain't no such thing as ghosts.

Ghost stories, we have plenty. They're easy to find, too. Every town has some legends—lakes made of tears, phantom hitchhikers, mean ol' men or ladies too ornery for heaven and too obnoxious for hell, and houses that resist occupation with all their supernatural might. There are the ghostly folktales as well, that serve as reminders to keep one's children in one's sight at all times lest they end up eaten. Of course, some of these stories are also warnings *to* children to beware strangers or get enough sleep. Ghost stories even evolve into modern urban legends, which have their own social purposes. "Stay away from that fast-food restaurant, you'll regret it" is one.

The ghost story doesn't even necessarily require a ghost. In "The Ash-Tree" by M. R. James, there is a curse and a witch and "an enormous spider, veinous and seared," but no real ghost. Even the spiders, despite their gigantism—"the size of a man's head"—aren't truly supernatural. They cannot travel much farther than the titular tree in which they live, so the curse is easily avoided by staying out of the room with the tree-facing window, and they die in flames like any other sort of everyday arachnid. Most ghosts aren't so easy to get rid of, because of what they represent: regret, nostalgia, hunger for another chance to get it right, and warnings to the curious. So we keep telling stories to one another, and we keep telling ourselves that they're just stories. True stories.

There are enough ghost stories out there, and enough desire for them, that pretty much every locality and region has its own cottage industry dedicated to publishing the local variations. Sadly, most of these books of "true" ghost stories tend to be . . . bad. The local university folklorist can't write much more than term papers on the local ghosts. The "paranormal investigator" with his electronic stud finder recalibrated to find ghosts instead of pieces of wood, hell, he can barely *think,* much less write a compelling story. It wasn't high technology or modern rationality that exiled most ghost stories to books nobody reads—it was sheer bad writing. Most of the short stories just didn't scare us anymore. The same way every city and town has been rationalized, bureaucratized, and Starbuckized into a homogeneous territory of tedium, the ghost story, too, has been rendered safe for sale to daytrippers, safe for presentation alongside "local" taffy (made centrally in a giant factory a thousand miles away) and the world's largest ball of twine.

And yet, ghost stories cannot ever be made completely safe, because we are not ever safe. There are old houses one shouldn't enter, hitchhikers one shouldn't stop for, bits of forest a little too easy to get turned around in. Children wander off, and sometimes they don't come back, but those innocent photos on the milk cartoons and the MISSING continue to haunt. And even the most complacent members of the bourgeoisie have their fortunes, and often their homes, built on piles of metaphorical bones, if not always real ones. There are things we still don't know, though we know there are no ghosts and no monsters. Ghosts are in the gaps. Life is still haunted by death. But the stale, easily digested stories won't suffice. Enter *Haunted Legends.*

Our concept was simple: ask some of the best writers of horror and dark fantasy in the world to choose their favorite "true" regional ghost story, and to rescue it from the cobwebs of the local tourist gift shop or academic journal. The Double-Face Woman, the fox spirits of Vietnam, the specter of communism still haunting Russia in the form of Comrade Beria's ghost, we've got 'em. The famed vampires of Rhode Island, the haunted amusement park you may not have ever heard of if you're not from the Pacific Northwest, Australian shipwrecks, and the Indian ghost city of Fatehpur Sikri, we've got them, too. There ain't no such thing as ghosts, but warnings to the curious, of those we have plenty.

Boo!

—*Nick Mamatas*

RICHARD BOWES

Knickerbocker Holiday

Richard Bowes has written five novels, the most recent of which is the Nebula Award–nominated From the Files of the Time Rangers. *His most recent short-fiction collection is* Streetcar Dreams and Other Midnight Fancies *from PS Publications. He has won the World Fantasy, Lambda, International Horror Guild, and Million Writers Awards.*

Recent and forthcoming stories appear in The Magazine of Fantasy & Science Fiction, Electric Velocipede, Clarkesworld, *and* Fantasy *magazines and in the* Del Rey Book of Science Fiction and Fantasy, Year's Best Gay Stories 2008, Best Science Fiction and Fantasy, The Beastly Bride, Lovecraft Unbound, Fantasy Best of the Year 2009, Year's Best Fantasy, Best Horror of the Year, *and* Naked City *anthologies. Most of these stories are chapters in his novel in progress,* Dust Devil on a Quiet Street.

His home page is www.rickbowes.com.

Last Sunday night the Dutchman flew, the Headless Horseman rolled in from Sleepy Hollow. It happened when I paid a visit that was in part nostalgia, but in larger part morbid curiosity, to a corner of my degenerate youth. I even kissed the fingertips of a very bad old habit of mine and told myself it was for memory's sake.

A bunch of fellow survivors and I were hanging out in a tacky New York City bar with strong roots in our past. The gathering followed the kind of ceremony one gets to attend at a certain age; we'd just cleaned out the apartment of a late acquaintance.

Eddie Ackers was the deceased's name. He and I had never been close. Our tastes and interests didn't coincide and we hadn't seen each other since we'd had adjacent desks in the offices of Flying Dutchman Fashion Promotions, a small garment district ad agency, forty years before.

A couple of weeks back my friend the Major phoned and told me that Eddie had died suddenly. I assumed it was a heart attack and didn't press for details. The funeral was upstate in the Hudson Valley town he'd come from at a time that wasn't convenient for me to take off from my library job.

Then last Tuesday the Major phoned again to say that none of Eddie Ackers's ex-wives nor the son and daughter he'd produced along the way were interested in his effects. Eddie's sister was, but couldn't come down to the city. The Major seemed anxious for me to rejoin the old gang for an afternoon.

We call Barbara Lohr, Major Barbara or just the Major, because of her height, bearing, and commanding British accent. She told me, "The sister's sweet as can be but getting on in age, as we all will. You should have seen the Dutch church and the graveyard where Eddie was laid away—utter Sleepy Hollow. And," she added, "after we've done the right thing, I think we may all go out and get a bit sentimental."

A lot of my memories of Flying Dutchman Fashion Promotions and our boss, Bud Van Brunt, are far from pleasant. But recalling those days I felt there were loose ends, things that still bothered me. Since I don't drink, I brought along some Percocet left over from a recent dental episode. Of course I don't do drugs anymore either, but, hey, no one's perfect.

Sunday afternoon six of us gathered in Eddie's apartment. The Major I see all the time. Jay Glass writes music criticism for the *Wall Street Journal.* He and I have friends and interests in common, and have run into each other over the years. I'd come to the conclusion that Jay wasn't gay or straight, wasn't interested in music or anything but being at or near the center of attention.

The others were little Mimsey Friedman who writes fashion columns for *Harper's Bazaar,* Douglas Lotts who left the agency to go to graduate school and still teaches college in New Jersey, and Dawn Boothby, a girl from a good family who has a nice career in public relations. It had been awhile since I'd seen any of them.

The Major had organized the sorting and boxing, ordered pizza, and set us to work as we arrived. "Ceremonies for the dead, such as this, are the only real rituals in circles like ours," she announced. "Births, the few that occur in our set, are preplanned with hereditary diseases taken into account, sex selected, time and place of delivery finalized. Weddings, well they're pretty much just place markers in this day and age. But death, oh death, my dears, that's often a surprise and nearly always very final." Major Barbara writes long, critically celebrated fantasy novels and it shows.

We made it through a large chunk of Eddie Acker's possessions: bagged the clothes for the Salvation Army; boxed kitchen appliances, golf clubs, and trout fishing equipment to be shipped to his sister; and tossed away magazines with names like *Man Eater* featuring young ladies wearing lion and tiger masks and nothing else. None of us had seen anything quite like them.

As we worked, we talked a lot about our old boss, that legendary horror Bud Van Brunt.

"Satan in a Brooks Brothers gray flannel suit," the Major said.

"The scent of sulfur barely hidden by the Vitalis aftershave and gin breath," someone added.

When I thought of Bud Van Brunt, instead of his round, flushed face and big bald dome, I saw a pumpkin lit from within by flames. That image made me go into the bathroom and take half a Percocet. For the next couple of hours things had a nice, warm glow.

Eddie Ackers hardly got mentioned at all. "Poor Eddie," someone remarked when we were done packing him up. "Kind of an empty life."

"He endured ten or fifteen years at Flying Dutchman Fashion Promotions, and when Van Brunt was finally dragged off to hell, Eddie took over the business. I'm sure he considered that worth the price of his soul," Jay Glass replied.

"He was some kind of relative of Van Brunt's. A nephew-in-law, or something," I said.

"What do you say we adjourn?" asked the Major.

"Where to?" I asked.

"The Knickerbocker Holiday," she said. "Or 'Knicks' as they call it now. It's where dear Eddie breathed his last."

"Isn't that a little macabre?" Mimsey Friedman asked.

"He would have wanted us to go there. He may even be waiting for us," she added. Mimsey flinched, Jay Glass grimaced, but the rest of us chuckled.

It was already dark when we hit the street. The place where Eddie Ackers had last lived was one of those high-rise monstrosities recently sprouted along Sixth Avenue in the Twenties. "It's always a cozy occasion when you've beat the reaper and are in a celebratory mood," I said. By then I'd taken the other half of the Percocet.

A bit farther uptown, just below where Broadway crosses Sixth Avenue and forms Herald Square, is a block of low buildings that the wreckers have passed by. In their midst stands an ancient four-story, wide-front building with a huge neon KNICKS sign hanging out front.

"The building dates back to the 1840s. It got landmarked as a historic spot so it can't be torn down," said Jay Glass, who'd obviously done research. "That probably keeps anyone from trying to redevelop the rest of the block."

When we all were young and Manhattan was wonderment, the Knickerbocker Holiday Tavern on the outskirts of the jumping, vibrant Garment

District was an oasis for junior copywriters and assistant art directors. Back then the Knickerbocker had a colonial motif and the waitresses wore Dutch bonnets and wooden clogs that we'd all found delightfully campy.

Now the Garment District, with its thousands of employees and streets choked with racks of clothes, is a fading memory. And all that's left of Dutch New York is an occasional street or building with a name like Gansevoort, Stuyvesant, Roosevelt, Astor, or Vanderbilt.

We stood on the sidewalk and read the two brass plaques that flanked the door. One said, "On this site dating back to Dutch Colonial times was a roadhouse and coach stop." The other told us, "When Herald Square was the theater district, this building housed The Knickerbocker Holiday Tavern, an actors' gathering spot. George M. Cohan is said to have written 'Give My Regards to Broadway' while sitting at the bar."

Inside, KNICKS was all leather and steel. One large-screen TV showed the Giants playing football in West Coast sunshine. The other had guys in blazers with network emblems on them working out the meaning of the baseball playoffs. The sound was off. Sunday evenings were obviously a down time, the place was big and kind of empty.

We took a table in a secluded spot in the rear and looked around for something we could recognize. "They still have a couple of artifacts from the old roadhouse," the Major said. "That added to the charm of the old Knickerbocker. Here they just look out of place."

"Old New York was in no way charming," Jay said. "The American Revolution involved skullduggery and double-dealing, families divided, plenty of traitors and spies. Aaron Burr and Benedict Arnold both slept in the old roadhouse."

"Together?" several of us wanted to know. Jay grimaced at our stupidity and shut up. In retrospect we should have let him talk.

Our server, a dark young lady with long black hair, appeared, announced herself as Benicia, and took our drink orders. I ordered club soda. Major Barbara looked up at the last minute and said to her, "Pardon my asking. But by any chance were you on duty when there was an unfortunate episode with a patron a couple of weeks ago?"

Benicia's head jerked in surprise. "Yes. It was creepy but I'm sorry for him. He came in from the street, went right past the hostess. Happy Hour is a busy time and the place was crowded. The guy was flushed bright red and he was walking funny. I thought he was already drunk. The manager was headed his way and then the customer went flat on his face. They called EMS but he was dead. How did you hear about it?"

"We knew him. His name was Eddie Ackers."

"I'm so sorry," the server said.

"Where did he fall?" asked Major Barbara.

"Right about where you're sitting."

When she left, Doug Lotts asked, "What on earth led him to come here to die?"

"This would be the perfect spot for a Van Brunt relative to seek out in his last moments. I would imagine it has the strongest magic in the neighborhood," said the Major.

"Magic?" I asked, looking around. "Where?"

"Just because a sacred place has been defiled does not mean it's without power." She smiled an eldritch smile and I wondered what game was being played.

"Poor Eddie," Mimsey remarked. "Remember how Van Brunt used to ream him out in front of everyone?"

"Was there anybody the Flying Dutchman didn't do that to?" I asked, and remembered a face like a fist being thrust into mine and the words "Make the suit copy read like a man wrote it, you little pussy."

"Each and every one of us was told we were fired at least once a week," Dawn Boothby said.

Van Brunt's specialty was hiring those who could be had cheaply—kids in need of experience like my friends, people like Ackers who had been on the skids, young screwups like me who were being given one last chance in the Garment District.

His brochure described the company as "An Agency on Seventh Avenue and in the Heart of the U.S." What we did was provide flashy copy and artwork for dreary little department stores in the places around the country most of us had run away from.

Behind his back, everyone in the business called Van Brunt "The Flying Dutchman." His temper, even in an industry whose foundations rested on argument and insult, was a legend. At least once a day he'd threaten castration and death to someone he was talking with on the phone.

Jason said, "Remember how he'd end a conversation by screaming, 'It'll be hard for you to walk with my size eleven shoe lodged in your fucking colon'?"

"Dear God, what a bottom-feeder he was," the Major remarked. "And we were what he fed on."

The drinks arrived and for a couple of minutes there was silence.

Then Dawn Boothby asked, "Remember the two-page apron spread Van Blunt had me do for that place down in Georgia? I still remember coming in one morning just after I'd started to work for him and on my desk were pictures of these tacky aprons and a note from the Dutchman telling me that I should make the copy sing. About aprons! Who ever imagined that people still wore them? And what song do you sing about aprons? He must have demanded a hundred rewrites."

I caught a moment of amusement on the Major's face. She and Mimsey exchanged a glance. The apron ad was a joke they had played on Dawn. After all this time she still hadn't figured that out.

To change the subject, I said, "Remember when we discovered that the villain in the 'Legend of Sleepy Hollow,' the bully who chases Ichabod Crane out of town, is called Brom Bones but his real name is Van Brunt?"

"Bud talked about that in his rants," Mimsey said quietly. "How his family had money and Washington Irving had envied them and made up the story about his ancestor stealing Katrina Van Tassel. So the legend had some truth to it. On the other hand, around 1980 I was told he had died in the mental ward of a hospital and what he said could just have been insanity."

She looked troubled, and I remembered that it was an open secret back in the day that she and the Dutchman were having an affair. And I could easily imagine how awful that must have been.

Jay Glass sat beside her. They seemed to be very close and not really happy.

"Irving told his stories without any mention of the horrors of war," he said. "But the Hudson Valley town of Sleepy Hollow would have been just a few years removed from Indian raids and military occupation. The Headless Horseman was a local ghost story about a Hessian mercenary fighting for the British who lost his head to a cannonball and rode out each night to search for it."

The talk about war reminded me of one night back at the agency. Eddie Ackers and I were working very late, me trying to squeeze copy onto catalog pages and Eddie doing the picture mock-ups for a chain of department stores in the Pacific Northwest. Bud Van Brunt had left for the day but, of course, he came back, loaded. The top of his bald head was the bright scarlet it turned when he got smashed.

He immediately went after Eddie as one more of his wife's freeloading, worthless family. I kept my head down to avoid notice and because this was embarrassing.

The two fell into a quarrel about which war was tougher, WW2 or Korea. At one point Ackers said, "To be a hero in WW2 all you needed to do was get drafted. In Korea you had to die falling on a grenade to save the platoon for them to notice you."

Before Van Brunt could reply, Ackers got up and walked out saying he needed to take a break. I was surprised the Dutchman didn't tell him not to come back. But at that moment, I guess he needed him too much.

Instead he turned on me. Vietnam was at full boil at that moment, and he asked how I'd managed to dodge the draft. I'm sure he suspected they didn't want me because I was gay. He stood very close to me. Sharp as the moment it had happened, I remembered how he stuck his face near mine and whispered low, like this was a seduction, that I was a worthless pervert, a drug freak, and coward.

He was baiting me and coming on to me at the same time. I should have walked out, but I was in a chaotic living situation with a pair of people I loved, I was strung out, I needed the money. I wanted to run him through with the scissors on my desk.

Just then, some other part of his brain seemed to open up. He began talking about war and the red menace: Hessians leaping out of sewers with bayonets, commies parachuting out of the skies to conquer New York. This, too, was scary as hell and evoked pumpkin eyes lighted by candles and dark riders in the night. But it was routine; we'd all heard him do this stuff. Back then Jay Glass had said, "Past and future loop right over the present, like a skater making a figure eight on the ice." Glass had seemed fascinated by Van Brunt. That long ago night Ackers came back and said we needed to be left alone to finish the catalog.

The only part of this memory that I told to the rest of the table was, "Once I heard the Dutchman say that Mohawks were going to come down from Canada and take back New York. I was kind of impressed with his multidimensional paranoia."

"He had a bit of a time-dislocation problem. It's as if he came out of the past and into our future," said Glass.

"He'd had a very bad war," someone said. I doubted he'd had a bad war, Van Brunt had been an officer in occupied Europe and my guess was he'd enjoyed every bloody, bullying minute of it.

"And peace wasn't very satisfactory for him either," someone else added.

Then Benicia was back with another round of drinks and plates of chicken wings and fried mozzarella. I got up to look for the restroom. The Major was on her feet also and we wandered past the bar.

"Time dislocation is right," she said to me. "At first glance, with his red face and head, Van Brunt looked like a burgher in an old painting. But he had a monster inside him and when that emerged . . ." She went past the end of the very long bar and looked in a corner. "Remember this?" she asked.

Enclosed in glass, hung on the wall, was a pair of wooden Dutch doors. There was a plaque saying they were from the original roadhouse that had been torn down and replaced by this building. The doors, hundreds of years old, looked small and dingy. They had been displayed far more prominently when this was still the Knickerbocker Holiday Tavern.

"When the new owners bought the place," she said, "they had to promise to preserve certain historical aspects." Then she threw in, "You know, Jay thinks Brom Bones and his gang of night riders used to come down to the old roadhouse to raise real hell."

Shaking my head at Jay's obsession, I left her and went on to the restroom, which was modern standard issue, well lighted and with forced air to dry your hands. The old one had featured oaken stalls that could have accommodated carriage horses, and urinals so tall and deep a man could fall in and never be found.

I took a whole painkiller and chewed it for faster action. When I came out the door, I saw, on the wall just outside the kitchen, a picture that had hung behind the bar in the Knickerbocker Holiday. I'd spent lots of time studying it when I was supposed to be at work.

It showed the old inn, circa 1790 to judge from the clothes. It was a two-story building with an attic and weather vanes. A coach had pulled up in front. The coachman flirted with the maid as birds flew about in the trees, dogs lazed in the sun, the passengers filed through the Dutch doors, and fresh horses were led from the stables in back. A country church, a few scattered houses, a store, and a blacksmith's constituted a village just off Broadway, some miles north of the tiny city at the tip of Manhattan.

Staring at it, I noticed again that in the midst of all that summer light, the two center second-floor windows in the inn were both pitch dark.

"We used to sit here and wonder what lay behind those windows," Major Barbara spoke in my ear so suddenly that I jumped. "We conjectured about exotic Dutch voodoo. I remember you told me about a dream or hallucination you had about the place. Do you recall it?"

"I hadn't thought of it for a long while but it came back to me the other day when you called. In the dream I was standing outside the Knickerbocker but what I was looking at was the two-story structure from this picture. It was dark. The only light was one flickering over the door of the tavern.

"Then in the distance another light was swinging in the dark. Three toots of a horn and a night coach came rolling down Broadway. Right then a pair of lights suddenly went on in the two windows at the inn that are dark in the painting. For some reason that seemed so sinister it scared me."

A couple of details had slipped my mind but I remembered the fear.

"The old Knickerbocker was so odd, there was no problem believing that whatever was here before it was stranger still," she said. "Not like now." She gestured at the lights and flickering TV screens, a flight of wide stairs that hadn't been there in the old days. "They gutted the whole building."

We started back to the table. "They let me go upstairs in the old Knickerbocker Holiday, you know," Major Barbara told me. "They were doing repairs years ago, after you'd left the Flying Dutchman, long before this renovation. It was three stories of storage attic, basically: an amazing pile of brass spittoons, a canopied bed all chewed by rats. And one disturbing item . . ."

She trailed off. I raised my eyebrow in question.

"A large oil painting of a man in eighteenth-century Dutch burgher clothes," she whispered. "He looked exactly like Bud Van Brunt. And his expression in the picture was demonic, more twisted than the Dutchman at his worst."

I laughed and said, "Oh, please!" The Major looked very disappointed in me.

When we got back to the table, Dawn Boothby told us, "This has become a group therapy session."

Doug Lotts said, "I remember the day he insulted my copywriting, my manhood, and my taste in socks. Then, of course, he fired me. Except that time I really left and didn't go back." We all applauded

Little Mimsey Friedman downed a colorful drink. "I'd quit a perfectly great job in the promotions department at Lord and Taylor to get married. Then my first husband lost his job and never found another one, ever. To support us both I had to go looking for work. And there was *nothing*! Except, of course, for Van Brunt. A day he didn't drive me to tears was a day he considered wasted."

Everyone nodded and drank to that. Aside from Mimsey's favored position, she also knew more about fashion writing than anybody, including him. Flying Dutchman Promotions provided a weekly column, "Cut on a Bias," with fashion commentary, mild gossip, and plugs for clothes the stores were pushing.

Client stores could publish the column whole or in part in their local newspapers as advertising. Mimsey wrote that copy for a few years and used that experience as the basis for her very successful fashion career. She still does TV commentary for the spring fashion shows.

All eyes turned to me as I sipped seltzer water. "I was the hippie/faggot/junkie," I said, feeling loose and stoned. "No office was complete without one in those days." A couple of people chuckled. "Work for me was a constant round of abuse from Van Brunt. The thing that kept me coming back day after day until he finally fired me was that compared to what was happening down in the East Village where I lived, Flying Dutchman Promotions seemed calm and orderly."

Said the Major, "You would have been the very life and soul of the party if the Flying Dutchman had been a party. Myself, I needed money. Even compared to London, New York was expensive and I was working as a lowly editorial assistant. I thought everyone who worked in advertising made tons of money. Van Brunt hired me, he said, because he loved my accent and ridiculed me every day I worked there because of it. After a couple of years with him, I sold a very silly murder mystery to a publisher, walked into the office, and quit."

We went around the table and the rest added their personal stories. The Sunday-evening crowd, such as it was, had thinned out. Customers were sparse up front. The bartender and the server looked bored.

As I got up and stepped away from the table, I had the last of the pills in my hand. I wandered toward the rear, chewing it, sipping my flat soda water.

The velvet cord that would have blocked access to the upper floors hung on a hook. I went up the stairs quickly, not really thinking about what I was doing. The second floor was dimly lit but I could see a perfectly ordinary banquet/reception room. The Major was right about the building having been gutted. They must have raised the ceiling, probably taken most of the third story to do that.

The windows that would have overlooked the uninspiring streetscape were covered over. On all four walls were murals of vaguely "ye olde New York" themes: paintings of carriages and town houses, sailing ships in the harbor, all against the background of a city where church steeples still dominated the landscape. No old oils of the Dutchman were on view, however.

Then I heard a noise and looked around. A door I hadn't noticed swung open. A figure, big and bald, was backing through it: I saw Van Brunt and froze.

But that only lasted until the guy turned and was revealed as olive-skinned, possibly Latino, possibly Middle Eastern. He was burly, maybe thirty, with a shaved head and a cardboard box under one arm. He may have been the manager or maybe one of the owners.

He locked the door behind him—no doubt they used what remained of the upper floors as storage—and then saw me. "Hey, guy," the accent was hard to place. "We're closed up here."

Keeping the slight smile and careful distance of someone used to herding drunks, he gestured for me to precede him down the stairs. "Plenty of room here," he said as he walked past our table.

The Major caught all that, guessed where I'd been, and gave a satisfied little nod.

Jay Glass, waving a scotch and soda for emphasis, was saying, "I think Van Brunt had a curse handed down from Brom Bones, maybe earlier. But to him it wasn't a curse. He reveled in being as complete and utter a monster as possible. Where the ancestor won Katrina Van Tassel by evoking the Headless Horseman, he did the same with anybody who crossed his path."

The Major said, "We think of ghosts as coming from the past but maybe they exist altogether apart from Time."

The others nodded with sage, drunken understanding and I saw that the group session had gone to another place.

Mimsey Friedman spoke up. "I saw Van Brunt, maybe ten years ago." I was about to say he would have been dead for some years. Then I looked at everyone's intent expressions and shut up.

"My marriage to Joachim had finally crashed and burned," she said, and I remembered hearing she had broken up with a European designer about then. "Boris and John were wonderful to me. They have a lovely little farm on the Hudson near the Mohawk Valley and I stayed there a lot that summer.

"It's not a working farm of course, but they have gardens and a small herd of sheep, gray ones with lovely black faces—quite decorative—that graze in the fields. They had geese in a pond and an old retired New York City Police horse named Crispin, the gentlest animal in the world. He'd nuzzle you until you yielded up the sugar lumps he knew you had.

"They had a local man who came by and took care of the animals. I never much noticed him—he was quite anonymous. Then, at the end of the summer, he had to be away and he got someone to take his place. I remember it was a hazy August afternoon. There was thunder up in the mountains but no lightning or rain.

"I saw a figure walking across the pasture toward Crispin and something about him was so familiar. He noticed me at the same time, paused, and turned to look my way. It was Bud Van Brunt and he stared at me for a long moment like he knew who I was and wanted me to know he was there.

"I packed and left that day. Boris and John eventually persuaded me to come back and I never saw that man again. But it wasn't the same. Even Crispin seemed jumpy after that."

Everyone was silent, seemingly chilled. But I thought I knew what was afoot and smiled.

"I wonder," said the Major, "what Eddie Ackers saw the night he staggered in here to die." She was going to add more but at that moment, Benicia the server came over to the table and said, "Folks, I'm afraid we're closing a little early."

That broke the spell. Quite quickly for people in very late middle age who were all more than a bit smashed, we figured out the bill and got ourselves together to depart. It was a little past midnight but we were about the only customers.

Sunday nights are the one time Manhattan really does seem quiet and almost deserted. We said our farewells out front. Dawn and Doug both lived in New Jersey and hurried off to the Herald Square Path station assuring us that they'd be in touch.

Jay Glass and Mimsey shared a cab to the Upper East Side. They both seemed troubled—part of the act, I thought.

The Major and I lived downtown and we were going to walk. "What if the idea that Brom Bones scared Ichabod Crane with a carved and lighted pumpkin head was a scam?" she asked as we crossed the street. "What if he actually summoned the Headless Horseman?"

And I replied, "Nice performance from Mimsey. She, you, and I'm guessing Jay had fun running that return of Van Brunt scam on the rest of us. It reminds me of the old days."

She paused on the curb and looked down at me. "Back in the old days your sense of the uncanny was more acute. You had no trouble recognizing that there was evil in Bud Van Brunt. You'll have to take my word for it, but outside of a couple of hints I got from her at Eddie's funeral, I didn't hear Mimsey talk about this until tonight. Jay did once tell me he's convinced some great misdeed or evil occurred on the spot back in Colonial times. But he's obsessed with this subject."

I was amused.

"In fact," she said, "I wanted you here tonight because you were the one I worried about. I remembered how disturbed you were forty years ago about Van Brunt—we'd call it sexual harassment today. I remembered your dream of the night coach and the light in the windows. I thought maybe Van Brunt had his hooks into you as he did with Ackers."

To clear my head of this nonsense, I turned to look back at KNICKS in all its renovated tackiness. What I saw was a roadhouse in a country village. The only lights came from the stars, the waning half moon, and a pair of candles flickering in the middle windows of the inn.

In the moment that I stared, the lanterns on the night coach swung into sight. A couple of details of my old dream that I'd forgotten came back: the pumpkin-headed coachman in his box, the face of Van Brunt staring at me out the coach window.

"Instead," Major Barbara said, watching the way my jaw dropped, "it's Mimsey we have to worry about. That poor kid was desperate to support herself and that worthless first husband and Van Brunt got a bit of her soul. And from the way he's behaving, I'm afraid Jay Glass is another one Van Brunt seduced."

"Always at the center of things," I said, and felt the October chill and was no longer stoned. "But not us," I said.

"No. We're minor characters."

"Like Doug and Dawn."

"Yes," she said, "we lucky bystanders."

⚜ Afterword ⚜

Washington Irving's *The Legend of Sleepy Hollow* is the immediate background from which my story was drawn. Irving is believed to have combined elements of local New York tales about the vengeful ghosts of Indian chiefs with German folktales of the Night Rider. Writing about thirty-five years after the American Revolution, Irving set his story in the Hudson River valley of a generation before, not long after that war ended. He made his Headless Horseman a Hessian trooper searching for the head he lost to a cannon ball—a very recent ghost. In part he was trying to create an American mythology to match those of Europe. I've always been impressed by how well Irving succeeded. *The Legend of Sleepy Hollow* has become part of our folklore and, along with his *Rip Van Winkle*, largely defines the way we think of Dutch Colonial New York.

KAARON WARREN

That Girl

Kaaron Warren's first novel, Slights, *was published by Angry Robot Books in* 2009. *Her second,* Mistification, *came out later in the same year, and the third,* Walking the Tree, *will appear this year.*

Her award-winning short fiction has appeared in Poe, Paper Cities, Fantasy Magazine, *and many other venues in Australia and around the world. Her story "Ghost Jail," which first appeared in 2012, was reprinted in* The Apex Book of World SF, *and "The Blue Stream," her second published story, was reprinted in* Dead Souls.

Warren lives in Canberra, Australia, with her family.

St. Martin's was clean, you could say that at least. Apart from the fine mist of leg hair, that is. I watched as Sangeeta ("You know me. I am Sangeeta.") crawled through the women's legs, a long piece of thread hanging from between her teeth. She stroked a shin, a knee, looking for hairs to pluck.

"Come on, Sangeeta. All the ladies are bald, now. You'll have to find a dog." The head nurse was very kind when there were visitors, the inmates told me.

They sat along the wide verandah that wrapped around their dorm. Like many verandahs in Fiji, it acted as their social center. It was the only place in the hospital with comfortable chairs. The dining hall, in a collapsing once-white building behind the dorm, had hard chairs designed to make you eat quickly; the art therapy room, across the loosely pebbled driveway, had stools. This was one of the things I wanted to change; put comfy chairs in so the women could sit and stitch, or paint, or weave. At present they made small pandanus fans and carved turtles from soap to be sold at the annual bazaar. My funding covered a month, and came from a wealthy Australian woman who'd visited St. Martin's and been depressed at the state of the art therapy room, with paintings so old there was more dust than paint. They had no supplies at all. My benefactor hired me to sort out the physical therapy room, perhaps train the nurses in some art techniques. The nurses loved the sessions with me and used them to gossip, mostly.

Sangeeta dragged herself up using the band of my skirt. "You've got too many hairs in your eyebrows. And your lip is like a hairy worm."

I turned a stare on her and she shrank.

The head nurse said, "You comment on our guest's appearance? Are you perfect? There are things you will need to learn, Sangeeta. If you want to return to your life in Suva."

Sangeeta primped her hair. "I am a beauty therapist. Of course I am beautiful." Her face was deeply scarred by acne. Open wounds went septic so easily in the tropics. There was a red slash across her throat, vivid shiny skin, and two of her fingers were bent sideways. The fingernails were painted and chipped, bitten to the quick. "I studied in Australia. I married an Australian man but he went mad every full moon."

"Of course he did," the head nurse said. "He was cursed on your honeymoon at Raki Raki."

"He upset the witches. He didn't believe they were witches and took a photo of me kissing one of their pigs. Then he said I smelled like bacon and could not make love to me."

"You are blessed," one of the other inmates said. "You will die untouched."

"My second husband turned out to be gay," Sangeeta said, all the time the thread hanging from her mouth. She held the thread taut. "Can I pluck your hairs? Make you smooth?"

The other women set up a clamor, all wanting to do something for me. To me.

Only the old lady at the end of the verandah sat quietly, her lips moving. I walked over to her and bent my head down. "What is it, dear?" I said.

"I am that girl," she said. "I am that girl."

She was very thin. Her skin was wrinkled, looking like folds of brown velvet—a handmade soft toy for an ungrateful child.

"I am that girl," the old woman said. Not much else. She would demand more porridge if it were on, and sometimes sing if the prayer was in Hindi. I would learn all this in the next few days.

She grabbed at me with sharp fingernails. They should have been clean; everything else was here, but I saw a dark red ridge I didn't like. If she was a painter I would have guessed at Russet Red, but she was not a painter. A strong smell of bleach filled the air. I suspected it was their only cleaning fluid.

"What girl does she mean?"

The head nurse shook her head. "We don't know. Malvika has been saying that for a long time now. She's been here since she was a teenager. Appeared one night, they say. Filthy, torn up, you've never seen such a thing, the old nurse told me. Nobody wanted her. Her family said no thank you. She's not our worst, though." She put her hand on a mess of a girl curled in a chair. "This one here came out of the womb this way. Her family kept her in a small *bure* at the back of their house until she got pregnant. No one knows who the father was but they say it was a dog." The poor girl looked like she'd been grown in a jar. She was twisted and folded over herself and she chewed her lip as if it was food. My fingers itched to draw her, and the old woman, too. Not as part of my funding, but for pleasure. I paint the daily details of life, to make sense of the world and here the details were vast and many layered.

. . .

After the shift was over the head nurse took me to the suburb of Lami, where we looked at secondhand clothes that smelled so full of mold and mothballs you could never wash it out. We went into the dark, rotting shed that passed for a market. Piles of vegetable waste sat in their own sludge, but on the tables beautiful purple eggplant; hands of bananas; small, aromatic tomatoes. The nurse talked in Fijian to the stallholders and they smiled at me, nodding, welcoming.

"Artist!" one of them said. "Oh, *mangosa!*"

"*Mangosa* means smart," the head nurse said. "She says you are smart if you are an artist. There's the dog," she whispered. She pointed at an enormous yellow mongrel. He sat with his back against a post, his back legs stretched out, his front paws lolling. He sat like a man. I've never seen balls the size of those he displayed, bigger than cricket balls and a dark grayish pink.

"He's the one they say got poor Dog Girl pregnant. They say her children are running for local council." At last she laughed and it finally sank in she was joking. I felt thick, slow, and patronizing, that I would believe such a thing.

I paid for the vegetables and I paid for the taxi to drop her home and take me to my flat. Local wages are so low, my per diem from my Australian benefactor was higher than her weekly wage.

We passed St. Martin's on the way. "They are mental in there," the taxi driver said, tapping his forehead. When I didn't respond he twisted to look at me, the steering wheel turning about so we veered across into traffic coming the other way. "Mental crazy," he said. "Don't go in there."

He seemed chatty, so I asked him who he thought "that girl" might be. He looked at me in the mirror.

"It might mean anything to anyone."

"But what does it mean to you?"

"The same as it means to any taxi driver," he said. "In the story she never gets old. Fresh-faced, sparkle-eyed, she smells of mangoes in season. Not the skin part, the flesh, chopped up and sweet on the plate. She picks up a taxi near the handicraft market in town. It's always at five thirty-seven. A lot of us won't pick up a girl from there, then. She climbs into the backseat and gives you such a smile you feel your heart melt, all thought of your family gone."

"Have you seen her?"

"No, but my brother has. She asks to go to the cemetery, and if you pry and ask who is there, she will say, 'My mother.' You want to take her home and feed her. You keep driving and you can't help looking at her in the mirror because she is so beautiful. She wears no jewelry apart from a small pendant around her neck. It nestles just here." He touched his breastbone with a forefinger, then spread his fingers as if holding a breast.

"I think that's enough," I said.

"The pendant has a picture of Krisna, fat baby eating butter. You turn the corner to reach the graveyard and you wait for her to tell you where to pull in. You feel a great coldness but the door is closed. You turn around and she is gone. Nothing of her remains."

I shivered. It was an old story, true. But it frightened me.

Taxi drivers love to tell stories of the things they've seen, the people they've picked up. I dismissed it as an urban myth, but I heard it again, and again. Always a brother, or a best friend, and they always told it with a shiver, as if it hurt to talk.

·   ·   ·

On my next visit to St. Martin's I walked up to the old lady, Malvika. "I am that girl," she said. Between her breasts I saw a pendant, Krisna eating butter.

"You had a taxi ride?" I asked. "Is that right?"

"I . . ." She nodded.

"Will you walk with me? Let's walk. I have sweets." I whispered this last to her, not wanting the others to follow. All the women here walked slowly, their feet dragging on the floor, as if their feet were lead and they were too tired, too weak, to lift them each step. The women looked up at visitors but their eagerness was frightening. They wanted to tell you, give you their stories, and they wanted treats. Sweets to suck is mostly what they craved, sugar being the easiest addiction. Sugar ran out here because the women spooned it into their pockets, poked a wet finger in there during prayer or while they swept, then sucked that sugar off.

We walked across the driveway and around behind the art therapy room. I didn't want to sit inside on the hard stools. It was dusty and it stank of bananas and sweat in the room. I wasn't sure how I'd fix it but fix it I would have to. We found an old bench in the shade behind the building and sat down. "I told this many times," Malvika said. "A hundred. Two hundred. They stopped writing it down."

"I can write it down," I said. I took out my sketchbook but I didn't write; I drew.

"My mother died and Father was happy to find a girlfriend the next day. He didn't visit my mother's grave but at least he gave me money for a taxi. I finished my job at five thirty and went to see Mother before going home. There were not many taxis because everybody had finished work but this one stopped. This one." She closed her eyes. I thought of the head nurse's description of Malvika's arrival and my heart started to beat. I didn't need to hear this story; I would do nothing about it. But I wanted to hear it. I did. I wanted to hear of suffering and pain. I wanted to draw it on my paper, capture the detail of it.

"Tell me," I said.

"He was a nice man and asked me questions about work and school. Then he asked about boys and my body, words I didn't like. I was not brave enough to tell him to stop, but I didn't answer him.

"When we reached the cemetery he pulled right inside. It was raining and he said he didn't want me to get wet though of course I would, standing out there. He stopped the car and jumped out while I gathered my things. He opened the door for me and I thought that was kind. But he didn't let me out. No."

She squeezed her hands together. "He pushed into the backseat and he took what my husband should have had. He hit me many times. As he climbed out, I tried to get out the other door but he slammed my fingers. He dragged me out into the mud and forced my face down into it. Then he did more terrible things, tearing and hurting me."

She thrust her fingers into her pocket and brought them out covered with sugar. She sucked them.

"He picked me up and shoved me into the taxi. He could have left me there but he thought of a way to cover up his crime. He drove me up the hill to the hospital and dumped me here. I couldn't speak sense for two days and by then it was too late."

"And he invented the ghost story to explain where you had gone, in case people saw you getting in his taxi?"

The old lady looked at me and smiled. "I am that girl."

I thought, *You cling to your youth. You dream of being young again, before this happened to you.*

The head nurse came around the corner. "There you are! You shouldn't take her away. She is very unwell. Very fragile."

· · ·

I went home to paint in the afternoon light. Rain obliterated Suva Bay and was headed our way, so I had to work fast. My painting of Malvika disturbed me, because I had the sense of her as a young girl more strongly than of her as an old woman.

The hair on her chin. I knew there was a long, dark hair, but did it curl? Which side of her face was it on?

I hailed a taxi and had him stop at a roadside market, where I bought bananas and pawpaw with the change in my purse. Nobody would question me if I came with fruit.

Out of habit I asked the driver about That Girl. This one said, "She disappears. I can show you the place."

· · ·

I went to Malvika although it was close to dinnertime and the hospital didn't like a break in the routine. She sat outside the door of the dorm. The other inmates used the door at the end of the verandah.

She sat bolt upright, her eyes wide open. She didn't blink. Her mouth was open and saliva had dried around her lips.

"Omigod," I said. "She's dead."

The nurse stopped me. "No, she's in a state."

The old lady's eyes were reddened and dry. I stared into them, looking for a sign of life, but nothing. There was no pulse. No breath. I remembered nothing of my first-aid training and didn't want to put my mouth on her anyway.

"We must lay her flat," I said. I could do that much. The others watched me.

"You should leave her comfortable," Sangeeta said, shaking her head. She smelled of burnt hair.

"We must call the doctor," I said, but even as I spoke I was thinking, "Prussian Blue. If I mix Prussian Blue with Titanium White, water it down, I'll get her dead eyes. I'll paint an image of her as a young girl in there, then wipe it away and paint the blank."

"She's empty," the nurse whispered to me. "Her ghost is taking a holiday. She will be back. Just wait."

Five minutes passed and I knew I had to take charge. I called for the doctor on my cell phone. He said, "No hurry. The nurses will call for the morgue when they are ready."

I squatted beside Malvika. I wouldn't get this chance again. The hair on her chin; it didn't curl.

And it happened. After ten minutes, maybe fifteen, Malvika began to twitch, blink her eyes, then she curled over into a ball and rocked.

"She— Has a doctor examined her?"

"They are not interested."

"How often does this happen?"

"Sometimes. It rests her. She is happier for days afterward."

No one else seemed concerned and I wondered if it was my Western woman ways that made me so terrified of an old woman who could die and come back to life as if she was merely sleeping.

I sat quietly and sketched their nighttime routine. That calmed me. Malvika sat up, demanding sugar. Yellowish saliva trails covered her chin. Her lips were dry and cracked. Her eyes were still out of focus and almost purple, it seemed to me. Her left cheek was reddened, as if the blood had already started pooling there.

I sketched those marks of death.

· · ·

I didn't go back to St. Martin's for a while. I was offered a commission from a wealthy Frenchwoman and the lure of the money, plus the idea of having my work hang in France, convinced me to take it.

One afternoon, feeling frustrated with the pretty Frenchwoman's face, I pulled out my portrait of Malvika. It made me feel ill to look at it. I had not painted a dead woman before. In the background I had painted a clock, set at 5:37.

I thought of the taxi drivers and how easily they repeated the legend of the disappearing girl. How happily they unconsciously supported their rapist companion. I knew that I would not be able to finish my portrait of Malvika until I knew her as a young girl, traced her steps over and over again.

I began then a week, or was it two? Of catching taxis just after five, outside the handicraft center. I did it a dozen times, maybe more. Some of them told me proudly, "A lot of drivers won't pick up young girls from there. But I don't believe in ghosts."

One evening, the driver said, "You been shopping?" His eyes looked at me in the mirror but not at me. Beside me. I've always found cross-eyed people hard to talk to.

"Yes," I said, though I had no bags.

"You girls going dancing tonight?"

"Girls?"

"You and your friend." He nodded at me. Beside me.

I felt prickles down my right arm, as if someone had leaned close to me. I didn't believe there was anyone there, but I didn't want to look. I shifted nearer to the door, and turned my head.

Nothing. No one.

The driver said something in Hindi.

"I'm sorry, I don't speak Hindi," I said, but he spoke more, pausing now and then as you would in a conversation.

"Your friend is very shy," he said.

We turned up the road to the cemetery, heading for St. Martin's. I had to continue, my heart beat with it. We passed the cemetery, pulled into St. Martin's. The driver turned around.

"Where . . . is . . . your friend?" he shouted. He didn't look like a man who shouted. "Where is she? You pay me."

"Will you wait? I just want to see something."

He shook his head, already driving away as I shut the door. "Where is she? Where is that girl?"

· · ·

Malvika sucked her fingers at me. "Sugar? Sugar?"

No one had cleaned her up and I could see the marks of death clearly, the yellowish saliva on her chin, the purple color of her eyes. "Have you been away? Out?" I said.

She nodded. "I am that girl," and she smiled at me.

· · ·

I finished my portrait of Malvika. The paint is very thick because I painted her over and over again; young, old, dead. Young, old, dead. I could never decide which face captured her best.

Afterword

The legend on which I based my story is a simple one. A young girl hails a cab in Suva City and asks to be taken to the cemetery. When they reach her destination, she is gone. Taxi drivers tell this story to their passengers at night, to frighten them.

I chose this urban legend because, of all the stories I was told in a year of searching, this is one of only two shared ghost tales I heard. Most were very specific—this person haunting that village, and each teller had their own ghost story to tell.

The cemetery really is across the road from the psychiatric hospital, which exists as I describe it. Around the corner is the prison, which will likely figure in a future story.

My house looks over this cemetery. When I first moved in, I used to tell taxi drivers, "The house near the cemetery." I realized this frightened them; they checked their mirrors all the time, making the road even more dangerous than it usually is.

KIT REED

Akbar

Kit Reed's most recent novel, Enclave, *was published in 2009. Other recent novels by her are* The Baby Merchant, Dogs of Truth, *and* Thinner Than Thou. *Her short novel* Little Sisters of the Apocalypse *and the collection* Weird Women, Wired Women *were both finalists for the James Tiptree, Jr. Award.*

Her short fiction has been published in various anthologies and magazines, including Asimov's Science Fiction, The Magazine of Fantasy & Science Fiction, The Yale Review, Postscripts, *and* The Kenyon Review. *Her next short story collection,* What Wolves Know, *will be published in 2011.*

India is hard, even when it's your dream destination. Sara's mouth is dry and her lips are cracked; red dust blows around her ankles. She's never been so thirsty. For their tenth anniversary, Terry has picked her up and set her down on a ridge in the Rajasthani Desert.

"This is it," he says in a voice she does not recognize. "Akbar's ghost city."

Above them, the massive gate to the red sandstone fortress rises. Shaken, she whispers, "Who died?"

"I guess you could say the city did," he says, but his voice is charged with hope. "Fatehpur Sikri. Aren't you excited?"

"I think so. It's just so *different*." They've talked about this trip for years but now that they're here, she is unaccountably edgy.

"Isn't it great?" He takes her hands, waiting for her to be happy.

"Jet lag. That train. I'm not myself right now."

"India changes people," Terry says without explaining. "Come on, you'll be fine."

"I'm trying!" She loves Terry Kendall, but she can't shake the idea that he has brought her here for a reason.

. . .

Things have been strange between them ever since they reached the subcontinent. Sara can't for the life of her say what's changed, only that in this altered world where the quarter-moon hangs upside down, nothing is certain.

With people everywhere she looks and in places she never thought to look, nothing is private.

They fought their way through throngs in the airport and escaped in the closed car Terry had arranged for them, where Sara fell back, grateful for the glass that separated her from multitudes wanting God knows what from them, from the untold numbers living in overgrown lean-tos and huts lining the road into the city.

Their first night in Bombay was glorious. They slept through the day and ate superb Indian food in a rooftop restaurant high above the glittering harbor. At sunset they looked out through plate glass, watching as the shifting light played on layers of smoke rising from a thousand cooking fires in the city far below. Without guessing what burned outside the cow-dung houses in the neighborhoods where the poor lived, they watched the smoke and marveled. Then, in the elevator going down to their room, Terry said weirdly, "You know, there's a lot riding on this trip."

This startled her. "What . . ."

For whatever reasons, he wouldn't answer. For one specific, grievous reason their lives together have been hard, but Terry gives her a bright, hopeful grin. "I can't wait for you to see it!"

"Where are we going?"

"An amazing, special place." His face went through a lot of complicated maneuvers, none of which worked out. "Oh, honey. This will make all the difference."

This made her step away from him, squinting. Married ten years and nothing between them is clear. She and Terry have always had a strange relationship, half needy adoration, half power struggle. "What, Terry? What will?"

"Relax," he said, and his laugh made Sara wonder if there was such a thing as too joyful. "Let's live the legend."

What legend? She rummaged through what little she knew but all she could come up with were dimly remembered names: Brahma, Vishnu, Shiva, Ganesh, oh God, did she have it right, did she even have the right religion? She'd resisted doing homework for this trip and she'd rather die than ask Terry. This was not her country; she was not herself. She was too disrupted and ignorant to ask questions.

On the night train to New Delhi, Sara grappled with mystery and dislocation, compounded by the unbidden knowledge that in a country this far from home you are always the foreigner, and nothing is what you think. She was upset by the weirdness (Terry's), followed by the being sick (hers).

It was sudden and apparently endless. Dying inside, she looked down the hole at rushing tracks and faced death at dawn, armed with a tin cup and leaky faucet. Every cramp came as a sickening reminder of the babies she'd lost—twice, and the second time it almost killed her. She was alone in the house. It was abrupt, terrifying, so bloody that Terry promised never to put her through it again.

While she rocked with pain, odd trees and desert rushed by under astounding blue skies sliced by wheeling vultures and she saw that India was beautiful. She looked out the window at great stretches of the vast, changing world studded by villages and train stations overflowing with people. *If I could stay on the train, if I could stay inside anywhere*, she thought, *I'd be OK*, and felt guilty for thinking it.

Momentarily unshelled, rolling through New Delhi in an open car, she was overwhelmed by the noise—not that it was loud. That it came from so many sources. It was as if the entire country was breathing, groaning, tossing, grumbling because nobody was alone for long enough to get any sleep. She thought she could hear all the people in this great, sprawling country; they were all talking, all at once, unless they were wailing in despair—or singing—and the worst part was that she did not know which, or what any of it meant.

Oblivious, Terry grinned as if he expected her to walk into the unknown gladly and face the world of strangers smiling.

She didn't feel safe until sliding glass doors closed behind them, sealing out the city. After a night and a long day sleeping, after dinner in another elegant hotel restaurant, she felt strong enough to confront him. "What, Terry?" She needed to look into the man she thought she knew, and find out why they were here. "What do you mean, there's a lot riding on this?"

"Let's don't go back there," he said gently, "not now, when you're doing so well," because he had brought her here to help her get past the old losses. Acknowledged master of the old bait and switch, Terry lifted her with his voice. "Look." His wide gesture took in the indoor waterfall, the tiers of marble balconies where guests prowled with no beggars and no vendors to hound them, no disorderly street life to break the carefully polished surface.

"Terry, I need to know," she said, because she had questions. "I just . . ."

He opened a small velvet bag and her voice trailed off. Something fell into her hand. It was a ring. "I had this made for you today. Blue topaz."

"Oh." The stone caught the light. "Oh!"

"Happy anniversary."

Ten years. There were still those questions. Safely enclosed, poised at the bottom of the four-story waterfall, she told herself they could wait. If the trip could end here and now, while she was so happy, the questions could wait forever. She and Terry would eat and play inside the vast hotel, riding out at dusk to see monuments through sealed car windows, marveling at the sights as they zipped by and heading home before anything too bad could happen, they . . .

"We'd better crash. Car's coming at four a.m."

"Car?" Her belly trembled. *I can't.*

"Girl." Terry's tone said *of course you will,* but he softened it, diverting her with another velvet bag. Blue topaz earrings spilled into her hand like promises. "This is India!"

They headed out at first light—before the heat, too early for most of the city's millions. The streets were as empty as they'd ever be. As long as they were contained, Sara was OK: air-conditioning on full, hotel driver Ravi Singh nodding deferentially as he handed her into the car. Once they cleared the city their fierce, elegant Sikh driver turned into something else. He plunged through traffic like a warrior preparing to die in battle. He drove as if fixed on his place in the ranks of Sikh heroes.

Sara gasped as he swerved into the path of an oncoming semi to avoid a cow that had plopped down to rest on the tarmac. Shaken, she had to wonder what it all meant to Ravi Singh, how much hair he had—a lifetime's worth, twined under that yellow turban, she had read. Do Sikhs expect God to grab them by the hair and yank them up to heaven, or did she make up that part?

Which god? She didn't know. Driving, the Sikh presented a massive profile so stony that she was afraid to ask him.

Riding along in silence, she had time to wonder.

It was her fault she wasn't clear where Terry was taking her. She'd been tied up at work; she let him research this trip and he did all the planning. She told him she wanted to be surprised, but she was afraid. India was too big, rich with legends like kept secrets. People could be born here and spin out entire lifetimes in a place this rich and complicated without comprehending what it was. They could read and study, travel the length and breadth of their country and still not know any more than a fish knows about the ocean, so preparing, she'd just packed and walked out the door.

Now she was beggared by her ignorance. With Ravi closed and locked for the day, she touched her mate's arm. "About this legend we're living. Which one, Terry? Which one?" He never snored, so she knew he was pretending. They rode for hours. She gave in and slept until the car stopped and sudden stillness awoke her.

Ravi pulled the hand brake and got out to open the door for them. Heat rushed in. "From here, you walk. Where shall I wait?"

Like a seasoned tourist, Terry answered, "Jami Masjid. That's big mosque to you," he told her helpfully.

Don't pretend to know places you've never seen. If thoughts could kill. But why was she so angry? It didn't matter. She could say it out loud and he wouldn't hear her, not now that they were here. They spilled out on the scorching road like two peas dropped on a griddle. Because this was her last chance to find out, Sara turned to Ravi. "There is a legend about this place?"

He touched his joined hands to his forehead. "Salim Chisti."

"Who?"

Damn Terry, why did he look so pleased? He tapped the guidebook with that hopeful grin. "It's all in here."

She grimaced. "I was asking Mr. Singh."

"The emperor Akbar built this city to give thanks to the saint, and brought his people here." The driver sighed. "It has been empty for many years."

"Thanks for what?"

Anxious to get going, Terry preempted. "We have that, Sara. It's in the book."

"Sunset," the Sikh said, as if the timing was a given.

· · ·

The driver leaves them standing there in the strong sunlight, blinking. In the streets below, other tourists, vendors, beggars jostle—*all these people*—and Sara steps closer to Terry, as though to escape them; oddly, it's like stepping into the iris of a camera's eye just before it closes.

Something shifts. Time passes. Startled, Sara shakes herself, blinking. The light has changed.

"Terry, what are we doing here?"

"What do you think? Waiting in line for tickets."

Want.

She whirls. *Who spoke?*

The want.

"I don't see any line."

"Cool! We can just go in." He tugs at her hand. "Come on!"

She wants to, but it is worrisome. For the first time there are no guides clamoring, there's nobody begging, nobody selling curios or street food or— God!—water. Their car is gone, Ravi Singh is gone and the road that brought them to the ghost city is empty. For the first time since they landed on the teeming subcontinent they are alone. "Where is everybody?"

"Inside, I suppose." For the first time Terry sounds uncertain. "Unless it's some kind of holiday."

After the bustle and outcry, it's so eerily silent that Sara shudders. "Are we safe?" She is asking more than one question here, although Terry won't notice.

"Sara, it's a national monument! Don't you think these places are protected?"

"How am I supposed to know! I don't even know why we're here!"

He wants.

What? She turns to Terry. "Did you say something?"

"I said, this is it." His tone speaks of more than the city. At the top of the ramp, the gate waits like an open mouth. He pulls her through the vaulted gate and out into the sun-blasted courtyard. "Downtown Oz."

They always want.

Troubled, she turns to look at the ancient city. It is magnificent. Amazing. Deserted. Above the archway, outlining onion domes and minarets, fortress walls and the turrets, that wild blue sky is empty except for the white sun pasted overhead, blazing. What is it, noon? Later? "Oh." Blinded in spite of the hat, Ray-Bans, everything she marshaled to protect her, Sara gulps scalding air. "Oh!"

"It's . . ." Terry is trying to pick her up with his voice and put her down somewhere she never intended to be. "It's like . . ."

Reflexively, she tilts her water bottle. "It's hot."

"I don't know what it's like," he says happily, "it's just so beautiful."

She drinks and feels better. "It is."

"Like the emperor's wet dream of, I don't know, it's . . ." Then Terry goes that one step too far. "Oh Sara, let's bring the kids some day."

Dazzled by the light, momentarily seduced into dreaming, Sara comes back to herself with a jolt. "You promised," she cries, and this is as far as the discussion goes.

Sara Kendall grew up motherless, and takes her own losses as proof that she could die the same way. She won't die that way, not like her mother, not ever, but there is more. She can't open herself up to that kind of grief and misery, never again.

She has survived since then by keeping her elbows close to her sides. Given their history, one extra person in her life is her limit and Terry knows it. "Now," she says briskly because he still hasn't explained, "about this legend."

"The emperor Akbar made a pledge," her man says so glibly that she knows he isn't telling her everything. "*Sikri* means thanks, the emperor got what he wanted and that's why he built this city." Terry says all that and throws in a short history of the Moghul emperors, but doesn't say what Akbar was giving thanks for. Like a pitchman for some product he isn't ready to unveil, he retreats into the guidebook. "Says here it took years to build the fortress and the palaces, everything up here had to be hauled to the top of the ridge except the sandstone they carved out right here. I mean everything: marble and malachite, all the metal and rugs and furniture, tools and fuel, everything they needed. Bearers brought clothes and jewelry and weapons for the hundreds, everything it takes to run an empire, and when it was done all of Akbar's people came up, and there were hundreds— warriors and courtiers, wives and concubines, the slaves, then there were the animals . . ."

The heat is making her dizzy but Terry drones on like an amateur hypnotist until she cries, "Oh, Terry. Don't go all tour guide on me."

Listen.

She shivers. *Oh, don't!*

"The emperor's elephants," he finishes anyway. "Ravi let us out on an elephant ramp, they had ramps for the elephants to enter," he adds in a scholarly tone that makes her want to smack him. "You may not care about this stuff but he was the greatest of the Moghul emperors after Babur, and he— Look at the place! Akbar thought of everything."

"It's been a while since Akbar," Sara says. When he pitched this trip to her on a cool night in Providence, Terry never told her how hot it would be, or that she would be too limp and dehydrated and disoriented to enjoy it. She shuffles uneasily, stirring the red dust that blows across the courtyard and clings to the hairs on her bare arms, caking in her nostrils. "If he thought of everything, why is it so quiet?"

"It was amazing, it was beautiful, like some kind of heaven, with a water garden to cool it in the hot months. He had a system, but all those people, all those animals . . ." Terry sighs. "A few years up here and they just plain ran out of water."

She sighs. "The city died."

"Pretty much. It's just tourists now." He turns to face her, adding, "And pilgrims."

Pilgrims, yes. Sara twitches like a horse plagued by a bluefly, desperate to shake it off. **Pilgrims who want.** "What pilgrims?"

Instead of answering, Terry leads her out of the covered walkway, into the open. The light is blinding. White sunlight brings every outline into sharp relief—the cornices, domes and turrets, passages and intricately carved screens of red sandstone that set the margins of the emperor's ghost city. The great courtyard is alarmingly still. Nothing moves; there are none of the expected tourists dutifully shuffling through the shady corridors or striking poses for point-and-shoots or digital cameras; there are no guides for hire struggling to be first, no hopeful little hangers-on smiling their hardest, and no vendors offering food or water; parched as she is, she won't find either here in the deserted city. The silence is profoundly troubling. She touches his arm. "Terry, where is everybody?"

"What do you care? The place is ours!" With that laugh, he locks her fingers in his like a child begging her to come out and play. He leads her into another passageway screened by lacy red sandstone. "Look!"

When Terry finally lets go she steps back, studying the man who brought her to this beautiful, deserted place: familiar face, dark hair blowing, same Terry and yet she is thinking, *Do I know you?* They stand for a moment, looking out through stone fretwork at the surrounding desert.

"Everything Akbar had is ours!"

Her mouth is dry; her skin is dry. Even her eyeballs are drying out. "It is," she says, because he is waiting.

She doesn't know what the problem is yet, but there is a problem: Terry's urgency, the bizarre sense that the stones or something trapped within the stones is speaking. She is listening hard, but Terry's voice drowns out whatever she thought was speaking. "It says here that Akbar had five thousand concubines." He points. "I think that's the *zenana*, where he kept them all, but you know, of all those wives . . ." He considers. Decides it isn't time yet and doesn't finish.

He wants.

Alarmed, she looks here, there, *What could he want? I give him everything he wants.* She'd like to face the mysterious figure that seems to whisper but doesn't have a voice. She needs to argue. If she could catch someone following, some helpful soul keeping pace behind one of the intricate sandstone screens, some living human who seems to be telling her things only she can hear, she would feel better. At this point she'd even take an enemy bent on her destruction. A person. *That,* she thinks, *I could handle.* But there is only Terry.

She puts it to him. "What do you want, Terry?"

He is running on ahead and doesn't hear.

Weird, she thinks. *This is so weird,* in spite of which she finishes, "Some kind of sacrifice?"

More. Words float into her head—a warning. **They always want more.**

"What?"

Typical Terry: he deflects questions with information. "See that platform out there in the water? That's where Akbar sat when he was holding court outdoors. You had to go over the little bridges to talk to him. I bet it was hot!" Studying the book, he points.

"See those steps? Sometimes he sat up there, on that platform? And played games, using humans as pieces. We're standing on his game board." He leads her up the steps. "See the squares?" He turns her so they are side by side like a pair of dancers looking at the courtyard, where Akbar's design is laid out in stone. On the downbeat, he will spin her out. "He moved people around like living chess pieces."

Like the objects of his desires.

Terry finishes wistfully, "And he always won."

What? It isn't the wind she hears and it is not a voice, exactly, but something bent on being acknowledged. Warning:

Like you.

Like me? If this is a warning, what should she be afraid of? Their major issue is dead and Terry knows it. He promised, so what is this? Intent on their destination, he goes along reading entries on everything they pass like a teacher thrilled by the sound of his own voice. When she tries to slow him down, the man she thought she knew wields the book like a shield, deflecting questions.

As they go along for what seems like miles the sky overhead bleaches to the color of melting lead; she is exhausted and dying of thirst and yet Terry pulls her along on a string of words, reading like a believer mesmerized by the text. "The emperor brought craftsmen from all over the known world to build his city and the architecture is rich and varied, showing design elements drawn from every known religious building."

"Don't," she cries as he launches into yet another long passage. "Oh please, Terry. Don't!" For the first time in a marriage built on love, Sara wonders whether it will last. She bats words away with her hands; there is no way to explain without hurting him. *How can I listen with you reading, and so loud?*

They come to another red sandstone building. Sara groans with relief as they step into the shadows.

"And this," he says, and he is reading instead of looking, "is the Diwan-i-Khas, the hall where Akbar held audiences. He sat up there, at the top of that pillar, behind all those screens, so he could hear but not be seen, because he was the power here. When the emperor spoke, none of the subjects waiting down here could see him, but every one of them heard every word when he passed judgment, and the judgment came down loud and clear." He points. "See?"

For once Sara does as told. She follows his finger up the stone column that supports Akbar's screened pedestal. From down here the thing looks like an inverted Sno-cone or an upside-down wet dream of a wedding cake ornamented with what could be dangling . . . *Oh, good grief.* "He had audiences here?"

Oddly, Terry says, "Down here we could hear him speak, but we couldn't see him deciding."

We. This is troublesome. "Deciding what?"

Whatever he wanted.

Thank God you're back. Frightened, alone in a foreign country, Sara can't even guess which god she is thanking.

"Oh, all the important things."

The next thing she knows, Terry is climbing, scrambling up worn stairs to the balcony. "Where are you going, Terry?" She sees him running along above her. She calls, "What are you doing?" With a wave, he crosses one of the six bridges that lead to the emperor's platform and disappears into the central pod.

They always get what they want.

This makes Sara groan. Disturbed, increasingly anxious, she tries again to make him answer. "Terry, what are you *doing*?"

After much too long his voice comes from above and the blind, loving bastard is reading aloud from the guidebook, sitting up there in the pod:

"According to the legend, it says here that none of Akbar's wives could give him a male heir. Then travelers came to him bringing stories about a great Sufi saint, and so he came out here to the middle of the desert on a pilgrimage. He traveled a long way to sit at the feet of Shaikh Salim Chisti, and tell him of his great need, and then the saint . . ."

Her breath shudders. "Is that what you want?"

". . . prophesied that he would have a son, but the mother must be a Christian."

Words pour out of her like vomit. "You thoughtless, deceitful . . ." The noun eludes her and she blurts, "Is that all you want from me?"

Then the air cracks open. Something huge thunders in.

SO MANY WIVES, SO MANY WOMEN, SO MANY DIED AND NOT ONE SON TO CARRY ON MY RULE.

Deafened, she thinks, *This can't be Terry talking.* "Terry! Did you hear that? Terry?"

SALIM CHISTI GAVE ME THE MIRACLE . . .

The tremendous, powerful voice shakes her to the spine. "Terry!"

MIRIAM.

"What's that, Terry, what *is* it?"

Heedless, her husband goes on reading smoothly, as untouched and voluble as a talking head on NPR informing her: "Akbar searched until he found her and she bore him a son, the future Emperor Jehangir, and in gratitude, the emperor transferred his capital to the ridge at Sikri and built his new and splendid city here."

"Dammit, Terry, listen!"

Above her, hidden, her husband goes on as though he neither hears nor cares. Then, when she is at her most vulnerable, he stops short. "No, you listen." Then he cries, "Oh, Sara. Let's try again, I want it so much."

"I thought you loved me!"

Just then huge words roll out of nowhere, unbidden, piling up like stones closing an emperor's tomb. **IT IS BITTER, BUT EVERY MAN NEEDS A SON TO BURY HIM, AND SHE...**

As he speaks a sigh fills the audience hall and then dwindles. Terrified, frantic, Sara understands that her friend, her ghost, her familiar is receding. Her friend's last words come out in a dying fall. **Now you know.**

She calls out in a thin voice, "Miriam? Miriam, don't go!" but Miriam is nowhere now. It is as if she had never been.

She is alone with the men.

DO NOT ASK ME WHICH IS TRUTH AND WHICH IS LEGEND. GO.

Stone grates against stone, as though some huge trap is closing.

Staggered—no, overturned, Sara calls, "Akbar?"

But there is only Terry, scrambling out of the stone pod above her head and over the walkway to the balcony where she can see him. If Sara lives until she dies—and she will; if she thinks about this every day until she is an old, old woman, she will never figure out who or what just spoke to her.

What she will do, standing there in the bare, beautiful, audience hall in the emperor's ghost city at the top of a dry ridge in the Rajasthani Desert in northern India, waiting for her husband to scramble downstairs and come running toward her with his arms spread, is come to a decision.

He hurries back to her, grinning. "Well, what do you think?"

Sighing, she dissembles. "Let's don't do this right now, let's just enjoy what we have here."

When they step outside, orange-gold light staggers her. The sky is streaked with sunset. How long has it been? Swallowing sand, she clutches at her water bottle and finds it empty.

Terry takes no notice. He just hurries her along the ridge to the tomb of Salim Chisti. A sign in English tells them to take off their shoes before they enter the tomb, but Terry ignores it. Even though there's nobody around, Sara slips out of her sandals. The marble underfoot holds the heat of the day but drained and thirsty as she is, Sara is comforted by the long shadows. Terry looks up from the guidebook. "It says the sheikh is buried here."

Stunned by exhaustion, frantic, terrified, and raging, she rips the guidebook out of his hands and hurls it out into the plaza. Halting at the center of the tomb, Sara looks down at the spot, wondering. She thinks to pray, but has no idea what she would say or who she would be telling. They stand under the marble canopy and the world stops. It is as if they are in a vacuum. Terry takes her hand with a sweet grin. It is as though this is a done deal, and her heart turns over.

They turn to leave, shuffling out of the shadows and into the fading daylight. As they emerge from the marble tomb the air splits and in a sudden, terrifying rush, all India comes roaring in on them: tourists, beggars, guides, musicians, and vendors jostling for space in the courtyard of the giant mosque, the smell of red dust and food cooking and a large crowd gathering in a space that will never be big enough for them, accompanied by the ambient noise—the voice of India, but hyped and amplified. It's as if the great, rich, incomprehensible civilization is flexing like a tiger waking up from deep, preternatural sleep.

As they come down the steps into the slanting light Terry stretches dreamily and rubs his eyes the way he does when he realizes it's Sunday and hits the snooze button again.

For the first time today Sara runs ahead, wide-eyed, alert, and jangling. At the edge of the ridge, she sees a crowd gathering at the foot of the monumental gate to the mosque for some event—listed, she supposes, in Terry's stupid guidebook. Outside the city walls, she knows, Ravi Singh is waiting with the car to take them back to safety but for whatever reasons, she is not done here. Instead she elbows her way closer, to see what the crowd is waiting for. There are figures standing on the top of the heavily ornamented gate, poised above . . . what? Sara thinks the people on top of that are fixed on something in the courtyard, but she can't see what's at the bottom.

Then somebody grabs her arm and she turns. It's a kid in a T-shirt and cut-offs—fourteen? sixteen?—one of many kid daredevils hustling tourists for . . . *What do you want?* She doesn't know. At the gate something just happened; a shout goes up.

"Maaa-am, maaa'm, see me jump into the pretty water."

She doesn't hear; she hears but doesn't understand. He's at her elbow now, a raggedy kid. "Only forty rupees."

"What?"

"For forty rupees I will jump into the pretty water," the boy tells her, pointing to the massive gate. "Come and see. See me jump into the pretty water."

Sand fills her mouth but she manages, "Water?"

"Only forty rupees."

"Of course," she says, crushing a hundred into his hand. "When?"

"Now!" The boy breaks for the gate, but he isn't fast enough.

Dazzled, Sara grabs the tail of his shirt and darts after him, running where he runs no matter how he tries to shake her off, climbing where he climbs, sobbing as she scrambles up the stones behind him.

"Ma'am. Ma'am!" The boy turns on her, trying his best to get free, but excited and mystified, compelled, she clings tighter. He almost escapes when the torn T-shirt starts to give way but Sara adjusts her grip, locking strong fingers around his ankle.

He can't go up. She won't let go. They are at a little impasse here on the rocks. She is the beggar now. "Please."

Wild-eyed, the boy gasps, "What do you want?"

"I don't know!"

Below them, diminished by perspective, Terry runs in circles, calling her to come down.

Hanging on to the rock with one hand, the boy gropes in his pocket and throws money, shaking his head: *No.* "Take it back!"

Shivering, she absorbs their position on the rocks, the distance to the top, the fact that she can't see the water below, can't tell how big the surface is or how deep it is or what happens to those who plunge; she does not know where this child will land, or what she thinks she is doing, only that at the bottom, there will be water.

At the bottom another boy cries, "Only forty rupees . . ."

Gripping tight, excited and hopeful, she tells this one, "A thousand rupees if you take me with you."

🪔 Afterword 🪔

Back in the day I was lucky enough to end up at the top of a plateau in
the Rajasthani Desert outside Agra, wandering through India's famous
ghost city. The red sandstone city is rich with elegantly carved sandstone
screens and marble mosques—and for hundreds of years, it's been deserted.

A ghost city, founded on an old Indian legend. What could be better?
According to legend, the sixteenth-century Moghul emperor Akbar had
a starter set of wives and daughters, but no sons to carry on the line.

Travelers brought tales of a Sufi saint who was known to perform
miracles, and Akbar made a pilgrimage into the desert to find him. Re-
vered as a mystic, Salim Chisti blessed Akbar and told him a Christian
woman would give him a son. He named the boy Salim, after his benefactor. Salim grew up to become the emperor Jahangir. Shah Jahan built
the Red Fort, Agra, and the Taj Mahal. As a gesture of thanks to Salim
Chisti, Akbar built the city of Fatehpur Sikri on the site of his camp and
moved all his wives and courtiers to the top of this plateau in the middle
of the desert, where they lived in splendor until—what was he thinking?—
they ran out of water and abandoned the city to red dust and the desert
winds. The Tomb of Salim Chisti lies just inside one of the gates to the
great ghost city.

STEVEN PIRIE

The Spring Heel

Steven Pirie lives in Liverpool, England, with his wife, Ann, and their small son, James. His fiction has appeared in many magazines and anthologies around the world. His comic fantasy novel, Digging Up Donald, *came out in paperback in 2007, and he's finishing up related (although not sequel)* Burying Brian.

More information may be found at Steve's website: www.stevenpirie.com.

Sometimes Ruth closes her eyes. But it's hard to dream when the tree bark is rough against her shoulders; when *he's* thrusting away, not caring she might need lubrication, not bothered she might be bleeding down her thigh.

"Do you kiss, love?" *he* says.

"No," says Ruth. "Never."

He buries his mouth into her neck. At least Ruth knows *he* won't be long now. She stares out into the park dusk over *his* back. It's dark under the trees; nothing moves but the whores and the rats. No lights shine behind the windows of the big Victorian houses that line the park driveway. No one lives here anymore and most of the houses are in ruin.

As *he* grunts, Ruth stares up at the slate roofs, stained yellow by the glow of the city lights on the clouds, darkest only where the slates have fallen through. And there's a figure up there. Even from down here Ruth sees its face is twisted, grinning or scowling, she's not sure, and it twirls arms and legs as if dancing on the rooftops. Its limbs are spindly, gangly, too long.

Ruth rubs her eyes and stares again. The figure is gone.

He slips out, spent and panting. "You sure you don't kiss, love? I like a bit of a kiss when I'm done."

But Ruth is already pulling up her pants to leave.

⋅　⋅　⋅

It's Tuesday morning and the mission hall is full. The fat women behind the tea urn dole out tea and toast and scornful looks. They shake their jowls as

Ruth passes. They know what Ruth is. Ruth hates the Mission, but in the day, if she's moved on from her restless sleep behind the bins to the rear of the Easy Rider bicycle shop on the High Street, there's nowhere else to go. She's long since learned the church opens its doors only partially to girls like her.

Ruth takes tea and pushes through the rut of unwashed bodies toward the alcove under the stairs. She can hide here, in the dim light. Ruth is more at home in the dark. The priest is less likely to spot her and try to save her. She shivers; how Father Thomas might save her by soaping her breasts in the bath she doesn't care to know.

The Runt's here, as is Basil and Lass. Basil surreptitiously tips alcohol into Ruth's tea.

"It's a bit early for tea without gin, what," he says. Lass grips his arm as if she's feared to let go. "I always say PG Tips alone is no way to start the day."

"You'll get us thrown out," says Lass.

The Runt grins and glances around. "Fuckin' hope so," he says. "This place is ripe today, even by my stench. I hear they're going to knock it down. They've found asbestos, and even shit like us are protected from asbestos. I hear there're holes in the roof."

Ruth splutters on her tea. For an instant, she's back in the park, and the devil is dancing on the rooftops, leaping between the broken chimney stacks and grinning down at her. Too long, those legs; too sticklike; too hot, that stare.

"There was someone on the roof last night," Ruth says, distantly.

"Of the mission?" says The Runt.

"No, on the houses in the park, a strange gangly bloke leaping about. He stared down at me, and his stare burned my face. It made me piss myself."

"How the devil did he get up there?" says Basil.

"Don't know, but when I looked back he'd gone."

"That's the Spring Heel," says Lass. "Everybody's talking about him. You've seen Spring Heel Jack."

"Doesn't that mean you're going to die or something?" says The Runt. "Doesn't he go round slitting prostitutes' throats?"

Basil kicks The Runt's shin. "It means too much bloody gin in the tea, old boy. Besides, that's the Ripper you're thinking of."

"Well, they're all the same, aren't they?"

Lass grips Basil tighter. "You should look for a beau like mine to look after you," she says. "Or find another patch to work, somewhere away from the park."

Somewhere away from the park. Ruth bows her head. She stares downward at the carpet and the top of The Runt's head, both balding and tattered. What is there for her away from the park? She has nothing but the tuft of intrigue between her legs. What can she do but dodge the pimps and the sadists?

She glances at Basil—a penniless tramp who believes himself aristocracy—and at Lass—simple and trusting but utterly devoid of self-esteem, who'd quite literally die were she cast adrift from the lifeboat that is Basil's arm. And The Runt, well, hunched and dwarfed and painfully ugly, what hope is there for him? What hope for any of them?

"I have to work the park," says Ruth. "It's all I know."

· · ·

That night business is slow. The path lamps are out, and there's a damp curtain over the park, a blanket that's more than the early September mists alone. The night is cool, and men aren't so keen to drop their pants on cool nights. She'll need to find somewhere inside soon, and that usually means paying a pimp. Pimps mean hidden bruises. Pimps mean the drug culture that's always scared Ruth. Better to remember what she did the night before, even if it was to fuck balding old men who know they'll never pull skirt any other way again. And better to have full use of the legs when one of the mad bastards holds a knife on her.

Ruth walks slowly along the park paths. With the mist and the smothering silence, she thinks she could be back in Victorian days. Simpler times when even whores were treated as people. The gentlemen would tip their hat and thank you, Basil had told her, and throw a coin or two's gratuity as they clambered aboard their hansom cabs. A world away, thinks Ruth. Now they just wipe their dicks on her skirt and run.

Ruth pauses, convinced she hears footsteps behind. It's not unusual for a punter to follow her for a while; to build up courage if it's a first time, or to convince himself she's not working with thugs, or the police, or both.

"Looking for business?" Ruth stares into the gloom.

There is someone there, lurking, ill-defined in the dusk. He's wheezing, but that's not unusual. They may be old men, lung-rattling ancients after a final fling at death's door. They may be young boys, panting as they ejaculate in their pants and run off with a story for their mates. It takes all sorts and Ruth's seen them all.

"Twenty quid for full; ten for hand; I don't do oral and I don't kiss. Anything else, well, it depends."

He looms from the darkness. He's little more than a blur as he passes. Ruth staggers as she's knocked backwards. The grass is muddy and she slips. The air smells sulphurous and rotten. Ruth's dress clings cold and wet to her thighs.

"Leave me alone," she yells.

The man returns, leaping gazellelike in front of her. As he jumps he turns his head toward her. His skin glows putrid green. His teeth are yellowed in an angular jaw. His eyes are bulging in his head. The sulphurous stench is a wind behind him. He laughs, cruel and guttural.

"Go away. I have a pimp. He'll cut you."

Thirty feet? Forty? Even in the pitch darkness Ruth sees him leaping lit from within like a will o' the wisp for her. He turns and heads directly for Ruth. She cowers, covering her head with her hands instinctively, but he leaps again at the last and soars away into the night sky. The dreadful wind washes over her. She can taste its smell and hear its colour.

Ruth sits panting upon the ground.

·   ·   ·

There's always confession in the church on Wednesdays. Basil says absolving sins midweek gives Father Thomas Sunday afternoons off. Lass clings to his arm, gazes up at him and nods.

"You're so clever, Basil," she says. "You know everything."

Ruth hesitates by the confessional booth. She's never seen anything to believe in with the supernatural, on either side for good or evil. It's always seemed to her to be Ruth and *the world,* and in such a titanic struggle between both there seemed little room for higher powers and greater wonders. But when the devil displays on the darkest of nights, when he dances just for her and her alone, when his stench grips her throat and burns her nose, then to where does she turn?

"I've got nothing to confess," says The Runt. "Fuckin' pure, me, pure as the driven slush."

Basil grips Ruth's arm. "Are you sure you want to do this, old thing?

I mean, Mad Maud went to confession and it lasted a week. She came out all drained and disjointed, like it was only her sins holding her together."

Basil offers Ruth brandy and she takes a swig. She doesn't do neat alcohol and it sears her throat. Homeless, barely destitute, it's hard enough to stay clean to attract punters as it is without stinking of spirits. Without that barest of self-control Ruth knows she'll be dead in a gutter by Thursday.

"I have to talk to someone," says Ruth. "Someone in the church. Someone who knows about these things."

"Father Thomas will want to soap your tits," says Lass.

The Runt grins. "Aye, and I could do that for you without all the Christian mumbo-jumbo."

"I have to find out if it's the devil," says Ruth. "I have to learn what it wants from me."

. . .

Ruth steps through, into the confessional booth. It's calm inside, serene such that it takes her breath away. It's an alien landscape and she's disorientated, as if she's stepped through onto the moon. A single candle flickers briefly and settles. At first Ruth thinks she's alone, but in the stillness she hears Father Thomas shuffle behind the thick, velvet curtain.

"Well, child?" he says at last.

Ruth is shaking. "I don't know what I'm supposed to say."

"You've never confessed your sins before?"

"I don't know what my sins are."

"We all know what our sins are, child, if we're really true to ourselves in looking."

Ruth sighs. "I've seen the devil, Father. It came leaping at me from the darkness. I breathed its fetid breath."

There's a pause before Father Thomas draws back the curtain. He looks flushed of face. "In a metaphorical sense, of course?"

"It knocked me to the ground, and flew off laughing, and the smell, well, I can still taste it now."

Father Thomas shakes his head. He stares down at Ruth's lap, and she covers herself with a palm. Slowly, nervously, she raises and lowers the hem of her skirt.

"I need help, Father, quickly."

"Come through and I'll run a bath." Father Thomas stands briskly. His ears are pink warm. "Cleanliness is next to godliness. You'll need your sins washing away. We'll get you from those dirty clothes and the devil will soon seem far, far away."

.   .   .

Ruth doesn't work that night. She lingers at the edge of the park, closer to the main road traffic and the late-night revellers that she can leap toward should the demon return.

"When will we see the devil?" says The Runt.

"I told you he'd want to get you undressed," says Lass. As usual she's lodged on Basil's arm, but he's well fried on vodka and gin, and it's no longer certain who is holding whom. "Though it's what he's doing fumbling about in his gowns with his other hand that makes me shudder."

Ruth speaks quietly. She's more alone in her head than she's ever been. "Father Thomas only wanted what *he* wanted. He said I was delusional. He had no idea what I was talking about. How can the church not know about the devil? How can the church not care about me if I reach out to it?"

Lass breaks free from Basil's arm. It's the first time Ruth has ever seen them not conjoined. Lass lifts Ruth's chin with a finger and looks into her eyes. Lass's pupils are flecked green and brown and gold; it adds a depth to her stare Ruth has never seen before.

"The church is self-serving," says Lass. "I know, because I've been abused by Father Thomas and his kind, too. He washed away my sins, once." Lass grins. "And limped for a week for his trouble. But this isn't the devil, this is the Spring Heel. There's a difference, I know. Be true to yourself, Ruth, and perhaps the Spring Heel can help you if you call to him."

"I say, summon the devil?" says Basil. "What fun."

"But why would I want to call so hideous a creature?"

"And where do we find him?" says The Runt.

"We must look to the rooftops." Basil points upward and stumbles through the effort. "I've heard tell the Spring Heel can leap the moon."

.   .   .

If the Spring Heel came that night, he was little more than a shadow that shrieked once across the high clouds. It's four in the morning and Ruth is no nearer to discovering herself. Lass, when back connected to Basil at the arm, loses all the lucent insight she'd displayed earlier. It's as if Basil is leaching her personality, and Ruth has long since grown impatient questioning her about the Spring Heel. Basil is so drunk he can barely breathe. The Runt stands twitching in his sleep in a nearby doorway.

Ruth pauses at the park gates. To the east, a hint of dawn lingers behind the black treetops. It could be dawn, or an onrushing fire to consume the world, thinks Ruth. She shivers, though she's not cold. There was a time when she'd see only the beauty of the dawn, not fear what the new day might bring. There was a time when demons and monsters were just the stuff of nightmares and fairy tales, of fears that flew before the light of day.

But now *he's* out there, somewhere, this ghostly devil dancing on the trees or the rooftops or the clouds or the moon. Perhaps he's close by, watching her from some high eyrie. Perhaps he's ready to swoop down and carry her off to some unspeakable Hell. Ruth reaches beneath her skirt and scratches at a rash developing on her labia. She sighs. Every man that's ever used her has taken her partway there anyway.

· · ·

It's signing-on day, and the DSS on Lord Street is full. Ruth sits silently waiting while Basil and Lass queue for handouts. Ruth's chair bleeds rubber foam to the piss-stained carpet from an ugly gash in its plastic. It can barely support her weight, but then neither can Ruth. Her vision is spinning and her neck is warm. She's been sick down her dress, and there's likely more to come.

Above a sign that says *Benefit Fraud Is Everyone's Problem,* an old television set hangs from the ceiling on dulled chains. Ruth peers up at it, squinting to focus. The colours are washy and *wrong,* and the picture fights roll and black static.

On the screen, some wanker in a sharp suit spreads news of a world bent on Ruth's exclusion. Her world is the park, the bins behind Easy Rider, the mission's soup kitchen, and little else. Hers is a rock pool that's barely heard of the ocean.

Ruth closes her eyes, but the television plays on behind her lids. The Spring Heel leaps in; his screen entrance could be Spider-Man camp, all comic book perspective and improbable acrobatic acts had Ruth not seen for herself his leaps and bounds.

Spring Heel's face fills the screen on Ruth's eyelids. His own eyes bulge, all spider veins and weeping, yellowed fluid. He tilts his head and there's a rim of fire on his lips. When he speaks, his words are disjointed as if they fall into Ruth's head from far away.

"I'll be taking you with me, Ruth," he says. "See if I don't."

Ruth falls forward from her chair. She's unconscious before she hits the floor.

· · ·

A twilight world, lost inside Ruth's head. Shapes fade and loom; colours swirl. She's in the park, but it's hardly the same park she knows so intimately. The air smells of wood smoke, and gas lamps hiss and bathe the strolling gentry with a tallow glow. Between the lamps the stars burn fiercely in darker skies.

Ruth reaches down and smoothes her petticoats. These are fine garments, silken to the touch. No one has pulled out and ejaculated on these skirts. No one has wiped piss and snot and God knows what on these gowns. She feels a hand grasp her wrist from behind, and she's lifted with ease from the ground. Ruth leaps, instinctively in step with her bearer's giant strides, until they're like two ice dancers soaring gracefully as one. Below her, the lamps swirl and fall away. Ruth feels the night air cool and damp on her brow.

"Is this what you want, Ruth?" says the Spring Heel.

Ruth shivers. She stares down at Victorian Liverpool bustling far, far below her feet. With each bound, the Spring Heel takes her higher, farther away from the pimps and pushers, away from the users and abusers; away from the Ruth she once was and farther toward the narrow thoroughfares and simpler times.

"Yes," Ruth whispers. She grips the Spring Heel tighter. "It's what I want."

Ruth turns her head. The Spring Heel's breath is a fire on his lips, but for an instant he could be Basil, or Lass, or even The Runt.

"You'd leave them all to be here?" says the Spring Heel.

"I could bring them with me."

"You could if they'll come."

· · ·

Ruth wakes, startled. The ward is hospital-warm, sickly stifling, and Ruth gasps for breath.

"She's awake," says The Runt. "About fuckin' time. I hate hospitals, me; hospitals are bad for the health."

Basil and Lass, entwined as ever, turn as one from the window.

"You gave us quite a turn, old thing," says Basil. "I thought we'd damned well lost you."

Lass smiles. "But not yet," she says. "Not quite yet, eh?"

The smell of the park lingers. Ruth still tastes the fiery breath of the Spring Heel on her lips. The white line of his grip fades around her wrist.

"Where did he go?" says Ruth.

"Who?" says The Runt.

"The Spring Heel."

A nurse enters the room. The Runt's ripe, and Basil swigs the last dreg of his brandy, and the nurse makes no attempt to disguise her contempt. She waves her arms. "Everyone, out, the girl needs rest."

Lass runs a hand over Ruth's brow. She stares down into Ruth's eyes. "I think he'll come back for you later," she says. "And when he does, then you should go fearlessly with him. It's what we all do whenever the mood to go back takes us, and that's more and more these days. There's less and less here for us now."

Ruth smiles and nods. She thinks she understands. Everyone secretly yearns for simpler times.

When the Spring Heel comes, he no longer looks the terrible demon to Ruth. Instead he's a glowing light of salvation. He's love, and Faith, and Hope, and all that Ruth needs. Together they stand paused at the opened hospital window. The evening is cool and the street below glistens with earlier rains.

Ruth can see the headline now: *Spring Heel Jack Lures Woman to Death Fall.*

Even as they leap, Ruth blows a kiss across time and space to The Runt, to Basil, and most of all to Lass. Perhaps she'll see them again one day, when they chance to journey back to better days. But for now Ruth strolls through the gas-lit park lanes with the gentry. She's at home in simpler times, and here she knows enough to live life away from prostitution, away from itchy labia, away from madmen with knives.

When she reaches the park gates, Ruth does not pause. She walks away slowly, deliberately. She no longer needs giant leaps to know where she's going. She glances skyward and sees the merest hint of the Spring Heel on his evening prowl.

"You're much misunderstood, sir," Ruth whispers to no one but the night and the devilish glow dancing amongst the chimney pots.

For an instant Ruth wonders if she's really there. Is this her Heaven, and her body lies broken against some hospital wall?

Ruth shakes her head. It doesn't matter. This is where she's at peace.

"Long may you leap, Mr Spring Heel," she says. "Your wonders to per-form."

Afterword

I've always been fascinated by the Spring Heel Jack legends. I love the way Jack was somehow able to show himself in great leaps and bounds even during daylight and yet still remain elusive and mysterious. I tried to mimic this in the story; to have the Spring Heel's appearances seem fleeting, as if he's almost incidental to Ruth's tale, yet at the same time to reveal him as a catalyst to bring on Ruth's (apparent) salvation. I added a little creative license to suggest that in Ruth's ragtag friends perhaps the Spring Heel didn't quite work alone. Living in Liverpool, where a great many of Jack's appearances came, also makes the legend special to me.

CAITLÍN R. KIERNAN

As Red as Red

Caitlín R. Kiernan is the author of seven novels, including the award-winning Threshold *and, most recently,* Daughter of Hounds *and* The Red Tree. *Her short fiction has been collected in* Tales of Pain and Wonder; From Weird and Distant Shores; To Charles Fort, with Love; Alabaster; *and* A Is for Alien. *Her erotica has been collected in three volumes:* Frog Toes and Tentacles, Tales from the Woeful Platypus, *and* Confessions of a Five-Chambered Heart. *She is currently beginning work on her eighth novel. She lives in Providence, Rhode Island.*

1

"So, you believe in vampires?" she asks, then takes another sip of her coffee and looks out at the rain pelting Thames Street beyond the café window. It's been pissing rain for almost an hour, a cold, stinging shower on an overcast afternoon near the end of March, a bitter Newport afternoon that would have been equally at home in January or February. But at least it's not pissing snow.

I put my own cup down—tea, not coffee—and stare across the booth at her for a moment or two before answering. "No," I tell Abby Gladding. "But, quite clearly, those people in Exeter who saw to it that Mercy Brown's body was exhumed, the ones who cut out her heart and burned it, clearly *they* believed in vampires. And that's what I'm studying, the psychology behind that hysteria, behind the superstitions."

"It was so long ago," she replies, and smiles. There's no foreshadowing in that smile, not even in hindsight. It surely isn't a predatory smile. There's nothing malevolent, or hungry, or feral in the expression. She just watches the rain and smiles, as though something I've said amuses her.

"Not really," I say, glancing down at my steaming cup. "Not so long ago as people might *like* to think. The Mercy Brown incident, that was in 1892, and the most recent case of purported vampirism in the Northeast I've been able to pin down dates from sometime in 1898, a mere hundred and eleven years ago."

Her smile lingers, and she traces a circle in the condensation on the plate-glass window, then traces another circle inside it.

"We're not so far removed from the villagers with their torches and pitchforks, from old Cotton Mather and his bunch. That's what you're saying."

"Well, not exactly, but . . ." and when I trail off, she turns her head toward me, and her blue-grey eyes seem as cold as the low-slung sky above Newport. You could almost freeze to death in eyes like those, I think, and I take another sip of my lukewarm Earl Grey with lemon. Her eyes seem somehow brighter than they should in the dim light of the coffeehouse, so there's your foreshadowing, I suppose, if you're the sort who needs it.

"You're pretty far from Exeter, Ms. Howard," she says, and takes another sip of her coffee. And me, I'm sitting here wishing we were talking about almost anything but Rhode Island vampires and the hysteria of crowds, tuberculosis, and the master's thesis I'd be defending at the end of May. It had been months since I'd had anything even resembling a date, and I didn't want to squander the next half hour or so talking shop.

"I think I've turned up something interesting," I tell her, because I can't think of any subtle way to steer the conversation in another direction. "A case no one's documented before, right here in Newport."

She smiles that smile again, and yeah, maybe I'm talking about violated corpses and rituals to keep the dead in the ground, but my mind's somewhere else. Even lesbian graduate students get horny now and then.

"I got a tip from a folklorist up at Brown," I say. "Seems maybe there was an incident here in 1785 or thereabouts. If it checks out, I might be onto the oldest case of suspected vampirism resulting in an exhumation anywhere in New England. So, now I'm trying to verify the rumors. But there's precious little to go on. Chasing vampires, it's not like studying the Salem witch trials, where you have all those court records, the indictments and depositions and what have you. Instead, it's necessary to spend a lot of time sifting and sorting fact from fiction, and, usually, there's not much of either to work with."

She nods, then glances back toward the big window and the rain. "Be a feather in your cap, though. If it's not just a rumor, I mean."

"Yes," I reply. "Yes, it certainly would."

And here, there's an unsettling wave of not-quite déjà vu, something closer to dissociation, perhaps, and for a few dizzying seconds I feel as if I'm watching this conversation, a voyeur listening in, or I'm only remembering it, but in no way actually, presently, taking part in it. And, too, the coffeehouse and our talk and the rain outside seem a lot less concrete—less *here and now*—than does the morning before. One day that might as well be the next, and it's raining, either way.

I'm standing alone on Bowen's Wharf, staring out past the masts crowded into the marina at sleek white sailboats skimming over the glittering water, and there's the silhouette of Goat Island, half hidden in the fog. I'm about to turn and walk back up the hill to Washington Square and the library, about to leave the gaudy, Disney World concessions catering to the tastes of tourists and return to the comforting maze of ancient gabled houses lining winding, narrow streets. And that's when I see her for the first time. She's standing alone near the "seal safari" kiosk, staring at a faded sign, at black-and-white photographs of harbor seals with eyes like the puppies and little girls from those hideous Margaret Keane paintings. She's wearing an old peacoat and shiny green galoshes that look new, but there's nothing on her head, and she doesn't have an umbrella. Her long black hair hangs wet and limp, and when she looks at me, it frames her pale face.

Then it passes, the blip or glitch in my psyche, and I've snapped back, into myself, into *this* present. I'm sitting across the booth from her once more, and the air smells almost oppressively of freshly roasted and freshly ground coffee beans.

"I'm sure it has a lot of secrets, this town," she says, fixing me again with those blue-grey eyes and smiling that irreproachable smile of hers.

"Can't swing a dead cat," I say, and she laughs.

"Well, did it ever work?" Abby asks. "I mean, digging up the dead, desecrating their mortal remains to appease the living. Did it tend to do the trick?"

"No," I reply. "Of course not. But that's beside the point. People do strange things when they're scared."

And there's more, mostly more questions from her about Colonial-era vampirism, Newport's urban legends, and my research as a folklorist. I'm grateful that she's kind or polite enough not to ask the usual "you mean people get paid for this sort of thing" questions. She tells me a werewolf story dating back to the 1800s, a local priest supposedly locked away in the Portsmouth Poor Asylum after he committed a particularly gruesome murder, how he was spared the gallows because people believed he was a werewolf and so not in control of his actions. She even tells me about seeing his nameless grave in a cemetery up in Middletown, his tombstone bearing the head of a wolf. And I'm polite enough not to tell her that I've heard this one before.

Finally, I notice that it's stopped raining. "I really ought to get back to work," I say, and she nods and suggests that we should have dinner sometime soon. I agree, but we don't set a date. She has my cell number, after all, so we can figure that out later. She also mentions a movie playing at Jane Pickens that she hasn't seen and thinks I might enjoy. I leave her sitting there in the booth, in her peacoat and green galoshes, and she orders another cup of coffee as I'm exiting the café. On the way back to the library, I see a tree filled with noisy, cawing crows, and for some reason it reminds me of Abby Gladding.

2.

That was Monday, and there's nothing the least bit remarkable about Tuesday. I make the commute from Providence to Newport, crossing the East Passage of Narragansett Bay to Conanicut Island, and then the West Passage to Aquidneck Island and Newport. Most of the day is spent at the Redwood Library and Athenaeum on Bellevue, shut away with my newspaper clippings and microfiche, with frail yellowed books that were printed before the Revolutionary War. I wear the white cotton gloves they give me for handling archival materials, and make several pages of handwritten notes, pertaining primarily to the treatment of cases of consumption in Newport during the first two decades of the eighteenth century.

The library is open late on Tuesdays, and I don't leave until sometime after seven p.m. But nothing I find gets me any nearer to confirming that a corpse believed to have belonged to a vampire was exhumed from the Common Burying Ground in 1785. On the long drive home, I try not to think about the fact that she hasn't called, or my growing suspicion that she likely never will. I have a can of ravioli and a beer for dinner. I half watch something forgettable on television. I take a hot shower and brush my teeth. If there are any dreams—good, bad, or otherwise—they're nothing I recall upon waking. The day is sunny, and not quite as cold, and I do my best to summon a few shoddy scraps of optimism, enough to get me out the door and into the car.

But by the time I reach the library in Newport, I've got a headache, what feels like the beginnings of a migraine, railroad spikes in both my eyes, and I'm wishing I'd stayed in bed. I find a comfortable seat in the Roderick Terry Reading Room, one of the armchairs upholstered with dark green leather, and leave my sunglasses on while I flip through books pulled randomly from the shelf on my right. Novels by William Kennedy and Elia Kazan, familiar, friendly books, but trying to focus on the words only makes my head hurt worse. I return *The Arrangement* to its slot on the shelf, and pick up something called *Thousand Cranes* by a Japanese author, Yasunari Kawabata.

I don't open the book, but I don't reshelve it, either. It rests there in my lap, and I sit beneath the octagonal skylight with my eyes closed for a while. Five minutes maybe, maybe more, and the only sounds are muffled footsteps, the turning of pages, an old man clearing his throat, a passing police siren, one of the librarians at the front desk whispering a little louder than usual. Or maybe the migraine magnifies her voice and only makes it seem that way. In fact, all these small, unremarkable sounds seem magnified, if only by the quiet of the library.

When I open my eyes, I have to blink a few times to bring the room back into focus. So I don't immediately notice the woman standing outside the window, looking in at me. Or only looking *in,* and I just happen to be in her line of sight. Maybe she's looking at nothing in particular, or at the bronze statue of Pheidippides perched on its wooden pedestal. Perhaps she's looking for someone else, someone who isn't me. The window is on the opposite side of the library from where I'm sitting, forty feet or so away. But even at that distance, I'm almost certain that the pale face and lank black hair belong to Abby Gladding. I raise a hand, half waving to her, but if she sees me, she doesn't acknowledge having seen me. She just stands there, perfectly still, staring in.

I get to my feet, and the copy of *Thousand Cranes* slides off my lap; the noise the book makes when it hits the floor is enough that a couple of people look up from their magazines and glare at me. I offer them an apologetic gesture—part shrug and part sheepish frown—and they shake their heads, almost in unison, and go back to reading. When I glance at the window again, the black-haired woman is no longer there. Suddenly, my headache is much worse (probably from standing so quickly, I think), and I feel a sudden, dizzying rush of adrenaline. No, it's more than that. I feel afraid. My heart races, and my mouth has gone very dry. Any plans I might have harbored of going outside to see if the woman looking in actually was Abby vanish immediately, and I sit down again. If it was her, I reason, then she'll come inside.

So I wait, and, very slowly, my pulse returns to its normal rhythm, but the adrenaline leaves me feeling jittery, and the pain behind my eyes doesn't get any better. I pick the novel by Yasunari Kawabata up off the floor and place it back upon the shelf. Leaning over makes my head pound even worse, and I'm starting to feel nauseous. I consider going to the restrooms, near the circulation desk, but part of me is still afraid, for whatever reason, and it seems to be the part of me that controls my legs. I stay in the seat and wait for the woman from the window to walk into the Roderick Terry Reading Room. I wait for her to be Abby, and I expect to hear her green galoshes squeaking against the lacquered hardwood. She'll say that she thought about calling, but then figured that I'd be in the library, so of course my phone would be switched off. She'll say something about the weather, and she'll want to know if I'm still up for dinner and the movie. I'll tell her about the migraine, and maybe she'll offer me Excedrin or Tylenol. Our hushed conversation will annoy someone, and he or she will shush us. We'll laugh about it later on.

But Abby doesn't appear, and so I sit for a while, gazing across the wide room at the window, a tree *outside* the window, at the houses lined up neat and tidy along Redwood Street. On Wednesday, the library is open until eight, but I leave as soon as I feel well enough to drive back to Providence.

3.

It's Thursday, and I'm sitting in that same green armchair in the Roderick Terry Reading Room. It's only 11:26 a.m., and already I understand that I've lost the day. I have no days to spare, but already, I know that the research that I should get done today isn't going to happen. Last night was too filled with uneasy dreaming, and this morning I can't concentrate. It's hard to think about anything but the nightmares, and the face of Abby Gladding at the window; her blue eyes, her black hair. And yes, I have grown quite certain that it *was* her face I saw peering in, and that she was peering in *at* me.

She hasn't called (and I didn't get her number, assuming she has one). An hour ago, I walked along the Newport waterfront looking for her, to no avail. I stood awhile beside the "seal safari" kiosk, hoping, irrationally I suppose, that she might turn up. I smoked a cigarette, and stood there in the cold, watching the sunlight on the bay, listening to traffic and the wind and a giggling flock of gray seagulls. Just before I gave up and made my way back to the library, I noticed dog tracks in a muddy patch of ground near the kiosk. I thought that they seemed unusually large, and I couldn't help but recall the café on Monday and Abby relating the story of the werewolf priest buried in Middletown. But lots of people in Newport have big dogs, and they walk them along the wharf.

I'm sitting in the green leather chair, and there's a manila folder of photocopies and computer printouts in my lap. I've been picking through them, pretending this is work. It isn't. There's nothing in the folder I haven't read five or ten times over, nothing that hasn't been cited by other academics chasing stories of New England vampires. On top of the stack is "The 'Vampires' of Rhode Island," from *Yankee* magazine, October 1970. Beneath that, "They Burned Her Heart . . . Was Mercy Brown a Vampire?" from the *Narragansett Times,* October 25, 1979, and from the *Providence Sunday Journal,* also October 1979, "Did They Hear the Vampire Whisper?" So many of these popular pieces have October dates, a testament to journalism's attitude toward the subject, which it clearly views as nothing more than a convenient skeleton to pull from the closet every Halloween, something to dust off and trot out for laughs.

Salem has its witches. Sleepy Hollow its headless Hessian mercenary. And Rhode Island has its consumptive, consuming phantoms—Mercy Brown, Sarah Tillinghast, Nellie Vaughn, Ruth Ellen Rose, and all the rest. Beneath the *Providence Sunday Journal* piece is a black-and-white photograph I took a couple of years ago, Nellie Vaughn's vandalized headstone, with its infamous inscription: "I am waiting and watching for you." I stare at the photograph for a moment or two, and set it aside. Beneath it there's a copy of another October article, "When the Wind Howls and the Trees Moan," also from the *Providence Sunday Journal.* I close the manila folder and try not to stare at the window across the room.

It is only a window, and it only looks out on trees and houses and sunlight.

I open the folder again, and read from a much older article, "The Animistic Vampire in New England" from *American Anthropologist*, published in 1896, only four years after the Mercy Brown incident. I read it silently, to myself, but catch my lips moving:

> In New England the vampire superstition is unknown by its proper name. It is believed that consumption is not a physical but spiritual disease, obsession, or visitation; that as long as the body of a dead consumptive relative has blood in its heart it is proof that an occult influence steals from it for death and is at work draining the blood of the living into the heart of the dead and causing his rapid decline.

I close the folder again and return it to its place in my book bag. And then I stand and cross the wide reading room to the window and the alcove where I saw, or only thought I saw, Abby looking in at me. There's a marble bust of Cicero on the window ledge, and I've been staring out at the leafless trees and the brown grass, the sidewalk and the street, for several minutes before I notice the smudges on the pane of glass, only inches from my face. Sometime recently, when the window was wet, a finger traced a circle there, and then traced a circle within that first circle. When the glass dried, these smudges were left behind. And I remember Monday afternoon at the coffeehouse, Abby tracing an identical symbol (if "symbol" is the appropriate word here) in the condensation on the window while we talked and watched the rain.

I press my palm to the glass, which is much colder than I'd expected.

In my dream, I stood at another window, at the end of a long hallway, and looked down at the North Burial Ground. With some difficulty, I opened the window, hoping the air outside would be fresher than the stale air in the hallway. It was, and I thought it smelled faintly of clover and strawberries. And there was music. I saw Abby then, standing beneath a tree, playing a violin. The music was very beautiful, though very sad, and completely unfamiliar. She drew the bow slowly across the strings, and I realized that somehow the music was shaping the night. There were clouds sailing past above the cemetery, and the chords she drew from the violin changed the shapes of those clouds, and also seemed to dictate the speed at which they moved. The moon was bloated, and shone an unhealthy shade of ivory, and the whole sky writhed like a Van Gogh painting. I wondered why she didn't tell me that she plays the violin.

Behind me, something clattered to the floor, and I looked over my shoulder. But there was only the long hallway, leading off into perfect darkness, leading back the way I'd apparently come. When I turned again to the open window and the cemetery, the music had ceased, and Abby was gone. What had taken her place, it might almost have passed for a large dog. It sat near the tree, amid row after row of tilted headstones, charcoal-colored slate, white marble, a few cut from slabs of reddish sandstone mined from Massachusetts or Connecticut. I was reminded of a platoon of drunken soldiers, lined up for a battle they knew they were going to lose.

I have never liked writing down my dreams.

It is late Thursday morning, almost noon, and I pull my hand back from the cold, smudged windowpane. I have to be in Providence for an evening lecture, and I gather my things and leave the Redwood Library and Athenaeum. On the drive back to the city, I do my best to stop thinking about the nightmare, my best not to dwell on what I saw sitting beneath the tree, after the music stopped and Abby Gladding disappeared. My best isn't good enough.

4.

The lecture goes well, quite a bit better than I'd expected it would, better, probably, than it had a right to, all things considered. "Mercy Brown as Inspiration for Bram Stoker's *Dracula*," presented to the Rhode Island Historical Society, and, somehow, I even manage not to make a fool of myself answering questions afterward. It helps that I've answered these same questions so many times in the past. For example:

"I'm assuming you've also drawn connections between the Mercy Brown incident and Sheridan Le Fanu's *Carmilla*?"

"There are similarities, certainly, but so far as I know, no one has been able to demonstrate conclusively that Le Fanu knew of the New England phenomena. And, of course, the publication of *Carmilla* predates the exhumation of Mercy Brown's body by twenty years."

"Still, he might have known of the earlier cases."

"Certainly. He may well have. However, I have no *evidence* that he did."

But, the entire time, my mind is elsewhere, back across the water in Newport, in that coffeehouse on Thames, and the Redwood Library, and standing in a dream hallway, looking down on my subconscious rendering of the Common Burying Ground. A woman playing a violin beneath a tree. A woman with whom I have only actually spoken once, but about whom I cannot stop thinking.

It is believed that consumption is not a physical but spiritual disease, obsession, or visitation . . .

After the lecture, and the questions, after introductions are made and notable, influential hands are shaken, when I can finally slip away without seeming either rude or unprofessional, I spend an hour or so walking alone on College Hill. It's a cold, clear night, and I follow Benevolent Street west to Benefit and turn north. There's comfort in the uneven, buckled bricks of the sidewalk, in the bare limbs of the trees, in all the softly glowing windows. I pause at the granite steps leading up to the front door of what historians call the Stephen Harris House, built in 1764. One hundred and sixty years later, H. P. Lovecraft called this the "Babbitt House" and used it as the setting for an odd tale of lycanthropy and vampirism. I know this huge yellow house well. And I know, too, the four hand-painted signs nailed up on the gatepost, all of them in French. From the sidewalk, by the electric glow of a nearby streetlamp, I can make out only the top half of the third sign in the series; the rest are lost in the gloom—*Oubliez le Chien.* Forget the Dog.

I start walking again, heading home to my tiny, cluttered apartment, only a couple of blocks east on Prospect. The side streets are notoriously steep, and I've been in better shape. I haven't gone twenty-five yards before I'm winded and have a nasty stitch in my side. I lean against a stone wall, cursing the cigarettes and the exercise I can't be bothered with, trying to catch my breath. The freezing air makes my sinuses and teeth ache. It burns my throat like whiskey.

And this is when I glimpse a sudden blur from out the corner of my right eye, hardly *more* than a blur. An impression or the shadow of something large and black, moving quickly across the street. It's no more than ten feet away from me, but downhill, back toward Benefit. By the time I turn to get a better look, it's gone, and I'm already beginning to doubt I saw anything, except, possibly, a stray dog.

I linger here a moment, squinting into the darkness and the yellow-orange sodium-vapor pool of streetlight that the blur seemed to cross before it disappeared. I want to laugh at myself, because I can actually feel the prick of goose bumps along my forearms, and the short, fine hairs at the nape of my neck standing on end. I've blundered into a horror-movie cliché, and I can't help but be reminded of Val Lewton's *Cat People*, the scene where Jane Rudolph walks quickly past Central Park, stalked by a vengeful Simone Simon, only to be rescued at the last possible moment by the fortuitous arrival of a city bus. But I know there's no helpful bus coming to intervene on my behalf, and, more importantly, I understand full fucking well that this night holds nothing more menacing than what my overstimulated imagination has put there. I turn away from the streetlight and continue up the hill toward home. And I do not have to *pretend* that I don't hear footsteps following me, or the clack of claws on concrete, because I *don't*. The quick shadow, the peripheral blur, it was only a moment's misapprehension, no more than a trick of my exhausted, preoccupied mind, filled with the evening's morbid banter.

Oubliez le Chien.

Fifteen minutes later, I'm locking the front door of my apartment behind me. I make a hot cup of chamomile tea, which I drink standing at the kitchen counter. I'm in bed shortly after ten o'clock. By then, I've managed to completely dismiss whatever I only thought I saw crossing Jenckes Street.

5.

"Open your eyes, Ms. Howard," Abby Gladding says, and I do. Her voice does not in any way command me to open my eyes, and it is perfectly clear that I have a choice in the matter. But there's a certain *je ne sais quoi* in the delivery, the inflection and intonation, in the measured conveyance of these four syllables, that makes it impossible for me to keep my eyes closed. It's not yet dawn, but sunrise cannot be very far away, and I am lying in my bed. I cannot say whether I am awake or dreaming, or if possibly I am stranded in some liminal state that is neither one nor the other. I am immediately conscious of an unseen weight bearing down painfully upon my chest, and I am having difficulty breathing.

"I promised that I'd call on you," she says, and, with great effort, I turn my head toward the sound of her voice, my cheek pressing deeply into my pillow. I am aware now that I am all but paralyzed, perhaps by the same force pushing down on my chest, and I strain for any glimpse of her. But there's only the bedside table, the clock radio and reading lamp and ashtray, an overcrowded bookcase with sagging shelves, and the floral calico wallpaper that came with the apartment. If I could move my arms, I would switch on the lamp. If I could move, I'd sit up, and maybe I would be able to breathe again.

And then I think that she must surely be singing, though her song has no words. There is no need for mere lyrics, not when texture and timbre, harmony and melody, are sufficient to unmake the mundane artifacts that comprise my bedroom, wiping aside the here and now that belie what I am meant to see, in this fleeting moment. And even as the wall and the bookshelf and the table beside my bed dissolve and fall away, I understand that her music is drawing me deeper into sleep again, though I must have been very nearly awake when she told me to open my eyes. I have no time to worry over apparent contradictions, and I can't move my head to look away from what she means for me to see.

There's nothing to be afraid of, I think, and *No more here than in any bad dream.* But I find the thought carries no conviction whatsoever. It's even less substantial than the dissolving wallpaper and bookcase.

And now I'm looking at the weed-choked shore of a misty pond or swamp, a bog or tidal marsh. The light is so dim it might be dusk, or it might be dawn, or merely an overcast day. There are huge trees bending low near the water, which seems almost perfectly smooth and the green of polished malachite. I hear frogs, hidden among the moss and reeds, the ferns and skunk cabbages, and now the calls of birds form a counterpoint to Abby's voice. Except, seeing her standing ankle deep in that stagnant green pool, I also see that she isn't singing. The music is coming from the violin braced against her shoulder, from the bow and strings and the movement of her left hand along the fingerboard of the instrument. She has her back to me, but I don't need to see her face to know it's her. Her black hair hangs down almost to her hips. And only now do I realize that she's naked.

Abruptly, she stops playing, and her arms fall to her sides, the violin in her left hand, the bow in her right. The tip of the bow breaks the surface of the pool, and ripples in concentric rings race away from it.

"I wear this rough garment to deceive," she says, and, at that, all the birds and frogs fall silent. "Aren't you the clever girl? Aren't you canny? I would not think appearances would so easily lead you astray."

No words escape my rigid, sleeping jaws, but she hears me all the same, my answer that needs no voice, and she turns to face me. Her eyes are golden, not blue. And in the low light, they briefly flash a bright, iridescent yellow. She smiles, showing me teeth as sharp as razors, and then she quotes from the Gospel of Matthew.

"Inwardly, they were ravening wolves," she says to me, though her tone is not unkind. "You've seen all that you need to see, and probably more, I'd wager." And with this, she turns away again, turning to face the fog shrouding the wide green pool. As I watch, helpless to divert my gaze or even shut my eyes, she lets the violin and bow slip from her hands; they fall into the water with quiet splashes. The bow sinks, though the violin floats. And then she goes down on all fours. She laps at the pool, and her hair has begun to writhe like a nest of serpents.

And now I'm awake, disoriented and my chest aching, gasping for air as if a moment before I was drowning and have just been pulled to the safety of dry land. The wallpaper is only dingy calico again, and the bookcase is only a bookcase. The clock radio and the lamp and the ashtray sit in their appointed places upon the bedside table.

The sheets are soaked through with sweat, and I'm shivering. I sit up, my back braced against the headboard, and my eyes go to the second-story window on the other side of the small room. The sun is still down, but it's a little lighter out there than it is in the bedroom. And for a fraction of a moment, clearly silhouetted against that false dawn, I see the head and shoulders of a young woman. I also see the muzzle and alert ears of a wolf, and that golden eyeshine watching me. Then it's gone, she or it, whichever pronoun might best apply. It doesn't seem to matter. Because now I do know exactly what I'm looking for, and I know that I've seen it before, years before I first caught sight of Abby Gladding standing in the rain without an umbrella.

6.

Friday morning I drive back to Newport, and it doesn't take me long at all to find what I'm looking for. It's just a little ways south of the chain-link fence dividing the North Burial Ground from the older Common Burying Ground and Island Cemetery. I turn off Warner Street onto the rutted, unpaved road winding between the indistinct rows of monuments. I find a place that's wide enough to pull over and park. The trees have only just begun to bud, and their bare limbs are stark against a sky so blue-white it hurts my eyes to look directly into it. The grass is mostly still brown from long months of snow and frost, though there are small clumps of new green showing here and there.

The cemetery has been in use since 1640 or so. There are three Colonial era governors buried here (one a delegate to the Continental Congress), along with the founder of Freemasonry in Rhode Island, a signatory to the Declaration of Independence, various Civil War generals, lighthouse keepers, and hundreds of African slaves stolen from Gambia and Sierra Leone, the Gold and Ivory coasts and brought to Newport in the heyday of whaling and the Rhode Island rum trade. The grave of Abby Gladding is marked by a weathered slate headstone, badly scabbed over with lichen. But, despite the centuries, the shallow inscription is still easy enough to read:

HERE LYETH INTERED Y^e BODY

OF ABBY MARY GLADDING

DAUGHTER OF SOLOMON GLADDING ^{esq}

& MARY HIS WYFE WHO

DEPARTED THIS LIFE Y^e 2^d DAY OF

SEPT 1785 AGED 22 YEARS

SHE WAS DROWN'D & DEPARTED & SLEEPS

ZECH 4:1 NEITHER SHALL THEY WEAR

A HAIRY GARMENT TO DECEIVE

Above the inscription, in place of the usual death's head, is a crude carving of a violin. I sit down in the dry, dead grass in front of the marker, and I don't know how long I've been sitting there when I hear crows cawing. I look over my shoulder, and there's a tree back toward Farewell Street filled with the big black birds. They watch me, and I take that as my cue to leave. I know now that I have to go back to the library, that whatever remains of this mystery is waiting for me there. I might find it tucked away in an old journal, a newspaper clipping, or in crumbling church records. I only know I'll find it, because now I have the missing pieces. But there is an odd reluctance to leave the grave of Abby Gladding. There's no fear in me, no shock or stubborn disbelief at what I've discovered or at its impossible ramifications. And some part of me notes the oddness of this, that I am not afraid. I leave her alone in that narrow house, watched over by the wary crows, and go back to my car. Less than fifteen minutes later I'm in the Redwood Library, asking for anything they can find on a Solomon Gladding, and his daughter, Abby.

"Are you sick?" the librarian asks, and I wonder what she sees in my face, in my eyes, to elicit such a question. "Are you feeling well?"

"I'm fine," I assure her. "I was up a little too late last night, that's all. A little too much to drink, most likely."

She nods, and I smile.

"Well, then. I'll see what we might have," she says, and, cutting to the chase, it ends with a short article that appeared in the *Newport Mercury* early in November 1785, hardly more than two months after Abby Gladding's death. It begins, "We hear a ftrange account from laft Thursday evening, the Night of the 3rd of November, of a body difinterred from its Grave and coffin. This most peculiar occurrence was undertaken at the beheft of the father of the deceafed young woman therein buried, a circumftance making the affair even ftranger ftill." What follows is a description of a ritual that will be familiar to anyone who has read of the 1892 Mercy Brown case from Exeter, or the much earlier exhumation of Nancy Young (summer of 1827), or other purported New England "vampires."

In September, Abby Gladding's body was discovered in Newport Harbor by a local fisherman, and it was determined that she had drowned. The body was in an advanced state of decay, leading me to wonder if the date of the headstone is meant to be the date the body was found, not the date of her death. There were persistent rumors that the daughter of Samuel Gladding, a local merchant, had taken her own life. She is said to have been a "child of singular and morbid temperament," who had recently refused a marriage proposal by the eldest son of another Newport merchant, Ebenezer Burrill. There was also back-fence talk that Abby had practiced witchcraft in the woods bordering the town, and that she would play her violin (a gift from her mother) to summon "voracious wolves and other such dæmons to do her bidding."

Very shortly after her death, her youngest sister, Susan, suddenly fell ill.

This was in October, and the girl was dead before the end of the month. Her symptoms, like those of Mercy Brown's stricken family members, can readily be identified as late-stage tuberculosis. What is peculiar here is that Abby doesn't appear to have suffered any such wasting disease herself, and the speed with which Susan became ill and died is also atypical of consumption. Even as Susan fought for her life, Abby's mother, Mary, fell ill, and it was in hope of saving his wife that Solomon Gladding agreed to the exhumation of his daughter's body. The article in the *Newport Mercury* speculates that he'd learned of this ritual and folk remedy from a Jamaican slave woman.

At sunrise, with the aid of several other men, some apparently family members, the grave was opened, and all present were horrified to see "the body fresh as the day it was confighed to God," her cheeks "flufhed with colour and lufterous." The liver and heart were duly cut out, and both were discovered to contain clotted blood, which Solomon had been told would prove that Abby was rising from her grave each night to steal the blood of her mother and sister. The heart was burned in a fire kindled in the cemetery, the ashes mixed with water, and the mother drank the mixture. The body of Abby was turned facedown in her casket, and an iron stake was driven through her back to insure that the restless spirit would be unable to find its way out of the grave. Nonetheless, according to parish records from Trinity Church, Mary Gladding died before Christmas. Her father fell ill a few months later, and died in August of 1786.

And I find one more thing that I will put down here. Scribbled in sepia ink, in the left-hand margin of the newspaper page containing the account of the exhumation of Abby Gladding is the phrase *Jé-rouge,* or "red eyes," which I've learned is a Haitian term denoting werewolfery and cannibalism. Below that word, in the same spidery hand, is written "As white as snow, as red as red, as green as briers, as black as coal." There is no date or signature accompanying these notations.

And now it is almost Friday night, and I sit alone on a wooden bench at Bowen's Wharf, not too far from the kiosk advertising daily boat tours to view fat, doe-eyed seals sunning themselves on the rocky beaches ringing Narragansett Bay. I sit here and watch the sun going down, shivering because I left home this morning without my coat. I do not expect to see Abby Gladding, tonight or ever again. But I've come here, anyway, and I may come again tomorrow evening.

I will not include the 1785 disinterment in my thesis, no matter how many feathers it might earn for my cap. I mean never to speak of it again. What I have written here, I suspect I'll destroy it later on. It has only been written for me, and for me alone. If Abby was trying to speak *through* me, to find a larger audience, she'll have to find another mouthpiece. I watch a lobster boat heading out for the night. I light a cigarette, and eye the herring gulls wheeling above the marina.

Afterword

"Closer to home, there is Rhode Island's own 'phantom dog of Fort Wetherill' in Jamestown. Less renowned, perhaps, than its cousin to the west, sightings of this dog are also reputed to portend doom. In Tiverton, there are reports of a 'pitch black dog' that has been seen to transform itself into the figure of a woman, who then proceeds to play a violin before vanishing. Similarly, though less musically inclined, is the shape-shifting black dog of Newport, which also transforms itself into a woman who is given to peering in through windows."

—Charles L. Harvey, *The Red Tree*

EKATERINA SEDIA

Tin Cans

Ekaterina Sedia resides in the Pinelands of New Jersey. Her critically acclaimed novels, The Secret History of Moscow *and* The Alchemy of Stone, *were published by Prime Books. Her next one,* The House of Discarded Dreams, *is coming out in 2010. Her short stories have sold to* Analog, Baen's Universe, Dark Wisdom, *and* Clarkesworld, *as well as* Japanese Dreams *and* Magic in the Mirrorstone *anthologies. Visit her at* www.ekaterinasedia.com.

I am an old man—too old to really care. My wife died on the day the Moscow Olympics opened, and my dick had not done anything interesting since the too optimistic Chechen independence. I shock people when I tell them how young I was when the battleship *Aurora* gave its fateful blast announcing the Revolution. And yet life feels so short, and this is why I'm telling you this story.

My grand-nephew Danila—smug and slippery, like all young people nowadays, convinced they know the score even though they don't know shit, and I always get an urge to take off my belt and wail some humility on their asses—called and asked if I needed a job. Tunisian embassy, he said, easy enough. Night watchman duty only, since for business hours they had their own guards, tall and square-chested, shining and black like well-polished boots, their teeth like piano keys. You get to guard at night, old man, old husk, when no one would see you.

Now, I needed a job; of course I did, who didn't? After the horrible and hungry 1990s, even years later, I was just one blind drunken stagger of the inflation away from picking empty bottles in the streets or playing my accordion by the subway station. So of course I said yes, even though Danila's combination of ignorance and smarm irritated me deeply, just like many things did—and it wasn't my age, it was these stupid times.

. . .

The embassy was located in Malaya Nikitskaya, in a large mansion surrounded by a park with nice shady trees and flower beds, all tucked away behind a thirty-foot brick fence. I saw it often enough. The fence, I mean. I had never been inside before the day of my interview. All I knew about Tunisia was that they used to be Carthage at some point, very long ago, and that they used to have Hannibal and his elephants—I thought of elephants in the zoo when I paused by the flower beds to straighten my jacket and adjust the bar ribbons on my lapel. There used to be a time when war was good and sensible, or at the very least there were elephants involved.

There were no lines snaking around the building, like you would see at the American embassy—not surprising really, because no one wanted to immigrate to Tunisia and everyone was gagging for Brooklyn. I've been, I traveled—and I don't know why anyone would voluntarily live in Brighton Beach, that sad and gray throwback to the provincial towns of the USSR in the seventies, fringed by the dirty hem of a particularly desperate ocean. The irony is of course that every time you're running from something, it follows you around, like a tin can tied to a dog's shaggy tail. Those Brooklyn inhabitants, they brought everything they hated with them.

That was the only reason I stayed here, in this cursed country, in this cursed house, and now stood at the threshold, staring at the blue uniforms and shining buttons of two strapping Tunisians—guards or attachés, I wasn't sure—and I wasn't running anywhere, not to Brooklyn, nor to distant and bright Tunisia with its ochre sands and suffocating nights. Instead, I said, "I heard you're hiring night watchmen."

They showed me in and let me fill out the application. There were no pens, and I filled it out with the stubby pencil I usually carried with me, wetting its blunt soapy tip on my tongue every few letters—this way, my words came out bright and convincing. As much as it chafed me, I put Danila's name as a reference.

They called me the next day to offer me the job, and told me to come by after hours two days later.

It was May then. May with its late sunsets and long inky shadows, pooling darkness underneath the blooming lilac bushes, and clanging of trams reaching into the courtyard of the house in Malaya Nikitskaya from the cruel and dirty world beyond its walls. I entered in a shuffling slow walk—not the walk of old age, but of experience.

And yet, soon enough there I was. As soon as the wrought-iron gates

slammed shut behind my back, I felt cut off from everything, as if I had really
escaped into glorious Carthage squeezed into a five-storied mansion and the
small garden surrounding it. A tall diplomat and his wife, her head wrapped
in a colorful scarf, strolled arm in arm, as out of place in Moscow as I would
be in Tunisia. They did not notice me, of course—after you reach a certain
age, people's eyes slide right off of you, afraid that the sight of you will cor-
rupt and age their vision, and who wants that?

So I started at the embassy—guarding empty corridors, strolling with my
flashlight along the short but convoluted paths in the garden, ascending and
descending stairs in no particular order. Sometimes I saw one diplomat or
another walking down the hall to the bathroom, their eyes half-closed and
filled with sleep. They moved right past me, and I knew better than to say
anything, because who wants to be acknowledged while hurrying to the
john in the middle of the night. So I pretended that I was invisible, until the
day I saw the naked girl.

. . .

Of course I knew whose house it was—whose house it used to be. I remembered Lavrenty Beria's arrest, back in the fifties, his fat sausage fingers on
the buttonless fly, holding up his pants. Khrushchev was so afraid of him, he
instructed Marshal Zhukov and his men who made the arrest to cut off the
buttons so that his terrible hands would be occupied. It should've been comi-
cal, but it was terrible instead, those small ridiculous motions of the man
whose name no one said aloud, for fear of summoning him. Worse than
Stalin, they said, and after Stalin was dead they dared to arrest Beria, his right
hand, citing some ridiculous excuses like British espionage and imaginary
plots. The man who murdered Russians, Georgians, Polacks with equal and
indiscriminating efficiency when he was the head of NKVD, before it softened up into the KGB. And there he was then, being led out of the Presidium
session, unclean and repulsive like a carrion fly.

He was shot soon after, they said, but it was still murder; at least, I thought
so, seeking to if not justify then comprehend, thinking around and around
and hastening my step involuntarily.

Sometimes the attachés, while rushing for the bathrooms, left their doors
ajar, illuminated by the brass sconces on the walls, their semicircles of light
snatching the buttery gloss of mahogany furniture and the slightly indecent

spillage of stiff linen, the burden of excess. But mostly I walked the hallways, thinking of everything that happened in this house, so I wasn't all that surprised or shocked when I first saw the naked girl.

She must've been barely thirteen—her breasts uncomfortable little hillocks, her hips narrow and long. She ran down the hall, and I guessed that she did not belong—she did not seem Tunisian, or alive, for that matter. She just ran, her mouth a black distorted silent hole in her face, her eyes bruised. Her hair, shoulder-length, wheat-colored, streamed behind her, and I remember the hollow on the side of her smooth lean hip, the way it reflected light from my flashlight, the working of ropy muscles under her smooth skin. Oh, she really ran, her heels digging into the hardwood floors as if they were soft dirt, her fists pumping.

I followed her with the beam of my flashlight. I stopped dead in my tracks, did not dare to think about it yet, just watched and felt my breathing grow lighter. She reached the end of the hallway and I expected her to disappear or take off up or down the stairs, or turn around; instead, she stopped just before the stairwell, and started striking the air in front of her with both fists, as if there was a door.

She turned once, her face half-melting in the deluge of ghost tears, her fists still pummeling against the invisible door, but without conviction, her heart ready to give out. Then an invisible but rough hand jerked her away from the door—I could not see who was doing it, but I saw her feet leave the ground, and then she was dragged along the hardwood floors through the nearest closed door.

I stood in the hallway for a while, letting it all sink in. Of course I knew who she was—not her name or anything, but what happened to her. I stared at the locked door; I knew that behind it the consul and his wife slept in a four-postered bed. And yet, in the very same bed, there was that ghost girl, hairs on her thin arms standing on end and her mouth still torn by a scream, invisible hands pressing her face into a pillow, her legs jerking and kicking at the invisible assailant. . . . I was almost relieved that I could not see him, even though the moment I turned and started down the hallway again, his bespectacled face slowly materialized, like a photo being developed, on the inside of my eyelids, and I could not shake the sense of his presence until the sun rose.

· · ·

I soon found a routine with my new job: all night I walked through the stairwells and the corridors, sometimes dodging the ghosts of girls—there were so many, so many, all of them between twelve and eighteen, all of them terrible in their nudity—and the living diplomats who stayed at the embassy stumbling past the soft shine of their gold-plated fixtures on their way to the bathrooms. In the mornings, I went to a small coffeehouse to have a cup of very hot and sweet and black coffee with a thick layer of sludge in the bottom. I drank it in deliberate sips and thought of the heavy doors with iron bolts and the basement with too many chambers and lopsided cement walls no one dared to disturb because of what they were afraid to find buried under and inside of them. And then I hurried home, in case my son decided to call from his time zone eight hours behind, before he went to bed.

You know that you're old when your children are old, when they have heart trouble and sciatica, when their hearing is going too so that both of you yell into the shell of the phone receiver. But most often, he doesn't call—and I do not blame him, I wouldn't call me either. He hadn't forgiven and he never fully will, except maybe on his deathbed—and it saddens me to think that he might be arriving there before me, like it saddens me that my grandchildren cannot read Cyrillic.

I come home and wait for the phone to speak to me in its low sentimental treble, and then I go to bed. I close my eyes and I watch the images from the previous night. I watch seven girls, none of whom can be older than fourteen, all on their hands and knees in a circle, their heads pressed together, their naked bottoms raised high, I watch them flinch away from the invisible presence that circles and circles them, endlessly. I think that I can feel the gust of Beria's stroll on my face, but that too passes.

I only turn away when one of them jerks as her leg rises high in the air—and from the depressions on the ghostly flesh I know that there's a hand seizing her by the ankle. He drags her away from the circle as she tries to kick with her free foot, grabbing at the long nap of the rug, as her elbows and breasts leave troughs in it, as her fingers tangle in the Persian luxury and then let go with the breaking of already short nails. I turn away because I know what happens next, and even though I cannot see him, I cannot watch.

Morning comes eventually, and always at the time when I begin to lose hope that the sun will ever rise again. I swear to myself that I will not come back here, *Never again,* I whisper—the same oath I gave to myself back before the war, and just like back then I know that I will break it over and over, every night.

On my way out of the light blue embassy house, I occasionally run into the cook, a Pakistani who has been working there for a few years. We sometimes stop for a smoke and he tells me about a bag of bones he found in the wall behind the stove some years back. He offers to show it to me but I refuse politely, scared of the stupid urban legend about a man who buys a hot dog and inside finds his wife's finger bone with her wedding ring still on. The ghosts are bad enough.

During this time, my son only called once. He complained at length, speaking hastily, as if trying to prevent me from talking back. I waited. I did not really expect him to talk about things we did not talk about—why he left or why he never told his wife where I was working. In turn, I made sympathetic noises and never mentioned how angry I was that his emigration back in the seventies fucked me over. What was the point? I did not blame him for his mother's death, and he didn't blame me for anything. He just complained that his grandkids don't understand Russian. I don't even remember what they, or their parents, my own grandchildren, look like.

When he was done talking, I went to bed and even slept until the voices of children outside woke me in the early afternoon. They always carried so far in this weather, those first warm days of not-quite summer, and I lay awake on my back listening to the high-pitched squealing outside, too warm in my long underwear. And if your life is like mine—if it's as long as mine, that is—then you find yourself thinking about a lot of shit. You start remembering the terrible sludge of life at the bottom of your memory, and if you stir it by too much thinking, too much listening to the shouts and bicycle bells outside, then woe is you, and the ghosts of teenage girls will keep you up all night and all day.

.   .   .

The cars NKVD drove were called black ravens, named for both color and the ominous nature of their arrival in one's neighborhood. Narodniy Komissariat Vnutrennih Del—it's a habit, to sound out the entire name in my head. Abbreviations just don't terrify me. The modern yellow canaries of the police seemed harmless in comparison, quaint even. But those black ravens . . . I remembered the sinister yellow beams of the headlights like I remembered the squeaking of leather against leather, uniform against the seats, like I remembered the roundness of the hard wheel under my gloved hands.

Being a chauffer was never a prestigious job, but driving him—driving Beria—filled one with quiet dread. I remember the blue dusk and the snowdrifts of late February, the bright pinpricks of the streetlamps as they lit up ahead of my car, one by one, as if running from us—from him, I think. I have never done anything wrong, but my neck prickles with freshly cut hairs, and my head sweats under my leather cap. I can feel his gaze on me, like a touch of greasy fingers. Funny, that: one can live ninety years, such a long life, and still shiver in the warm May afternoon just thinking about that one February night.

It started to snow soon after the streetlights all flickered on, lining along the facades of the houses—all old mansions, being in the center of the city and all, painted pale blues and yellows and greens. The flight of the lights reminded me of a poem I read some years ago; only I could not remember it but tried nonetheless—anything to avoid the sensation of the sticky unclean stare on the back of my head, at the base of my skull, and I felt cold, as if a gun barrel rested there.

"Slow down," he tells me in a soft voice. There's no one but him in the car, and I am grateful for small mercies, I am grateful that except for directions he does not talk to me.

I slow down. The wind is kicking up the snow and it writhes, serpentine, close to the ground, barely reaching up high enough to get snagged in the lights of the car beams.

"Turn off the lights."

I do, and then I see her—bundled up in an old, moth-eaten fur coat, her head swaddled in a thick kerchief. I recognize her—Ninochka, a neighbor who is rumored to be a bit addled in the head, but she always says hello to me and she is always friendly. The coat and kerchief disfigure and bloat her as she trundles through the snow, her walk waddling in her thick felt boots that look like they used to belong to her grandfather. I hope that this misshapen, ugly disguise would be enough to save her.

I pick up the speed slightly, to save her, to drive past her and perhaps find another girl walking home from work late, find another one—someone I do not know, and it is unfair that I am so willing to trade one for another but here we are—just God please, let us pass her. In my head, I make deals with

God, promises I would never be able to keep. I do not know why it's so important, but it feels that if I could just save her, just this one, then things would be all right again, the world would be revealed as a little bit just and at least somewhat sensible. Just this one, please, God.

"Slow down," he says again, and I feel the leather on the back of my seat shift as he grips the top of it. "Stop right there." He points just ahead, at the pool of darkness between two cones of light, where the snow changes color from white to blue. The wind is swirling around his shoes as he steps out, and the girl, Ninochka, looks up for the first time. She does not recognize him—not at first, not later when she is sobbing quietly in the backseat of the car, her arms twisted behind her so that she cannot even wipe her face and her tears drip off the reddened tip of her nose, like a melting icicle. I still cannot remember the poem—something about the running streetlights, and I concentrate on the elusive rhythm and stare straight ahead, until I stop by the wrought-iron gates of his house and let him and Ninochka out. I am not allowed beyond that point, being just a chauffer and not an NKVD man. I am grateful.

·   ·   ·

So I thought that my presence in the sky-blue house was not coincidental, and the fact that I kept seeing the dead naked girls everywhere I looked meant something. I tried to not look into their faces, not when they were clumped, heads together, in a circle. I did not need to see their faces to know that Ninochka was somewhere among them, a transparent long-limbed apparition being hauled off into some secret dungeon to undergo things best not thought about—and I squeezed my eyes shut and shook my head, just not to think about that, not to think.

My son was a dissident, and to him there was no poison more bitter than the knowledge that his father used to work for NKVD, used to turn people in, used to sit on people's tribunals that condemned enemies of the state. His shame for my sins forced his pointless flight into the place that offered none of the freedoms it had previously promised, the illusory comforts of the familiar language and the same conversations, of the slowly corrupting English words and the joys of capitalism as small and trivial as the cockroaches in a Brighton Beach kitchen. He still does not see the irony in that.

But he does manage to feel superior to me; he feels like he is better because he's not the one with naked dead girls chasing him through dreams and working hours, crowding in his head during the precious few minutes of leisure. The bar ribbons of all my medals and orders are of no consequence, as if there had been no war after the slow stealthy drives through the streets. Seasons changed but not the girls, forever trapped in the precarious land between adolescence and maturity, as if there were no victories and marching through mud all the way to Germany and back, as if there was nothing else after these girls. Time stopped in 1938, I suspect, and now it just keeps replaying in the house in Malaya Nikitskaya. And I cannot look away and I cannot quit the job in the embassy—not until I either figure out why this is happening or decide that I do not care enough to find out.

·   ·   ·

I remember the last week I worked in the Tunisian embassy. The dead girls infected everything, and even the diplomats and the security saw them out of the corners of their eyes—I saw them tossing up their heads on the way to the bathroom, their eyes wide and awake like those of spooked horses. The girls—long-limbed, bruised-pale—ran down every hallway, their faces looming up from every stairwell, every corner, every glass of sweet dark tea the Pakistani cook brewed for me in the mornings.

The diplomats whispered in their strange tongue, the tongue, I imagined, that remained unchanged since Hannibal and his elephants. I guessed that the girls were getting to them too, and for a brief while I was relating to these foreign dignitaries. Then they decided to deal with the problem, something I had not really considered, content in my unrelenting terror. They decided to take apart the fake partitions in the basement.

I was told not to come to work for a few days, and that damn near killed me. I could not sleep at night, thinking of the pale wraiths streaming in the dark paneled hallways of the sky-blue house. But the heart, the heart of it were all these dead girls, and I worried about them—I feared that they would exorcise them, would chase them away, leaving me no reason to ever go back, no reason to wake up every day, shave, leave the house. I could not know whether the semblance of life granted to them was torturous, and yet I hoped that they would survive.

They did not. When I came back, I found the basement devoid of its fake cement partitions, and the bricks in the basement walls were held together with fresh mortar. The corridors and the rooms were empty too—I often turned, having imagined a flick of movement on the periphery of my vision.

I looked into the empty rooms, hoping to catch a glimpse of long legs shredding the air into long, sickle-shaped slivers.

I found them after morning came and the cook offered me the usual glass of tea, dark and sweet and fragrant.

"They found all these bones," he told me, his voice regretful. "Even more than my bag, the one I told you about before."

"Where did they take them?"

He shrugged and shook his head, opening his arms palms-out in a pantomime of sincere puzzlement. I already knew that they were not in the house, because of course I already looked everywhere I could look without disturbing any of the diplomats' sleep.

Before I left for the day, I looked in the yard. It was so quiet there, so separate from the world outside. So peaceful. I found the skulls lined under the trees behind the building, where the graveled path traveled between the house and the wall.

I looked at the row of skulls, all of them with one hole through the base, and I regretted that I had never seen Ninochka's face among the silent wraiths. I did not know which of these skulls was hers; all of them looked at me with the black holes of their sockets, and I thought I heard the faint rattling of the bullets inside them, the clattering that grew louder like that of the tin cans dragging behind a running dog.

I turned away and walked toward the gates, trying to keep my steps slow and calm, trying to ignore the rattling of the skulls that had been dragging behind me for the last sixty years.

🙎 Afterword 🙎

Lavrentiy Pavlovich Beria is one of the most shadowy and controversial figures of Russian history, so it is not surprising that his former address figures in many ghost stories. There is a phantom limousine that stops by his house every night, and then there are the ghosts inside. Among all the different versions of this legend, I chose the most horrific. The actual life of Beria is just as shrouded in mystery, horror, and contradictory reports—the stories of kidnappings and rapes coexist with legends of giant meat grinders and other infernal torture devices in his basement; little hard evidence was found for any of them. Even his role in history is not entirely free of controversy—most know him as Stalin's butcher, but some argue that after Stalin's death he was on the forefront of reformism.

For me, this story was an opportunity to talk not only about a great evil, but of regular people complicit in it. How does one live after something like that?

JOHN MANTOOTH

Shoebox Train Wreck

John Mantooth teaches seventh-grade English and drives a school bus in central Alabama. His short stories have appeared in Shroud, Feral Fiction, Shimmer, *and* Fantasy. *Currently, he's finishing up his master's thesis: a collection of Southern noir about hard men, dead babies, and vehicular collisions.*

I imagined Suzy running across a great expanse of prairie, hair swept back by the wind, mouth opened to a laughing smile. For the prairie I used cut grass from the yard, taking time to glue each blade to the inside of the shoebox. Above her, cotton-ball clouds hang beneath an orange-peel sun. On either side are the things she loved in life: Skittles; Barbie dolls, represented by tiny, color cut-outs from *Girls' Life Magazine;* miniature plastic puppy dogs I found at a garage sale; and a beaded necklace, each bead painstakingly looped along a filament of thread no larger than a wisp of hair. Her hair, or so I like to imagine.

As for Suzy herself, I found her at the flea market, a glorious little figurine at the bottom of a box of toys. I knew the second I saw her. Something about the eyes, the smile, the windswept hair. It was Suzy.

I found the others in much the same way. Oh, not all of them were ready-made like Suzy. I had to piece Samantha together from old action figures, but eventually, I got her right.

When I started them, three years ago, just after the wreck, I had plans of calling the parents, the families, inviting them over to my room, showing them what I'd done, how hard I'd worked to denounce that day, to make their children alive again. I imagined them impressed, murmuring to each other, pointing at the level of detail, marveling at how I seemed to get everything just right. There would be tears, of course, but I'd wrap them up with hugs, and the tears would never hit the ground. Instead I would soak them all up in the folds of my shirt, so that when the families left, I could hang it in my closet unwashed, and touch it each day, another reminder of what I'd wrought.

Today, I stand inside my room and survey the six shoeboxes, wondering what might be done. I can think of nothing new, so I go to them one at a time, starting with Michael, ending with Suzy—Adriana, Phillip, Adam, and Samantha in between—the order I see them when I dream. I listen, their voices welling up from deep inside the boxes, soft sounds like murmuring wind. Leaning closer, I mold the sounds into words and they become a chant I cannot understand. But later, when the house is silent and I'm in my bed, drifting freely from sleep to waking and back again, I'm able to just make out what they are saying:

The dead do not haunt the living.

. . .

I thought about moving. After all, how many train engineers would stay in the same community where they caused such tragedy? Besides, by the time I got around to putting my house on the market, I'd already started the shoeboxes, and I needed to be here on the south side of San Antonio to finish them. Not that anyone has ever bothered me much about it. Most people assumed that the bus driver, Jake Crowley, was at fault because he put a shotgun in his mouth three hours after the wreck and blew off the top of his head.

Nowadays, if people talk about the accident at all, they speak of phantom trains and ghostly images of Crowley prowling the crossing at Buck's Creek with a lantern looking for all the children he lost. There's also a widespread belief that parking your car on the tracks where the accident occurred will cause the spirits of those six children to push your vehicle to safety. Teenagers like this last one. It's common enough to see them heading by the carload out to Buck's Creek with six-packs of beer and bags of Gold Medal flour to sift like dust over their back bumpers. Drunk enough, they can convince themselves of anything, even that the demarcations in the flour are the prints of angelic fingers rather than where moths have landed, drawn to the warm glow of the taillights.

And even though I haven't touched a drop of alcohol since the day of the wreck, I can believe it too.

. . .

Inside Phillip's box I have laid smooth strips of hardwood, oiled and polished to a shine. Over these, I've painted lines and erected miniature hoops. Phillip would be a senior now, if he had lived. He would have been a varsity basket-ball player, a good one, according to his coaches. The article the newspaper ran after the accident quoted the varsity coach as saying that Phillip was one of the middle school players he had already pegged for a college scholarship.

When I stare into his shoebox like I am doing now, I can almost hear the crowd behind him, cheering him on, insisting he live.

And sometimes I can lose my hold on this world, like roots slipping through the soil. When this happens I see him move. I see him play. And for a time, he does live again.

.   .   .

The thing that pleases me the most about my dioramas is that they represent an ordered place where violence cannot intervene. Here, I keep the children safe through diligence and attention to detail. They are invulnerable here, impervious to the awful winds of fate. Here, trains do not run, nor buses stall. Here, towns are not consumed by grief.

.   .   .

I've slept a dreamless sleep until my eyes open and see the blinking clock beside my bed. The room is dark, and it must still be hours before morning. Heaving myself out of bed, I go to the window and see that the yard is a wasteland of trash and tree branches. Earlier in the night, a great elm in my front yard cracked in two, and one side has fallen against a power line caus-ing random electrical sparks. They look like silver eels, whipcracking in a black sea.

I hear a knock at my front door. A moment later I'm peering through the peephole at James, my brakeman at the time of the accident.

Like me, James had been drunk the day of the accident, and like me, he'd been able to act sober enough at the scene of the wreck, when everybody was shouting questions at us. In fact, he'd been the first one to come to my defense during the inquiry. "Wasn't anything Arch could do. Everybody knows that the county commission should have put a crossing arm at Buck's Creek a long time ago. In my opinion, no engineer could have avoided that accident."

James and I fell out of touch after the wreck, mostly due to my own guilt and anger. But also because there seemed to exist between us a kind of physi-cal knowledge, an unspoken bludgeon. Whenever we were together, it hurt. I stopped answering the phone when he called. Once, I met him on the street on my way home from the library. We both pretended not to see the other. It was an unwritten pact, and we understood the parameters: suffer alone.

Now he's outside my door, having braved a thunderstorm in the middle of the night.

I'd heard he was sick with cancer, but even that doesn't prepare me for the way he looks. His body is smaller, his collarbone protruding out and around his neck like some obscene bone scarf. His hands are crossed in front of him, clasped together like clusters of hooks that have become accidentally entangled. His arms droop like fishing line, so skeletal and long, I wonder how he moves them, as the muscles are so deteriorated, they appear to have vanished. When he speaks, his teeth—what's left of them—smile of their own accord, a crooked pumpkin grin.

"Arch," he says. "Can I come in?"

I step aside and he shuffles past into my living room.

I sit down, gesturing to the couch for him.

Outside, a rush of rain begins again, so loud against my tin roof, I wonder how I slept through it the first time.

"I got some things to tell you, Arch."

Lightning flashes, making the room go white and then black as my power goes off for good. It's so dark James is nothing more than a shadow across the room.

"What we did, getting drunk on the train . . . You feel like a murderer. But that's over. For the longest time I wanted to go back to the day I lied and take it back. I wanted to go to jail. Die there. But I couldn't. You understand?"

"Yeah," I say. "I understand."

"Those kids down at the tracks. I talked to them. They want me to tell you something."

"Don't do this, James."

"They want you to understand. They're not still here because they want to be." He speaks calmly, oblivious to my rising anger.

"It's because I put them there, right, James? You were only the brakeman, ultimately not responsible for any of this. Isn't that the deal?" I'm across the room, reaching for him before I know what I'm doing. Grasping his shirt in my fist, I try to pull him to his feet. But he's heavy, way too heavy for a man his size. A flash of lightning lets me glimpse his dark eyes; they're unexpressive, calm.

"Let them go, Arch."

He seems about to say more when a barrage of lightning lashes the house, illuminating the room in a series of repeating flashes as if a million cameras are being snapped in an instant. When the room goes dark again, James is gone; I can't see him at all. His shirt is still balled in my fist. In desperation I pull hard on it, trying to find him, trying to pull myself back to him, but it's no use. His shirt rips. My fist holds something, but I can't see what. My head aches. Thunder pounds around me. The room spins, and I lose my grip on consciousness.

. . .

The next morning, sun streams in my window so brightly I can barely keep my eyes open.

The clock next to me blinks 12:00. I shade my eyes and peer out into the yard where the elm is split open. The power company is there, already working on the broken line.

I feel wasted, tired beyond all reason, as if I did not sleep at all. James's visit is still etched in my memory. But what had he wanted to tell me?

A dream, I decide. Then I realize something is clenched inside my fist. Opening my hand, I find a solitary button.

. . .

I confirm James's death with a quick phone call. According to his wife, Beth, he died last night in the midst of the storm.

"I'm sorry for your loss," I say.

"James told me the truth, Arch. He told me about being drunk."

"Beth . . ."

"I hated him. I wanted him to go to jail. Then the next day I wanted him to be with me forever. Back and forth like that. It was a long time before I forgave him. Even longer before he forgave himself."

"It wasn't his fault, Beth. It was mine."

"Nobody can carry that by themselves."

"Ever wonder who decides?" I ask her.

"Decides?"

"Decides which kids are due to die? Which bus will stall on the tracks? Before the accident, I'd been drunk dozens of times on that train. None of those mattered."

"Arch . . ."

"And how many children's deaths had I heard about before the wreck? Hundreds at least. All you have to do is turn on the nightly news and you'll get your fill. But you know what? I shrugged them off. Paid them no mind. It was like they didn't matter. But it changes. It all changes when you're driving the train that hits the bus. They're not just children anymore. They're your children."

.   .   .

I begin James's box the next day. I construct James out of a clothespin and spindly bits of wire. His head is the button I managed to keep from my dreamlike encounter with him.

Painstakingly, I build a little train and Popsicle-stick tracks. Placing James inside without me feels strange, but I do it anyway. I create a grayscale sky and dot the landscape with trees made from old bottlebrushes. Finally, I fashion the school bus from an old Cheerios box and place it on the tracks, just ahead of the train.

The day of the accident, in a shoebox. I feel like God, except powerless to stop the past.

.   .   .

A few days later I hear a whistle blow. I step outside on my back deck and study the trees behind my house, as if they are somehow responsible for the noise. I know somewhere behind those trees are the tracks where the accident occurred, but they are miles away, too far for me to hear a train.

Yet I can't deny the sound. I go back inside, into my sanctuary, and sit in front of my dioramas, waiting for the calm feeling to come over me, the feeling that lets me believe I am in control and the children in these boxes are not dead.

But I can hear the whistle here too. If anything, it's louder, more insistent, blaring, demanding that I do something. But what?

Closing my eyes, I try to go back to the night I dreamed of James.

What did he want? What had been so important?

Let them go, Arch.

"They won't let me go," I say.

Then another voice. A voice from my dream. A child's voice. *The dead do not haunt the living.*

"Yes they do," I say. "They haunt me."

The train whistle is louder.

I remember the day of the wreck, watching the trees as they scraped the sky. They looked like claws; the earth trying to peel back heaven.

That's what I was looking at when the one-hundred-car payload I was pulling began to wrap itself snakelike around the blind curve, and I saw the school bus stalled out on the tracks. One minute I had been drunk, perfectly content with the world, and the next I was cold sober and stricken with such bone-numbing panic I literally felt helpless, stuck inside my own skin.

If I even considered blowing the whistle, I don't remember it. What I do remember is thinking I had to stop the train. This thought was followed closely by the cold realization that I couldn't stop it, not in time to avoid a collision.

I never thought about bailing. It's nothing to be proud of, but I did stay with the train.

By the time I engaged the brakes, the train was on top of the bus.

There was a ground-shaking smack followed by the rending of metal on metal, the sickening scrape of steel, and then a single scream, which died almost as soon as it rang out, extinguished like a snuffed match. The train kept going, barely shuddering as it bisected the bus, sloughing off the front and back like great rocks tumbling from a precipice.

When it was over, one thing stood out. I never blew the whistle.

But someone is blowing it now.

. . .

Later that evening, I take my pickup truck out to the tracks, to Buck's Creek where the accident occurred. In back I have a bag of flour.

When I arrive, another car, a convertible, full of teenagers, is already there. They've parked on the tracks, powdered the bumper with copious amounts of flour, and now they wait, throwing back beers and laughing, pretending to hear noises behind them. They ignore me.

I wait too. An hour passes and the evening drops a veil over the sky, creating a hazy glow that is almost as silver as it is black. The stars are above me in draft, barely bright enough to be seen. Off in the woods an owl hoots, marking time, until the moment comes when the last inches of daylight are shooed away by shadows, and I see them gleaming in the almost darkness, six shapes, rising out of the earth. So slowly it's as if they've choreographed their movements with the setting sun.

By full dark, I can recognize them all; they line up in the order I have set for them in my room: Michael, Adriana, Phillip, Adam, Samantha, and Suzy. Suzy is not smiling. Phillip does not look pleased or full of athletic potential as he does inside my shoebox. Michael, Adrianna, Adam, and Samantha all look tired.

The children reach out for the car in front of them, their fingers barely grazing the bumper. They don't push as much as touch, and the car, already in neutral I suppose, rolls off the tracks. The teenagers inside laugh out loud. Somebody snorts and spews beer all over the others. A girl says, "Oh hell no. That did not just happen." A big kid with long straight hair and a beer in his hand jumps out and runs around to the back. "Holy shit, guys! Holeeee shit! Come look." They file out to look at the flour and the fingerprints of the children I killed. Yet they cannot see the children who stand on the tracks as if they are unsure what to do with themselves now.

One of them, Suzy, turns around and seems to see me. Her face is distraught, shining silver like the face of the moon on a clear night. Her eyes meet mine, and I hear the voice again. Her voice: *The dead do not haunt the living.*

Slowly, they reform their line in the center of the tracks. They stand, resolutely facing east, waiting for the train that will kill them all over again. Within seconds I spot smoke, snaking in thin columns over the tree line. The acrid smell of diesel fills my lungs. The earth beneath my feet begins to thrum.

The train appears, heaving forward like some hound unleashed from hell. The children are erased, obliterated, sent back to the soil from which they rose, sentenced to re-form and live again, however briefly the next night and the night after that and on and on until . . .

I let them go.

Driving away, into the shadowed dusk, I finally understand. The dead really don't haunt the living. The living haunt the dead.

. . .

I'll build a fire. Let the flames lick the bottom of the pines and watch the smoke curl heavenward. Then, one at a time, I will bring them out, toss them into the fire, turn away as they burn.

Last, I'll come to James's box. Keeping his button in my hand, I'll burn the rest. The fire will give off the sweet smell of death and no more lingering, a final scent, like the odor of chrysanthemums after a long rain.

Breathing in the air, I'll take a moment to think how the world never gives you what you expect. Like ghosts. Me keeping *them* around. I'll laugh at this thought and try to take some lesson from my anguish and the way it results in more anguish, an endless cycle, forever rolling over on itself until there is no proper way to tell where the cycle begins or, much less, where it will end.

After I've stood for a long while, I'll open my hand, palm up, and stare down at the button. I'll consider keeping it, one last token, one more way to hold on. I'll want a drink. But ignoring that desire, I'll close my eyes, and in the tilting darkness, cast the button into the fire. When I open them again, all of this will seem half-remembered, a fever-dream of little worlds. I'll turn back to my house, and when I go inside, I'll begin the real battle of living with myself and what I've done.

Afterword

As a school bus driver, I was drawn to the legend of San Antonio's "Ghost Children." Train tracks are anathema to bus drivers, and stalling on the tracks while an oncoming train bears down on you is something we fear in the silences of our routes, long after the last child has been safely delivered home. Telling the story from the train engineer's point of view was one of those writing surprises that happen without explanation, but in retrospect, now seems inevitable.

In researching the legend and legends like it, I found myself wondering how the principals involved in such an accident would feel about their true tragedies playing second fiddle to these maudlin legends. Soon, I was mulling over issues like guilt and forgiveness and how even sentimental ghost stories might have something to teach us about ourselves and the way we deal with tragedy, communal guilt, and personal recovery.

CATHERYNNE M. VALENTE

Fifteen Panels Depicting the Sadness of the Baku and the Jotai

Born in the Pacific Northwest in 1979, Catherynne M. Valente is the author of more than a dozen works of fiction and poetry, including Palimpsest, the Orphan's Tales *series, and the crowd-funded phenomenon* The Girl Who Circumnavigated Fairyland in a Ship of Her Own Making. *She is the winner of the Tiptree Award, the Mythopoeic Award, the Rhysling Award, and the Million Writers Award. She was a finalist for the World Fantasy Award in 2007 and 2009. As of this writing, she is a finalist for the Lambda, Andre Norton, and Hugo Awards to be awarded in 2010. She lives on an island off the coast of Maine with her partner, two dogs, and an enormous cat.*

What She Whispered

When you, sweet sleeper, wake in the morning, one arm thrown over your golden-sticky eyes, sheets a-mangle, your dreams still flit through you, ragged, full of holes. You can remember the man with the yellow eyes, but not why he chased you. You can remember the hawk-footed woman on your roof, but not what she whispered.

That is my fault. I could not help it. I tromped through you in the night, and ate up your dreams, a moth through wool. I didn't want them all, only the sweetest veins, like fat marbling a slab of ruby meat, the marrowy slick of what she whispered, why he ran.

I am a rowling thing—my snout raises up toward the moon to catch the scent of your sweat. I show my flat teeth to the night wind. I beg permission of your bedclothes to curl up in the curve of your stomach, to gnaw on your shoulders, your breasts, your eyelids. I must open up a hole in you, to crawl through to the red place where your dreams spool out.

You put your arm around me in the night. Do you remember? My belly was taut and black, a tapir's belly, a tapir's snout snuffling for your breath as a pig for truffles. You were my truffle, my thick, earthy mushroom. You were delicious, and I thank you for my supper.

A Jewel We May Not Gnaw

At dawn, blue light shines on my woolly stump-tail. I catch the tin-patched 6:17 commuter train from your house to my home, deep in the Paradise of the Pure Land. My friend Yatsuhashi lumbers aboard at your aunt's house, the one with the wide white porch. She is fat and full of your aunt's dreams of straddling her supervisor while he recites Basho. She takes her seat in the empty car; I take mine. She sits up and her tapir-body unfolds neatly along three creases to become the body of a respectable businessman in a respectable black suit. I, too, unfold, and straighten my tie. The attendant brings cups of hot, sweet *matcha,* but we refrain, straining at the pelt with the night-feast. If you saw us, you would not think we had snorted and snuggled against you all through the dark and moony hours. You would think: *there go two wealthy and reputable gentlemen, off to their decent, clean desks in the city.*

But we have worked our shifts already, and we aim toward home, hurtle toward it, home to the peach tree of immortality and the pearl-troughs of enlightened discourse, where we will disgorge our meals for the pleasure of eating them again.

"Kabu," says Yatsuhashi, though she knows my full name is Akakabu. She insists on the familiar because she has no manners. "Do you think dreams taste more like cherries or more like salmon roe? I can never decide."

"With respect, Yatsuhashi-san, the comparison with roe is not at all apt. Recall that at the bottom of a dream is a hard jewel we may not gnaw, the jewel of the sleeping soul, clung with dream-meat and sugar. Roe is sweet and soft and bursts on the tongue in a shower of golden salt—how rare is the roe-dream! Only the very young and the very old have no pit on which we may break our teeth if we are not careful."

"Of course you are right, Kabu. But I cannot escape the feeling of fishiness; the dreams of sex-starved aunts wriggle in me so!"

That is my friend's way of talking. Many Baku talk like this, because they are not sensible, and all they eat all night are the kinds of dreams that do not agree with a tapir's stomach: drunken dreams, fever dreams, sickness dreams, the dreams of enfeebled children. These are so rich it is hard to resist, like a tiny table set with a cake so moist it wets the cloth, but they make a Baku babble and walk into walls.

Disembark for Yokosuka-Chuo Station.

The mechanical voice is slim and soft and breathy, a dream-voice. I approve. I obey.

The Paradise of the Pure Land

Does it surprise you that Pure Land has a train station? It has many. We are subtle, we who inhabit this place—not only Baku but many other beasts and *tsukumogami* and dragons and maidens with the moon in their hair and bodhisattva with bare feet. We let humans build grey, stocky towers in the Gardens of Right Practice; we let them bring great gun-bristled ships to the Lotus Harbor; we let them pave the Avenue of Yellow Smoke and set up pachinko parlors there. We let them call Pure Land Yokosuka, and we watched the Butterflies of Perfect Thought sizzle on the neon of their nightclub advertisements. We were clever—we are safe, a dream in their sleeping, hidden beneath a human city, where no one, not even their soldiers with golden buttons, will ever think to look for heavenly pavilions. It is not that there is no sadness in the Paradise of the Pure Land. On the contrary, we must all report for sadness once in our long, endless, peach-saturated lives, so that we may have something hard and terrible to hold against the beauty of the Pure Land. No one likes to talk about their sadness, but we have all reported on schedule, and done our duty. I want to tell you about mine, I want you to dream about it, but manners make it difficult to get to the point. I have an apartment above Blue Street in the Paradise of the Pure Land. The street does not really have a name—it has a number—but the humans thoughtfully paved it with sparkling blue stones, perhaps in some instinctive nod to our tastes, and so we and they call it Blue Street, for we are all of us together sagacious folk. From my window I can see the bay, the green water foamed with trash so that each wave is tipped with beer bottles, cellophane, detergent boxes, swollen manga, orange rinds. Beneath the surface is an improbable depository of bicycles, dumped by poor souls who could not parse out the arcane laws of garbage removal—our nature does shine through in places, and complexity of order is paramount in the pure land of contemplation. Jellyfish tangle in the wheel spokes, confused, translucent, lost.

I am lost, too. I have mistaken a bicycle wheel for safe harbor. No one is perfect.

Close Your Eyes

It would be better if you closed your eyes. I relate more easily with the sleeping. If you could dream my story, I could lumber along the low river of your spine, snuffling out the parts that are too horrible, too radiant, too private for your witness. I could eat them weeping into your brainpan, and you would wake remembering only salt.

I don't suppose you are tired. No? Ah, well. Suffice it to say I loved a creature, and that creature is no more. It is the sort of thing dreams were invented to wrangle.

Bashfulness or the Night Wind

My love was owned by a white woman. She and I met at work, as all modern lovers do, while I was on my nightly rounds. I had curled into the white woman's arms and fixed my teeth to her mouth, working at her throat, pulling up the jellied marrow of her little housely terrors. Westerners do not have the most complex palate. She dreamed of a husband in a white uniform, a husband with a sword at his hip and also an oily black gun, a cap of gold, eyes of silver. The husband touched the sea and it glowed phosphorescent green, sickly. He did not smile at her; I ate his smile. I saw her over the shoulder of the sad little wife. She was tall and dark, standing in the corner as though she guarded her mistress's sleep. Her figure was angular, her expression still as a soldier's.

Rafu, my Rafu! How I have pored over that first glimpse, held it in my paws, packed it into a box with tears and red tissue, taken it out to warm me when the stars had frozen! I rested my chin on the Western woman's shoulder, gazing at the golden-black thing that I did not yet know was Rafu. She bowed slightly. Her hinges creaked. The silk of her panels fluttered slightly in bashfulness or the night wind. A willowy green slip hung half over her face—my Rafu was a folding screen, a silk monster of beauty like statues. A *jotai,* a screen so old that one day she woke up and had a name and an address and an internal monologue. You earn these things after one hundred years or so. The world owes them to you, if you survive it. "What are you doing here, glory-of-the-evening, in this pretty pale devil's house?"

Rafu fluttered again. There were golden tigers playing on the silk where her thighs might be. They batted at floaty, cloud-bound kanji like mice.

To Conceal Her from Her Life

"Her name is Milo," whispered my not-yet-beloved. "Her father wanted a boy. I was a present from her friend Chieko, who chose in her youth to be kind to the navy wives because they are worse than children: mute, lost, dead, rigid with stupidity, which is their only defense. Chieko loved *mikon* oranges and had a mole on her left breast. Once a boy kissed it without permission under a persimmon tree, and Chieko never forgot it—she burned warmer and brighter in that moment than she ever did again. Her mother, Kayo, whose favorite perfume was made from lotus and lemon-water, who had a husband whose face was always red and three miscarriages only I witnessed—I never told anyone—bought me from a teahouse in Yokohama, where I belonged to a little girl who turned into an old woman as if by magic. She was called Bachiko and all her kimono were pink with black cherry blossoms. She drank in secret, squatting in the secret shade of me, drinking silver things until she was sick. Her great-aunt, Aoi, loved a man from England who did not love her back, and so she married a ginger farmer whose fingers burned her, and had no children. Aoi found me in a shop in Kamakura, by the sea, and thought that I would suffice to conceal her from her life. I have had much time to consider women. Milo is no worse than any of them."

"Her dreams taste like the white membranes of limes." Rafu shrugged, a peculiar raising and dropping of her slats. "She is sad. She does not speak Japanese. Her husband went to the desert months and months ago. Every day she goes to the market and brings back chocolate, a peach, and a salmon rice-ball for her dinner. She sits and eats and stares at the wall. Sometimes she watches television. Sometimes she walks three miles to Blue Street to look at necklaces in the window that she wishes someone would buy for her. Sometimes she walks along the pier to see the sunken bicycles, pinged into ruin by invisible arrows of battleship-sonar, crusted over with rust and coral. She likes to pet people's dogs as they walk them. That is her whole life. What should she dream of?"

"Something better."

Dancing Down the Windows

It is not that I thirsted for Milo's dreams. I could have had better from any rice-cooker salesman on Blue Street, marbled with darkness and longing for kisses like maple sap. But Rafu stood in the shadows of Milo's house, wrapped in the grassy yellow green perfume of new tatami, showing the stars through her skin, laughing when I told her the jokes Yatsuhashi had snorted to me on the morning train. I rocked on my haunches below her, and showed her all the things I could be: tapir, tiger, salaryman, shadow, water.

I forgot to fix my mouth to the sailor's wife. Her sawdust-dreams did not glisten. She cried in her sleep, chasing ships I wished to know nothing of, lost in her tired colonial despair.

I lost weight, as lovers will do.

On the seventh night I knew my Rafu, I unfolded into a silk screen with lonely tapirs drinking from a moonlit stream painted on my panels. I wanted so to please her. We stood side by side, saying nothing, content. Delicate snow came dancing down the windows. Milo slept on her mat below us, and did not see our still, silent lovemaking.

"I can do that, too," said Rafu coquettishly, when we had finished and sweat shone like water on our screens. "I can fold up into a tapir, a tiger, a salaryman, shadow, water. A girl."

"Show me!"

"Not yet," she demurred.

Because of Her Nakedness

"Come away from this tailless old alley cat," I begged my Rafu, resplendent in the night, golden against the dark. "I have an apartment above Blue Street—I will never throw clothing over you. I will show you the secret

Peacocks of Right Intention, who make their nests in the Admiral's mansion and peck at him when he orders his men to stand in ridiculous lines and speak the nonsense of demonkind. He cannot see them—the poor man thinks he has eczema. It is an excellent joke. I will take you walking through the Carnival of Right Livelihood, and we will eat black sugar burnt in the Ovens of Contentment. You can take the Baku-train with me every night, and continue your study of women—I will eat only the dreams of women for your sake! Into the pachinko parlors we will go, hoof in hinge, and in the plinking of those silver balls we alone will hear the clicking movements of stars in perfect orbit, and know that nothing is chance."

Rafu blushed—her panels blossomed with scarlet as though she could bleed. Milo snored and turned over in her sleep, murmuring in phantom agony, her brown hair caught in her wet mouth. Rafu watched her, tipping slightly toward the woman. "No, Akakabu, passion of my elderly years! I love her. I love her, and I will never leave her."

"How can you love such a thing?"

"I love her because of her nakedness, Kabu. She has stood before me and peeled off all her clothes until she was utterly defenseless, her breasts and her shoulders and her lonely sex all for me, for my view, my love, my pity. I know that she had her tongue pierced when she was a girl, but took it out when she married. I know that her right breast is somewhat larger than her left, that she has a birthmark at the base of her spine as though someone punched her, and that she has stretch marks on her belly, but no children, for there is nothing here for her to do but eat. These are such precious things to know! I knew them about Chieko, and Kayo, and Bachiko, and Aoi, too. They all showed me their bodies, and how the world stamped itself onto them. I have not even seen your body the way my mistresses show me theirs. She has been naked before me, Kabu, and I will not abandon a naked girl to the cold."

First Ladies

I admit I was angry, that it was my fault, in the end. I begrudged Rafu her naked women, her secret lovemaking in lonely houses full of women who would never see the green and purple of the Peacocks of Right Intention. I wanted to show my *jotai* that a Baku, too, can know a human that way, and better, for no one is ever so naked as in their dreams, where everything shameful and bright glistens like sweet fat over bone.

I curled up into Milo's heavy sleeping arms, snarling at Rafu, gloating, taking up that flaccid Western mouth in mine and sucking down all her old, buried things, her grief and her loneliness and her cream-thick guilt, her tawdry affair in Okinawa, her lost lover who used to kiss her toes as though she were an angel that might confer blessing. I ate it all, greedily, slovenly. I ate her husband who left her, his sword and his gun and his curling, saluting smile. I writhed against Milo, my black tapir-belly taut with her, hard and swollen, grinding into her, sliding off the hard little cherry pit at the base of her dreams, scraping at it, breaking my teeth on the stone of her soul.

Rafu turned away from me in shame.

Milo wrapped her arms around me and opened her eyes. "All the other wives have First Ladies' names," she whispered, her voice sand-slurred with sleep. "Hillary, Laura, Eleanor, Pat, Libby. What's wrong with me?"

"You were supposed to be a boy," I said cruelly, because I chose to be cruel, "if you had been born as you were meant to, you would get to march about with a fine rifle and shoot at things and drink whiskey and have a lovely time, and no one would ever have left you."

"Oh," Milo said with finality, as though it had finally been explained to her satisfaction. She fell asleep again.

Creatures of Stomach

I am sure it has happened before. We are creatures of stomach, after all. My mother told me when I was small and spotted that the first Baku was nothing but a great violet-translucent stomach, maybe with a bit of esophagus, and it floated over rooftops on stormy days, descending to cover sleepers like a blanket and draw up all their dreams into itself with perfect retention. In those days, no one remembered their dreams at all, so deft was the Baku in its slurping of them.

That Baku surely was blameless, but I am not. I ate too much Milo; I was so full of her my hiccups turned into anchors and dolphins and swam away through the night. Rafu rustled disgust—her gold flushed a jaundiced yellow, so deep was her disapproval of my gluttony.

I only did it to hurt you, my silken love, my Rafu, my vanished adored. I think that makes it better.

I tottered on my fat paws, skidding on the slick tatami, drunk, queasy. My skin felt too thick; I wanted to take it off, to go naked before Rafu and be loved as the women in her life had been. I deserved that, didn't I? I careened into a wooden candlestick, bounced off a low table of red wood, bruised my snout on Rafu's corner; she clattered to the floor.

I threw up on the grass mats and lolled in my decrepitude beside my waste.

The Unrushed Familiarity of a Husband

A man lay on the floor. The substance of my retching. I vomited up Milo's dream, and it lay on the floor in a white uniform streaked with the silvery stuff of my digestion: tears, the honey of lost days, sweat, night-semen. His officer's cap tumbled off onto the tatami; his hair was wet and matted like a newborn.

He stirred; Rafu held her slats together in terror, as silent as she could be. The man crawled to Milo's sleeping shape and curled into it as I had done, with the unrushed familiarity of a husband, or a frequent Baku. He kissed her hair, left streaks of silver on her neck. I watched from the shadows as he called her name and she rolled into waking, rolled into him, her face unfolding into a smile as I sometimes unfold into a man. "How are you here?" she marveled, as well she might.

"I missed you," he murmured, slurred, unsure of English, as well he might be, having been in my stomach a moment previously. *Liar,* I thought. "I've been so lonely," Milo sighed. "I hate it here. Can't we go home?"

"Yes, of course. Tomorrow." He was not listening to her. The sailor pulled at her frumpy nightgown, pulling her grayish, threadbare underthings away, pulling his sex from his crisp white trousers, clung with silvery dream-glue. She moaned a little, frightened, half-asleep yet.

"It's so strange," he gasped as he thrust awkwardly into her, with all the grace of an elephant falling upon a hapless antelope. "I was in the desert just a moment ago. Everything smelled like oil and sand. There were men on a raft; they shot at us, and all around them the sea was angry, blue and green, phosphorescent with spilled fuel and algae, it glowed and the men's faces were so hollow."

Milo began to cry silently. Her body lurched with his motion.

"We shot back, we had to. I pulled their bodies out of the glowing water." He started to laugh roughly, pushing faster against her. "And it was so weird, their skin just came off in my hands, like a coat. So soft, like they were made of nothing, with nothing inside, and all we pulled out was skin and blood, no men at all."

"Don't laugh, it scares me," whispered Milo. Her husband put his hands against her ears as if to blot out the sound of his laughter, which spiraled up and higher and further and faster, until water came from his mouth and his hands, water pouring into her, the salt-sea scouring her, shells and fish and sand and blood splashing out of him, into her ears, into her womb, into her mouth. She spluttered, coughed—he pushed the sea through her, and her lips became as blue as the waves, her hair streamed like kelp, his fingers left purple anemones on her ribs. "Aren't you happy I'm back? Why don't you kiss me? Don't you love me?" And he kissed her, over and over, wet, salty smacks in the dark, and above the sound of them I could hear Rafu crying, huddled like discarded furniture against the concrete wall.

You Can't Love Meat

The dream-vomit sat cross-legged on the floor, waiting for someone to serve him tea. Milo lay broken by him, her face swollen, water dribbling from her mouth.

"Your name is Kabu. Akakabu," he said slowly to me. A child might well know its father. "Is my name Lieutenant?"

"No." I walked out of the shadow of the American television stand and sat on my haunches next to him. "Your name is Gabriel Salas, but you're not him, not really."

"No, I know that. If I were Gabriel Salas I would still be in the desert, and the sea would be glowing, and I would be able to see cities in the distance, full of crumbling and canny birds."

"You're a dream. Do you understand that?"

"Whose dream?"

"Your wife's. Look at what she dreams you will do to her, and what you have done in her dreaming."

The dream-sailor looked down at his wife. His expression was blank. "I loved her."

"Yes."

"I don't love her anymore. You can't love meat."

"That's your business."

"What do I do now, Akakabu?"

"This is the Paradise of the Pure Land. You might start with Right Thought. This is also Yokosuka. You might start with burying your wife and lighting incense for her."

"That does not sound like something I would do. Instead, I am hungry."

"You are hungry because you came out of me, and I am always hungry."

"I am going to the city, then. To eat things I like."

"What sort of things do you like?"

Lieutenant Gabriel Salas cocked his head thoughtfully to one side. He picked up his officer's cap and put it on. "Peacocks. Butterflies. Black sugar. Right Thought."

He strode from the house, his spine straight and proud, his steps turning south toward Blue Street.

When he had gone, Rafu crawled from the corner of the room, her slats digging into the tatami. As she dragged herself the slats of fine dark wood became fingers breaking their nails on the woven grass, her silk screens became shoulders, a stomach, a strong back. She stood up, unfolding into a woman with long, hinged arms, accordioning out from her sweet torso in hanging, tiger-painted screens that ended in graceful hands. She sank down over Milo's drowned body.

"Save her," my Rafu wept. "Save her because of her nakedness, how bare she was before me, and how I loved her smaller breast."

"It's no good, concealer-of-my-heart. I only know how to eat things."

Because You Are New

The Paradise of the Pure Land exists within Yokosuka as hair caught in a brush. The teeth of the city rise tall through the tangles and think nothing of them, but deep in the comb, long onyx strands wind and snarl. It is, of course, possible to yank all these strands free with a pitiless fist. They will not protest.

Rafu and I followed the dream of Gabriel through Yoshikura-Chuo and along the highway, though the wet, dank tunnel and up the jungled terraces. He was not hard to follow, being loud and foreign. He ate cherry trees along the way, opening his jaw and swallowing them whole as I might. When he reached the city, he seized in one hand a Peacock of Right Intention, squirming blue and green, and in the other a young girl coming home from a date with an enlisted American on the sprawling grey base. He shoved each into his mouth like two legs of one golden chicken.

On Blue Street, he ate hats, belts, rice cookers, kerosene lamps, lightbulbs, expensive Italian shoes, the Grocers of Perfect Balance, aquariums, streetlamps, Prostitutes of Pure Mind, the Motorcycles of Holy Judgment. Rafu wrinkled her new nose and clapped her screen-arms.

"Is this what you are like, on the inside?" she said.

"This is what everyone is like on the inside," I sighed.

"It's not what I'm like!"

"That is because you are new. You did not have a stomach for one hundred years. You are only just learning how to fill it. You do not yet know it can never be filled."

Just ahead of us, the dream-Gabriel unhinged his jaw and swallowed a drink machine. It expired with a red whine. "Will he eat us all?"

"Yes," I said calmly. "He is a dream; he does not know this is not a dream. His real self is somewhere impossibly hot, dreaming of his soft, plain wife who is not named after a First Lady. He eats up the world with a grey boat and a fine cap. Dreams are more literal. More honest."

"Why are you not afraid?"

"Because I know a thing about the Pure Land he does not." Rafu took my tapir-form into her screen-arms and kissed my ardent snout. I unfolded into a man in her arms, to match her, to please her. I wanted so to please her.

A Perfect Shard of Gold

There is no more sacred place in the Pure Land of Yokosuka than the pink palaces of the pachinko parlors. I would have taken Rafu there, to meditate with me in the blue haze of the electronic screens and the heady cigar smoke. Here, the bodhisattva practice Right Gambling, prone before the unyielding goddesses of luck, their throats ecstatic and bare. One by one, the dream-Lieutenant ate them from the ceiling, the green-limbed seraphs of Perfect Chance, sucking their toes down into his throat. Their screams were shattered by the crash and fall of silver balls. The old, shrunken men turning the wheels of the glittering machines did not move—they see nothing of the Pure Land, even when the sun rises over the harbor and grants each citizen of the Right City a perfect shard of gold. He is a dream; I am a dream; we are all dreams, and the flashing arcade-lights blind them.

Gabriel laughed, a thick, fatty sound, a gargle, a chortle. The parlor erupted in jackpots and high scores. The goddesses who held back and gave forth at their whim had gone into his great, insatiable belly and held back no more.

"Please," said Rafu softly. The old men shouted for joy, jostled each other, shook fists at the perplexed proprietor. Rafu's voice barely sounded among them, but Gabriel turned toward her in hunger, his lips scarlet with secret blood. "Do you remember," said Rafu, sliding toward him, "how Milo's toe was broken when she was six, running too fast after her friends through the forest behind her house? How it is still crooked, and aches, and how you used to rub it for her during thunderstorms until she was well? Do you remember how her waist curved so sweetly in, how her mouth tasted, how even when she had the flu she smelled like childhood to you, clean and innocent and permanent?"

"No," growled the dream-Gabriel.

"Do you remember how her fingers still had calluses, even though she stopped playing the guitar so long ago? How her hair looked when it was tangled, when it was smooth? How her belly sloped, how her birthmark looked, how her ears curved?"

"No," growled the dream-Gabriel. "Instead, I want to eat you. Then I'll remember those things."

"Why are you doing this?"

Gabriel shrugged. "What else is there to do when you visit a foreign country?" He turned to bite down on a crippled old woman with a cane and a bend in her back like a stair. Her skinny arms were full of silver pachinko balls. She was winning, of course she was winning. His invisible teeth shattered on her dry old skull, scraping off her jaw. She smiled quietly to herself.

"There is a pit in every dream that cannot be eaten," I said to Rafu. I was so tired. This was a lesson for baby Baku. "It will break you if you try it. Naturally it is the most delicious thing in a dream, and we have all had to learn to curb our desire for it. And in the dream of the Pure Land, the dream Yokosuka dreams waking and sleeping, an old woman sits in a pachinko parlor, our indestructible core, indestructible because she does not know she is the sweetest thing in the world."

The dream of Gabriel was breaking apart, spilling the silver dream fluid onto the floor, shuddering, shaking, crying out for help. I did not care.

But Rafu opened her arms to him, and ah, I should have known—we are each slaves to our own natures, even in the Paradise of the Pure Land, especially here, and if I know only how to eat, she knows only how to conceal, how to hide a thing from shame. Her arms flipped open, square screen by square screen, and she enveloped him so suddenly he could not move, clapped him up entirely in herself, all wall of golden Rafu.

The dream-Gabriel sobbed in her grasp. The things he had devoured began to tear out of him: hats, belts, rice cookers, kerosene lamps, lightbulbs, expensive Italian shoes, the Grocers of Perfect Balance, aquariums, streetlamps, Prostitutes of Pure Mind, the Motorcycles of Holy Judgment. The Seven Goddesses of Perfect Chance. They burst from him in his weakness—and burst through the body of Rafu, which was no more than silk, not really, leaving her skin hanging, ragged, torn threads fluttering in the breeze of falling silver.

Then I Woke Up

It was only a dream. Sometimes they say that, at the end of stories, in the land where Milo was born. *And then I woke up—it was only a dream.* Stories here do not end like that. I cannot wake up. I do not sleep.

Milo cannot wake up. If she could, she would see in her house: a low table of red wood, several windows, a television, chocolate, a peach, a salmon rice-ball, and her friend Chieko's screen, shattered as though a cannonball struck it, in a broken pile on the tatami. If she could wake up, she would have to get a new one—they can always get a new anything, these humans. Only you can wake up, out of all of us, and be relieved. You can assure yourself that we never really existed, that Yokosuka is only a broken old military town, that folding screens never speak with voices like thread spooling. I will leave it all intact for you.

I am fasting now, anyway. I have my penance to pay.

. . .

Yet eating dreams is an essential act of waste management in the Paradise of the Pure Land. I did my duty. I swallowed the wreckage of the dream-vomit I spilled out of myself, and also the wreckage of Milo, sodden with seawater. I cleaned everything up, don't you see? It's all just the way it was before.

On the 6:17 commuter train, Yatsuhashi told me a joke about a geisha who wouldn't wear her wig. It rambled and was not funny. Yatsuhashi-san is an idiot. The apartment above Blue Street is empty because she is gone. She was never here, of course—I never brought her to my threshold, I never served her tea with the exquisite abasement of which I am capable. I never showed her the jellyfish. But once there was a glowing cord between our houses, hers tatami-golden and tall, just down the hill from Anjinsuka Station, mine clean and neat as dreams cannot be, polished with a spongey, devoted snout. But in dreams, one can feel the absence of a thing that never was, and so can I.

Rafu will never come here now; the emptiness is permanent.

The Paradise of the Pure Land remains. It is bigger than all of us, and notices nothing. It sprawls by the sea, a reef of light, and as I trundle down the leaf-strewn length of Blue Street, the whole of the Pure Land turns to you as if to say something, something important, something profound.

. . .

And then you wake up. After all, it is only a dream.

ஃ Afterword ஃ

I lived in Japan for two years as the wife of a naval officer, and it was one of the strangest, loneliest times of my life. For a Westerner, Japan is liter- ally the world of magical reality, everything unexplained, most things surreal. Yokosuka itself is a depressed military town, with little joy or fanfare to share with visitors. To prepare myself, being the kind of girl I am, I read reams of Japanese fairy tales and mythology. I'm not sure this made it any easier. It was in that reading that I came across the *tsukumo-gami,* a species of beasties that are born when an inanimate object turns one hundred years old. There are many kinds: stirrups, tea kettles, swords, shoes, folding screens. Folding screens have always seemed like such intimate objects to me, I was fascinated with the idea of a living one—and when imagining what a *jotai* might witness in its time, my mind re-turned again and again to the lonely navy wife, adrift in Japan, tilting toward suicide. That she might be saved from her ghosts by the resident demons of Japan seemed only right.

CAROLYN TURGEON

La Llorona

Carolyn Turgeon is the author of two novels, Rain Village *and* Godmother: The Secret Cinderella Story. *Her third,* The Mermaid, *a retelling of the original little mermaid story, is forthcoming in 2011.*

Her website is carolynturgeon.com.

Karen had come alone, on a whim, to this city full of lovers. Saw a special in the Sunday paper and thought, *that . . . that's what I need now.* The promise of Mexico: bird cages and parrots and sweeping flowers that tumbled over rooftops and along fences, margaritas and sand, tile floors and churches. Something to remind her: there is more than this, this heartbreak, now.

Already, on her first afternoon, she'd bought three little boxes with crosses and Marys on the lids, a pair of long silver earrings with Mayan gods carved into them, and an array of Day of the Dead figurines—dancing mermaid skeletons and glass frames filled with tiny dried rosebuds—to place around her apartment back in New York. She'd put on a summer dress and sandals, right in the middle of December, and treated herself to dinner at the place the hotel manager, Marco, said was the best in town. She'd had a plate of fish with sliced avocado on the side, trying not to feel strange or self-conscious as the lovers murmured around her, as the waiters looked at her sadly and brought her extra sweets. In this place so full of couples walking down the street wrapped around each other, their arms a-tangle, she knew she was a spectacle: a lone thirty-five-year-old woman wearing a bright red shoulder-baring dress, her dark hair pulled back and fastened with pins, her nails the color of berries. She'd wanted to feel alive, beautiful, and she ate slowly, sipping her cocktail. Wondering if this is how it would be from now on, wondering if she could live with that, if she could maybe even be happy alone.

But it was her dreams that would not let her forget, and that first night she woke up choking, sure that water was filling her lungs. The white sheets twisted around her.

She shot up in bed, gasping for air, and it took several long moments for her to remember where she was, for the room to appear faintly around her. The tile floor gleaming in the moonlight, the outline of bougainvillea and gardenia outside her open window. The sound of the surf.

Slowly, Karen got out of bed, went to the window, and leaned out. The sky was a clear inky black and smattered with stars. The perfumed air was warm on her face. She stared out at the water, black like oil in the night. And there, on the sand, she saw a woman walking slowly along the edge of the water, wearing a white dress that hung to her ankles. She stood for a while, watching the woman, letting the tears stream down her face. Feeling strangely soothed.

. . .

On her second day she took a tour to some Mayan ruins nearby. She signed up on a whim after overhearing a waiter telling a young Japanese couple about it at breakfast. Why not. She was up for anything. And it seemed wonderful, an adventure, sitting on the rickety bus with a thick romance novel clutched in her hand, about to be immersed in an ancient culture that had nothing to do with her own life. In front of her, the Japanese couple sat, the man's dark hands stroking the woman's bleached blond hair. His thick fingers moved through the bright strands as they chatted on in their own language, light and sweet-sounding, between the bus's loud rumbling and the tour guide's occasional instructions to the group.

She tried not to think about her last trip with Tim, when the two of them had taken a bus from Florence to San Gimignano. That had been a different kind of immersion—the pair of them throwing themselves into medieval Italy as a way to come closer together, to save themselves, what was left of them. Of course, by then it had been too late. She'd been in a haze of grief the whole time, both of them had, and not even the gorgeous landscape, the grapevines and the hills and the crumbling pathways, could tear them out of it.

Karen stayed at the edge of the tour group and only half listened, preferring to let the sun sink into her skin, to imagine herself in this other time, other universe. She bought a glass of *horchata* at one of the food stands lining the site, and a hot *churro* wrapped in waxed paper. She sipped slowly—it was like drinking rice pudding—and took in the ancient stones, the grass and dirt surrounding the crumbling structures. What would it have been like, to live here, then, and not now? She ate the churro, let the hot sugared dough melt against her tongue, and wondered: Would this loss have felt different, then? Imagined all the other lives she could have had, selves she could have been. How many others had gone through what she had? It was as basic as these stones, this grass. This sun that felt so good against her skin.

They returned to the hotel in late afternoon. Other tours were returning then, too, and Karen found herself looking for the woman in white from the night before, but there was no sign of her amid all the laughing couples.

She was sleepy from the sun and the walking when she made her way down to the spa for the massage appointment she'd scheduled when she signed up for the tour. She was going all out today, she'd decided, a massage followed by a long, beautiful dinner—*carnitas,* maybe *mole* or *tamales,* more of that perfect soft avocado, that perfect *salsa verde,* a bottle of wine.

The masseur was young and handsome, a strong Mexican boy with white white teeth. She was almost nervous as she slipped off her clothes and under the thin sheet, and at first she curled inward at the feel of his palms on her shoulders. This was the most intimate she'd been with another person in at least a year. His fingers pressing into her back, rubbing warm oil down the line of her spine. A bliss unfurled from deep in her body.

She'd forgotten what this was like, the pleasure of being touched.

·   ·   ·

Later, the same dreams woke her. Her lungs filling, clawing and clawing for breath, at a surface that seemed miles away.

She sat up and the grief came at her like a fist. Like a boulder landing right on her chest. It could still be like this, now: his face in front of her, his tiny hands, the long eyelashes she used to run her fingertips along. Back and forth, back and forth.

What was she doing here, wandering around the ruins of cultures she knew nothing about? Eating avocado and getting massages from handsome young Mexicans? How could she do anything at all, when her son was dead?

She stood up, stumbled to the window. The grief came over her in waves, and she knew she just had to grit her teeth and get through it.

After a while, she saw movement down by the water, a flash of white. It was the woman again, from the night before, in the same white dress, her straight black hair flowing down her back.

The moment Karen saw her, a strange calm entered into her, as it had the night before. Maybe it was because this woman, too, had lost something. Karen could feel it, as if this feeling connected them as surely as a wire stretched between them.

She squinted, tried to make out more details of the woman. Something told her the woman in white was alone, even though the likelihood of that, here, was slim. Probably she was just a tourist with a touch of insomnia. Any minute now she would turn back to the hotel, join her lover in bed.

. . .

Breakfast was served out on the veranda, overlooking the water. Piles of fresh fruit—bananas, mangoes, papaya—and fresh juice and *huevos a la mexicana* and *chilaquiles* and *cornettos con dulce de leche* and *café con leche* and *licuado de batata* laid out on long tables.

Karen sat alone, looking for the woman in white. The veranda was crowded with people. A handsome older Mexican couple, the woman with that Sophia Loren quality Karen had always wished she could pull off, the low-cut top and a scarf around her neck. The Japanese couple from the tour, sitting with another couple now, probably American. A redhead with a much older man, obviously wealthy and definitely not her father. A very blond, very German family.

Then a young woman with long black hair entered, wearing a white top and a pair of loose cotton pants.

Karen stood up immediately, and went to her. "Excuse me," she said to the girl, "were you walking down by the water late last night?"

The girl drew back in surprise—*how strange*, Karen thought—and then vigorously shook her head. "Oh no, señora," she said. "No."

"Well, I was—"

Before she could finish her sentence, the girl whispered an apology in Spanish and quickly darted back into the hotel.

Karen stared after her, confused. She noticed the Sophia Loren couple staring at her. The moment she looked back at them, they shifted their eyes, almost in unison, and didn't look at her again.

She shook it off, the strangeness, and returned to her breakfast. She was too used to New York, she thought. One thing was certain: she couldn't be farther from New York now.

She spent the day at the beach, reading her romance novel, getting lost in a world of kings and queens and secret, passionate affairs. Around her, people laughed and rubbed lotion onto each other's backs, couples ran into the water hand in hand, women walked around topless in bikini bottoms. She was starting to feel oppressed by all this physical affection and display. She felt much lonelier than she had before, and thought of another massage before deciding there was something distasteful in it. Pathetic. What she really needed, she thought, was to get laid.

She laughed out loud. She couldn't even imagine it.

. . .

Early that evening Karen returned to her room, determined to talk to the woman in white tonight, at least see her up close. After a few pages of her novel she got up and checked the window, but all she saw was the moon, the sky, the black water, the outline of the bougainvillea and gardenia, swaying back and forth. Finally, just after midnight, the woman appeared. Again in the white dress, walking slowly up and down the deserted beach.

Karen rushed out of bed and ran out to the hallway, out the door, across the tile veranda that led to the beach. The air was surprisingly cool, and she shivered slightly. The night was gorgeous. She stopped just to take it in: the velvet sky strewn with stars and a moon full to bursting, the silvery dark water reflecting the moon back up to the sky.

For a moment Karen felt pure joy.

Then she snapped to, and hurried down to the sand. She walked right up to the water, letting it run over her bare feet, and looked up and down the beach. There was no one there. It was completely deserted. Not even footprints in the wet sand.

She stayed by the water for a while. Running her hands through the water, imagining what lay within it, underneath the black surface.

But the woman did not return.

. . .

The next morning, as Karen was stepping out of the shower, there was a knock at the door. She wrapped herself in one of the plush hotel robes, went and opened the door a sliver, and peeked out. The maid, Irene, was standing in the hall.

"Oh, I'll be leaving in a few minutes," Karen said, smiling. "Thank you."

"Yes, señora," Irene said. "But . . . I have something to tell you."

"Yes?" Karen looked at her.

"Forgive me, señora. But you need to be careful, not walk alone at night."

"What do you mean?" She was aware of the sharp edge to her tone, and immediately felt guilty. "Here, come in."

Irene walked into the room, clearly uncomfortable. She stood by the bed, stiff in her pink uniform, and looked up at Karen. She was at least half a foot shorter than she was, Karen thought.

"I jus— I, my husband, he saw you last night, by the water, and it's not good. He wanted me to tell you. None of us here, we all stay away, at night. Believe me, it's better to stay here at night, inside."

Karen laughed. "Oh, but the beach is so beautiful at night, Irene. It's so crowded in the daytime, and at night it's like another world." She couldn't help thinking: *I'm from New York.* This was a pristine little beach town in Mexico. How dangerous could it be?

"No," Irene said. "It's no good. Believe me, señora. Bad things have happened. I tell you this from my heart."

Karen was about to respond, and then just nodded. Maybe there had been a few crimes down by the water. Maybe she shouldn't be so cocky. She knew the woman meant well. "Thank you," she said, smiling. "I appreciate it."

"You're welcome."

Irene smiled back at her, her face a mass of wonderful lines. She turned, and Karen watched her tiny, strong frame as she moved out of the room.

Things are certainly strange here, she thought as she pulled on a tank top and leggings. Today she'd decided to take a Pilates classes at the spa. It would be good for her. Exercise was another thing she'd abandoned, since even before Ethan was born. She'd never lost all the baby weight, either.

Heading to the spa, she noticed a few people giving her strange looks. The Sophia Loren woman from the day before, the dark-haired woman who was clearly a hotel employee, and a few scattered others. Karen was used to this by now, of course, being a woman alone, but now she saw something menacing in their looks she hadn't noticed before. Even a hint of fear?

Didn't she?

She shook her head. She was getting paranoid.

The Pilates class was challenging but she was able to get through it.

Afterward she felt relieved and proud of herself. She'd be able to lose this weight when she returned to New York. She *would* lose it, she decided. And maybe, eventually, start dating again. When she was ready.

For the first time in a long while, it seemed like there might be a day when Karen would be ready.

That afternoon, she put on a floppy hat and just wandered. Past the shops and town, past a few churches, into some side roads. She liked the little houses here, the colorful shrines in the front yards filled with Marys and candles and garlands and saints, the bursting flowers. She passed a group of young children playing at the end of the street and she paused for a moment, smiling. For a second she imagined Ethan there with them, kicking the ball to the tiny girl in braids. She let herself imagine what he might have been like at five, six, ten. Would his lashes have stayed long, like a girl's? Little Elizabeth Taylor eyes, her mother had called them.

The thoughts were strangely comforting, as if he were somehow close by, as though there was a part of him really there, playing in the dusty street. What if she just stayed in this town, this part of Mexico, she thought suddenly. Just dropped out of her life and stayed here? Wasn't it possible? Sometimes people just dropped out of their lives and started new ones, didn't they? In New York she made well into six figures, had a sweeping loft in Tribeca. What if she sold the loft, cashed in the 401K, emptied her bank account? She'd never have to work again.

She wandered back into town, through the farmer's market with its piles of fruit and vegetables, its stands with the sublime smell of steaming meat wafting out from them, the paintings made on bark, the silver jewelry and thick, brightly colored skirts. She bought a plate of fish tacos and ate them as she walked, washing them down with a bottle of ice-cold Mexican beer with a wedge of lime floating in it.

Maybe she could stay here, start a new life. Be someone new.

She took her time, exploring everything.

·   ·   ·

That night Karen waited again for the woman in white. Just before midnight, she threw a shawl around her shoulders, slipped into her tennis shoes, and went outside. She walked along the veranda, watching the silvery, moonlit water, breathing in salt and perfume and sea. Irene's husband was likely watching her from some window—he probably worked in the kitchen, or in the garden out front; she imagined they must live there, somewhere in the hotel—but she didn't care.

Karen stepped carefully down to the sand. Listening to the sound of the water. She could get used to this sound, day and night, the constant breathing. She picked up a shell, felt its smooth, ridged surface. Took off her shoes and squashed her feet in the sand.

She'd almost forgotten about the woman altogether when she heard the sound of crying. She looked around, saw a flash of white in her periphery.

Karen turned then, and the woman in white was standing right there, facing the water. Not more than a few yards away. How hadn't she noticed her? Yet there she was, in the flesh, oblivious to Karen's presence.

She was younger than Karen had suspected. The woman's skin smooth and brown, her hair thick, black, shiny in the light of the moon. The perfect curve of her cheek just barely visible, wet with tears.

Karen stood still, almost afraid to breathe, as the woman bent down and ran her fingers along the surface of the water.

The woman's grief was so palpable, it was as if it carried over to Karen as well, like the breeze, the sound of the waves, the scent of the flowers and the water. She felt it move over her, and it was surprising, how comforting it was. Like it reached into a secret place in her, and held it.

For a moment, then, she let it all return to her. The crushing sadness, the pure pain of losing her baby boy.

And somehow, right here, right now, it was okay.

She knelt down on the sand, put her head in her hands, and missed him, and it was okay. The thought came to her with a strange force: *he's here.* Ethan. He was with her, here. His pain was gone, the wound that had filled his little body, healed. He was at peace now. He was so close.

She cried there on the sand, letting it all push through her, and when she finally looked up again the woman was gone.

Above, the sky was a deep blue-black, almost as if it'd been painted.

Karen wanted to kick herself for not having said anything to the woman, for not having tried to comfort her. The way the woman had, without knowing it, comforted her.

· · ·

The next morning Karen called the front desk for fresh towels. Irene arrived at the door a few minutes later.

"Are you ready for me to do your room, señora?" she asked, placing the towels on the unmade bed.

"In a little bit," Karen said. "I'm leaving soon. But first I wanted to ask you about someone."

Irene smiled. "Oh yes? And who is he?"

Karen laughed. "Not a he, a she."

"A she?" Irene raised her eyebrows.

"No, no. I'm just curious. I've seen this woman at the beach, at night. Always alone, walking along the water."

Irene's face changed then, became serious. "You have not gone down there again, have you, señora? At night? You must not go down there at night."

"No no no, I've just seen her, from my window. Do you know who I mean?"

Irene backed away, toward the door. "What does she look like?"

"A woman with long black hair, wearing a white dress. Very beautiful. And always alone."

Karen couldn't understand the way Irene was looking at her. Like she'd just sprouted fins and shark's teeth.

"Irene," Karen said. "It is just a woman! She's not going to mug me or rape me, believe me. She seems very sad. I think she's always crying."

"That woman," Irene said, not looking at her now, "is La Llorona. The crying lady. To see her . . . It is not good, to see her."

"You're not making any sense, Irene."

"La Llorona, she . . . she is dead, señora."

Karen just looked at the maid. She could see Irene was serious, that she believed what she was saying. This really was another world, here. Despite herself, a chill went through her. The ancient part of her believed in such things.

"That doesn't make sense," she said, and was annoyed to hear her own voice waver. More firmly: "The woman I saw was as alive as we are."

"Señora, listen to me. These things I say, they are true. You do not believe me, but you must understand. It is very dangerous for you. You stay inside, when the sun goes down."

"Irene, you're saying the woman I saw is a ghost? Is that what you want me to believe?"

The woman had just appeared, out of thin air, hadn't she? She shook the thought away. Since when did she listen to superstitious old ladies?

Irene took her hand, stared up at her intently. "Yes, señora. The woman you saw is La Llorona. She is a bad woman. She killed her own children. Her husband abandoned her for another woman, and she killed them to punish him. Now she wants to find them. You say she was crying. This is why."

Suddenly, despite herself, she was shivering, as if the room had gone cold.

Irene continued. "They say she appears to people when they're going to die. That is why you stay away from the water at night. She is always there, looking for her children."

Karen pulled her hand out of Irene's and sat down on the bed, hardly able to breathe. *Looking for her children. She killed her own children.*

She forced herself to sound calm. "Thank you, Irene," she said. "I will be careful."

"Good, señora." Irene nodded. "Good. I leave you now. I will come back."

"Thank you," she repeated, watching the maid leave the room. Everything was so strange here. The woman in white appearing and then disappearing. Or had she? She couldn't quite remember. Karen was so distracted here, between the mesmerizing beauty of the sea and sky, the other tourists, the locals, and her own memories. And Ethan—Ethan!—who seemed so close to her here.

My God, she had loved him. From the moment they put him in her arms, his fragile little body, she'd loved him with a ferocity she'd had no idea she was capable of. She'd understood every cliché about motherhood at that moment. She would have died for him, one thousand times over. She would have done anything for him.

And she had, hadn't she? Tried everything to save him. Everything the doctors had told her, to a T. There was not one more thing she could have done.

And he'd just gotten sicker, more and more consumed by a pain that seemed to extend past his wretched, suffering little body, that seemed to fill the entire world.

Her baby, screaming with pain, day and night.

. . .

By late afternoon Karen was sick to her stomach. She skipped dinner and took to her bed, clutching her belly. Immediately she was pulled into dreams, the same dreams, over and over, that she'd had every night since she'd arrived: the water pulling her down, filling her lungs, her baby there, at the surface, and she can't get to him, she claws through the water but it just pulls her deeper as he cries and cries.

Karen awoke to the sound of crying. She didn't know how much time had passed. Just vague memories of dreams and darkness, water. Her son.

She opened her eyes. The first thing she saw was the outline of the bougainvillea and gardenia against the star-spattered sky. Beautiful. She smelled the perfume, felt the warm breeze.

And then a face, right in her window, watching her, a woman's face surrounded by thick black hair.

She screamed, sat up.

But there was no one there. Only the bougainvillea and gardenia.

She heard a voice then, a child's voice, a soft cry.

"Ethan?"

There was a flash in the corner of the room, and then nothing.

"Ethan!"

She leapt out of bed. Frantic. Her baby boy! He was here! She'd known it, sensed it, she knew she'd come here for a reason, something had drawn her here. Made her pick up the Sunday paper—when had she last bought a Sunday paper?—and open it to that page, see that ad, and decide, on a whim, to just fly to a Mexican resort alone on a vacation. She'd taken all that time off to care for Ethan those last months, to cart him from doctor to doctor, to take him for every kind of treatment, even driving him out to a "healer" upstate who'd rubbed him with oils and claimed to pull the sickness out of him with his bare hands, and then there was the last, sad, pathetic trip she and Tim had taken to Italy, as if everything between them hadn't died the moment that fucking doctor said "cancer" and then, here, now, a year later she'd seen this ad promising "romance," promising "bliss" and "adventure," and without hesitation she'd called a travel agent, put in her last-minute vacation request—of course they'd give it to her, even during the busiest month of the year, even though every person in her group would have to work so much harder with her gone, because *her baby had died of fucking cancer*—and then there she was, filling a suitcase with prebaby sundresses she doubted even fit her anymore and heading to JFK.

Now she knew why.

She heard his cry again, and now it came from outside, outside her window.

She pulled on her clothes and ran into the hall, out the door and onto the veranda, down to the sand and water.

"Ethan!"

He was here, she knew it. Where was he?

"Karen."

The voice was soft, kind. She turned, and the woman in white stood in front of her. Tears streamed down the woman's face, yet she was smiling. She was beautiful. Karen had never seen a woman more beautiful, or more sad. She felt a peace move through her, the same sense of calm.

"Karen, it's okay," the woman said. "He is here."

"Ethan?"

"Yes. Yes." La Llorona smiled. "He's here. Follow me." As she spoke, she moved backwards in the water. She looked just like the Marys in the front yards, the Marys carved into the boxes Karen had bought at market. Radiant and pure.

"Full of grace," Karen whispered. The water spread in front of her, silver under the moon, magical under the huge star-spattered sky. The air full of flowers, the smell of those luminous white flowers. What could be more wonderful than this? This gorgeous night, this peace blossoming inside her, her baby boy returned to her. She couldn't wait, couldn't wait to see him again.

La Llorona moved back into the water, spreading her arms on either side of her, her white gown shifting in the faint breeze.

Karen followed her, into the water. "Where is he?" she asked. She tried to see below the surface, but it was so dark, too dark to see anything at all. "Is he here?" Her feet sank into sludge as she waded farther out.

"He was in so much pain," La Llorona said.

"Yes," she whispered. "Yes." The water turned colder as they walked.

"You sent him to a better place, where there is no pain at all."

"Yes," she said, moving closer to La Llorona, to her son—where was he? "He was suffering so much. I couldn't let him suffer."

"I know, my child." La Llorona's hands on hers, pulling her. "Come."

La Llorona said something else, but her voice was too soft for Karen to hear. And then La Llorona's arms were around her, and they were falling together into the sea. Water filled her lungs, she thrashed and clawed, unable to breathe, and then La Llorona, too, was gone, and there was nothing under the surface of the water, nothing at all, and she was falling and alone, the way she had been ever since he died, and she remembered those first moments when she'd held him in her arms and he'd looked up at her with those Elizabeth Taylor eyes, and she'd thought *I will do anything for you, anything at all.*

She saw him then. Coming toward her. Smiling, and happy, and whole. Her son.

·   ·   ·

The stars were brighter than she'd ever seen them, the sky right on top of her. Karen blinked. Sat up.

She was on the beach again, staring out at the black water. She had no idea what had happened.

She twisted her head and looked back at the hotel. Took in the sprawling veranda with the bougainvillea dripping down, the small trees with dark leaves and blooming gardenias, the luxurious, sprawling building itself. A few windows were still lit. Behind one, she could see the silhouette of a couple embracing. Behind another, a lone woman staring up at the sky. She followed the woman's gaze to the lush, almost-full moon.

Something wasn't right.

She looked back to the water, to her son. "What is it, Ethan?" she whispered. She stood up and walked slowly along the shore, slowly enough for him to follow along.

A breeze swept over her, ruffling her long white dress, her black hair. She breathed it in. But there was something missing. The perfume. There was no perfume. No heady scent of gardenia. She couldn't smell any of it. She couldn't even feel the breeze on her skin.

"Shhhh."

She turned, and La Llorona was there, suddenly, looking right at her with those wet, black eyes.

"It's okay, Karen," La Llorona said. "You're not alone anymore."

"I know," Karen said. "Look." She pointed to the water, to where her son was playing, laughing, but now there were other children, too, alongside him. Hundreds of them, maybe thousands, in the water. As many children as there were stars in the sky.

She looked back to La Llorona, confused, and now she saw, stretching out behind her, countless other women, all of them crying, reaching out toward the water, toward their children.

For a moment Karen felt panic, terror.

And then it passed, and she understood, and the most glorious sense of joy entered her.

She was home now. Tears of pure joy fell down her face. It was all so beautiful. Her son was laughing, and she was home.

❧ Afterword ❧

La Llorona—"the crying lady"—is a popular legend in Central and South America about a ghost woman who wanders about looking for her children (whom she had drowned in life, either to win or punish her lover), weeping. Multiple versions of the tale exist. In some, she can only be seen by people who are about to die. I liked the idea of another grieving woman going to Mexico to heal, seeing La Llorona, and finding comfort in her, a feeling of peace within the horror.

CARRIE LABEN

Face Like a Monkey

Carrie Laben was raised near Buffalo, New York, in a place best described as "about a mile from Six Flags." After stints in Ithaca and Brooklyn, she now lives in Montana, where she is working toward her MFA. She spends her spare time bird-ogling. Her short stories have appeared in Clarkesworld, Apex Digest, ChiZine, *and the* Phantom *anthology; she is currently at work on a novel.*

To this day they say it was just a bird, some kind of big ugly Mexican stork. Only I looked these storks up at the library and they're white. So that's bullshit. The Devil Bird was black.

My aunt Mary, my mother's sister, saw it two or three days after it first made the news. She was driving back from our place in the dusk after spending all afternoon helping Momma address wedding invitations—this was just before Momma married Walter—and as she passed the Stewarts' hayfield, she saw something moving and stepped on the brakes, assuming that it was one of their idiot dogs and might run out into the road.

And something did come out into the road—not running, but flying low, a shadow just above her headlights that flapped loosely and turned, as it passed over her hood, to stare her right in the face. That was what she kept repeating, when she had driven back to our house and scared Momma nearly to death banging on the door. That it had looked in her face.

She wouldn't sit down, and so Momma wouldn't sit down either, and so we all kept circling the kitchen, Aunt Mary pacing and Momma doing that pregnant-lady waddle that still makes me nervous to this day—they always look like they're going to fall over, and I know I'll be blamed if I don't catch them—and me dodging from corner to corner, trying not to get in the way.

"I wish Walter was here," Momma said, holding her belly. "I hate to think of him driving around out there with something on the roads. It's bad enough I have to worry about drunks and drug smugglers or who knows what, and now this."

"It had red eyes," Aunt Mary repeated, though I couldn't see the need; Momma was upset enough. But Momma hugged her. "A face like some kind of monkey. And a tail, pointed on the end. Tell me what it could be but the Devil?"

"Maybe it was a pterodactyl?" Walter had brought me a book on dinosaurs not long before and I was showing off.

"Go upstairs, Jimmy," Momma said.

"If it's a pterodactyl, they eat fish. They won't hurt us. Or Mr. Lyon."

"I said get upstairs."

She hadn't said where upstairs, so I sat in the hall in the dark where I could still hear them, just in case anything interesting happened. But they were quiet for a long time, and then Aunt Mary said, "I have to get home." She sounded like she might cry.

"You can't drive while you're all worked up like this—look at you, you're still shaking."

"Mom and Pop are probably tearing their hair out. They expected me half an hour ago."

"Call them and say you're staying the night here."

"They won't believe me. If I tell them what I saw, I mean." By now I was pretty sure she was crying, and I was grateful that Momma had had the foresight to send me away when she did.

"So tell them it took longer to do the invitations than we thought. We'll do a few more, so it won't be lying."

"They think I'm spending too much time on the wedding already."

"They wouldn't want you running into a ditch."

"I have to go home. You know how they get."

By then I was pretty sure no fresh pterodactyl details were going to emerge, and the floor was getting uncomfortable, so I went to my room and set up an observation post by the window at the foot of my bed, flashlight in hand, waiting for Remington and Max to bark so I could get a glimpse of the pterodactyl. I figured there was no way I was ever going to fall asleep. But somehow I still found myself waking up when it was time for cartoons in the morning.

I was watching Wile E. Coyote get hammered into an accordion by the sheepdog that he'd be saying "Goodnight, Ralph" to before the next commercial when Momma came from the kitchen. She had a cup of Folger's in one hand and a bowl of cornflakes in the other. She handed the cornflakes to me and plopped onto the couch, which sagged; the spoon rattled in her coffee cup.

She took a long pull of the coffee and we lost ourselves in the coyote's sufferings, and then in ads for the *Six Million Dollar Man* and Cocoa Puffs, and then in Bugs Bunny's acrobatic evasions of Yosemite Sam. Only after Sam, his mustache-ends singed, had given way to the next commercial did Momma set the coffee cup on the floor and put her arm around me.

"Mr. Lyon will be staying with us tonight," she said rapidly. "He'll get your bed, so you'll have to sleep on the floor of my room."

"Aw, Ma." I knew I didn't stand much of any chance of seeing a ptero-dactyl from the ground floor, even if Momma would let me sit up, which she wouldn't.

"It'll be like camping out," she said.

"Well, could I camp out? In the backyard? I won't get scared and I won't bother you guys and I won't try to start a campfire this time."

"No!" She must have felt me flinch, because she squeezed my shoulder. "Honey, it's not safe. The Stewarts saw that thing fly over their barn last night, and this morning one of their cows is dead."

"Can I go see?"

"The only thing you're going to go see is the sink." She pulled her arm away and picked up the coffee again. "I need all my canning jars washed, and you just won yourself a ticket to wash them. Go to see a dead cow? Honestly. Like you've never seen one before." She lifted herself back to her feet, shaking her head. "You can wait until the next cartoon is over, then you get your rear end in the kitchen."

Even back then, Momma had a lot of canning jars—they were wedding presents from when she'd married my father, so even though they were just old mason jars, she would get upset if one of them got broken. It was disre-spectful to his memory, or bad luck, or both. So it took me most of the morning to get through washing and rinsing and drying them all. For lunch we had eggs in baskets, which was one of my favorites, and I thought about asking to go up to the Stewarts' again, carefully, so that she at least wouldn't come up with more chores for me. But just as I thought I had figured out how to ask, the phone rang.

"Get that for me, sweetie, would you? If it's about a bill or like that, I can't come to the phone."

But it was Aunt Mary, so Momma had to get to her feet again, leaving her eggs half-eaten. I lurked in the doorway, waiting to ask my carefully-formulated question.

Momma listened for quite a long time, and then she said, "But why?" and then, "But Pop's got a gun too," and then, "Look, I know they don't like what me and Walter did, but we're doing our best . . ." and then, "Jesus, Mary!" and I tripped backwards through the doorway because it was so strange to hear her swear.

Momma seemed surprised at herself too; she was silent for a long time, and she was quiet when she finally said, "OK, all right. I'm sorry," and I crept away upstairs—I wasn't going to bug her about dead cows just then.

I was in my room, looking at my book trying to get an idea of what I would see if I saw the pterodactyl, when Walter showed up. I saw his truck pull into the driveway, and ran downstairs to show him; I wanted to show him that I'd put his gift to good use. I liked Walter a lot, and didn't understand why Pop and Grandma and Aunt Mary didn't—sure, he had slightly longer hair than me or Pop, but he drove a truck with a U.S. Geological Survey logo on the side and to my eyes that made him sort of like a kind of police, or something, and surely that canceled out long hair.

When I got down the stairs, he was busy talking to Momma in a low voice and I didn't think it would be a good idea to interrupt.

"Pack up an overnight bag, Jimmy," Momma said when she heard me on the stairs. "We're all going to your grandparents' house."

By the time I got outside with my things, Walter had already loaded the dogs in the truck and Momma was sitting in the passenger seat, looking back at the house like she expected it to fall down when we got out of sight.

We drove through the pounding afternoon sun and I strained my neck trying to scan both sides of the road at once for traces of the pterodactyl, but I saw nothing but grass and steers and the occasional tree. Walter drove in silence—he wasn't his usual happy self, and even in my pterodactyl-crazed state that made me a little nervous—one hand resting on the curve of Momma's belly. I wondered if Walter thought the bird was the Devil. It didn't seem like him. He'd taught me that toads couldn't give me warts, and which snakes I actually needed to be afraid of and which I could leave alone. I couldn't picture him scared of a dinosaur, any more than my dad would have been.

It was half an hour to the old ranch house where Pop and Grandma and

Aunt Mary lived. Remington and Max were as glad to get out of the back of the truck as I was, and before I'd peeled myself from the vinyl of the seat they ran toward the shade of the house and the place where the leaky hose left a little moisture.

As they reached it, though, instead of plunging in and rolling with belly-to-the-sky glee like they usually did, they slowed, sniffed, and then backed away. Walter tried to put them back into the truck but they didn't like that idea either, and went all skittish, and he had to hold both their collars.

Pop, leaning in the doorway, nodded. His old hound Lucy was lurking behind him, tail tucked in, rather than laying in her usual spot by the driveway.

"So, you came too?"

The dogs were giving Walter a lot of trouble; he didn't look up. "I figured if the situation is that serious you'd be glad of all the help you can get." He wrangled Max into sitting down, but Remington was still acting peculiar.

"Whatever it is, they don't like it," he said as he came unsteadily down the steps toward us. "What about you, Jimmy my boy? You scared of that Devil Bird?"

"No, sir." He took my shoulder, and I smiled.

"You wouldn't have let it get your momma, now would you have?"

"No, sir!" I wanted to tell him that it was a pterodactyl, but the first time I'd told him about the dinosaur book he'd dismissed it as nonsense.

"I should give you my gun, now that you're the man of the house." I glanced up at him—a chance to shoot a pterodactyl would be beyond my wildest dreams—but he wasn't looking at me, he was looking at Momma. "Anyway, your grandmother has some Cokes in the icebox, go inside and have yourself one."

Inside it was dark and a little cooler, and Grandma and Aunt Mary sat by the radio. I pulled out a Coke and sat by them, listening to the radio announcer describe how the Big Bird, as they called it with a laugh, had scared one Alverico Guajardo out of his trailer by running into the side of it. Bright red eyes, the man said, the size of silver dollars, a face like a gorilla, but with a long beak, wings like a bat, definitely a pterodactyl clue; I couldn't wait to tell Walter. Apparently a lot of the Mexicans a little farther south had been seeing it for years, or so they said. Every time the DJs laughed, Aunt Mary would flinch, but she never said anything.

Walter and Momma and Pop still hadn't come in by the time I finished my Coke. The DJs had gone on to talk about the weather and the boring stuff that the state legislature was up to. I stood up and made for the door, but Grandma caught me by the wrist.

"Give an old lady a hand with these," she said, pushing a bowl of wax beans into my arms as she rose. "Thank you, Jimmy. You're a good boy."

So she went outside, while I sat in one of the kitchen chairs, snapping beans and wishing for a breeze, or another Coke, or anything more exciting to do than listening to ads for Gold Medal flour and watching the blue-bottles circle suicidally around the fly strip. Aunt Mary still didn't speak, and when I looked over at her bowl she'd only snapped three or four beans.

I was nearly half-finished with my beans when the dogs started barking like mad. I jumped up, dropping the bowl onto the table, and ran for the front door.

But there was no red-eyed pterodactyl, not even a dark shadow overhead. Just Momma and Pop and Grandma and Walter, standing by the trucks yelling at each other. The dogs leaped in circles and barked, clearly confused about which side they were meant to be on.

"Just because you've ruined your own life doesn't mean you have any right to put Mary in a position where people will talk about her," Grandma said angrily.

"What are they going to say?" Momma said, her voice wobbly. "That she remembered that blood is thicker than water? Because some folks around here should."

"Says you." Pop didn't raise his voice; he dropped it to almost a growl. "You're the one who wants to take that boy away from us and from all his father's kin because you've got no more sense than a cow and you can't lie in the bed you made!"

Walter, angrier than I had ever seen him, took a step toward Pop, but Momma held her arm out to block him. "It's no good for me or Jimmy here, Pop. You know it. Even before all this. The bills are piling up, and . . ."

"And you think that running away will change the fact that life is hard?" Grandma said. "You go, you leave the boy. At least here he'll be with decent people." She took a step toward Momma, and for a moment I thought she might slap her. She'd slapped her before, though never in front of Walter, and I didn't want to see what would happen.

I stepped backwards, thinking to run back inside and go back to the beans and the radio. But I stepped on Aunt Mary's foot and yelped. She'd come up behind me in silence.

"The beans fell off the table," she said flatly, and everyone looked up at us.

I leaped off the steps, evaded Pop's reaching hand, and ran full-speed into the neighboring cornfield.

I'd gone a long way and my legs and arms were well scratched by weeds and I was sweaty and itching with pollen before I realized that none of them were still chasing me. I threw myself to the ground between the rows of towering corn plants and looked up at the tiny slivers of sky that appeared between the deep-green leaves.

No one had said anything to me about moving. Before, I would have thought it was a great adventure. But I didn't want Aunt Mary and the Stewart kids to keep having shots at the pterodactyl when they didn't know any better than to think it was evil, and me never ever see it. That wasn't fair.

I must have dozed off, hot and upset and itchy as I was, because I woke up to slanting late-afternoon light and the sound of rustling leaves. Someone was in the field, a few rows over from me. Pop's voice called my name.

He still sounded angry, though, so I kept quiet and still. If they found me I could always say I hadn't heard him. All cornfields muffled sound, and this one more so than most; judging by where the stalks were trembling, Pop was only a few rows over, but he sounded miles away.

It was only when the voice and movement drifted away to the west that I began to think that I should get home. I was hungry, and I would have killed for another one of those Cokes. And if Pop was out here being angry, he wasn't at the house being angry.

I started off confidently, in the opposite direction from that Pop had taken, cutting across the rows. I was past caring if I knocked down some stalks—they could blame that on deer or raccoons or the Devil Bird for all I cared.

The field went on and on. I didn't remember having come in this far—either I'd been running a lot faster than I thought, or I was going in the wrong direction. I angled myself south a little—that was definitely the way that home had to be, and there was no mistaking the cardinal points now. Even deep in the corn the sun's slant was obvious.

Letting alone the Coke, I would have been happy for a drink from the garden hose or even an irrigation ditch by now. Down among the stalks, fragments of twilight were starting to appear, and crickets were stirring to life—not to mention mosquitoes. Every few steps I had to shake and slap myself.

Surely Pop heard me moving and was coming back for me now. Surely the others were looking too. Surely the dogs could smell me. I stopped to listen.

Somewhere far away, Pop yelled again. It was hard to be absolutely sure, but I moved toward where I thought I heard him.

Suddenly, I felt a rush of air against my shoulders. The shadow swept over, and I looked up, and there it was.

My pterodactyl dreams fell apart around me. It had feathers, dusty black feathers that ended in wing tips like fingers clawing the air in slow strokes. It had a long spear of a beak, and a face like something that had rotted in a dry barn, grimacing without lips. And the red eyes that Aunt Mary had cried about.

It didn't look down at me, it passed over and away. I watched it go, the long tail sweeping behind it, ending in a club that almost makes me wistful today, because if I'd only seen that, I could have gone on hoping for a pterodactyl a little longer. Then it was out of sight, blocked by the tall tassels of the corn.

I didn't remember falling, but I was on my butt in the dust. Scrambling to my feet, I found my hands scraped. I had to get out of the corn. I wanted my mother. I ran.

Somewhere, where I couldn't judge, a long strangled cry rose into the dusk. A coyote, I thought. Then, no, Pop.

A few seconds later, I ran through a last row of corn and stumbled on the bank of an irrigation ditch. Frogs leaped like a forty-gun salute, and I skidded to a stop just short of joining them in the water. Somewhere someone—not Pop, Walter—was calling my name, and this time I opened my mouth to call back.

It hit me square between the shoulders, and not only was it not a pterodactyl, it was the Devil, just like Aunt Mary had said. The claw that seized the back of my head was hot and rough and as flexible and cruel as any hand. It was pushing me facedown into the mud, I squirmed but it was heavier than any bird ever had a right to be and I was pinned, blinded by grass and ready to choke. My fingers dug at the ground pointlessly.

I thought of Momma. And then I heard her. She was screaming for me, screaming like her heart would break, and I worried, she wasn't supposed to get upset.

Suddenly, the weight on the back of my head vanished as though it had never been. I was pulled to my feet, and I wiped the mud from my eyes and scanned the sky desperately. But the Devil Bird was gone.

Walter, behind me, gave me a shake. "Jimmy. Jimmy, can you breathe? Talk to us."

Momma was in front of me. She stared, white and panting, until I ran to her and buried my faced against her side and sobbed like mad. Walter said, "Lucy!" and she looked down at me and nodded, stroking my hair.

She held me as we lurched together back to the house, and never let me fall.

Pop's heart attack made the news because of the Devil Bird connection, and there were a lot of people at the funeral that I'd never met, even a couple of kids from the university at Houston. Aunt Mary yelled at some of them in the street until Grandma took her by the arm and pulled her away, and after that she went back to acting normal.

A few weeks later, Momma and Walter, who told me to call him Walter and that I had been the bravest kid he'd ever seen, got married in the courthouse, and I was officially adopted and was James Earl Lyons, and it wasn't long after that that we were putting as much as we could in Walter's truck and heading for Portland, Oregon. Momma only brought three of the canning jars, and she always kept flowers in them from then on. None of us ever went back. Momma didn't go to Grandma's funeral. She would tell me sometimes that she was sorry, but I never knew for what.

Sometimes, even to this day, people call me, wanting to hear it all again, and I indulge them. Unless they say they it was a stork.

Afterword

The Big Bird of Texas was the subject of a spate of sightings and rumors that caused a local panic in the Brownsville, Texas, area in 1976. It had a disconcerting habit of buzzing houses and cars; witness descriptions varied, but many included the detail that the creature had a naked head, "like a monkey" or "like a reptile." The sightings eventually tapered off, but reports of something strange flying around Texas have continued sporadically down to the present. Whether the Big Bird was natural or supernatural, whether it was bird, Thunderbird, pterodactyl, or kin to the Mothman, is still a subject of debate among cryptozoologists. I tend to suspect it was a Mexican stork.

Stork or something else, though, what fascinated me was how this out-of-context creature (and others like it, from Chupacabra to the Dover Demon) became a nucleus around which different narratives could crystallize—narratives that had more to do with the unspoken pressures and paranoias of peoples' everyday lives than with the substance, if any, of what they'd seen.

The Big Bird never attacked a human being directly; I have borrowed that detail, and the nickname "Devil Bird," from another alleged giant-bird sighting that took place in Illinois in 1977, in which a ten-year-old boy was supposedly seized and briefly lifted about two feet off the ground in front of multiple witnesses.

JEFFREY FORD

Down Atsion Road

Jeffrey Ford is the author of the novels The Physiognomy, Memoranda, The Beyond, The Portrait of Mrs. Charbuque, The Girl in the Glass, *and* The Shadow Year. *His short fiction has been published in three collections:* The Fantasy Writer's Assistant, The Empire of Ice Cream, *and* The Drowned Life. *His fiction has won* The World Fantasy Award, The Nebula Award, The Edgar Allan Poe Award, *and* Grand Prix de l'Imaginaire. *He lives in New Jersey with his wife and two sons and teaches literature and writing at Brookdale Community College.*

I live along the edge of the Pine Barrens in South Jersey, 1.1 million acres of dense, ancient forest, cedar lakes, cranberry bogs, orchids, and sugar sand. Black bear, fox, bobcat, coyote, and some say cougar. There are ghost towns from the Revolution, dilapidated shacks and crumbling shot towers that can only be reached by canoe. I've hiked through much of it in my years, and still I get a feeling that some uneasy sentience pervades its enormity. If I'm quite a distance from the trailhead where my car is parked and twilight drops suddenly, as it does out there, I feel a twist of panic at the thought of meeting night in those woods. You will, of course, have heard of the Jersey Devil. He's for the tourists. The place is thick with legends far more bizarre and profound. If you learn how to look and you're lucky, you might even witness one being born.

Sixteen years ago, when my wife and I and our two sons—one in second grade, one not yet in kindergarten—first moved to Medford Lakes, I noticed, every once in a while, this strange old guy stomping around town. He was thin and bald and had a big gray beard with hawk feathers tied into it. His head was long, with droopy eyes and a persistent smile. He pumped his arms vigorously, almost marching. Rain or shine, summer or winter, he wore a ratty, tan raincoat, an old pair of Bermuda shorts, black sneakers, and a red sweatshirt that bore the logo of the seventies soft rock band Bread. Every time I passed him in the car, it looked like he was talking to himself.

Then one day I was picking up a pizza in town, and he was in the shop, sitting alone at a table, a paper plate with pizza crusts in front of him. He studied me warily, whispering under his breath, as I passed on the way to the counter. Behind me, a woman and her girl came in. When he saw the little girl, the old guy pulled a brown velour sac from somewhere in his coat. He opened it and took something out. I was watching all this from the counter and wondered if something crazy was about to go down, but the mother let go of the girl's hand. The old guy slipped out of his seat onto one knee. The kid walked over to him, and he gave her what looked like a small, hand-carved wooden deer. The mother said, "What do you say, Helen?" The kid said, "Thank you." The old guy laughed and slapped the tabletop.

About a week later, Lynn and I were at the lake down the street from our house one evening. We'd taken a thermos of coffee and sat on a blanket, watching the sun go down behind the trees while the kids messed around at the water's edge. A neighbor of ours, Dave, who we'd met a few weeks earlier, was out walking his dog, so he came over and joined us, sitting on the sand. We talked for a while about the school board, about the plan to dredge lower Aetna Lake, he gave us his usual religious rap, and then I asked him, "Hey, who's that crazy old guy in the raincoat I see around town?"

He smiled. "That's Crackpop," he said.

"Crackpop?" said Lynn, and we broke up.

"His name's Sherman Gretts, but the kids call him Crackpop."

"He's on crack?" I asked.

"He just seems like he's on crack," said Dave. "A few years ago this kid who lives about two blocks over from where your house is, Duane Geppi, he's in my older son's class, overheard his father, who works down at the gas station, call the old guy a 'crackpot.' Duane thought he said 'Crackpop,' and called him that ever since. Now all the kids call him that. I think it's perfect."

"What else do you know about him?" I asked.

"Nothing, really. He's an artist or something. Lives all the way down Atsion Road by the lake."

"That's a long walk," said Lynn.

"Eight miles," said Dave.

"He seems deranged," I said.

"He probably is," said Dave, "but from what I hear, he's not a bad guy."

As time went on, and we settled into our life in Medford Lakes, I'd see Crackpop now and then trudging along under a good head of steam, jabbering away, the raincoat flapping. I always wondered how old the guy was. He looked to me to be in his sixties, but with all that walking he did, keeping him in shape, he could have been a lot older. Lynn also started bringing me reports of him. On her way to work and back she'd take Atsion Road to get to Route 206, and every couple of days she'd spot him going east or west or sitting somewhere in among the trees.

For our first Christmas in town, Lynn and I were invited to a party. The couple whose house it was at had a son in our older son's class. I met a lot of people from town and beyond, and we drank and shot the breeze. When the living room got too crowded and hot, I stepped out into the backyard to have a cigarette. It was lightly snowing, but it wasn't all that cold. I was only out there for a minute before the door opened and this older woman, a little heavyset but tall, with white hair came out and lit up. I introduced myself, and she told me her name was Ginny Sanger.

I talked to her for quite a while. Eventually she said she was an amateur historian. The origins of the area had always interested me, so I asked her when it had been settled.

"Well, the first people were, of course, the Lenape, the grandfather tribe of all the Algonquin nation," she said. "They go way back here. The first Europeans, you're talking early-1600s, Swedish trappers. Stuyvesant came in 1655 and shooed the Swedes out. The English eventually kicked the Dutch out."

"What got you into the history?" I asked.

"After my husband died, I really had nothing to do. He left me with plenty of money, so I didn't have to work. One summer day, about seven years ago, I went over to Atsion Lake for a swim. Do you know where I mean?" she asked, pointing east.

I nodded.

"I was out in the lake swimming around, and I stepped on something sharp. I knew I had to find whatever it was; there were a lot of kids in the water that day. I reached down to the bottom and felt this big piece of metal. Bringing it up, I saw it was a flat rusted figure of an Indian in a big headdress shooting a bow and arrow. He was attached at the feet to about a four-inch shaft. It was pretty corroded, but you could definitely make out the form."

"So that got you started?" I said.

"No, what got me started was my neighbor told me to take the thing over to Sherman, who lived just a little way up Atsion Road from us."

"Sherman?" I said. The name rang a bell but I couldn't place it.

"You've seen him. The old guy with the raincoat."

"You know him?" I said.

"Everybody up that way knows him. I took the Indian to him, and he told me that it was an ornament for a weather vane and had been forged in the Iron Works at Atsion Village, probably in the mid-1800s. He started telling me stories about the early settlers and the Lenape. We sat all afternoon on the screened back porch of that crazy house of his, sipping iced tea from blue tin cups, and he told me about a place called Hanover Furnace, a story from the time of the settlers that involved a description of how iron was made, an evil spirit of the woods, and the last Lenape Sachem."

"From seeing him around town, I got the impression he's kind of out of it."

"Well . . . ," she said.

Lynn came out looking for me then, ready to split. I introduced her to Ginny and we quickly said good-bye and left through the back gate. On our way home in the snow, we walked around the lake and I told her what the old woman had said about Sherman Gretts.

Months went by, and I was deep into writing a book, so I didn't go out much. Crackpop was about the last thing on my mind, until one Friday evening in February. Lynn came home and told me that in the morning on her way to work she saw the old man going into a house down by the end of Atsion Road. "I never noticed the place before," she said. "And I can't believe I didn't because it's bright yellow."

The thought of Crackpop in a yellow house made me smile.

"You've got to see it, though," she said. "I always thought, when I passed, that there were trees, like tall dogwood, growing around it, but today, when I saw him and knew it was his place, it became clear to me that they're not trees but sculptures made of limbs and pieces of trees. He's got like an army of tree-beings in his yard."

Saturday we drove out Atsion and Lynn slowed down as we passed the sagging yellow house. The sculptures were primitive, writhing forms like Munch's *Scream* made of twisted magnolia wood. "Jeez," I said, and made her turn around and pass it twice again.

Crackpop appeared in and disappeared from my life well into the spring. I didn't see him as frequently as I had at other times, and when I did spot him, I thought of his sculptures, and studied him closely. During the summer's first thunderstorm, I caught him tromping along Lenape Trail toward the Pizza Shop. The rain was beating down, and he was drenched. The two cars in front of me, one right after the other, hit the puddle along the edge of the road, sending a sheet of water up over him. He never slowed down or even acknowledged what had happened, but stayed on parade, jabbering away. A few weeks passed then where I didn't see him, and out of the blue at dinner I asked Lynn if she had. She said she saw him coming out of the woods down by 206 one night on her way home.

That first summer, we spent a lot of time at the lake with the kids. On the weekends we cooked out and then, as the sun was setting, we'd walk the twisting trails of town. The dark brought a certain coolness and the breezes would ripple through the oak leaves, carrying scents of wisteria and pine. The kids ran after toads, and every now and then someone would appear out of the dark.

Late one night, in the middle of July, we crossed the dirt bridge that spans a section of upper Aetna Lake. I had my younger son on my shoulders and Lynn had his older brother by the hand. We approached a bench that faced the water, and just as we drew up to it, I was startled by the sudden bright orange glow of a cigarette. The spot was cast in deeper shadow by a stand of oaks, and the figure was invisible until the ash glowed and momentarily lit up a face. I did a double take when I saw that it was Ginny Sanger.

I said hello to her and reminded Lynn we'd met her at the Christmas party. The old woman said that she was visiting the couple who'd had the party and while they were getting the kids ready for bed, she decided to duck out for a walk. "I like this spot," she said.

"We're trying to get these two guys home before they both fall asleep on us," I said.

"We're losing the race," said Lynn.

"I see you have to go," said Ginny as she stamped out her cigarette. Now it was perfectly dark under the oaks. "But I never got a chance to finish telling you how I got into the local history."

"Yeah, you told me it was that guy, Sherman," I said.

"That's true," she told me. "I started reading books and going to lectures on the area after talking to him. This is the part I wanted to tell you, though. From my own study and from having related some of Sherman's stories to a Lenni-Lenape storyteller I met at a conference, it became clear to me that Mr. Gretts was making everything up. The place names were right and some of the details, but in all the texts I've scoured I never saw any of the things he's spoken to me about." There was a moment of silence and then she laughed.

"That's pretty interesting," I said, and an image of Crackpop marched through my thoughts.

Ginny nodded. "Sherman spends a lot of time in the woods," she said. "One of his big things is, and he always whispers this one to me, like someone he doesn't want to might be listening, that there is still a band of Lenape roaming the Pine Barrens, living the old way like it was before the Europeans. 'They've always been there,' he says."

I would have liked to have heard more, but we had to get back home. As we trudged along, now each holding a sleeping kid, passing beneath tall pines on a carpet of needles, Lynn said, "I bet Ginny tried to corroborate Crackpop's story about the band of Indians hiding in the barrens with that Lenape storyteller."

"So?" I said.

"Say the storyteller was in on it, and he told her he'd never heard of it in order to keep people from searching for his ancestors?"

"Don't you think Crackpop's just nuts?" I said.

"Of course," she said.

. . .

It was early November and Atsion Road was littered with yellow leaves the same color as Crackpop's house. I drove to the end of the road, looked both ways, crossed over Route 206 and entered a dirt driveway with a steep incline. The car dipped down and then ascended a little hill. On the other side of that hill I could see a grass parking area and beyond that the steeple of a church from behind the trees. There were two other cars there but no one in sight. I parked, got out, and put my jacket on. It was cool and there was a strong breeze.

I was only twenty yards from the trailhead. I'd done some research of my own and knew that if I'd had the time and fortitude that trail would've taken me through the heart of the Pine Barrens and ended fifty miles later, at Batsto, another early Iron settlement where they'd made shot for the

Revolution. I started into the woods. About a hundred yards later, off to my left, there was a large clearing, and sitting in the middle of it was a white church. I'd read up on it. The Samuel Richards Church, a Quaker establishment built in 1828. Richards had owned the foundry at Atsion Village. His mansion still stood over by the lake.

There was a graveyard next to the building, the stones planted in concentric circles. At the far end of it was the most enormous oak I'd ever seen. The tree was ancient, and the way it stood there, barren of leaves against the blue sky, made me feel as if it could be thinking. I walked into the graveyard and looked at the markers. They were thin, with an arch at the top and made of some white stone that could have been marble or limestone. I read some of the names and dates that were still legible, the oldest being 1809. Some disaster took four of the Andrews family in one day. As I walked back to the trail, I looked quickly over my shoulder at the oak.

I walked a mile or more that first time in the Barrens and saw no one. Finally, at a place where a stream ran alongside the trail, I stopped, surrounded by endless pine and oak. Red and yellow leaves covered the underbrush. It was so quiet that when the wind blew I could hear the pines creaking as they swayed. Off at a distance, a crow cawed. Right then I felt something curl in my chest, and I turned around and started back. I saw deer watching me from deeper in among the trees.

Back in my car, I went up the dirt hill and crossed Route 206. On my way up Atsion toward home, I spotted a large, hand-painted sign on the side of the road. In bright green on an orange background it read ART SHOW TODAY! ALL WELCOME! Then I saw it was at Crackpop's house, and I was pulling over. There were a number of cars parked along Atsion and more pulled up into the lot next to the house. When I got out of my car, I saw people in the backyard and smelled a barbecue.

I passed beneath the writhing tree giants in front and went around back. There were more of the crazy sculptures in the big backyard and from their twisted hands hung paintings and mobiles made from animal bones. Some people sat under them smoking pot and pretty much everybody there had an open beer. People just nodded to me and smiled. Kids and teenagers and old people, black, white, and a woman made up like an Arab sheikh in white robes. When I passed the grill a young guy with a goatee and tattoos all over his arms, holding a spatula, offered me a hot dog. I accepted and moved on, strolling around from painting to painting.

Crackpop was no Picasso, but the images were sort of charming in their neokindergarten style. They were all depictions of events in the Barrens—Indians and deer and settlers hunting wild turkey. There was one of a burial beneath a giant oak, and a whole series of what looked like demons. I felt self-conscious there, so I lit a cigarette and strolled closer to the house. When the music, Faron Young's "Hello Walls," scratching away on an old Victrola ended, I heard a woman call my name. I looked around.

"In here," I heard her say, and I turned and looked into the shadow of a screened porch I was standing near.

"Who is that?" I said, shading my eyes to try to see.

"Ginny Sanger," came the voice.

I walked over to the concrete block that stood where steps should have, hoisted myself up, and opened the screen door. My eyes adjusted, and I saw Ginny sitting in a redwood lawn chair next to Crackpop, who wore some kind of animal pelt over his shoulders; a red, white, and blue headband; and his usual getup. He had a joint between his fingers that was as thick as a cigar.

Ginny introduced me and said, "This is Sherman Gretts, the artist." I stepped over and shook the old man's hand.

"Seen you at the pizza place," he said.

I nodded. "I was looking at your paintings," I said.

"Want to buy one?" he asked, and laughed.

"How much?" I said.

He motioned for me to sit down in the empty chair next to his. I did. He passed me the joint and I took a hit. Ginny took it from me. Gretts leaned close and said, "She tells me that you're a writer."

"I am," I said.

"Why do you write?" he asked.

"Because I like to," I told him, and he laughed.

He stubbed the joint out and said, "OK, you want to witness something?"

"What do you mean?"

"I'll give you a painting if you bear witness to me. Ginny'll be my other witness."

"To what?" I asked.

"I'll show you," he said. He reached down beside his chair and lifted into his lap a rolled up pink bath towel. He laid it on the coffee table in front of us. "First thing, you gotta listen to me," he said.

I nodded.

"Back in 1836, a book titled *The American Nations,* written by this gent Constantine Samuel Rafinesque-Schmaltz, was published. In it Rafinesque, as he was known here, claimed to have had revealed to him by the Lenape a copy of the Wallum Olam, a book written on tree bark in ancient pictographs, telling the narrative of how the Lenape had arrived in the area from far away due to a great flood. " The old man took a beer off the table, snapped it open, and handed it to me.

"Rafinesque even hinted that some of the scenes had shown the early Lenape beginnings in Siberia. By the time the book came out, though, he said the actual Wallum Olam had been destroyed in a fire, but assured the reading public that the reprinted pictographs in his book were authentic. But of course they weren't. Of course they weren't." Here Crackpop went silent for a moment and leaned back in his seat.

I glanced over at Ginny and she winked at me.

"His was a fraud," the old man began again. "But like so many things labeled false, it holds some pieces of truth. I'm telling you the Wallam Olam is a real thing Let's just say that I have contact with a certain sect of the Lenape who guard the real Wallam Olam at the dark heart of the forest. What I'm going to show you is a page of it." Sherman put his yellow-nailed hand out and unrolled the towel. Within it was a roll of the thinnest piece of birch bark, so supple it appeared to have the texture of cloth. It was off-white and in the center was a black drawing of a giant turtle with a man straddling its back.

"You didn't make that, Sherman?" asked Ginny with a stoned smile.

"Oh, it's real," he said. "If they find out I took it, they'll send a Mahtantu after me."

"What's that?" I asked.

"A kind of demon," said Ginny.

"You didn't notice this when you came in I bet, but my house is surrounded by a small concrete gutter full of water. I keep a pump running twenty-four/seven in it so the demons can't get in. I was taught that evil spirits can't cross running water."

"What happens when you leave the house?" I asked.

"I have to be really careful, perform rituals and such before I go out. I can't mess up."

"What's the chances of that?" I asked.

"I can do it," he said, "but the question is, can you two? Remember, you're my witnesses. If you tell anyone outside of this protected area, even in a whisper, about what I've shown you, they'll know I took it and it won't matter how careful I am. So you've got to promise not to tell anyone."

"OK," I said. "It's a deal." I stood up and shook his hand. I said a quick good-bye to Ginny, thanked the old man, and split, almost missing the concrete block on the way down. Crackpop said I could take a painting, and as much as I wanted to just get out of there, I had to stop and consider it. The old man was truly insane, and his slow revelation of it on the porch gave me the creeps, not to mention old Ginny smoking a joint and secretly mocking him to me. On the other hand, I knew that years later if I didn't have something tangible to attach to this story when I told it, no one would believe me. I grabbed the rendering of the oak tree burial from the hand of a tree-being. As I relieved it of the picture's weight, the wooden giant moved as if stretching. All the way home, with that painting in the backseat, I kept checking the rearview mirror.

Lynn took one look at the painting and said "No," so I hung it in my office. Later that night, in bed, she asked me about my walk. I told her about the church and the art show. I really wanted to tell her about the bizarre episode of my bearing witness, but I swear I didn't. And the fact that I didn't followed me into sleep.

Time passed, a couple of years, and both kids were in school and Lynn and I were both working. The Curse of Crackpop wasn't the worst that could happen and so the whole thing faded pretty quickly from my thoughts. Occasionally I'd see him on the move, and I'd wonder what rituals he'd performed in order to walk so far from home. At other times, I'd notice the painting hanging in my office, and that would make me think of him as well. All this was fleeting, though, in the onrush of our lives. Through all of it, even drunk at the holidays or stoned with old friends, I kept the old man's secret.

More time passed, and the whole thing was as prevalent in my thoughts as my third birthday party, when one night Lynn came home from work pretty upset. She was trembling slightly.

"Crackpop," she said. "I almost hit him. He's drunk or something, stumbling around in the middle of Atsion Road."

"Uh-oh," I said.

"Fuck him. I almost hit a tree trying to avoid him."

"What should we do?"

"What are you going to do?" she said. "Stay out of it."

"Somebody's gonna hit him," I said.

"He's popped his last crack," said Lynn. She picked up the phone and called the local cops.

Maybe a month after that, I heard, in a matter of two weeks from different neighbors and the guy at the 7-Eleven, that Crackpop had a meltdown at the pizza place, engaging in some unwelcome bellowing, then he was spotted weaving along Atsion one afternoon, literally frothing at the mouth, after that a car did hit a tree, trying to avoid him, though no one was injured. This chain of events ended in his being hit and killed one night by a semi. Our neighbor, Dave, told us about it at the beach. He knew one of the cops who was called to the scene. "Gretts was completely obliterated," he said.

I waited a few months out of some strange sense of respect, and then I told Lynn at the end of summer. We sat out back on the screened porch, having coffee by candlelight. The crickets were strong and the night was cool. When I finished telling her about my bearing witness to Crackpop, the first thing she said was, "Does that mean Ginny told someone and the old man was possessed by a demon?"

I laughed. "I didn't think of that," I said.

Soon after, there was another fatal accident down on Atsion. Four high school kids in a white Windstar, drunk and high, veered off the road into a large oak tree. The driver was killed instantly, the two in the back died later, and only the front passenger, having been thrown from the vehicle, lived. That person was Duane Geppi, and when he finally came to, he swore to the cops that it was Crackpop, back from the dead, who had come lunging out of the shadows at the van. That story made the rounds. I heard it from a number of different people and told it to more. Hence a legend was born.

Weird old guy, hit by a truck on Atsion, comes back from the dead to walk the road, seeking revenge against the world that shunned him. Reports of his ill-intentioned specter showed up frequently in the local paper around Halloween, and I heard from my older son that kids sometimes drove out that way toward the lake, hoping for an encounter. Eventually, Crackpop's house burned down in a fire of "mysterious origins," as it was reported. They didn't know the half of it.

What really scared me was something else entirely. That question Lynn had asked me about whether Ginny might have given away the old man's secret came back to me every time I'd see the oak tree painting in my office. I knew the only way I could find out whether she had or not was to meet her face-to-face. I believed that even if she lied to me when I asked her, I'd be able to detect the truth in her expression. I called the couple who'd had us to our first Christmas party in town, where I'd met Ginny, and spoke to the wife. I told her I wanted to get Ginny Sanger's phone number. She said she didn't know who I was talking about. I described the stately older woman with white hair, and she said, "I can tell you for sure, we don't know anyone like that."

"She doesn't visit you sometimes? She lives down Atsion."

"You must be thinking about one of your books," she said, laughed, and hung up.

I scoured the phone book, paid for an Internet trace, stopped and talked to old people when I'd see them out in their yards along Atsion Road. Nobody had ever heard of Ginny Sanger. I took some solace in the fact that Lynn attested to having met her. There wasn't a Sanger in the county, though. It took me years to figure it out, my kids are in college now, but I had the answer hanging in front of me the whole time.

I found her yesterday, in the circular cemetery next to the white church. The giant oak looking on, I scraped some moss off one of the stones and there she was. Virginia Sanger, Born 1770—Died 1828. Like I said to Lynn, don't ask me to explain. I don't understand my own part in what had happened, let alone Ginny's. What I was fairly certain of, though, was that, if I went into that church and went through their archive, I'd find some thread of a story about her, a sketch, a letter, and then there'd be no end to it—legend giving way to legend, like a hydra. That's the way it is here. The mind of the place manifesting in human legends that intersect and interbreed into a vast invisible wilderness all their own. We really only live along the edge of the Pine Barrens, but, still, for whatever reason, that spirit reached out and gathered us in.

❧ Afterword ☙

The Jersey Devil isn't the weirdest thing in New Jersey by a long shot. As a matter of fact, I have neighbors that make him look like a patsy. The creature has gotten the most publicity, though, which is a shame because there are literally hundreds of legends that exist in and around the Pine Barrens. There's The White Stag, The Black Doctor, The Atco Phantom, Captain Kidd at Reed's Bay, The Rabbit Woman, Jerry Munyhon (a kind of Barrens wizard who, when turned down for a job at Hanover Furnace, cast a spell and filled it with black and white crows), more ghosts from every era than you can shake a stick at, and that's not mentioning any of the Lenape legends.

If you live here for a while and keep your eyes and ears open to these tales, as I do, being a writer of the fantastic, it soon becomes evident that there is something about the place that engenders legend. Part of this has to do with the enormity of the wilderness, its loneliness and mazelike quality, but I think the main reason is that there is some kind of sentient energy at its heart, as if it was conscious and scheming, imbuing the lives of those who live in it or near it with some measure of its primordial consciousness. The feeling is palpable. I've only felt this from a landscape in one other place I've been: the Scottish Highlands. I spent ten days there once in a cottage near the Isle of Skye. The place was remarkably beautiful, but haunted. There was a pervasive feeling of melancholy and loneliness mixed into the spectacular views of the mountains and lochs. I definitely felt as if the place was alive, like some sleeping giant, dreaming. "Down Atsion Road" is my attempt to chronicle the supernatural influence of the Barrens. Believe me when I tell you that most of this story is true, and the parts that aren't are the incidentals. The strange wilderness has been shaping legends since humanity first set foot here. They crisscross and interconnect like a web. Through them, it communicates with us. Consider this, a vast piece of real estate in the Northeast, within commuting distance of New York City, remains virtually untouched. Think of the money it would be worth to developers, think of the towns and malls and roads that could be cut into it. As other landscapes fall to the onslaught of "progress," the Barrens has retained itself. Pretty damn cunning, if you ask me.

GARY A. BRAUNBECK

Return to Mariabronn

Gary A. Braunbeck is the author of nineteen books, among them the acclaimed novel In Silent Graves, the first novel in the ongoing Cedar Hill Cycle. His fiction has been translated into Japanese, French, Italian, Russian, and German. Nearly two hundred of his short stories have appeared in various publications, including The Magazine of Fantasy & Science Fiction and The Year's Best Fantasy and Horror. He was born in Newark, Ohio, the city that serves as the model for the fictitious Cedar Hill in many of his stories. As an editor, Gary completed the latest installment of the Masques anthology series created by Jerry Williamson, Masques V, after Jerry became too ill to continue, and also coedited (with Hank Schwaeble) the Bram Stoker Award–winning anthology Five Strokes to Midnight. Gary's work has been honored with five Bram Stoker Awards, an International Horror Guild Award, three Shocklines "Shocker" Awards, a Dark Scribe Magazine Black Quill Award, and a World Fantasy Award nomination. Visit him online at www.garybraunbeck.com.

There you are. I see you at night.

    .   .   .

Lorena notices right away that Rudy is out of sorts. He always took a stool right smack in the middle of the counter—"I like being close to the action," he'd say. "And if there's no action, I like looking at you and *imagining* some action." Why she hasn't slapped his face after all this time, she can't say. Maybe it's because he always blushes like a little boy who's just told his first dirty joke whenever he tries one of his bad lines on her. There's something sweet about his attempts at crude trucker humor, and that always makes her smile.

But tonight Rudy sits at the far end of the counter, near the bathrooms, the worst seat in the diner. He's been tight-lipped, shaky, and anxious. This is not the same man she's been serving and flirting with for the past couple of years, and she's not sure if it's a good idea to ask him about anything *too* personal. Still, he looks like he's about to crack apart. Lorena finishes refilling everyone's coffee and drifts down to Rudy.

"I gotta tell you, Rude"—the nickname usually gets a grin out of him, but not tonight—"I didn't expect to see you with the weather and the roads the way they been. You musta drove like a bat out of hell."

Rudy attempts a smile, doesn't quite make it, and silently pushes his coffee cup toward her. Lorena fills it again. When Rudy reaches for it, she puts her free hand on top of his and squeezes. "What's up with you tonight,

Rude? Usually by this time you've propositioned me at least three times. You never know . . . tonight I might say 'yes.'"

Rudy looks at her, at the other customers in the diner, and then speaks; his voice is a fragile, sad, frightened thing: "I think I might've done something terrible tonight, Lorena. I didn't *mean* to, but . . ." He looks at her with eyes so full of mute pleading that Lorena feels her throat tighten. She can't remember if she's ever seen a man so lonely.

"What is it, Rudy? You can tell me."

"I don't know," he whispers. "I . . . I kinda really like you—why do you think this is always the first place I stop when I leave on a run and the last place I stop on the way back?"

Lorena feels herself blush a little. "I figured you was just the shy type."

"Your opinion of me means a lot, and I . . . I don't want that ruined."

Lorena puts the coffeepot back on the burner and tells the cook and the other waitress that she's taking her fifteen-minute break. She picks up Rudy's coffee cup and half-eaten sandwich and gestures for him to follow her over to one of the far empty booths.

Once they're situated and sitting across from one another, Lorena sits back, folds her arms across her chest, and says, "Okay, Rudy, here it is: I like you, too, and I think a lot of you, think you're an okay guy. I done things that I ain't really proud of, either, so I try not to judge anybody. So, c'mon—out with it."

Rudy doesn't look at her as he begins talking. Even when describing the worst of it, he never makes eye contact. Lorena has to lean forward and turn her good ear in his direction in order to make out the words. It's hard for her to pay attention to his story at one point because she's stunned by the tears that are forming in his eyes. But she listens, and feels sick.

Rudy finishes his story, sips at his now-cold coffee, and finally looks at her. Something in him touches her, and she moves over to sit beside him, using a paper napkin to wipe his face.

"Rudy, you gotta listen to me, hon, okay? If it hadn't been you, it woulda been somebody else. Sounds to me like they was pretty determined."

"But, *Christ*, Lorena, I . . . I . . ." He takes hold of her hand. "Am I a bad man?"

"No, you're not. A bad man wouldn't be feeling the way you are." She

then cups his face in both of her hands. "You listen to this, Rudy, and you
listen good.

"*Yes . . .*"

.   .   .

"Dude, I'm serious—you *gotta* hear what I got on my digital voice recorder
last night."

"Oh, for the love of— Look, I'm begging you, find a woman, download
porn, start collecting Precious Moments figurines—*something else,* all right?
This goddamn ghost chasing of yours is wearing really thin. You're out
there alone in the middle of the night and— Hell, I worry about you, okay?"

"Please? Just listen, and I swear if you think it's bullshit, if you still think
it's a waste of my time and money, I'll drop it, okay?"

"Fine. Let's hear it."

Click. Hiss. *Where have you been? I've missed you.* Hiss. Hiss. (Very softly,
sounds of distant traffic nearly obscuring the words.) *Dance with me?* Click.

"Well?"

"Jesus."

.   .   .

The O'Henry Ballroom is crowded that night, the orchestra in rare form as
they play "You Came Along" and "Love in Bloom" and "(I Can't Imagine)
Me Without You" (one of her favorite new songs), but her escort for the evening has had far too much to drink and is getting somewhat fresh. She
reaches behind her and grabs his left hand, pulling it up to the small of her
back where it's supposed to be, and hopes that he understands. He doesn't,
and soon his hands are slipping again, touching her in the most inappropri-
ate of ways, and at last she breaks away and slaps his face.

"*Please* stop doing that!"

He glares at her, rubbing his check. Around them several couples have
stopped dancing and are staring at them.

"I'm afraid I don't know what you mean," he says.

She looks around at the staring faces and feels herself turning red. She
realizes then that she should have stayed home and listened to *The Shadow*
with her parents. That new actor, Orson Welles, oh, his voice! Instead, she
is here, being made a spectacle of because her escort was a drunkard and a
masher.

"I wish for you to take me home now, if you please."

He steps toward her, gripping her shoulders. When he speaks, his words are thick and slurred. "I am not going to take you anywhere . . . 'cept back to our table. Let's have another drink an' settle down."

She tries to free herself of his grip but he's quite strong. Finally, she stomps on his right foot. He cries out, releases her, and stumbles backward.

"You will take me home *now*!"

"I will most certainly not. If you wish to go, then *go*! Have a nice walk." With that, he turns away and stumbles through the dancers until he disappears somewhere in the throng of swaying bodies. Fighting back tears of humiliation and anger, she twirls around and walks off the dance floor toward the doors. Her face is puffy, red, and tear-streaked. Maybe the cold air will help.

She pushes open the doors and glides out into the harsh winter night. Less than a mile. She has strong legs, a dancer's legs, and knows that she can make it. Yes, she'll be freezing by the time she comes through the front door, but her mother and father will be there. Warm cocoa, perhaps some soup. Father's heavy coat and a place by the fire. Soft music on the radio. Is *Gershwin Presents* on tonight? (She hopes so.)

Crossing her arms over her midsection, she takes an icy breath and moves out toward the road, her white dress blending into the swirling snow.

. . .

The State Police find the car in the spring, after the first thaw. It's on its roof far off to the side of Archer Avenue, not far from Resurrection Cemetery, at the bottom of the incline where the winter snow always piles high to hide the carcasses of animals that crawl into the foliage to die, the litter tossed by teenagers as they drive too fast around the bend, and even, sometimes, the bodies of vagrants who curl up with newspaper blankets in the shadows thinking they'll be on their way in the morning, after they've rested.

The entire driver's side of the car is smashed in, the door and part of the front missing.

"Looks like the damn thing got hit with a wrecking ball," remarks one of the officers.

His partner shakes his head. "Never had a chance. At least the license plate is still attached."

The officers call in it in. They are instructed to make a search of the immediate area, which turns up nothing.

. . .

The old man wakes at four in the morning and lies there staring at the ceiling. He hates the way the patterns in the plaster form an endless overlapping series of swirls. They look too much like snow caught in the merciless winter winds coming at a windshield late at night, an endless assault of white that not even the windshield wipers can fight against. White . . . so much white.

He sits up, swings his legs over the side of the bed, and presses his feet against the cold floor. Looking over his shoulder, he stares at the half of the bed where his wife used to sleep. Dear Henrietta, now six years in the grave. She would know what to say, how to rub his shoulders *just so,* relaxing him, whispering *It's all right, honey, it's all in the past, you know it was an accident. . . .* But she's gone, and the children are grown with kids of their own. Sure, they call and visit often, he has pinochle with the guys at the Eagles on Thursdays, but he's going to be eighty-nine next birthday—a "spry" eighty-nine, as his children and grandchildren always remind him—but on nights like this, nights that have become more and more frequent the past few months, he wakes at some god-awful hour and is all too aware of his aches, his pains, the little snaps and crackles made by his bones when he moves, the silence of the house and the world outside . . . and he wishes that silence would extend to his conscience. Shouldn't he have started becoming absent-minded by now? An old fart who can't remember if the underwear goes on before the pants. Too bad an old man can't choose *what* to forget.

He shuffles over to the window, pulling back the curtain. It's beginning to snow; not much at the moment, just a few light flurries, but if the Weather Channel is right, this part of the Midwest is going to be under a good nine inches in the next forty-eight hours. He wonders if the snow will be as heavy and merciless as it was on that night. He looks back to the empty place in the bed. "I can't live with it anymore, my dear girl. I have to go back." For a moment he imagines Henrietta sitting there, the covers pulled up around her shoulders—she always did chill easily in winter—smiling at him, a smile tinged with sadness at the edges, and finally he imagines her wonderful voice as she says: *You do what you need to, honey. You deserve some peace.* "Thank you," he whispers to the emptiness. He looks out the window again. "I left a big part of me on Archer Avenue back in '37. I remember Bing

Crosby was singing 'Black Moonlight' when I started to go around that bend. I remember all the snow—God, there was so much snow against the windshield. The wipers couldn't keep up.

"I should've slowed down, or pulled off to the side and waited for it to clear up. Lord, I was driving Mom and Dad's Imperial! Chrysler used to make their cars like tanks back then. I could have waited it out. I was just a kid, you know? I shouldn't've . . ." His voice fades away as he hears another voice, not that of his wife, whisper from the memory of a dream: *There you are. I see you at night.*

He wanders over to the bookshelf and takes from it an old edition of Hesse's *Narcissus and Goldmund,* one of his favorite novels. He sits on the edge of the bed on Henrietta's side and leafs through the pages, stopping to read a favorite paragraph here, a memorable dialogue exchange there, all the while shaking his head. He looks at his late wife's pillow. "I don't know why, my dear girl, but I just suddenly thought of the two of them—Narcissus and Goldmund . . . how they became friends and the different paths their lives took, Narcissus remaining at the monastery of Mariabronn to become its Abbot John, while Goldmund set off to live the life of an adventurer and artist.

"I was always moved by the final chapters—I don't know if I ever told you this, so pardon me if I'm repeating myself—but there you have Goldmund, who's squandered and prostituted his artistic talents, led a life of self-indulgence and debauchery, only to wind up waiting to be hanged as a thief. And like the deus ex machina I suspect it was intended to be, along comes Narcissus to help him escape and bring him back to Mariabronn where Goldmund, sick and dying, is forgiven by Narcissus. Knowing his time is short, Goldmund sets about creating his last genuine work of art, a Madonna fashioned after the image of Lydia, his one true love, whose heart and spirit he had broken. He finds forgiveness in his heart for himself, my dear girl, because he uses all of his love and regret and guilt to perfectly fashion the Madonna's image. And when Goldmund at last sees Lydia's face again, he knows that he is forgiven, and so can die at peace with himself." He closes the book with a loud snap. "That's probably about as close to sentimentality as Hesse ever came.

"It seems to me now, my dear girl, that unlike fiction, one has to fashion one's own deus ex machina if forgiveness is to be found."

He rises from the bed, his hand pushing against Henrietta's pillow, then replaces the book on the shelf, and begins preparations for his trip.

.   .   .

"I got more than just that on here. I talked to a guy who's seen her."

"Let's hear that, too, then."

Click. Hiss. The sound of muffled voices and the ping! of glasses being slid into an overhead rack. A louder voice calls, "Two more pitchers for table seven!" A bartender shouts, "Regular or Light?" Hiss. The sound of a man clearing his throat. Then: "Is that thing on?"

"It sure is."

"Huh. Don't look like no tape recorder I ever seen."

"It doesn't use tape. It's a digital recorder."

"You don't say? Well, I'll be. Makes you wonder what they'll come up with next."

"So . . . you said that you met her one night?"

"Oh, I sure did! Told the story many times. Was even on TV once."

"Would you mind telling it again now?"

"Not at all. Nice of you to not think I'm some kinda kook."

"I believe the stories. So, please . . ."

.   .   .

As the winch pulls taut and the tow truck begins moving the demolished car up the incline, the State Police detective looks at the man standing next to him and says: "Mind if I ask you another question?"

The other man shakes his head and wipes something from one of his eyes. "I don't know what else I can tell you but, okay."

"Do you have any idea what he was doing all the way out here? I mean, a man his age had to've known that driving from Ohio to here in the middle of winter was risky. I just can't help but think he was really determined to do something or see someone. Do you have *any* ideas?"

The other man shakes his head once again. "I swear to you, I don't have the slightest clue."

Something in the man's voice makes it clear to the detective that he's lying. The detective begins to speak, thinks better of it, and stands in silence. No reason to push the poor guy.

.   .   .

She's made it as far as the bend in Archer Avenue when she hears the sound of a car, but the wind makes it impossible to tell from which direction the vehicle is approaching. She decides it doesn't matter. She can barely feel her feet or hands. Even if the car is going in the opposite direction, no one with a soul and an ounce of compassion would leave her out in the cold, not on this night.

She moves toward the middle of the road and begins looking both in front of and behind her, then begins waving her arms. Soon, she sees the glow of headlights coming around the bend straight toward her. Oh, how wonderful! They *are* going in her direction. She opens her mouth to shout at the driver and steps to the side, away from the oncoming vehicle, but a sudden gust of wind causes her to lose her balance and her white shoes slip on a patch of black ice and she gasps, spins, and stumbles into the path of the car.

. . .

"Sis? It's Joseph. Listen, I'm over at Dad's house and— What?"

"I said, do you know what time it is?"

"Yes, and I'm sorry, but I've been trying to call Dad for the last three days and haven't gotten an answer."

"Oh, God. Is he all right?"

"He's not even *here*! The car's gone. He left an envelope for us with a bunch of stuff in it—a copy of his will, his bank book, his stock certificates, the deed to the house—he made it out to you—and . . . and there's a letter."

"What's it say?"

"No, not over the phone. Can you come over? I called the police and I have to wait here."

"I'll be there in an hour. Are you okay?"

"*Hell*, no. But thanks for asking."

"Where do you suppose he could've gone?"

"When you get here. I'll tell you everything when you get here."

. . .

The driver of the semi doesn't see the parked car until he's right on top of it, and by then there's no time to hit the brakes or swerve, not on this road and not with all the black ice. The front of his truck slams into the car and pushes it along the road for several yards, sparks flying, shattered glass spitting up against his windshield, before finally smashing into a snowman in the middle of the road, splattering it all over before the car at last dislodges and rolls down the incline by the side of the road.

The driver beats his steering wheel and screams a torrent of profanities, but does not stop. The snow and wind are coming in almost full force now, and if he's late with this delivery, it's his ass.

Stupid asshole should've known better than to park there in this weather, anyway, he thinks. What kind of nutcase leaves their car and goes to build a fucking snowman *in the middle of the road?*

A few miles later, the driver notices the blood in a few of the larger, icy clumps of snow that have lodged up against the center of the windshield, in that no-man's-land the wipers can never quite reach.

Oh, God, please . . . please, no.

He eases off to the side of the road and parks the semi, then grabs a flashlight from under the seat, opens the door, stands on the running board, and shines the light onto the hood.

Blood and hair. There is blood and hair in the clumps of ice and snow. He shakes his head. No, it was just a snowman, that's all. Snowmen don't bleed. It must've been a bird. Yeah, that's it. He must have hit a bird and not noticed.

Birds don't have hair, whispers something in the back of his conscience, where the light doesn't quite reach.

"No," Rudy says out loud. "No. It was a bird. Snowmen don't bleed." And that helps. Not a lot, but some. So he drives on, his hands shaking, knowing that it couldn't have been a bird but telling himself it was, anyway, over and over, knowing full well that this is going to haunt him for the rest of his life.

. . .

"—well, she was a sweet thing, no denying that. Long blond hair and the prettiest face. She kind of reminded me of my youngest daughter. Anyway, she was at the Willowbrook—used to be the O'Henry years ago, until the new owners bought it and decided things needed to be, you know, updated and such.

"She come over and asked me for a dance and I figured, why not, she was awful courteous—not like the girls these days—and we had ourselves a nice little dance. Oh, you should've seen how she was dressed! Long white dress, real fancylike, and shoes to match. I know this sounds corny as hell, but she looked like some of them paintings you see of angels.

"Thing was . . . she was awful *cold,* even though it was only autumn. The small of her back, her hands, her cheeks. Real cold. My wife, she's kind of cold-blooded—not in *that* way, she's a sweetheart, but brother, sometimes her touch is like ice—she says it's 'cause of her circulation problems . . . shit, where was I? Oh, yeah.

"This gal was *real* cold, so I offer her my jacket. She thanks me for being such a gentleman, and I drape my jacket over her shoulders. She asks me if I could give her a ride home and I say sure thing. We're driving along a little ways and she asks me to go down Archer Avenue. I oblige her request and we're driving along and talking about the weather, the way the Willowbrook has changed over the years, stuff like that, and then we come up on Resurrection Cemetery and she asks me to stop. I think it's a bit odd but I stop anyway.

"She gives me back my coat and thanks me for being a gentleman, then she gets out and starts walking toward the cemetery gates. Here it is, ten thirty at night, and she's headin' into the boneyard. I call to her that the cemetery's closed and that she really ought to get back in the car so I can take her home. That's when she turns and looks at me and smiles and says, 'I am home.' Then she just . . . faded away into nothing.

"That's when I knew who she was, and believe you me, I damn near wet myself. I mean, you hear all the stories about her, but you never expect that *you'll* . . . you know what I mean. Ain't a day goes by that I don't think of her. Makes a body wanna cry, it does, thinking about the way she died, out there all alone on that road, middle of winter. Son-of-a-bitch what hit her didn't even stop. I hope to hell whoever it was, if they're still alive, I hope to hell they ain't had a moment's peace.

"She was a damned sweet girl, and she deserved better than that, you know?"

· · ·

The old man impresses himself; he's only had to stop twice along the ten-plus-hour drive to make water. The last time, he went outside, writing his name in the snow like he used to do when he was a child. He even laughed while doing so, the first real laugh he's had in at least twenty years.

But he's made it, despite the damn snow and wind. Three times he's almost been knocked off the road by the wind. The radio said there were "blizzardlike conditions" coming, but that hasn't stopped him.

And now he's finally back here, after all the years, after all the bad dreams, after a lifetime. Archer Avenue. But this time, *this* time he drives slowly. This time he'll see her before it's too late. This time he'll stop. This time he'll make it right and hope that will be enough.

He turns the radio to a local "beautiful music" station. Truth in advertising, for once. It's Big Band night tonight. Glenn Miller. Stan Kenton. Spike Jones and His City Slickers. This music suits the old man just fine and dandy, yessir. Just as long as they don't play any Bing Crosby, especially "Black Moonlight."

He slowly rounds the bend and hits the straight stretch dense with trees on either side, some of them obscuring the steep incline off to the side of the road. He knows that if he's not careful, he will drive off and fall a good seven feet where no other passing cars can see him. He has to be careful now. Like he should have been back in '37.

A flicker in the headlights as several swirls of snow dance up onto the hood and skitter across until they explode against the windshield. But this time he's got the defrost on high; this time he's got the expensive wipers that are going a mile a minute; this time, he's careful. He drives up and down the road for one hour, two hours, and only notices the gas gauge nearing **E** halfway through the third hour.

"Where are you?" he asks the snow and darkness. He wasn't expecting an answer, but, still, he's heard the stories about this road, about the other people who have seen her, talked with her, given her a ride home.

"Where are you?" he asks again, this time much louder than before. He pulls over to the side of the road, taking care to stay as far away from the incline as possible. Too much of the car is still jutting out into the passing lane, but he doesn't care. He presses his forehead against his hands, takes a deep breath, and then turns off the engine.

For a little while he sits there, staring out into the freezing night as the snow whips about the car. He's so tired, so very tired. He imagines that he sees two medieval men on horseback in the distance, making their way back to the monastery where the creation of a final masterpiece patiently waits for one of them.

He opens the car door, climbs out, and begins walking up the road toward Resurrection Cemetery. His knees ache and his legs are weak, but at least he's wearing his good winter coat, his good winter gloves, and the heavenly wool cap Henrietta had given him on the last Christmas she was alive.

He's only a few hundred yards from the cemetery gates when he can't walk any farther. He stops, kneels down, and makes a snowball. The snow is thick and heavy enough to pack well, and with a laugh he sets about making a snowwoman, forgetting that he's now in the middle of the road. It takes him nearly forty minutes to fashion her, and by the time he's finished his hands are nearly frozen, even with the gloves. There is no time for her face, but that's fine because he remembers that face with startling clarity. He's never forgotten even a single detail.

He steps back and smiles at her, then holds out his arms.

"May I have this dance?" he asks his creation.

And there he stands, arms extended, eyes blinking against the wind and snow, until at last he hears the roar and the collision and the metallic scrape and the shattering of glass. He moves closer to her, touching her cold skin—didn't everyone always say that her touch was cold? Poor girl. Poor little thing.

He stands there, smiling, as the lights and roar and sparks screaming down on them form a marvelous winter aura around her. He closes his eyes. *There you are,* he thinks. He does not tremble. *I see you at night.* He holds his breath. He holds his breath. He holds his breath. He holds

❧ Afterword ❧

In 1968 a local radio station in Newark ran an "old-time radio" program every Friday night that included at least one episode of *Lights Out, Haunted: Stories of the Supernatural, The Price of Fear,* and *Macabre,* to name but a few. One night the program featured Lucille Fletcher's classic story "The Hitchhiker," and it scared the eight-year-old me silly, and from that night on, I was a ghost-story junkie. Tales of phantom drivers, phantom passengers, phantom roads and cars, were my particular favorites. The idea of being alone on the road at night, in your car while *something* supernatural and not at all nice followed you or, worse, was in the car *with* you, tantalized my young imagination. When it came time to write a story for *Haunted Legends* I knew immediately that I was going

to write a story about a road ghost, and reshaping the legend of Resurrection Mary was too enticing to pass up. And I'd always wanted to try
my hand at writing a ghost story wherein the ghost never makes an appearance. Except through guilt, of course. Guilt is a ghost all its own.

ERZEBET YELLOWBOY

Following Double-Face Woman

Erzebet YellowBoy is the editor of Cabinet des Fées, *a journal of fairy-tale fiction, and the founder of Papaveria Press, a private press specializing in handbound limited editions of mythic poetry and prose. Her stories and poems have appeared in* Fantasy Magazine, Jabberwocky, Goblin Fruit, Mythic Delirium, Electric Velocipede, *and others, and her second novel,* Sleeping Helena, *is being published in 2010. For more information, visit her website at www.erzebet.com.*

There is a blizzard rolling in. It flattens the sagebrush and sends the last few ragged tumbleweeds hurtling into the fence around the house. In these frigid hours the word on the street is this: there's a narc among us; Jax went to the hospital throwing up blood; the police are organizing a Meth Task Force and holding their first public meeting tonight. I wonder if she's bold enough to go.

Em and I are huddled on the couch, wrapped in a blanket, watching the light flicker on the old black-and-white tilting in the corner. We weren't invited to the meeting. None of us on this side of town ever will be, never mind that every other house on our block stinks of ten thousand cats. Never mind the scarecrows, the broken bones, and the babies crying at night. It isn't really a problem until it becomes one for them.

Their doctors discuss the root of the problem, their law determines how they deal with the problem, they talk in circles around the problem and they'll probably be talking still when the problem walks in on them. The fools will never see her coming. I know all about her, though I wish Double-Face Woman had never walked down my block. I told my baby sister Em, if you see her, run, but Em didn't believe. Em and I used to be close, but Em never did listen to me.

That's the real problem. Not enough people believe in her these days. It has always been her way to lead us from the path of thoughtful living. There *was* one, once. We used to walk it. My grandmother told me this, before she went home to the stars. She told me all about Double-Face Woman. I thought she was making it up. Though the path was long overgrown, I should have listened, too.

The path may be gone but Double-Face Woman is right here, right now. We no longer recognize her and so she gets us all. Before, she'd go after the boys, tempt them and tease them with strands of her hair or the doe-look in her eye. Our ancestors knew the stories. They knew not to follow Double-Face Woman. We, on the other hand, open our arms because what they believed, we've forgotten.

She was the most beautiful woman alive, so the story goes, and too proud of it. She tried to seduce the sun from the sky and was punished. Her beautiful face was halved, and half made hideous, but that did not stop her. She made her way out of the cottonwood copses and the wide plains. She walks now to and through the small towns, once watering holes for the wagon trains, and from there into cities, barrios, and ghettoes. She seduces us all as she goes. Now she is everyone's problem. Double-Face Woman has done what we cannot; she has crossed all barriers and boundaries of color, class, and kind. Not too shabby for a legend. I want to laugh, but there's nothing funny about it.

She got me a long time ago. I was just a girl, skipping school, like Em is now, hanging out with my friends, cousins, and aunties, as carefree as any child. It was a slow and scorching day and we were playing with the old frayed garden hose when she walked by. Maybe if I'd turned back to the game she would have kept on going. I didn't. I stared at her as she passed. She was everything I was not, dark as the clay with hair the color of a starless night. I couldn't look away. She turned her head and looked back at me with a sly, sideways eye. I was hooked.

She showed me her beautiful face, dark and dusky, half hidden behind strands of bark-black hair. Her lips were luscious and I wanted to kiss them, but instead she handed me a pipe and I drew in the smoke for her, all for her. I didn't know any better. We never do, or maybe we do and we just don't care. I know I couldn't resist. I followed her.

I watched the ground below my feet change from cracked granite to tar, to puncture-vine streaming across rock and sand as the dry heat of summer formed a wall around me. I wonder now if the very air knew I was heading toward danger and wanted to stop me from reaching it. Every so often I glanced at the back of her as she walked on ahead of me, her gait gliding, each step placed so delicately before the other, like a deer moving through the world of men. Her hair was wild and free; it poured down into the small of her back and fell below it to where soft buckskin rippled over her thighs. The bright-patterned beadwork on her dress belonged in a museum, not here among the dust and rubble-strewn streets.

I followed her all the way to the abandoned lot at the end of the block, where Indian paint and sage grows side by side among the husked-out remains of cars and trucks, left to rust and decay. She sat down on a rock and I sat beside her. She raised that pipe to my lips and held the match over it for me, all for me. She never once looked me in the face, and now I know why. She was hiding half of her own, saving the truth for later. I inhaled. When I opened my eyes, she was gone.

Here, little girl, she may as well have said, *have a treat.* And I did, and it was good, and I forgot for a while that I was a speck of dirt on clean, white linen and I knew the feeling that comes with being singled out for something good. She loved me.

Now, however many years later, Em looks to me for guidance, but I haven't got any to give her. I'm always out chasing that pipe. It is too late for me, I tell her. You've got to find the path on your own. I don't even know where to look for it.

Maybe I could have found my way, but I've been too busy looking for Double-Face Woman. That's the way it works. She shows us the side that photographs well, the side that calls us with the curve of cheek and lash. We look around—will anyone see us? We look back and there she is, still smiling, still waiting just for us. Maybe it's her scent or the steps she weaves on the crumbling sidewalk. I don't know. All I know is how good she makes me feel.

After she'd gone and I was done running in circles, back and forth, thoughts racing and then finally coming to rest on a single point—her face—I went looking for her again. Again and again until finally, she was all there was. I could see her on every step and in every window. I could knock on any door and she'd be there, pipe in hand, waiting just for me.

I go home sometimes and there Em is, waiting just for me. Em does not have such a beautiful face. Em tries to talk to me, but I have no time. Sleep, and find her again. That's my life. Sometimes Em wants to go with me when I search for Double-Face Woman and I say, no Em, you stay here. I'll be right back. If she grabs on to my sleeve I push her away, maybe a little too hard, and I turn my face so I don't see the tears she bravely tries to hide from me. From me, her big sister. I never came right back.

One day as I was sitting on the sofa, feebly looking for a half-full bottle of whatever was lying around, my old friend Seal walked in. We called him Seal because he was slippery, he never got caught for his crimes. I could tell he'd seen her, too.

"Gotta smoke?" he said, and he didn't mean her kind.

"Yeah." I tossed him my bag of tobacco and watched him work it into a brittle paper with fingers bone-thin. He pulled a pack of matches out of his pocket and the flame threw shadows under his eyes. I could see the wall through his skin.

"How ya been?" he asked, and I told him. "You?" I asked when I was done.

"Just passing through," he said. "I wanted to show you something."

I watched as he took that lit cigarette and passed it through his hand—through it—and back again. I was too dried out to cry, but I would have if I could. My good friend had followed Double-Face Woman. He followed her all the way home.

He left me then, and not by way of the door. As if to make his point, he slowly faded in front of me, his particles winking out like stars in the night sky. I got up and went looking for her.

That's when I began to notice the other ghosts. One in every crowd, every gathering. Their clothes were more ragged than most and their eyes glowed. They smoked and drank whatever they were offered, just like anyone else, and maybe everyone else was too drunk or high to notice they were ghosts. Even at my highest, I saw them. They smiled at me, co-conspirators, as though they knew something I knew but wouldn't admit.

They made me think about things I hadn't before considered. I wondered if they, on the other side of town, saw the ghosts, if the ghosts went to those meetings and whispered things into those cold, pale ears. I wondered if the ghosts might be heard, the way we were not. Every time I saw Double-Face Woman, I checked her skin. She was always beautiful, always ripe and as solid as any tree. I grew to ignore the ghosts, to avoid their smiles. I forgot about them after a while. After a little more time with her pipe.

Until that last time. All was well; all was as it always was. She held out the pipe, I took it, put the flame to it, inhaled. She was watching; she always watched, she reveled with us, though her own lips never touched the stem.

I closed my eyes and breathed in the rush. When I opened them, Double-Face Woman had turned her ugly face toward me.

Let me tell you about her ugly face. She only shows it when we are so far gone there is no longer any way back. Then she turns, and so much for the photograph. By the time she shows her other face, it is too late to run. In that face I saw what I'd become.

I went home and slept for three days. When I came to my senses, it was my turn to wait. I sat in the cold house for days, shaking, laughing, pulling at my hair and picking at my face. Every time a floorboard creaked I was sure it was Em, come home at last. Every time a car drove by, I went to the window to watch it. Finally, I gave up. My little sister wasn't coming back and I could wait no longer. Double-Face Woman was out there waiting for me.

I looked everywhere and couldn't find her, but I saw Em the other day, out walking the streets with her friends. I saw one of the girls reach into her pocket and pull something out, something she showed to the others in the half-concealed cup of her palm. Oh, Em. I didn't have to see it. I knew it was her pipe. I watched the girls turn down an alley and would have cried if I could, but there were no tears left in me.

The television flickers, the wind howls by a window held together with tape. Em is curled up in my arms. She is so small, so fragile. I look at my own skin and hair; no one will ever follow me. What beauty I ever had is long gone. I look down at Em and catch her watching me, just like I once watched Double-Face Woman, before she turned her head. I want to say to Em, no, older sisters are not to be followed. But of course what really happens is this: you and Double-Face Woman look at each other and when you turn away, there she is.

Afterword

Double-Face Woman, akin to Deer Woman, is a figure of Native American myth who historically haunted the forests and plains in order to lure unwary travelers from the path with her stunning beauty. Once in her clutches, she revealed her hideous nature, but by then it was too late for rescue. This story is a product of my time in the west, where I witnessed firsthand the effects of methamphetamine abuse on the young Native American population. It was obvious that Double-Face Woman was more than a myth. She was right there with all of us.

M. K. HOBSON

Oaks Park

M. K. Hobson's first professional sale was to SCI FICTION *in 2003. Since then, her stories have appeared in a wide variety of publications and anthologies, including* Realms of Fantasy, The Magazine of Fantasy & Science Fiction, Interzone, Strange Horizons, *and* Polyphony 5 & 6. *Her debut novel,* The Native Star, *a saga of magic and romance set in 1870s America, was recently published.*

For more information, check out her website, www.demimonde.com, and blog, mkhobson.livejournal.com. She lives in Oregon with her husband and daughter.

You are thirty-nine years old and you are a woman and a mother, and you've just avoided saying something to your husband that would cause a fight. Summer is almost over, though the days are still long and the evenings still warm and heavy with the sound of insects, and this makes you feel desperate, but you don't know why. You have a daughter that you already don't understand even though she is only twelve. Even your own life is puzzling to you, you move in a fog of mild discontent, whatever ability you ever had to make a decision or form an opinion lost to the endless consensus of family, the compromises of marriage, every day covering you like a sheet with holes cut out.

.   .   .

Your daughter has friends all over the neighborhood, tanned scuffed elastic creatures, each as wild and improbable as she. They are like another species. They come from nowhere, they come up from behind you and you never hear them coming. They all look alike. They lounge on couches inside cool dark houses hiding from daylight's glare, watching Nick for Teens and sipping Capri Suns, crushing packages of ramen and eating the crumbled noodles raw. They leave a trail of wrappers and crumbs. One day your daughter is prompted by her best girlfriend, a girl who looks exactly like your daughter, to ask "Can you take us to Oaks Park?" and you say "If you clean your room," knowing that she will never clean her room so you will never have to take her to Oaks Park.

.   .   .

Later, you hear your daughter talking to two more of her friends, a boy and a girl who look exactly like her, scraped knees and dark tanned skin and corn-silk hair and T-shirts that assert their unswerving allegiance to an anime show. They are all sitting in the shade of the porch, eating Popsicles, dripping bright-colored sugarwater on the worn treads.

"Oaks Park is haunted," one of them says. "Someone died there and the ghost wanders around."

You listen closely. You haven't heard this story before. You want to ask, *Who died there? Is there really a ghost? What does it look like?* But none of the kids on the porch have these questions, so they are not asked and not answered. The kids run into the streets and seize their bikes, leaving behind wrappers and sticks and puddles of sugary sweetness for ants to swarm over.

· · ·

You turn to the Internet.

Oaks Park is a modest amusement park located 3.5 miles (6 km) south of downtown Portland, Oregon, in the United States.

The park was built by the Oregon Water Power and Railway Company and opened in 1905, when trolley parks were often constructed along streetcar lines.

The large wooden roller-skating rink is open year-round. The centerpiece is the largest remaining pipe organ installed in a skating rink in the world.

As of December 2005, Keith Fortune is at the organ's console providing music for skaters on Thursdays and Sundays.

It's all ragtimey, bandstands and box lunches, women in gored skirts and men in straw boater hats. You find bits of information about the flyscreened dance hall and how the floor of the roller-skating rink is on floating pontoons so it can stay above water when the Willamette River floods. There is nothing about a dead child or a ghost. The absence of such information makes you feel better. The vague anxiety you have been feeling eases. Your husband comes home, and you avoid talking about something that would upset you both, and you make dinner and eat it in front of the television, closing the curtains against the summer sunlight that blazes long into the night.

· · ·

The next day you receive an e-mail from a young man named Chuck. He works at Oaks Park. You've already forgotten that you e-mailed him—Internet time works like that. But when the message pops into your e-mail box you suddenly remember filling out a Web form marked "history questions." Your message was brief.

Is there a ghost that haunts Oaks Park?

Chuck's e-mailed reply is just as brief.

Some people have reported seeing the ghost of a girl, about 12 years old. She's dressed in seventies-era clothing. She steals cotton candy from the snack bar and rides the rides. The Octopus is her favorite.

Your fingers type a furious question in response:

Is she happy?

But you don't hit send, because you know that Chuck won't know the answer and you already do.

.   .   .

The last time you went to Oaks Park you were twelve and it was 1977.

You remember riding in the backseat of the Dodge Dart, American steel bullying across the narrow Sellwood Bridge, sweltering heat pouring in through all four open windows.

Your hands are sticky and you are wearing Haggar shorts and a Garanimals T-shirt from the Sears Surplus over by Lloyd Center. Your hair is cornsilk blond and your skin is brown and scratched, scabs everywhere like a map of stars.

Your parents are brittle, recovering from a nightlong fight. This is your reward, your battle pay, your assurance that everything in the world is perfect.

Your dad's profile is sleek and handsome and brutal. Your mom's face is soft and young beneath a smooth Dorothy Hamill cut, her eyes watchful behind huge amber sunglasses. Your legs stick to the vinyl. "Hotel California" plays on the radio.

Your parents park the car under knobby, diseased trees. The small parking lot seems like it's in the wrong place; you get to it by driving past a caretaker's shack and a shop with old ride parts jumbled before it. You approach the park from behind, like you're sneaking up on it, stepping carefully over cracked mounds where tree roots have broken the asphalt. You leave your parents behind to mutter between themselves. That's the only time they talk, these days—when they think you can't hear.

To get to the new rides you have to pass the old midway, abandoned attractions that have been shut down for years. The old buildings are regal in their decay, silvered wood and peeling paint, bulb-broken light fixtures clotted with nests and twigs, cottonwood fluff piled in unswept corners.

One tilting building has a gigantic round doorway, like a giant storm drain, all boarded up. You run up to it, peek through the boards, peer into the darkness. The cool air coming from inside smells of mold. Your parents call you away, to where the new rides are—the steel-spiderweb Ferris wheel, the carousel with its cracked menagerie of dragons and rabbits, the erector-set roller coaster of rusted bolts and oil-smeared wood. A vast go-kart track sprawls to the north, belching gas fumes and the smell of baking rubber; beyond it, a fetid river lowland, a swamp filled with abandoned cars and frayed tires. There's a neon sign for a ride called the Fly-O but the ride that's actually there is the Octopus, spinning arms swinging bulbous black seats like fists.

While you are standing in line to ride the Octopus, you see a boy and girl in the shade of the snack bar. She is wearing a haltertop and baby-blue shorts, and she has long smooth hair that gleams down her back. She has one thumb hooked in the top of her shorts, and a velour prize monkey under her arm. The boy has tight curly hair, and he is leaning against her, his thumbs stroking the sides of her ribs. You are eating popcorn. You don't understand them and you know, suddenly, that you don't want to understand them. You never want to understand them. Your father has gone off somewhere, and you are alone with your mother. You watch her watch them. She understands them. There is betrayal and regret on her face.

The sun is still beating down but you feel cold. The line is moving, and it is almost your turn to get on the Octopus, but you know that there are clouds coming in, and you know that it will rain, and it will get cold. Your parents will fight again and again and again. And school will start and you will have a new teacher in a room with waxed floors, and you will wear new clothes and then it will be Christmas and then spring and then summer again, and then high school and then college and then you will be far far away from here, far from where old wise buildings keep the order of time. You will be the girl with the straight shiny hair or you will be the curly-haired boy in cutoffs, betrayed. You will be your parents. You will be thirty-nine years old, and a woman, and a mother, and nothing will make any sense but it will all hurt. You see it all in one shambling terrifying moment, you see that everything will go on and on, spinning.

.   .   .

You ride the Octopus with your mother. Then you run away.

You find a deserted place, a trash-strewn nook behind the bumper cars near the old line of bathrooms. You hide there, legs drawn up to your chest. You rest your forehead on your knees, and you close your eyes.

You imagine a ghost, a shell, a hollow creature that can be buffeted and molded, pliant as your mother when your father's bulbous fists swing around and around, yielding as the girl with long smooth hair, the curly-haired boy looming over her like a cloud over the sun. You pretend someone else out into the world. You send her in your place. *You can't ever come back,* you whisper to her. You tell yourself it's like a game. A game of hide and seek. You will hide from time and fear and betrayal and regret. Someone else goes home in the car with your parents, someone new and formless, some-one who feels no fear because she feels nothing. As insubstantial as mist, as air under a sheet. You will stay at Oaks Park. You will sleep during the hot-test part of the day and at night, when the lights come on, the buildings will whisper their secrets to you and they will keep you safe forever.

.   .   .

You are thirty-nine years old and you are a woman and a mother.

You wake up after a night of unsettling dreams, whirling spinning dreams full of screaming and blurred lights and the smell of burnt sugar, and you have a fight with your husband. You tell him he's the worst decision you ever made. You tell him you wish you'd never married him. You tell him you never loved him. You tell him you hate him, and when you tell him this, you feel the sickening truth of it. You scream at each other for hours, and you're both late for work, and your daughter is late for school.

You drive her, and she cowers in the backseat and you feel, rather than see, the anxiety on her face. You understand it completely. You remember it, the fear of everything falling apart. The memory is strange and alien. It is a fear that is supposed to belong to someone else, someone like you.

You don't go in to work. You come home and sit on the couch in your front room, heat beating against the walls of the house. You draw curtains against it, you move the air with fans, but it's so terribly hot. You drowse, but every time you nod off you dream of boarded up buildings and peeling paint. The buildings are empty. You thought they held secrets, you thought they were wise. But they contain nothing. They are as empty as you are. You wake screaming.

Late in the afternoon, you drive to Oaks Park.

The air is still and sunny. You make the turn off the Sellwood Bridge at sunset, the dazzling light making your eyes tear. You drive along the road that leads to the park, fluff from the cottonwood trees glistening in the golden air. A stiff breeze from the Willamette makes faded nylon pennants ripple. The lights have been turned on, but you can't see them, not yet.

Everything has changed. The big flat expanse of cracked blacktop where the go-karts used to be is now acres of smoothly paved parking. The swamp is now wetland and there are multiuse trails and urban hiking areas threaded throughout it. Everything is smaller. Most of the rides you remember are gone, even the Tilt-o-Whirl with its evil clown faces—you never liked it, it gave you a headache and made you feel sick and it smelled like diesel. The erector-set roller coaster has been replaced by something plastic and candy-colored that has a loop-de-loop. You pass what used to be the Haunted Mine, and remember that it used to scare you, but now it is called The Lewis and Clark Adventure and beavers jump out at you instead of skeletons. It's all bad hand-me-down funtastic carnival rides with cheap graphics of secondhand superheroes. Alternative rock spews from the speakers.

All the old boarded-up rides are gone, razed. Where they once stood, picnic space has been cleared for corporate picnics and soccer team parties.

You buy popcorn from the snack bar. Made in China, it comes in a foil bag and is very stale. You sit on one of the old green wooden benches and wait for it to get dark. You see her before she sees you. She's wearing Haggar shorts and a Garanimals T-shirt from Sears Surplus. She has a chunk of cotton candy in her hand. She's all eyes, wandering through the crowd in the watchful way of lost children, her brow creased with anxiety. You watch her until she sees you, watch her face light with perfect joy and relief. Feelings wrap around you like a winter coat. Anger. Resentment. Bitterness. Regret. She runs to you, clutching grubby hands at your clothing. She buries a dirty face in your stomach and breaks, brave wary watchfulness dissolving into sobs. She wails and moans, a lost child found, and you pet her back and say soft soothing things to her. She clings to you, and people are watching, making sympathetic clucking sounds. You savor this moment. You hold on to it for as long as you can. You think of your daughter and you remember a million looks on her face that you couldn't interpret. You understand them all now. You remember a hundred times you hated your husband, your life, your job . . . even your own child.

I want to go home, she sobs into your stomach, against your shirt. *I want to go home.*

You want to take her home. You want to put her in the backseat of your car, and let her fall asleep, exhausted by her ordeal. You would drive home, and when you got there, she would be gone, melted into the car, melted back into you. You would be whole again. Oaks Park would have one less ghost, and you would have one more.

And there would be another fight and another and another, and you would see the infinity of days stretch before you again, and you would see the looks your daughter gives you, and understand them for what they are—disgust, pity, shame. And maybe you would hurt her, hurt her so much that she would make her own ghost, and this whole terrible wheel would turn again, this carnival wheel, this gut-wrenching loop-de-loop.

You can't take her home.

Dread of what you will have to do makes all the small muscles in your body ache. You can't think about it. You will have to just do it. Your hands will have to rescue you. You take her hand and walk. She is content to be pulled along, compliant and humbled, nose running. You are walking in the direction of the old parking lot at the back of the park. But you are really walking to the place behind the bumper cars, behind the bathrooms. It is the same as it was twenty-seven years ago, trash-strewn with the same trash, the same cottonwood fluff.

You pull her down beside you and you take her in your arms and hold her tight, cradling her for a few minutes more, telling her how brave she's been. She talks fast, sentences like broken sticks: she didn't mean to, it was just a game, she didn't mean to get lost, she was scared, she was looking for you.

You murmur *shh, shh* in her ear as your fingers find the kitchen knife you have brought from home.

You pull the knife across her smooth brown throat. She gushes, but it is not blood. She bleeds time, a million golden sunsets and white illuminated nights, and she bleeds fear, the shambling shadow of the eternal, dark and molasseslike. She bleeds regret. She thrashes in your arms, making betrayed noises, animal noises. She deflates. She melts. Then she is nothing but a pile of dirty old clothes from Sears Surplus. You hide these beneath the trash.

Walking back to your car, you are trembling, but it is only a physical thing. Your mind is calm, and everything feels vague and unknowable again. Your accustomed numbness returns, and you know that everything will be all right.

She will stay at Oaks Park. She will ride the rides and steal cotton candy. But she will be someone else, someone new and formless, someone who feels all the terror that you should share. As insubstantial as mist, as air under a sheet. She will sleep during the hottest part of the day and at night, when the lights come on, she will search watchfully through crowds for the mother she didn't mean to lose and a life she didn't mean to surrender.

You leave her to her haunts.

You return to yours.

Afterword

When I was looking for a ghost story to retell, I focused on my home state of Oregon. Oregon doesn't want for great ghost stories (a lighthouse haunted by a murdered sea captain, a ghostly flushing toilet, a revenant cow that wrecks cars on old Highway 97), but I was captivated by a single tantalizing entry about Oaks Park:

"This amusement park, built in 1890, has been plagued with a ghostly apparition of a lone child in 1970s style clothing for over 20 years."

I found that same surreal squib all over the Internet, obviously cut and pasted from the same source, never elaborated on. The opacity was oddly chilling, as was the fact that the story was so precisely contemporary to my own experience. I was often at Oaks Park in the 1970s, a lone child clutching a paper cone of cotton candy. Maybe I met the child who became a ghost? Could I have spoken to her? Could I have *been* her? The story arose swiftly from that juxtaposition of the surreal and the personal. More than anything, I tried to capture a feeling of timeless disquiet, of discovering that ghosts might be closer than you think, in places you'd never imagine.

STEPHEN DEDMAN

For Those in Peril on the Sea

Stephen Dedman is the author of four novels—The Art of Arrow Cutting, Shadows Bite, Foreign Bodies, and A Fistful of Data—and more than one hundred twenty short stories published in an eclectic range of magazines and anthologies.

He teaches creative writing at the University of Western Australia and is co-owner of Fantastic Planet bookshop in Perth.

For more information, check out his website: www.stephendedman.com.

Workers at the Kayser Shipyards said the *George M. Shriver* was jinxed long before she sailed, or possessed, or infested with gremlins. But no one spoke of seeing a ghost until much later.

· · ·

Dugan gritted his teeth as another tarantula crawled up his leg. The spiders ranged from the size of his thumbnail to larger than his palm, and he'd been promised that none of them were any more venomous than wasps and much less likely to bite, but that didn't make it any easier to stand there without flinching. He'd also been told that if he killed any of the spiders, their cost would be taken out of the prize pool at the end of the show. His tattoos, and the hair on his legs and chest, hid most of his gooseflesh, but he couldn't help but shudder as he felt something tickle him just below the hip, or just above where he thought his boxer shorts ended.

Instead of glancing down at the dozens of spiders inside his private hell—a coffin-sized Perspex booth—he stared into the chamber next to his. Langley stood there at attention, as erect and impassive as a cigar-store Indian or a grenadier guard outside Buckingham Palace. The ex-soldier didn't seem to be afraid of anything . . . at least, anything that the producers had thrown at them. Dugan suspected that he had at least one crippling fear: a pathological terror of failure, of showing any sign of weakness.

It's going to be you or me, in the end, thought Dugan, as a cave spider with a seven-inch leg span dropped onto his shoulder—the one marked with the one percent symbol and the Harley-Davidson logo with purple wings, not the one he'd briefly considered having tattooed with a cobweb pattern while in maximum security. *It'll be down to us,* he silently repeated as though it were a mantra. *All of the others will break before we do.*

He saw frantic movement in the corner of his field of view, and turned his head. One of the women was beating on the walls of her booth, obviously too panicked to remember the phrase that would get her out. Dugan smiled, though he was careful not to open his mouth. Once the first person quit, the timer started, and that meant there was only ninety minutes of this nightmare to go. He wondered what would be next.

· · ·

Beck looked at the spreadsheet, and grimaced. *Worst Nightmare* seemed to be living up to its name, at least as far as he was concerned. "You've got to be fucking kidding," he groaned. "I wouldn't try to shoot a thirty-second ad on this sort of budget."

"That," said the accountant, "is because you've gone overbudget on almost every episode, to the tune of one million three thousand and seventeen dollars, while the ratings have been in the fucking toilet." She handed over another printout. "We've had to drop the price of those thirty-second ads so low they're barely paying the electricity bill. We'd be doing better with a rerun of *Gilligan's Island.* The only reason you're still on the fucking air is the Australian content rules."

Beck couldn't argue with that. Reality TV had been a godsend for the networks—making money from product placement and the telcos who were making money out of people texting their votes, and costing much less to produce than drama or even sitcoms because the payment for the performers averaged out to less than minimum wage . . . and so, when Beck had approached the network with the proposal for *Worst Nightmare*—a hybrid of *Survivor* and *Fear Factor,* with more than a hint of the old Japanese game show *Endurance*—they'd jumped at it. Unfortunately, they'd also given the greenlight to no less than six other reality shows, audiences had already begun to switch off, and the last episode of *Worst Nightmare* had suffered the ultimate indignity: losing in the ratings to all the other free-to-air stations, including the foreign-language service.

The problem, Beck suspected, was that not enough viewers liked the remaining contestants, and had realized that none of them were likely to die or even be badly injured: waivers and insurance could only cover so much.

And while they were frequently humiliated, the contenders who'd made it through the first two weeks were so stolid that the show was falling flat—about as scary, Beck thought gloomily, as the remake of *The Haunting,* but with much less eye candy. The budget restrictions meant that he couldn't even afford to bring in even the most obscure celebrities as guest stars.

He looked at the spreadsheet again, then took out his smartphone and did some calculations. The only area where it seemed possible to make cuts was in travel and accommodation. Whittling down the number of contestants faster than expected might not save them in the ratings, but it would save them a little money. And he could change the schedule to reduce the number of flights . . . no, even that wouldn't be enough. "I'll think of something," he said.

"You'd better," she purred. "If the show gets axed . . ." She didn't need to finish the sentence. Beck nodded, and walked out.

.   .   .

A few of the workers cheered as the *George M. Shriver* slid down the slipway and into the sea; others waited to see whether it would sink or explode. After three minutes, it had done neither, and the foreman called out, "Coffee break. Smoke 'em if you got 'em," and lit up a Lucky Strike.

Assembling the hull of a Liberty Ship typically took ten days; for the *George M. Shriver,* this had dragged out to six weeks because of equipment failure and accidents. Many of the accidents the foreman had put down to the workers hurrying to finish building the cursed thing and be rid of it—and absenteeism was making matters worse, with men finding excuses not to expose themselves to the jinx. It was whispered that the ship either exuded bad luck or attracted it like a gigantic magnet. Now that the cursed thing was gone, the foreman reflected, maybe things would return to normal.

Most of the absentees returned within the next week, except for the few who'd been injured while building the *Shriver,* and two who were never seen at the shipyard again.

.   .   .

Beck spent the evening looking through a catalog of horror movies in search of frightening situations he could inflict on *Worst Nightmare*'s contestants on his reduced budget. After a few minutes of going through the book in alphabetical order as far as *The Blair Witch Project,* he began opening it at random. *Phantasm.* Different versions of *Ghost Ship. The Premature Burial*—no, he'd already done that in episode seven. *Freddy vs. Jason. The Seventh Victim. Halloween III*. He picked up his whiskey glass, found it empty, and walked over to the bar. Before he reached it, he had an idea that had him rushing back to his laptop to write it down. Then he reopened the spreadsheet, and began chuckling.

The prize for the winning contestant was one million dollars, and he was contracted for another eight episodes. If no one won the million, that would almost cover his cost overruns, without requiring him to trim over a hundred thousand from the budget of each episode. If he could do both, of course, then even better.

He looked at the contracts, and found that if any of the contestants defaulted on a particular task, he could reduce the prize pool and penalize all of them. And most of the endurance tests had a minimum time as well, and he could set the limits on those as high as he liked. Now to find something, preferably local, that would be cheap, scary, and could be made to stretch out over at least a week.

. . .

"A haunted ship?" Langley laughed. "After all we've been through, you think we're going to be scared of *ghosts*?"

Beck looked around the room at the remaining four contestants, out of the original thirteen. Langley, ex-Special forces; Dugan, an outlaw biker with a long prison record; Syverson, a stunt performer; and Moss, a professional dominatrix. "It's not just a question of what scares *you*," said the producer. "A lot of the audience is going to find this scary, and that's just as important. More so, even, in terms of the ratings. And even if you all get through this one without any of you dropping out, there'll be at least one more test after this."

Syverson looked suspicious. "What sort of condition is the ship in?"

"Oh, it's a wreck," Beck replied cheerfully. "About the same sort of shape as the *Titanic*, except it's mostly above the water. You won't have to sail it anywhere; just camp aboard for a few days. And nights, of course. We'll give you sleeping bags, food, water . . . the rest is up to you. Everything else you need to know is in those envelopes."

Dugan looked sullen; Beck knew that the biker was so badly dyslexic as to be barely literate. They watched as the others opened the bulging envelopes and looked at the information sheets, photos and maps. "The *Alkimos*," said Langley. "I've heard of that. It's off the west coast, near Yanchep."

Moss raised a pierced eyebrow. "You been there?"

"No, but I had friends who went diving near there. They didn't see any ghosts, and nothing happened to them. Well, not then, anyway." The others stared at him, waiting for him to finish. "They got divorced, she got cancer, and he tried to kill himself by wrapping his car around a tree . . . but all of that happened years later, a long way from the ship, and it would've happened anyway whether they'd been there or not. Right?"

"Aren't you a little ray of sunshine," muttered Moss.

"You'll be driving out there tomorrow," said Beck. "Langley, you know how to handle an outboard?"

"Sure."

"Good. You'll be taking them the rest of the way. Try not to lose anybody, okay?"

. . .

The *George M. Shriver* spent most of World War II in dry-dock, undergoing repairs. Crewman reported hearing barking, and joked that the ship was haunted by a ghostly dog, though no one ever claimed to have seen it.

In 1961, after a collision with another ship, the accident-prone *Shriver* was sold to a Norwegian firm and renamed the *Viggo Hansteen*. A few months later, it was sold again and renamed the *Alkimos*. In March 1963, it struck a reef off the coast of western Australia. It was refloated, and towed into Fremantle harbour for repairs, but mysteriously caught fire in May and was almost gutted.

The *Alkimos* was impounded. The unlucky owner paid to have it released, then hired a tug to have it towed to Hong Kong for further repairs. On its second day out of Fremantle, the tug and the ship were battered by huge waves lashed up by an unexpected storm. The towline snapped, and the *Alkimos* drifted back toward shore into another reef.

Several attempts were made that year to salvage the ship; all were plagued by accidents, and failed. The crew of the tugboat *Pacific Star* came closest to success, but were also plagued by mechanical mishaps, and operations were temporarily put on hold when the owner of their company died.

The *Pacific Star*'s captain called in a Catholic priest to exorcise the *Alkimos* before they made their next salvage attempt. A heavy swell lifted the *Alkimos* off the rocks, and the *Pacific Star* began towing it back toward Fremantle. Before they'd gone two miles, another ship pulled up alongside them, the captain was arrested for unpaid debts and the tug impounded. The *Alkimos* was anchored offshore, but another heavy swell snapped the anchor chain and it drifted back toward the shore. Crewmen from the *Star,* stationed aboard the *Alkimos* as guards, reported seeing a man in oilskins and a sou'wester walk across the main deck and through a closed door.

. . .

The sea off Two Rocks was choppy, and Moss leaned over the edge of the inflatable boat to vomit. To her disgust and Dugan's amusement, the wind blew much of it back onto her anorak. The wreck, clearly visible from miles down the beach in good weather, was now obscured by rain. The bow of the ship seemed largely intact back as far as the bridge and the engine room, but the stern end had been stripped down to its skeleton and gutted.

Beck had wanted the four to approach the ship by night, but the network's lawyers had vetoed this. One camera crew had followed them in a larger boat, while another watched on from a hill near the shore. Beck had tried to squeeze enough money out of the budget to pay for a helicopter to give a better view of the top of the wreck, but was now relieved that this had been impossible: they were running hours behind schedule, and even had they found a pilot willing to fly in such dire and unpredictable weather, the cost would have blown out the budget, and the chances of getting any useable footage were slim. As it was, Langley had reached the wreck before Beck and the second crew were in position, and had had to wait until they were set up for the shot. Moss's stomach was empty by now, but she was still dry-heaving as they sailed in half-circles around the *Alkimos,* looking for the best place to moor the boat. Radio reception between the boats and the second crew was frequently interrupted by static, and often barely audible.

Beck watched the boats through binoculars, without leaving the comfort of the Range Rover. This, he thought, was going better than he'd hoped. He was fairly sure that neither Dugan nor Langley were going to opt out yet, nor would Syverson, but Moss might still quit. She had a small cult following, but not enough of a demographic to lift the show's ratings high enough to compensate. It was a pity, he thought, that the stripper-turned-wrestler hadn't coped with the spiders as well as she had with carrying handfuls of snakes.

Langley and Syverson had both been given helmet cameras, and were the first to climb aboard the rusting hulk. It had taken them several attempts to get a line attached to the ship, as the swell kept carrying their inflatable out of range, but finally they had a sufficiently secure rope that Syverson was able to abseil up the side and clamber up onto the deck. The feed from the cameras was spotty, and the editor was probably going to demand overtime trying to get the necessary amount of useable vision and sound, but that, Beck thought cheerfully, would give the episode a sort of *Blair Witch* ambience, and anything that went wrong could be blamed on ghosts.

The producer smiled. Word had gotten out among the crew that the series might be canceled, which meant it would have reached the competitors as well. And Dugan, he knew, was desperate for money—possibly desperate enough to kill someone, once it came down to the last two contestants—and Beck was fairly confident that the biker would be one of the last two. The other would probably be Langley, who was trained in the same sort of dirty fighting as Dugan and would be more than a match for him, unless the biker could take him completely by surprise and do enough damage in one blow to gain the advantage. Not that it mattered enormously to Beck. He doubted that Dugan had read and understood the contract well enough to have realized that if any of the contestants were charged with a crime because of their actions during the production of the show, they forfeited any prize money that might be coming to them. It wouldn't even matter whether they were convicted or acquitted or pleaded self-defense, and if they tried to sue the network later they'd be lucky to get a cent.

He turned to the crew. "How's it looking?"

"Bad," said the cameraman, while the sound engineer made a thumbs-down gesture. "Even without the rain and the light levels. At this distance, I can hardly tell them apart. And the forecast is for even worse weather ahead—a big storm front headed down this way."

Beck pouted. "Maybe we'll get some useable footage from the helmet cameras. Bill?"

The sound engineer grimaced. "You're going to need a voice-over. All I'm getting is thumping, crashing, swearing, wind noise, waves, seagulls, interference, and what sounds like a dog barking."

"A dog?" Beck repeated incredulously.

"That's what it sounds like. Maybe one of 'em has a dog in their back-pack. Or I guess it could be a seal. But whatever it is, I don't think it's happy."

• • •

Syverson was the first to haul himself, cautiously, over the *Alkimos*'s railings and onto the deck. Both were slippery from the rain, but neither collapsed under his weight, and he relaxed slightly and turned to Langley. "Area's secure, capt'n."

"You hope," muttered the ex-soldier as he climbed over the rails. He scanned the wreck, the helmet camera panning slowly across the expanse of rusted steel and choppy iron-gray water. Then he shrugged and looked over the gunwale to the boat. "Okay, you can come up now." He watched as Moss, still seasick, struggled with the ascender on the line he'd just used.

"I thought she'd be good with knots," said Syverson, obviously amused; then, when Langley didn't reply, said, "Can I ask you a question?"

"Go ahead."

"You said a friend of yours tried to kill himself. You mean he survived?"

"Sort of. He hit the tree, all right, and went through the windshield, but it didn't kill him."

"He didn't try again?"

"He couldn't. He's paralyzed from the neck down. He's asked the doctors to euthanize him, but none of them will."

"Jesus," Syverson breathed. Langley turned to look at him, realizing it was the first time since shooting had begun on *Worst Nightmare* that he'd seen Syverson actually looking scared. Maybe he found paralysis more frightening than death. Then the stuntman chuckled, and Langley glanced back at the boat, which was drifting away from the ship. Dugan had grabbed the line, but seemed unsure whether to stay with the inflatable or swarm up the rope.

"Maybe the ghost doesn't want him aboard," said Syverson.

"We should be so lucky. That asshole wants the money too bad to give up." He watched as the ex-biker made his decision and jumped out of the boat into the sea, still holding the rope—then vanished beneath the waves.

• • •

In March 1969, Herbert Voight disappeared in an attempt to swim from Cottesloe to Rottnest Island.

Three weeks later, an escaped convict trying to hide on the *Alkimos* found Voight's skull inexplicably lodged in the wreckage of the engine room.

.   .   .

Syverson cheered ironically as Dugan's head—minus his climbing helmet and mounted camera—reappeared above the churning sea. The ex-biker hauled himself hand over hand along the rope until he could brace his feet against the side of the ship, then began trying to climb. He half-swung half-scrambled across the hull toward the other line as though trying to grab hold of it—or Moss, who'd paused halfway up the hull in case he needed rescuing. Langley swore under his breath, and began pulling on Moss's rope, lifting her out of Dugan's reach. Dugan swore as his boot slipped on the wet metal and he swung back the other way like a pendulum.

"You want me to give him a hand?" asked Syverson, but Langley seemed to have gone deaf. He continued to haul on Moss's line until her hand appeared above the level of the deck, when he leaned over the railing and grabbed her wrist. The rail shed wet flakes of rust, but it didn't break, even when Moss rested her full weight on it.

"Thanks," she gasped as she flopped down onto the rain-slick deck.

"No worries," Langley mumbled, and looked down at Dugan, who was still struggling to climb up the hull.

The camera crew had taken their inflatable boat in tow, and were also following the ex-biker's slow and unsteady progress. Moss picked herself up, then looked around. "What a fucking dump," she announced. "They couldn't have found a haunted hotel?"

Syverson smiled. "I guess it's home until we can afford something better. Of course, you could always call Beck and ask for another room . . ." He tapped the radio mike on the lanyard around his neck. "Testing, testing . . ."

Moss sighed. "Nah, this'll do. I just hope the toilets work." She glanced at Dugan as he hooked an elbow over the railing. "Glad you could join us," she lied.

He scowled at her as he clambered onto the deck, then unzipped one of the pockets of his scuffed leather jacket and pulled out a small waterproof case, from which he removed a pack of Camels and a Zippo lighter. "Okay," he said, after he'd lit up, a hand over the cigarette to shelter it from the wind and the rain, "what the fuck do we do now?"

"For one thing, you'd better be careful where you throw that butt," said

Moss. "I've been reading about this place. There are still drums of tar or oil or something on board, and one of them caught fire back in the seventies. Spontaneously, they think."

"Sure it wasn't the ghost?" asked Dugan, and guffawed.

"I'll ask him if I see him," said Langley. "And to answer your other question, I suggest we check out the cabins and see if we can find four that are still reasonably intact. Unless anybody has a better idea?"

No one did, so they splashed their way back to what remained of the boat deck, cautiously grabbing handholds where they could. Dugan laughed as he found a cabin door marked "Wipers," next to the toilets. "Now that's what I call a shitty job," he crowed, then opened the door and looked inside. No light came through the walls or rain through the ceiling, so he swung his flashlight around, then grunted. "I've stayed in worse," he said. "If nobody else wants this one, I'll take it."

"Fine," said Moss. Dugan unbuckled his backpack and dropped it onto the floor with a dull clang. The other three left him there and continued searching. The wind and the rain had eased off enough that they could talk without shouting, though the dark clouds suggested that worse weather was on the way.

"What else did you find out about this place?" asked Langley.

"A few facts and a shipload of rumours and legends. Some say a welder got sealed into the hull before it was launched—either by accident or because he'd fallen behind paying a loan shark. Some say it was two, or a security guard and a watchdog. One website said that the ghost is of a smuggler who was thrown overboard after he'd cheated some of his accomplices. And there's supposed to have been a murder-suicide on board, during the war." She opened the door of another cabin and looked inside: it, too, seemed mostly intact, though it smelled no better than the previous one. "Hard to tell how much of that is bullshit. But since it was stranded here, the ship's been bad news financially for anyone who's tried to salvage her. Even when they tried selling her for scrap, they only got halfway through dismantling her when another fire broke out—though I don't know what there was left to burn by then." She looked more closely at the door. "Do you think we can lock these? Or bar them, at least?"

"Maybe," said Langley, "but what if we can't open them again? How will you get out?"

"Do you think that's more of a problem than someone getting in?"

"You mean Dugan?" The ex-soldier shrugged. "I don't think he'll try anything while there are still so many of us here, and we're all wired and have cameras—"

"Except him," Moss pointed out.

"—but if you like, I'll take the cabin next to yours, and if you need any help, bang on the wall, or scream, or whatever. But don't get too energetic: this old tub looks like it might fall apart at any moment." He glanced at his watch. "You still feeling nauseous? It's lunchtime."

Moss gagged. "You go ahead and eat," she said. "I think I'll just take a nap."

. . .

Beck had given Langley a walkie-talkie so they could ask to be taken off the ship, but had forbidden the competitors to bring any other electronic devices. Langley, who had considerable experience of sitting around waiting for something to happen while in remote areas, had protested briefly about being deprived of his PDA, but had enough foresight to pack a miniature deck of cards and a pocket-sized chess set among the other survival gear in his bug-out bag. He was playing solitaire when the door suddenly opened and the wind scattered the cards around the cabin. He looked up, but there was no one standing in the doorway—nor in the corridor, by the time he reached the doorway and looked outside. If someone was playing a prank, he thought, they were pretty damn good at moving quickly and silently: he wasn't sure he could have disappeared as effectively, for all his training. He shut the door again, then unhurriedly picked up the cards and shuffled them. He was halfway through another game when the door blew open again, and he wearily repeated the procedure. The rain had begun in earnest again, and he could hear a rumble of distant thunder over the wailing of the wind.

He had started two unsuccessful games (he hated to lose, but refused to cheat) and was coming to the conclusion that the third was going to be just as frustrating, when a frantic clanging and a muffled scream made him sit up. He ran toward the door, the cards forgotten, but the door refused to open. He continued to tug at the handle until it snapped off in his hand, at which point the door blew open as suddenly and forcibly as though it had been kicked, knocking him backwards. He recovered quickly, and scrambled out into the corridor before the door swung shut again.

The door to Moss's cabin was already open, and he looked inside and saw Moss, cocooned in her twisted sleeping bag and with her hair awry, arguing with Syverson. "Are you okay?" Langley demanded.

Moss turned to stare at him. "You, too? Yeah, I'm okay, apart from having my beauty sleep interrupted."

"That wasn't you screaming?"

"Not unless I did it in my sleep." She glanced at Syverson. "Did you hear screaming?"

He shook his head. "Clanging—I thought it might be you, banging on the door or the wall, but I guess it was just the wind. Sorry for disturbing you."

The two men returned to their own cabins. Langley tried propping the door shut with his backpack, but the wind continued to blow it open, and after a few minutes he decided to leave it that way, despite the cold draught. He gave up trying to play cards, and started a game of chess against himself. In a little over half an hour, he heard a metallic thumping again, and what sounded like a cry of "Noooooo."

He hurried into the corridor again, and wrestled with the door of Moss's cabin until Syverson arrived. The two forced their way through, and found Moss alone, still in her sleeping bag, and looking decidedly irritated. "What did you hear *this* time?"

"What did *you* hear?"

"I heard banging, but I knew it wasn't me, so . . . fuck, this is going to drive us crazy before long."

Syverson grimaced and nodded. "From exhaustion, if nothing else. Do you want one of us to stay in here with you?"

"No," she said, flatly. "It's nothing personal, it's not that I don't trust you; I just can't go to sleep when there's someone else in the room. Especially not if they're awake." Her tone became defensive. "It's not a phobia, it's just . . . I've never been able to do it. If one of you wants to sleep in here while I'm awake, I could cope with that, but not . . . no. And if I try staying awake, here, I'm going to start seeing things. Sorry."

"What if next time it really *is* Dugan?" asked Syverson.

"My door doesn't shut anymore," Langley replied. "He doesn't have to go past it to get here, but it's the shortest route. Besides, there's no reason to think he knows which is the right room; even if he was lucky enough to guess right first time, I don't think he could get in without one of us noticing him. But I think that once you've had enough sleep, Rachel, it'd be a good idea if we all *did* stay in the same room—preferably one with a door that shuts—while one of us slept."

Moss hesitated, then nodded.

"I have another idea," said Syverson. "Rather than just thumping, can we decide on some pattern or something that won't have us jumping every time a loose hatch or door, or whatever's causing the noise, bangs in the wind . . . not SOS, but something like that, something with a particular rhythm."

"Shave and a haircut, two bits?" suggested Moss, drily.

In the end, they decided on the *Star Wars* theme, and the two men walked out . . . but Langley waited outside Syverson's cabin before returning to his own. "You're sure you didn't hear screaming? Or voices?"

"Pretty sure. The banging was pretty loud, though, so that might have drowned them out. Why?"

"I don't think it was just the wind I heard."

"Don't tell me you're starting to believe in the ghost?"

"No. But I'm not sure I believe *her*, either, not with a million dollars riding on this." He muffled the microphone he wore around his neck by wrapping it in his fist. Syverson took the hint, and did the same. "And I think the producers want us to believe in the ghost badly enough that they might throw in a few sound effects or other tricks," Langley continued. "You've worked in movies, television . . . what do *you* think?"

"It's possible," Syverson admitted. "From what the crew has been saying, the show isn't rating all that well. Making it more exciting, even if it means faking something . . . I could see the producer trying something like that. We're not the only ones who have to worry about their competition."

"Hmm. Well, I'm not going to stand by and let Moss get hurt, but I wouldn't mind if she quit. I think Dugan's going to hang on until the bitter end."

"He must be scared of *something*," said Syverson. "Going back to jail?"

"Possible, but not easy to arrange," said Langley, but he looked thoughtful. Not all of the situations Beck had set up had been dangerous: some had merely been embarrassing or repulsive. Dugan hadn't balked at the strip poker, buying weird fetish porn from a sex shop, cross-dressing (with makeup, hairstyling and waxing), nude karaoke or eating food that even the former commando had found difficult to keep down. He seemed to be both homophobic and racist, but for a million dollars, Langley suspected the biker might even manage to overcome those prejudices briefly—possibly more easily than Langley would himself. Langley didn't know what else Beck might throw at them once they'd finished on the *Alkimos* . . . sweatboxes? Waterboarding? Stress positions? . . . and he would have been very happy for this exercise, uncomfortable as it was, to be the last thing they had to endure. "I have an idea, though. Rather than both of us waiting here in case Dugan decides to come after Moss, what if one of us took the cabin next to his, and kept a lookout for him that way? At least until Moss has finished her nap. And whoever stays can take your cabin; mine doesn't have a door anymore."

Syverson considered this. "Okay. You want to toss for it?"

"Do you have any coins?"

"Ah. No."

"'Sokay. I have a deck of cards. Low card goes."

There was a sudden clap of thunder, and Syverson jumped. "Jesus."

"I'll go get the cards."

· · ·

The camera crew on the hill stayed until after sunset, then drove back to Yanchep for dinner—except for Kelly, the assistant sound engineer, who sat in a tent half-listening to the static-riddled transmissions from the four on the *Alkimos*. She occasionally caught snatches of recognizable speech between thunderstorms, when the contestants braved the cold and emerged from the rusting hulk onto the deck, but for the most part the sound quality was so dire that she doubted any of it was useable. Dugan's was the worst, possibly because of its time in the water—not that he seemed to be engaging in much conversation, though she did occasionally hear him snore. She was glad the mikes also had their own recording media—not that she could imagine anyone watching reality TV shows for the dialogue. She poured herself another mug of terrible coffee from the thermos, and continued reading the apocryphal history of the *Alkimos* that Beck had left behind. The author claimed that the ghosts were the spirits of people reliving unimaginably horrific or agonizing deaths, trapped on the wrecked ship and conscious of nothing but their last moments replaying in a hellish closed loop. The final chapter described a séance supposedly held on the beach near the wreck by a group of students. Someone or something had moved a plastic cup across their Ouija board, warning them not to visit the wreck.

"'Is the ship cursed?'"

" 'YES'

" 'Is the ship haunted?'

" 'YES'

" 'Are you the ghost?'

" 'NO'

" 'What does the ghost want?'

" 'SOMBODY [sic] TO DIE'

" 'Why?'

" 'NEXT TO DIE ON SHIP BECOM [sic] NEW GHOST OLD GHOST SET FREE NEW GHOST HAUNT TILL—' "

Kelly jumped as she heard a resounding crash that seemed to echo for minutes, and she dropped the book and scrambled out of the tent. She stared into the darkness, but the wreck was just a slightly darker shadow in the dull gray sea. For a moment, she considered grabbing the walkie-talkie and asking if everything was okay, but Beck had made it clear that the contestants were not to be spoken to unless they initiated the conversation—in which case, they'd failed the exercise and lost their chance at the prize. The radio mikes were picking up what sounded like running, loud enough to drown out any speech except for a higher-pitched sound that might have been the wind but felt more like a scream.

.   .   .

Moss was the first to reach the door of Syverson's cabin. The crash, whatever it had been, had seemed to come from that direction, though the entire wreck felt as though it was still vibrating. "Andy?"

No answer—at least, none audible over the echoes of footsteps as Langley and Dugan came running through the corridors—and she pounded on the door with the butt of her flashlight. She tried the handle, then was pushed out of the way by Dugan. "What the fuck was that?" He pushed at the door, then stepped back and ran at it. The door swung open, and he stepped out onto nothing more than air. He swore loudly as he grabbed at the doorframe on his way down, and barely managed to catch it with his empty hand. He dropped his flashlight and grabbed the deck with his other hand, but the rusted metal groaned and flaked off as he fumbled for a firm grip. "Shit! Fuck! Help me!"

Langley stared downwards as the flashlight tumbled. The entire cabin—and not just the cabin, he realized, as he shone his own light around, but a whole section of the ship ending at that wall—had collapsed into the sea. There was jagged debris sticking above the waves, four or five meters below Dugan's feet; the fall was unlikely to be fatal, unless he landed very badly . . . or if medical assistance failed to arrive in time. He looked at Dugan's hands—the knuckles tattooed HARD and CORE—then at his own heavy combat boots, and wondered what the biker would do if their situations were reversed.

"If you fell," he said, just loudly enough to be heard over the thunderstorm, "would that count as leaving the ship, as far as the prize money went?"

Dugan blinked, then looked down. "For fuck's sake, give me a fucking hand!" He couldn't see Langley's expression, or Moss's—they were merely darker silhouettes against the cloudy sky—but he could tell that neither of them seemed eager to help him. "One of you! Please!"

As though in reply, there was a groan from the wreckage below. Langley blinked. "Andy?"

"*Please!*" Dugan repeated.

"Shut the fuck up," Langley growled, but he braced himself and grabbed Dugan by the wrist. It struck him, for the first time, just how much he hated the biker, but he also realized that he might need his help if he were to save Syverson. Dugan grabbed his forearm, and it occurred to Langley that this might be a ruse, an attempt to take *him* down, to haul him over the edge. He considered letting go—surely Moss would back up his version of events—and then Dugan grunted, and hauled himself upwards until his head and shoulders were back on the deck. Moss grabbed his other hand, and they dragged him back into the corridor. He lay there for a moment, then sat up.

"Andy?" Langley repeated, turning his attention back to the sea. He was vaguely aware that Dugan was now behind him, but felt that he had to take the risk. "Can you hear me?"

There came a frantic metallic banging, and Langley swung the flashlight beam around until he saw a hand protruding from behind a sheet of metal. "Are you okay?"

The response was too muffled to make out. "That had better be him, and not the ghost," said Moss.

"I'll risk it," said Langley. "Dugan, go and get the radio. Call for help."

The biker didn't move. "Why don't you go? Didn't they say that whoever used that to call for help was out of the game?"

"You asshole, *this isn't a game anymore*!"

"I'll go," said Moss. "You fuckers can argue later. Do we still have the climbing gear?"

"Yes. And get my bag, too. There's a signal flare in there, just in case the radio doesn't work."

Dugan scrambled to his feet and let her pass. "I'll go get the ropes," he said, sullenly. "But I'm not going to quit."

· · ·

"This is Moss to *Worst Nightmare*. Can you read me? Over."

Silence from the walkie-talkie. Langley held his breath, vaguely aware that he was sick with fear and in danger of vomiting. It occurred to him that if the radio didn't work, he'd have to use the flare, and if no one saw that . . . "This is the *Alkimos*. Can you—"

A crackle of static, barely audible over the wind, then, ". . . hardly hear . . ."

"Mayday! SOS! Help! Can you hear that? WE NEED HELP!"

". . . what . . ."

Langley grabbed the radio. "THIS IS *ALKIMOS*. PART OF THE SHIP HAS COLLAPSED AND SYVERSON IS TRAPPED UNDER THE WRECKAGE. HE'S STILL ALIVE, BUT NEEDS EVAC. DO YOU READ? OVER?"

". . . call Beck . . ."

"WE'LL NEED A WINCH AND A MEDIC. DO YOU COPY?"

"Medic. Copy," came the reply. "Did you say witch?"

"WINCH! WHISKEY INDIA NOVEMBER CHARLIE—"

"Winch," said Kelly. "Copy that. Over and out."

Langley sighed with relief, and handed the walkie-talkie back to Moss. "What do we do now?" asked Dugan. "Wait?"

"How much first aid do you know?"

"Basic," said Langley. "And that was a couple of years back."

"The same, but a *lot* of years back," said Dugan.

"I have a Level Three Certificate, and I used to be an enrolled nurse," said Moss, picking up the first-aid kit, then the ascender and rope. "How do I use this thing to get down there safely?"

"I'm not sure you *can* get down safely."

"I won't if I don't try."

Langley nodded. "Okay. You'll need a headlamp—I have one if you don't. Let's do it."

. . .

Langley hauled her back up onto the deck nearly half an hour later. "There's a boat and a chopper on its way," he said. "Divers on the launch as well as medics. Is he going to make it?"

"Well, he won't bleed to death or drown," she said. "And his head's above water—just. He can move his fingers, but can't feel his legs . . . at least one of which is broken."

"Spinal injuries?"

"It looks that way. I don't know whether he can be fixed."

Langley shook his head. "Fuck. I'm not sure he wouldn't rather be dead. I think I would be."

"At least this way he has a choice," said Moss, sharply. "Look, I'm going to go back to my room and get out of these wet clothes. Then I'm going to get a cabin near the other end of the ship. I suggest you do the same." She pointed at the microphone still slung around Langley's neck, then ran a finger across her own throat. He blinked, then nodded. He returned to his cabin, removed the microphone, then met the others in the corridor between the boiler casing and the galley.

"Okay," said Moss, without preamble. "I don't know whether the producers are going to drop me from the show because I used the radio, or because I left the ship to help Andy; if they do, I'll go straight to one of the other networks and try to sell them my story. It won't be worth a million, but it's got to be worth something. If they *don't* try to kick me off . . ." She drew a deep breath. "I say we split the money. A quarter million's enough for me."

"Four ways?" said Dugan.

"I think Andy's going to need it more than we do."

"You don't know what I need it for," replied the biker, heavily. "But I'll tell you what. I'll settle for half. The rest of you can sort the other half a mill out between yourselves."

"What makes you think—"

"Because I'm prepared to go the distance with this thing," snarled Dugan. "Are the two of you? I'm doing you a favour here."

"Pig's arse you are!" Moss snapped. "Sure, I want off this wreck, but I'm not—"

"Hold on a second," Langley interrupted. "Dugan, if you're so fucking confident, how about the three of us each take . . ." He calculated quickly. "Two hundred thousand. I have a deck of cards in my room. High card keeps the rest. You get it, you get your half mill and an extra fifty thou. We get it, we give half of it to Andy. Or to his wife, if he dies."

Dugan lit up a cigarette to give himself time to think, then he shook his head. "Nah. Life's mostly dealt me a shitty hand: I don't trust to luck anymore."

"Jesus," said Moss. "You think you've had—" She froze, and the other two looked around. There was a man standing at the T-junction, his face illuminated by the beam from Moss's headlamp. He wore a tight checked swimsuit and had a sheath knife strapped to his right shin, and he seemed to be laughing. Dugan took a step toward him, and he backed away through the wall and out of sight.

The three of them stood there for a moment, then Dugan laughed. "Ooh, I'm so fucking scared!" he said sarcastically. "Fuck it. I get half a mill, and the general can split the rest any way he likes, but that's my final offer." He took a drag on his cigarette, then added, "And I stay until the end."

"That's corporal," said Langley. "You're saying you want me to quit."

"I'm doing you a favour."

"I did a tour in Afghanistan, and you expect me to say I'm scared of a fucking *ghost*? Besides, do you really expect us to trust you to hand that money over after you get it?"

"Why should I trust *you*?"

"*I'm* not the one who's done time."

"That was for assault. And drugs." He took a long draw on his cigarette. "But I'm not a thief."

Moss looked from one to the other, and realized that neither of them was going to back down. She shook her head in disgust and walked back to the stern, waiting for the helicopter.

She was safely back at home, and Syverson was in hospital and in stable condition, when another storm hit the *Alkimos* three days later and the last rusted remains of the hull and deck collapsed into the sea.

. . .

Beck walked out of the inquest with his back straight and his head held high. The network had fired him because *Worst Nightmare* had ended its run early, but they'd decided not to sue him, and after the coroner had delivered his verdict on Langley's and Dugan's deaths, the crown prosecutor had announced that he had no intention of having anyone charged with negligent homicide. The production crew had confirmed that neither Langley nor Dugan had made any attempt to contact them to ask to be taken off the ship, either before or during the storm.

As far as the coroner could tell, the two men had been sitting in the galley, drinking coffee and playing cards, from the time Moss had left the ship until the ceiling collapsed on them with no apparent warning. Two large knives had also been discovered among the wreckage, but the pathologist who'd performed the autopsy had made it clear that neither body showed any signs of knife wounds.

As far as he could determine, he told the court, while both men might have survived and possibly even remained conscious for as long as an hour after the wreck had come crashing down on them, they seemed to have died within minutes of each other—quite possibly, at exactly the same time.

Afterword

The wreck of the *Alkimos* was a few hours' walk from my parents' home; it could easily be seen from the beach near the house, and on a few occasions I trudged along the beach to take a closer look at it, though I never swam out to the wreck, nor ever saw the ghost.

Most of the history of the ship given in this story is true—though on a few occasions, when the legend has contradicted the facts, I've printed the legend. Accounts vary as to exactly where Voight's skull was found, in or near the ship. The story Langley tells of his friends is based on those of visitors to the wreck who were later struck by similar misfortunes. And in 2007, the wreck did indeed collapse, leaving nothing remaining above water except the engine block.

The transcript of the séance, however, is fictitious—as are all of the characters, and (fortunately) *Worst Nightmare*. There was an attempt to produce *Fear Factor* in Australia, but it was canceled after only two episodes, and I will not pretend to mourn it. Some things should remain dead.

LILY HOANG

The Foxes

Lily Hoang is the author of the novels The Evolutionary Revolution, Invisible
Women, Changing, *and* Parabola, *winner of the Chiasmus Press Un-Doing
the Novel Contest.* Changing *received a PEN/Beyond Margins Award. She
is associate editor of Starcherone Books and coeditor of the anthology* 30
Under 30.

Now I know what you're thinking. Foxes aren't indigenous to Vietnam, but that's part of it. That's what makes this whole story memorable. And I want you to understand it wasn't just one or two foxes that appeared in that little village that day. No, hundreds of foxes circled the place, and they didn't leave until there was nothing left but flattened soil.

· · ·

This story starts like most stories do, as a memory. There was a time when Vietnam was a peaceful place. This was a very long time before today, long before Communism, long before my parents lived there. In this Vietnam, the people lived cooperatively. They worked in their fields during the mornings when it was cool and by midafternoon everyone retired to their homes for rest and study, but studying was nothing like it is today. Instead, people wandered from house to house, seeing what each person had to offer. If you felt like learning weaving, you would go to Co Thu's house. If you wanted to learn about the stars, you would visit Chu Sang's observatory. If you wanted to study the human body, you could go to the doctor's—Tiem Phuong—office. Of course, if you didn't feel like attending a lesson, you weren't forced to. You could simply rest, but most people enjoyed these lessons. It gave the citizens of this small village an opportunity to learn and build a level of appreciation for all forms of work.

Then, as most stories like this go, something happened. In this case, it was disease. Disease came into this village and killed almost everyone. It was a horrible sickness, one so grotesque that the villagers prayed for death. It wasn't the fear of a slow death that made the people wish for a quick one either. No, the people who had the disease felt such pain and looked so repulsive that those who were not sick prayed for murder. They prayed for quick deaths. They prayed to a God they had not yet met to take them.

Then, with the same ease with which it came, the disease left the small village. It left the village with exactly seven people, most of them malnourished and so crazy they had forgotten language and could think only of death. It was their method of survival. And so these seven survivors, unable to acknowledge that the disease had indeed left them, planned and plotted ways to kill. Luckily for them, the colonizers arrived at their village just in time to save them.

Children still play the Foxes game. I played it when I was a little girl. My parents played it when they were children, as did their parents, and so on, back through history.

These colonizers were much like all other colonizers. They had hair that blew yellow in the breeze and gold crosses around their necks and wrists that blinded our savage survivors. They spoke a language close to the one the village linguist, Chu Hien, had taught them so long ago. They remembered. Even after the disease had eaten most of their memories and ability to feel compassion, they remembered, and so these survivors allowed the colonizers into their homes. They explained as best they could with the patchwork of language they had left, that a plague had come and ransacked their entire village. They told the colonizers about the lives they'd led before the disease came, but the colonizers only heard Hail Mary's and prayers. It was not long before these seven survivors of the most deadly disease to have ever surfaced on this earth were hanged.

·   ·   ·

When my mother tells the story, she says, "The foxes haunt the country like memory. They are unrelenting and hard. They are calloused beasts."

When my father tells the story, he says, "The foxes are warriors. They are timed and tempered."

. . .

When you become infected with the disease, you know it immediately. Even though nothing happens for the first thirty-six hours—its incubation period—you know it. It's as though there's a sudden lucidity, an onset of self-understanding and self-realization, and it's as though all the mistakes you've ever made in your entire life simultaneously play around you, like a series of three-dimensional films playing all at once and you are both subject and viewer. Then, you know your death is coming. And you know that it's going to be brutal.

. . .

Khanh was a good boy. He was a diligent student, he worked hard, he loved his parents, he was never lazy. Often, when school was let out, he would run home to cook dinner for his parents. Even after dinner, he would insist on washing the dishes. Of course, his mother wouldn't allow this.

After dinner, Khanh would go back to his room where he'd study until his eyes could no longer focus. Even then, he would try to forge on for just another hour or two to maximize his time. He was the perfect Vietnamese son.

. . .

When my father tells the story, he says, "It was the disease that impregnated these women with a rage so powerful that they manipulated reincarnation to seek revenge." When my father tells the story, he says, "These seven women will not stop." He says, "Women, especially scorned women, can never recover: they will never be sated." It's hard to estimate, he tells me, but these women—these foxes—they've probably destroyed scores of villages, but because they are so thorough, it's impossible to know how many for sure. He says it could be hundreds. Maybe even thousands, but one thing is for sure, these foxes are real and they will keep on killing.

When my mother tells the story, she says, "It was the colonizers' cruelty that made the women come back as foxes." She says, "As long as Vietnam remains under the colonizers' rule, the foxes will continue to try to break down anything they build."

My mother isn't political, but she's telling a story so it's OK.

When my mother tells the story, she explains, "The foxes have been do-ing this for as long as Vietnam has been colonized." She says that they're systematic about it, that they go from village to village, killing and destroy-ing, that they're building up an army. My mother says, "They're not going to stop. They're never going to stop."

.   .   .

For thirty-six long hours, you have to relive the most painful times of your life. During this time, you have perfect memory—every color is the exact shade it was, every hair is in place—and you watch yourself stumble, you watch yourself fail, watch yourself suffer, you watch yourself knowing everything that will happen, everything that has happened. It's the embar-rassment, the pity that kills you. You wish yourself death, but it isn't that easy.

> In the game, seven little girls pretend to be foxes. They circle the rest of us. Then, through a series of winks, nods, and a few singing howls, they pick their new fox. They run in, salvage the lucky one, and kill the rest. Of course, they don't really kill us, but the one who's picked, well, she's practically our leader for that day. She's the one every single one of us want to be. She's the one that's been picked by the gods to survive.

During the incubation period, the disease makes you believe you're living the past all over again. You walk through the past in the present, such that you collide your present body into a building that exists today but you still continue walking, continue your course of motion as though the building is not there because from where you stand—in the past—it isn't. Those who are lucky walk into the ocean and drown themselves before the real pain of the disease starts. Most are not lucky. They end up with bruises, broken legs, and missing organs.

.   .   .

The fox is a hunter. She is a sly creature. She is beautiful and elegant.

. . .

One man, while reliving the murder of his wife, stabbed thirty-eight people, killing nearly half of them. He would have been tried and hung, except that everyone knew he had been merciful, killing those people so quickly and efficiently.

. . .

The only survivors were women, pregnant women. The women didn't even realize they were pregnant though. The disease had dissolved essential portions of their brain. One woman had no hippocampus; another lacked the entire frontal lobe of her brain. These women were a sight, nearly nine months pregnant and they could hardly walk, not because of the bulge of their bellies or the strain on their backs but because the disease had degenerated their legs such that they resembled the stalks of bok choy. The disease tattooed their skin with large purplish blotches and patches of acne that swelled under heat.

. . .

It was the colonizers who first realized these women were with child. The colonizers, being infinitely wise in their understandings of the world, once they realized that these women were pregnant, quickly ascertained that it was the disease—the devil—that had impregnated them.

. . .

But the fox can also be sexy. She can be svelte, her fur smooth. The fox has human eyes—compassionate and, sometimes, quite passionate indeed.

. . .

When Khanh was a little boy, he'd beg his mother to tell him ghost stories, the kind that would make a boy never be able to sleep because of the fright, but she wouldn't indulge him. She told him the truth is always scarier than fiction, and she told him that this very village, the one he was sleeping in right now, had a history to it that would haunt even the bravest little boy so strongly he would never be able to sleep again.

Taunted, Khanh asked for more, but his mother said, "Soon, my dear son. You're too young now, but soon enough, you will go to school, and I won't be able to protect you, even if I wanted to."

And it was true. She wasn't able to protect him at all.

The rules are simple: the seven most popular girls, or the ones with the most money or power, get to be the foxes. Everyone else must be the villagers. These girls, these fox-girls, they are the strong ones and they know it. They are more powerful than teachers or parents. They have the ability to give and take life. They are like gods, and all the other children treat them like it. It is a never-ending game. The fox-girls can come at any time. They can come while you're eating dinner or while you're sleeping. They can come while you're pissing or while you're studying. Any time. And you have to be ready to be taken or to die.

When these fox-girls come, they dance with translucent veils covering their bodies. When they kill you, a little part of you really does die because you had wished—you had prayed—that this time, they would finally pick you, but by the time you think about this, you're already dead. They've killed you.

The disease starts in the brain. If you're lucky, the disease will eat away the right part of the brain to cut off your senses. But most people aren't so lucky.

Once the disease is fully incubated, it attacks the skin. The disease manifests itself at first as a simple freckle or mole and within a minute or two the spot begins to burn. The sensation feels something akin to a little fleck of acid on flesh. Once one spot appears, ten more do too. Then, a hundred. Until you're covered with these tiny blood-filled freckles, each one burning with an icy intensity, that point where hot turns cold turns indescribable pain. But it doesn't stop there.

Luckily though, this is just a game and you can come back to life. You have an incredible opportunity. Next time, they could pick you. Next time, you can be reincarnated as a fox-girl.

The disease keeps these spots far enough from each other to keep the skin from sluicing off, and although you try to scrape your skin away, mutilation doesn't help. The burning burrows, until you can feel it in your muscles, these tiny pinpricks, and then in your bones. It's quite possible you can even feel it in your heart and brain, although there's no evidence to prove this either way.

Once the pain finds its way to the bones, the marrow begins to expand and contract, making the bones themselves elastic, and you can't walk. But you can't lay still either. The pain is too much for even the strongest of men to endure, and even then, the disease won't let the body die. It lets people writhe on the ground, and from afar, you could see inside their emaciated frames, and a slight pulsation: the bones breathing.

. . .

When I was a little girl, my parents used to tell me to behave or else the foxes would come eat me. Of course, I never doubted it and that scared me into good behavior. The thing is that my parents never stopped warning me about the foxes. To this day, my parents remind me the foxes are always nearby, that I can never escape from them, that it only takes them seeing me once for them to remember me forever. It's their sense of smell, they say, but deep down, I think we all know it's something much more sinister than that.

. . .

But of course, the foxes don't eat little kids. They don't care about them at all. These foxes, they're not really foxes. Yes, they take the form of the fox, they look like a fox, they press their bodies against the ground flat before pouncing on prey like a fox, but don't be deceived. These foxes have the disease in them. It's the disease that killed their whole village so long ago, the disease that just won't leave this place alone.

. . .

The colonizers were ruthless. When the seven surviving women emerged from the wreckage of dead bodies, the colonizers strapped them down to clean them, to see what was beneath all that crusted blood and dirt. And maybe it was because neither understood the language the other was speaking, but the women and the colonizers screamed hell until finally the women were gagged. Then, they were blindfolded. Then, they were whipped. Then, they were raped. Then, they were cleansed. And then, the cycle started all over again until the colonizers were sated. Then, these women—these seven strong women who survived the deadliest disease the earth ever saw—were hanged, and even after they were dead, the colonizers did not stop with the torture.

· · ·

When my father tells the story, I'm safe. My father says, "The foxes would never be interested in you. What they want most, these foxes, is to find a good father for their children. They want a man who will not kill them, one who will not be murdered by disease, and every day, they search for him, and luckily, my little girl, you're not a man."

When my mother tells the story, though, it's quite a bit different. Sure, it's mostly the same. There's disease and colonizers, murder and foxes, but in her version the foxes are much more vengeful. She says, "It's because of everything they've had to endure." And even though she insists that Vietnamese people, especially the women, can endure much more than anyone else and not complain or even hold grudges, what these women experienced deserved revenge. She says, "Even though Vietnamese people are not ones for violence, when pushed to a certain limit, it would be stupid—it would be suicide—not to push back."

· · ·

Khanh studied by candlelight not because his family didn't have electricity—because they did and he actually used that artificial light for illumination—but because he preferred to use the candle as a marker for time. Every night he would go through exactly three candles before going to bed. Before studying, he would place a sheet of paper around the middle of each candle to account for each of his six subjects. He was a dedicated student, but even more than that, he was dedicated to his parents, as all good Vietnamese boys are. He studied, not for himself, but for them, so that they would be proud to brag about his diligence.

· · ·

When my mother tells the story, she says, "The foxes want Vietnam to remain stagnant. They want things to be as they were in the past. They are selfish and close-minded."

When my father tells the story, he says, "The foxes are trying to save Vietnam from falling under the weight of desire."

· · ·

The foxes work as a group. Even though we can't hear or understand their language, it's evident that there must be a language because these foxes move as a singular force. Their movement is choreographed. It is an epic ballet where hundreds die for them to circle just one person, the one they want to claim as their own. And then, of course, another fox is born.

．　．　．

After the bodies were cleared, the colonizers modeled their new village after their homeland, which happened to be monarchical and capitalistic. This was handy because they—the colonizers—were the new monarchs. They were the rulers who should never be questioned. Even after the foxes had killed all the colonizers, even after generations of people had come and gone, the village never went back to that ideal restful collective.

．　．　．

The day Khanh's mother heard that the foxes had resurfaced, she knew they were coming for her son. It was not her maternal pride. It was instinct. She knew her son, so diligent and handsome, even though he had his small flaws, was the greatest boy born in the village in years. This was when she made her plan. She went to see all the other women in the village. She gave them cakes and sticky rice. She gave them any of her small treasures, if only they would promise to help her. The foxes were infamous. She knew they would come and they would kill everyone, and the only way any of them could survive was if they pushed back, hard.

．　．　．

After the disease enters your bone marrow, then things get really ugly. Once the marrow becomes elastic, it pushes against the hardened calcium of the bone until it begins to crack, but because of the disease, the bone can't quite break. Instead, the bone unwraps, layer by layer, but the layers are not clean. They splinter, the bones force their way to the surface, to the air, to breathe. You still don't die. Even then, you survive to suffer further.

．　．　．

But foxes *do* eat children. They eat boys and girls as easily as they eat women and men. They'll do it and they won't regret a thing.

The truth of it is that foxes will eat everything and everyone. They'll eat your entire village, and then, just as a gesture of kindness, they'll plow any freestanding structure into the earth to erase any hint of your existence. The foxes are demolishers. They want to do to you what the disease and the colonizers did to them. They do it without any remorse. They do it swiftly, but often, they pause for just long enough for you to understand what's happening. They do it to raise and then eradicate consciousness. They are vicious and cruel.

But they save one. With every village they destroy, their pack, their family grows, slowly. Now they have an army of foxes.

· · ·

Khanh's mother was diligent. She went from door to door and gathered the village women. She didn't know what to do. No one else did either, but they still gathered and talked. Each woman told her version of the fox legend. Khanh's mother thought that in the gaps of the different versions of the legends, there could be some secret, something to save them all, but as each woman spoke, it became evident that nothing could be done, that they were all doomed, and worst of all, it became clear the foxes would not choose her son to join them. The foxes didn't want men in their ranks; they didn't need another man to kill them all over again.

· · ·

The problem with the colonizers, which is a problem with all colonizers in general, is that the land they colonize is not their own. They don't know what belongs and what doesn't. They don't acknowledge the customs because they don't know them. So when the colonizers hanged those seven sick women, they didn't stop to think about the process of death, they didn't think about where the bodies should be interred, and they certainly didn't think of the possible repercussions.

But it wasn't out of malice that they hanged these women. That would be a complete misunderstanding. No, the colonizers were afraid. They were certain the devil was trapped in these women, behind the black flesh and protruding cage of bones.

The colonizers didn't notice that after they'd hanged the women the corpses just disappeared. With all those dead bodies in the village, the colonizers had so much to do, and these women, they were simply lost in the shuffle, and yet still, they should have noticed. But that was the way it was. These seven pregnant women, after surviving the disease and encountering these colonizers, after being hanged and certainly certified dead, simply vanished.

It was only a few weeks later that the foxes appeared. Of course, the colonizers didn't notice them either.

The fox-girls can choose anyone they like to be their new fox. Each new fox-girl has a different initiation, a rite of passage, into the world of the foxes. It is another long ritual involving ribbons and confetti, coal and water, but the new fox-girls never mind. They are overjoyed to be a part of the group, and each fox-girl secretly wonders if the real version is this much fun, if it really is like becoming a part of a new family.

The disease creates huge blisters on what is left of the body. They grow to the size of a fist. Inside, you can see little spots swimming in the pus. If you're conscious enough to see them, you know that those spots *are* the disease, but by the time the blisters come, your brain is already soup and the only thing you can actually think to feel is pain.

But the ones who are not chosen, for the entire week following their massacre, they cannot speak. Parents and teachers alike understand this rule. They allow for it. It is as though the entire country of Vietnam makes these allowances to pay credence to the foxes. It is their way to worship and pray that the foxes will stay far away from their village, no matter how big or small, how rich or poor it is.

Khanh's mother was right that the foxes had their eye on her house, but they didn't want her son. To them, he was a pathetic epitome of the colonizers. No, they wanted her.

The day the foxes attacked her village, it was silent.

The day the foxes attacked her village, the sun was out and shining brightly. The villagers knew something big was coming: the sun never lit their town with such clarity.

And then, they came. The foxes came.

· · ·

The night before the foxes came, all the women in the village dug small but deep holes around their houses. They placed sharp stakes at the bottom and covered them with straw and hay. They stocked their homes with gasoline and matches. They sharpened their knives and hid their children in rooms they'd built under their houses. These women were ready. The foxes would have a force to be reckoned with in them.

. . .

When my father tells the story, he says, "It was the colonizers that brought the disease." My father says, "The disease was like a warning sign." He says, "The disease was merciful to those it killed."

He says all of this and yet he took the colonizers' religion.

When my mother tells the story, she says, "The foxes can come at any time. You should always be ready."

. . .

The disease came only a week before the colonizers arrived. By the end of that week, only seven women survived. They were the ones the disease rejected.

. . .

The day the foxes arrived, the women hid their men and children. When the foxes arrived, only the women stood strong. The foxes came into their village and began killing.

Khanh's mother watched from her kitchen window as the foxes leapt over the holes, as they dodged the gasoline and matches. She watched as the foxes simultaneously pirouetted through their front windows. *It's beautiful,* she thought. She saw blood cascade, and she heard the foxes enter the basements. She heard the children and men scream and then, there was silence. It had all happened within minutes. She had barely breathed.

Then, before she even knew they were in her house, she too had a tail.

. . .

There are warning signs, but no one can decide what they are with any certainty. Some say that it becomes incredibly hot. Others say that insects swarm. Others insist that the night sky becomes devoid of any light.

Either way, it's clear that the foxes control nature.

. . .

When my mother tells the story, she tells me that my great-great-grandmother once saw a village the foxes hadn't completely demolished. My mother says, "She could barely tell it was a village. The houses all had large cracks running along their sides, where the foxes had rammed their heads with the force of earthquakes. Inside each house, the family was lined up—Mother and Father side by side, the children curled in the fetal position at their feet." She says, "Your great-great-grandmother saw one family and only one family where the mother was missing."

When my mother tells the story, she says, "The fields had nothing in them. They were mounds of dirt. There were no animals. There were no plants, not even grass. There weren't even insects. The whole town was nothing but collapsing buildings and dead people."

When my father tells the story, my mother's story has no credence. When my father tells the story, there are no surviving villages. Not even one.

· · ·

Khanh was a good boy. He was smart and loving, but he was not immune. The foxes killed him like they would anyone else. He was not special.

· · ·

My great-great-grandmother saw this when she was just a little girl. She also played the Foxes game. One day, she was chosen as the newest fox initiate, and as a reward, her fox friends took her to see this ransacked village. They took her to see her destiny. My great-great-grandmother, after seeing this, stopped talking. She could barely eat. Every time she closed her eyes, she saw all the dead faces, serene and accepting. She saw the one cocoon missing a piece and dreamt.

· · ·

The only time the foxes did not take a new fox with them was the very first time they killed. They were newly born, undeveloped, not fully sophisticated. Back then, they killed out of necessity. They killed for survival and revenge. They did not have a message. They did not have a politic. They simply wanted to ravage the men that had done the very same thing to them.

The first time the foxes killed, the colonizers had been settled for decades. They'd made children and dispersed them across the land. The foxes had waited too long, and as such, they decided, right then, right when they saw the faces of the colonizers, to devote the rest of their lives to fighting everything they'd created.

· · ·

Now, my children play the Foxes game. They run around and dance in these elaborate rituals. I don't remember my games being so sophisticated. When they run home to me, I tell them not to worry. I tell them that the foxes won't hurt them, that they're not real, but even as I say this, it takes all the strength I have not to show them my lush and beautiful tail.

Afterword

My parents have created this mythology about my childhood, one that I don't remember, one that I have no proof of whatsoever, but one of the most prominent mythologies tells the story of a little girl version of me with a bowl haircut. I'm young, although I'm not sure exactly how old I am. Surely, I am no older than three or four years old. I hold a book in my hand, a book of folktales written in both English and Vietnamese. When strangers come to my house, my parents put the book in my hand and I read. I read out loud. I read first in English. People ooh and aah. Then I read the very same story in Vietnamese. Then, everyone is speechless. They are amazed. I am a genius. I make my parents proud. I am proud that I can make them proud.

LAIRD BARRON

The Redfield Girls

Laird Barron's work has appeared in such publications as The Magazine of Fantasy & Science Fiction, SCIFICTION, Inferno: New Tales of Terror and the Supernatural, Poe: 19 New Tales Inspired by Edgar Allan Poe, The Del Rey Book of Science Fiction and Fantasy, *and* Lovecraft Unbound. *It has also been reprinted in numerous year's-best anthologies. His debut collection,* The Imago Sequence & Other Stories, *was the winner of the inaugural Shirley Jackson Award. Barron is an expatriate Alaskan currently at large in Washington State.*

1

Every autumn for a decade, several of the Redfield Girls, a close-knit sorority of veteran teachers from Redfield Memorial Middle School in Olympia, gathered for a minor road trip along the hinterlands of the Pacific Northwest. Traditionally, they rented a house in a rural, picturesque locale, such as the San Juan Islands or Cannon Beach, or Astoria, and settled in for a last long weekend of cribbage, books, and wine before their students came rushing into the halls, flushed and wild from summer vacation. Bernice Barber, Karla Gott, Dixie Thiess, and Li-Hua Ming comprised the core of the Redfield Girls. Li-Hua served as the school psychiatrist, and Karla and Dixie taught English—Karla was a staunch, card-bearing member of the Dead White Guys Club, while Dixie preferred Neruda and Borges. Their frequent arguments were excruciating or exquisite depending on how many glasses of merlot they'd downed. Both of them considered Bernice, the lone science teacher and devourer of clearance sale textbooks, a borderline stick in the mud. They meant this with great affection.

This was Bernice's year to choose their destination and she chose a rustic cabin on the shores of Lake Crescent on the Olympic Peninsula. The cabin belonged to the Bigfish Lodge and was situated a half mile from the main road in a stand of firs. There was no electricity, or indoor plumbing, although the building itself was rather comfortable and spacious and the caretakers kept the woodshed stocked. The man on the phone told her a lot of celebrities had stayed there—Frank Sinatra, Bing Crosby, Elizabeth Taylor, and at least one of the Kennedys. Even some mobsters and their molls.

Truth be told, Dixie *nagged* her into picking the lake. Left to her own devices, she would've happily settled for another weekend at Ocean Shores or Seaside. Dixie was having none of it: ever fascinated with the Port Angeles and the Sequim Valley, she pushed and pushed, and Bernice finally gave in. Her family homesteaded in the area during the 1920s, although most of them had scattered on the wind long since. She'd lived in Olympia since childhood, but Dad and Mom brought them up to the lake for a visit during the height of every summer. They pitched a tent at a campsite in the nearby park, and fished and swam in the lake. Dad barbecued and told ghost stories, because that's what one did when one spent a long, lonely night near the water. Bernice and her husband, Elmer, made a half dozen day trips over the years; none, however, since he passed away. Lately though, she thought of the lake often. She woke in a sweat, dreams vanishing like quicksilver.

The night before the Redfield Girls were to leave on the trip, there was a storm. She was startled by loud knocking on the front door. She hesitated to answer, and briefly lamented not adopting another big dog for protection after her black Lab, Norman, died. Living alone on a piece of wooded property outside of town, she seldom received random visitors—and certainly not in the wee hours. A familiar voice shouted her name. Her teenage niece Lourdes Blanchard had flown in unannounced from Paris.

Bernice ushered Lourdes inside, doing her best to conceal her annoyance. She enjoyed kids well enough. However, she jealously coveted those few weeks of freedom between summer and fall, and more importantly, her relationship with Lourdes was cool. The girl was bright and possessed a wry wit. Definitely not a prized combination in anyone under thirty.

Bernice suspected trouble at home. Her sister Nancy denied it during the livid, yet surreptitious phone call Bernice made after she'd tucked the girl into bed. Everything was fine, absolutely super—why was she asking? Lourdes saved a bit of money and decided to hop the international flight from Paris to Washington State, determined to embark upon a fandango of sorts. What was a mother to do? The child was stubborn—just like her favorite auntie.

"Well, you could've warned me, for starters," Bernice said. "Good God, Nance, I'm leaving with the Redfield Girls tomorrow—"

Nancy laughed as the connection crackled. "See, that's perfect. She's been clamoring to go with you on one of your little adventures. Sis? Sis? I'm losing the connection. Have fun—"

She was left clutching a dead phone. The timing was bizarre and seemed too eerie for coincidence. She'd had awful dreams several nights running; now, here was Lourdes on her doorstep, soaked to the bone, thunder and lightning at her back. It was almost as bad as the gothic horror novels Bernice had been reading to put herself to sleep. She couldn't very well send Lourdes packing, nor with any conscience leave her sitting at the house. So she gritted her teeth into a Miss America smile and said, "Guess what, kid? We're going to the mountains."

2.

The group arrived at the lake in the late afternoon. Somehow they'd managed to jam themselves, and all their luggage, into Dixie's rusted-out Subaru. The car was a hundred thousand miles past its expiration date and plastered with stickers like FREE TIBET, KILL YOUR TV, and VISUALIZE WHIRLED PEAS. They stopped at the lodge and picked up the cabin key and a complimentary fruit basket. From there it was a ten-minute drive through the woods to the cabin itself. While the others finished unpacking, Bernice slipped outside to sneak a cigarette. To her chagrin, Lourdes was waiting, elbows on the rail. Her niece was rapidly becoming a bad penny. Annoyingly, the other women didn't seem to mind her crashing the party. Perhaps their empty nests made them maudlin for the company of children.

"Aunt Dolly died here. This is where they found her." Lourdes squinted at the dark water thirty or so yards from the porch of the cabin.

"That's great-aunt to you." Bernice quickly pocketed her lighter and tried to figure how to beat a hasty retreat without appearing to flee the scene. "To be accurate, it probably happened closer to the western side. That's where they lived."

"But she's the Lady of the Lake?"

"Aunt Dolly was Aunt Dolly. She died an awful death. Cue the violins."

"And the ghost stories."

"Those, too. Nothing like enriching cultural heritage by giving the tavern drunks a cause célèbre to flap their lips about."

"Doesn't it make you sad? Even a little?"

"I wasn't alive in 1938. Jeez, I never knew the gal personally. How old do you think I am, anyway?"

Lourdes brushed back her hair. She was straw blond and lean, although she had her mother's eyes and mouth. Bernice had always wondered about the girl's fairness. On the maternal side, their great-grandparents were a heavy mix of Spanish and Klallam—just about everybody in the immediate family was thick and dark. Bernice had inherited high cheekbones and bronze skin and black hair, now turning to iron. She owned a pair of moccasins she never wore, and a collection of beads handed down from her elders that she kept locked in a box of similar trinkets.

A stretch of beach separated them and the lake. The lake was a scar one mile wide and ten miles long. The water splashed against the rocks, tossing reels of brown kelp. Clouds rolled across the sky. The sun was sinking and the water gleamed black with streaks of red. Night came early to the Peninsula in the fall. The terrain conspired with the dark. For the most part, one couldn't see a thing after sundown. The Douglass fir and western redwoods rose like ancient towers, and beneath the canopy all was cool and dim. Out there, simple homes were scattered through the foothills of Storm King Mountain in a chain of dirt tracks that eventually linked to the highway junction. This was logging country, farm country; field and stream, and overgrown woods full of nothing but birds and deer and the occasional lost camper.

An owl warbled and Bernice shivered. "Anyway. How'd this gnat get in your ear?"

"I read about it a long time ago in a newspaper clipping—I was helping Grandma sort through Grandpa's papers after he died. As we drove up here, I started thinking about the story. This place is so . . . forbidding. I mean, it's gorgeous, but beneath that, kind of stark. And . . . Dixie was telling me about it earlier when you were getting the key."

"That figures."

The younger woman pulled her shawl tight. "It's just so . . . awful."

"You said it, kid." Bernice called her niece "kid" even though Lourdes was seventeen and on her way to college in a couple of weeks. Depending upon the results of forthcoming exams, she'd train to be a magistrate, or at the very least a barrister. They grew up fast in Europe. Even so, the divide was too broad—Bernice was approaching fifty and she felt every mile in her bones. Chaperone to a sardonic, provocative little wiseacre seemed a hollow reward for another tough year at the office.

"There's another thing . . . I had a really bizarre dream about Aunt Dolly the other day. I was floating in a lake—not here, but somewhere warm—and she spoke to me. She was this white shape under the water. I knew it was her, though, and I heard her voice clearly."

"What did she say?"

"I don't remember. She was nice . . . except, something about the situation wasn't right, you know? Like she was trying to trick me. I woke in a sweat."

Bernice's flesh goose pimpled. Uncertain how to respond, she resisted the temptation to confide her own nightmares. "That is pretty weird, all right."

"I'm almost afraid to ask about the murder," Lourdes said.

"But not quite, eh?" They must be sharing a wavelength. What wavelength, though?

"I wish Mom had mentioned it."

"It's quite the campfire tale with your cousins. Grandpa Howard used to scare them with it every Halloween—"

"Way insensitive."

"Well, that's the other side of the family. Kissinger he isn't. Nancy never told you?"

"Frank discourages loose talk. He's a sensible fellow. Mom follows his lead." It was no secret Lourdes disliked her father. His name was Francois, but she called him Frank when talking to her friends. She'd pierced her navel and tattooed the U.S. flag on the small of her back to spite him. Ironically, his stepsons John and Frank thought Francois was the greatest thing since sliced baguettes.

Fair enough, if she hated him. Who knew what Nancy was thinking when she married the schmuck. Except, Bernice *did indeed* know what her sister had been thinking—Francois was a first-rate civil engineer; one of the best in Paris. After Bill died, Nancy only cared about security. Her two boys were in middle school at the time and Bill had been under the weight of a crippling mortgage, the bills for his chemotherapy. Bernice suspected she only got herself pregnant with Lourdes to seal the deal. It shouldn't irk her that Nancy had made the smart choice. When Bernice lost Elmer, she'd gone the other direction—dug in and accepted the role of widow. Eleven years and she hadn't remarried, hadn't even gone on a date. It was wrong to begrudge Nancy, but Lord help her, she did, and maybe that was why she resented poor Lourdes just a tiny bit—and maybe she was envious because she and Elmer put off having their own children and now it was far too late.

Lourdes said, "That's why you brought us up here, right? To tell the tale and give everyone a good scare?"

Bernice laughed to cover her mounting unease. "It hadn't occurred to me. I brought a bag of books and sunblock. We've got our evening cribbage tournaments. Hope you don't get too bored with us biddies."

"Dixie promised to go hiking with me tomorrow."

"Tomorrow?" Bernice detested hiking. The hills were steep, the bugs ravenous. She'd allowed her gym membership to lapse and piled on almost fifteen pounds since spring. No, hiking wasn't a welcome prospect. And to think she wasn't even consulted in the change of program. Dixie's treachery would not go unremarked.

"Tomorrow afternoon. Then she's driving us into Port Angeles for dinner at the Red Devil."

"That's a bar. Your parents—"

"The place serves fish and chips. Dixie says it's the best cod ever. Besides, there's no drinking age in France."

"Cripes," Bernice said. Her desire for a cigarette was almost violent, but she restricted herself to a couple of Virginia Slims a day, and only in secret. Lights came on in the cabin. Dixie stuck her head out a window to say dinner was up.

3.

Li-Hua made stir-fry and egg rolls over the gas range. She preferred traditional southern Chinese cuisine. A tough, sinewy woman, she'd endured a stint in a tire factory during the Cultural Revolution before escaping to college, and eventually from Hainan to the United States where she earned her doctorate. For years, Karla nagged her to write a memoir that would make Amy Tan seem like a piker. Li-Hua smiled wisely and said she'd probably retire and open a restaurant instead.

They ate garlic bread on the side and drank plenty of red wine Karla and her husband, Chuck, had brought home from a recent tour of Wenatchee vineyards. Normally the couple spent summer vacation scuba diving in Puget Sound. As Karla explained, "We went to the wineries because I've gotten too fat to fit into my wetsuit."

After dinner, Dixie turned down the kerosene lanterns and the five gathered near the hearth—Bernice and Li-Hua in the musty leather seats; Karla, Dixie, and Lourdes on their sleeping bags. The AM transistor played soft classical jazz. Karla quizzed Lourdes about her dreaded exams, the pros and cons of European track education versus the American scattershot approach.

Bernice half-listened to their conversation, wineglass balanced on her knee, as she lazily scrutinized the low split-beam rafters, the stuffed mallard and elk head trophies, and the dingy photographs of manly men posing beside hewn logs and mounds of slaughtered salmon. Darkness filled every window.

"You want to tell this?" Dixie said. "Your niece is pestering me."

"I know. She's been bugging the crap out of me, too."

"Oh, be nice, would you?" Karla said. She stirred the coals with a poker.

"Yeah, be nice," Dixie said while Lourdes didn't try hard to cover a smirk. Her cheeks were flushed. Dixie and Karla had given her a few glasses of wine. "Hey, they do it in France!" Dixie said when confronted.

"Go for it, then." Bernice shook her head. She was too drowsy and worn down to protest. She always enjoyed Dixie's rendition of the tale. Her friend once wrote an off-the-cuff essay called "Haunted Lake." It was subsequently published in the *Daily Olympian* and reprinted every couple of years around Halloween.

"If you insist."

"Hey, guys," Li-Hua said. "It may be bad luck to gossip about this so close to the sacred water."

"Come on," Dixie said.

Li-Hua frowned. "I'm serious. My feet got cold when you started talking. What if the spirits heard us and now they're watching? You don't know everything about these things. There are terrible mysteries."

"Whatever," Bernice said. She refused to admit the same chill creeping up her legs, as if dipped in a mist of dry ice. "Let nothing but fear . . ."

"Okeydokey. What's so special about the lake?" Karla dropped the poker and leaned toward Dixie with an expression of dubious interest.

"She's cursed." Dixie was solemn.

"That's what I'm saying," Li-Hua said.

"I get the feeling you Northlanders brought a lot of superstitious baggage from the Old World," Karla said, indicating Dixie's pronounced Norwegian ancestry.

"It's more than white man superstition, though. In the winter, thunderstorms boil down the valley, set fire to the high timber, tear the roofs off houses, and flood a hundred draws from here to Port Townsend." Dixie nodded to herself and sipped her drink, beginning to get into her narrative. "The wind *blows*. It lays its hammer on the waters of the lake, beats her until she bares rows of whitecap teeth. She's old, too, that one; a deep, dark Paleolithic well of glacial water. She was here an aeon before the Klallam settled along the valley in their huts and longhouses. The tribes never liked her. According to legend, the Klallam refused to paddle their canoes across Lake Crescent. This goes back to the ancient days when the Klallam were paddling just about everywhere. They believed the lake was full of demons who would drag them to the bottom for trespassing."

A gust rattled the windows and moaned in the chimney. Sparks flew around the grate and everybody but Dixie glanced into the shadowy corners of the room.

"Man, you're getting good at this," Bernice said drily.

"Keep going!" Lourdes said. She'd pulled her sweater over her nose so that only her eyes were revealed.

"I'd be quiet," Li-Hua said.

Dixie chuckled and handed her glass to Li-Hua. Li-Hua poured her another three fingers of wine and passed it back. "Oh, the locals *adore* stories—the eerie ones, the true crime ones, the ones that poke at the unknowable; and they do love their gossip. Everybody, and I mean everybody, has a favorite. The most famous tale you'll hear about Lake Crescent concerns the murder of poor waitress, Dolly Hanson. Of all the weird stories, the morbid campfire tales they tell the tourists on stormy nights around the hearth, 'The Lady of the Lake Murder' is the one everybody remembers.

"A tawdry piece of business, that saga. In the mid-thirties, the bar had grown into a popular resort for the rich townies and renamed Lake Crescent Lodge, although most of the locals stubbornly referred to it as Singer's Tavern. A few still do. According to legend, Dolly, who was Bernice's aunt,

of course, had just gotten divorced from her third husband, Hank, on account of his philandering ways—"

"And the fact he beat her within an inch of her life whenever he got a
snootful at the tavern," Bernice said.

"Yes, yes," Dixie said. "On the morning of the big Singer's Christmas
party of 1938, he strangled Dolly, tied some blocks to her, and dumped her
in the middle of the lake. The jerk went about his way as the resident merry
widower of Port Angeles until he eventually moved to California. People
suspected, people whispered, but Hank claimed his wife ran off to Alaska
with a salesman—or a sailor, depending on who's telling the tale—and no
one could prove otherwise."

"Some fishermen found her in 1945, washed up directly below the lodge.
That lake is deep and cold—there aren't any deeper or any colder in the continental U.S. The frigid alkaline water preserved Dolly pretty much fully
intact. She'd turned to soap."

"Soap? Like a soap carving, a sculpture?"

"Yes indeed. The cold caused a chemical reaction that softens the body,
yet keeps it intact to a point. A weird sort of mummification."

"That's freaky," Lourdes said.

Dixie chuckled. "Say, Bernie, wasn't it Bob Hall who identified her?
Yeah . . . Hall. A barber by trade, and part-time dentist, matched her dental
records. The young lady's teeth were perfectly preserved, you see. That was
curtains for old two-timing Hank. He was hanged in '49. That's just one
incident. Plenty more where that came from."

"More murders? More soap mummies?" Karla said.

"I suppose there could be more corpses. Deep as she is, the lake would
make a pretty convenient dump site. Folks are given to feuds here in the
hills. A lot of people have disappeared from this end of the Peninsula over
the years. Especially around the lake."

"Really? Like who?"

"All kinds. There was the married couple who bought a washing machine in Sequim and were last seen a mile or so from where we are right
now. Those two vanished in 1955 and it's still a mystery where they went.
Back in 2005, an amateur detective supposedly found the lid to the washer
in two hundred feet of water near a swimming hole called the Devil's Punch
Bowl. The kid got pretty excited about his find; he planned to come back

with more equipment and volunteers, but he hasn't, and I doubt he will. It wouldn't matter anyway. Then there's Ambulance point. An ambulance racing for the hospital crashed through a guardrail and went into the drink. The paramedics swam away from the wreck, but a logger strapped to a gurney in the back of the ambulance sure as hell didn't. Every year some diver uncovers the door handle to a Model A, the bumper from a Packard, the rims to something else. Bones? Undoubtedly, a reef of them exists somewhere in the deep. We won't find them, though. Like the old-timers say: the mistress keeps those close to her heart. Some say the souls of those taken are imprisoned in the forms of animals—coyotes and loons. When a coyote howls or a loon screams, they're crying to their old selves, the loved ones they've lost."

Lourdes's eyes were wide and gleaming. "You actually wrote an essay about this?"

"Yep."

"You must e-mail it to me when I get home!"

"You got it, kiddo."

Bernice was getting ready to turn in for the night when Dixie laughed with Lourdes and said, "That's a great idea. Bernie, you in?"

"On what?"

"A séance."

"I've studied the occult," Lourdes said with a self-conscious flush. "I know how to do this."

"Black magic an elective across the pond, is it?"

"No, me and some friends just play around with it for fun."

"She looks so normal, too," Bernice said to Karla and Li-Hua.

Li-Hua shook her head. "Forget about it. No way."

"I'm game," Karla said. "I attended a couple of séances in college. It's harmless. What night could be better?"

"Think of the memories," Dixie said. "When's the last time we've done anything wild?"

"Yeah, but you go to El Salvador while we effete gentry glut ourselves and sail around on yachts during summer vacation," Karla said. "Don't the locals believe in ghosts and such? Surely you see funky goings on?"

"From a distance. I'm not exactly brave."

"Pshaw. No way I could stomach the dozen inoculations you've gotta get to enter those countries. Nope, I'm white bread to the core."

"Well, I'm with Li-Hua. I'm tired and it's silly anyway." Bernice stood and went out to the porch. The wind ripped across the water and roared through the trees. She shielded her eyes from a blast of leaves and pine needles. Her hair came free of its barrette and she wondered how crazy that made her appear. Getting in a nightcap smoke was out of the question. She gave up, all but consumed with irritability. Her mood didn't improve when she slammed the door and threw the bolt and discovered Dixie, Karla, and Lourdes cross-legged in a semicircle on the floor.

Li-Hua had crawled into her bunk and sat in shadow, her arms folded. She patted the covers. "Quick, over here. Don't bother with them."

Bernice joined her friend. The two shared a blanket as the fire had diminished to fading coals and the room was colder by the moment. "This is simply . . ." she struggled for words. On one hand, the whole séance idea was unutterably juvenile—yet juxtaposed with her recent bout of nerves, the ominous locale, and the sudden storm, it gained weight, a sinister gravity. Finally, she said, "This is foolish," and was immediately struck by the double meaning of the word.

Ultimately, the ritual proved anticlimactic. Lourdes invoked the spirits of Aunt Dolly and others who'd drowned in the lake, inviting them to signal their presence, which of course they may or may not have done as it was difficult to discern much over the clattering shutters and the wind screeching in the eaves. Dixie, head bowed, almost fell over as she nodded off, eliciting chuckles from all present.

Things began to wind down after that. The cabin was quite warm and cozy and the wine did its trick to induce drowsiness. Again Bernice had decided not to mention her recent bad dreams that revolved around drowning and the ghost of her aunt bobbing to the surface of the lake like a bloated ice cube, then skating across the water, her face black as the occulted moon. Dixie would've laughed and said something about zombie ballerinas, while Karla raised an eyebrow and warned her to lay off the booze. Worst of all, Li-Hua was likely to take it seriously. *So, you've returned to face your childhood demons. Good for you!* No, no, no—far better to keep her mouth shut.

She fell asleep and dreamed of sinking into icy water, of drifting help-lessly as a white figure crowned in a Medusa snarl of hair reached for her. In the instant before she snapped awake tearing at her blankets and gasping for air, she saw her sister's face.

4.

Unhappily, so far as Bernice was concerned, they did indeed embark upon a hike along the cluttered beach directly after breakfast. The Redfield Girls had the shore to themselves, although there were a few small boats on the lake. The sky was flat and gray. It sprinkled occasionally, and a stiff breeze chopped the surface of the water. They picked their way until reaching the farthest point on the north side where a stream rushed over jumbled stones; shaggy bushes and low-hanging alders formed an impenetrable screen between shore and deep forest.

The women rested for a bit in a patch of golden light sifted from a knot-hole in the clouds. Bernice pulled off her shoe and poured out pebbles and sand, and scowled at the blister already puffing on her ankle.

"Don't tell me you thought we'd let you lead us to God's swimming hole and then hibernate all weekend." Dixie sat beside her on a log.

"That's precisely what I thought."

"Silly woman. Hiking is f-u-n!"

"Look at this damned thing on my foot and say that again."

Lourdes and Karla skipped pebbles across the water and laughed. Li-Hua came over and stared at Bernice's blister. "Maybe we should pop it? Let me."

"What the hell are you talking about?"

"You know, to drain the pus."

"For the love of—that's not what you do with a blister," Bernice said. She quickly stuck her shoe on before Li-Hua got any more ideas.

"Yeah, that's crazy talk. You just want to try one of your ancient herbal remedies and see if it works, or if her foot swells like a melon."

Li-Hua shrugged and grinned. She didn't think much of Western medi-cine, a prejudice that had been exacerbated by complications stemming from her hysterectomy, conducted at St. Peter Hospital. Her own grandmother had been an apothecary and lived in perfect health to one hundred and three.

"My husband knew an old fisherman who lived here." Li-Hua's husband, Hung, worked for the state as a cultural researcher. He'd assisted on a demographical study of the region and spent several weeks among the Klallam, and Norwegian and Dutch immigrants who'd lived nearby for decades. "Job Nilsson had a ramshackle cabin over one of these ridges. After Hung interviewed him, we brought him cases of canned goods and other supplies every winter until he passed away. It was sad."

"Yeesh," Dixie said. She'd gone to El Salvador and Nicaragua on many humanitarian missions. "I never knew, Li-Hua. You guys are wonderful." She sprang from her perch and hugged Li-Hua.

"Job wouldn't talk about the lake much. He stopped fishing here in 1973 and went to the river instead. He believed what the Klallam said: that demons were in here, swimming around, watching for intruders. He said most white people believed it was mainly ghosts of those who drowned haunted this place, but he thought that was wrong. Only a few corrupted souls linger here on earth. Or a few who get lost and forget who they are. The rest go to their reward, or punishment."

"Uh-huh," Bernice said. This conversation brought back the creepy feelings. She was frightened and that kindled the helpless anger.

"The spirits are great deceivers. They delight in causing pain and fear. Of course, the spirits are angry about the houses, the motor boats, the trash, and seek to lure anyone they can and drown them."

Bernice shook her head. "Last night you groused at us for telling tales. Now look at you go."

"The cat is out of the bag."

"Huh. Maybe you should put it *back* in the bag."

"That it? The codger was superstitious?" Dixie lighted a cigarette and Bernice's mouth watered.

"His brother Caleb drowned in the Devil's Punch Bowl. Four people saw him fall into the water and disappear. The body was lost, but Job claimed to meet something pretending to be his brother a year later. He was walking along the beach and saw him lying under a pile of driftwood. Job ran toward his brother's corpse, but when he reached it, Caleb sprang from the weeds and slithered into the water, laughing. Job was terrified when he realized the figure didn't really resemble his brother at all. And that's why he stopped fishing here."

"I hope he gave up on moonshine, too," Bernice said.

Lourdes was the one who spotted the rowboat. It lay grounded on the beach, partially obscured by a tangle of driftwood just below their cabin. The women gathered around and peeked inside. Nothing seemed amiss—the oars were stowed and only a pail or two of rainwater slopped beneath the floor-boards.

"It's a rental," Dixie said. "The lodges around here rent skiffs and canoes. Somebody forgot to tie it to the dock."

"I don't think so," Bernice said. The boat was weathered, its boards slightly warped, tinged green and gray. "This thing looks old." Actually, ancient might've been more accurate. It smelled of algae and wood rot.

"Yeah. Older than Andy Griffith," Karla said.

"Maybe it belongs to one of the locals."

"Anything's possible. We'll tell the lodge. Let them sort it out." Dixie tied the mooring rope to a half-buried stump and off they went.

5.

They stopped at the Bigfish to report the abandoned boat and use the show-ers, then drove into Port Angeles for dinner at the Red Devil. When they returned a few hours later, the moon was rising. Bernice and Karla lugged in wood for the fire. Li-Hua fixed hot chocolate and they drank it on the porch.

"The boat's still here," Lourdes said, indicating its dark bulk against the shining sliver of beach.

"Ah, they'll come get it in the morning," Bernice said. "Or not. Who cares."

"I know!" Dixie clapped for attention. "Let's take it for a spin."

"A spin? That would imply the existence of an outboard motor," Karla said.

"Yes, but we'll just use the manual override. It comes with oars."

"I've stuffed my face with entirely too much lobster to take that sugges-tion seriously."

"Don't look at me," Bernice said. "I mean it, Dix. Stop looking at me."

A few minutes later she and Lourdes were helping Dixie shove off.

Li-Hua and Karla waved from the shore, steadily shrinking to a pair of smudges as Dixie pulled on the oars. "Isn't this great?" she said.

Bernice perched in the bow, soon mesmerized by the slap of the oar blades dipping into the glassy surface, their steady creak in the metal eye rings. The boat surged forward and left the rising mist in tatters. She was disquieted by the sensation of floating over a hadal gulf, an insect prey to gargantuan forms lurking in the depths.

Dixie slogged midway to the far shore, then dropped the oars and let the boat drift. "Owwwie! That did it. Shoulda brought my driving gloves." She blew on her hands. "No worries. Bernie, ol' chum, how about 'bailing' us out here?"

"Dream on. This is your baby."

"Omigod, we'll be doomed to cruise these waters for eternity!"

"I'll do it," said Lourdes. The boat tipped precariously as she and Dixie switched places. "So, what do I do?" Dixie gave her a few pointers, and in moments they listed homeward, lurching drunkenly as Lourdes struggled to find her rhythm.

"We're going to capsize," Bernice said, only half joking as their wake churned and spray from the oars wet her hair.

"Uh-oh," Dixie said.

"What uh-oh?" Bernice said. The cabin was growing larger. She looked down again and water was rapidly filling the boat. Dixie was already ankle deep and bailing like mad with a small plastic bucket. "Good grief! It's the plug." All boats were fitted with a plug to drain bilge water when dry-docked. She scrambled aft, catching an oar in the shin. She plunged her arm to the elbow, felt around, searching for the hole, and found it, plug firmly in place.

Bubbles roiled about Lourdes's feet. "Guys . . ." She dropped the oars. Rowing was impossible now as the boat wallowed.

"Oh crap on a stick! I think it's coming apart!"

"We gotta swim for it," Dixie said. She'd already kicked off her shoes. "C'mon Bernie—get ready."

The shore was about seventy yards away. Not so far, but Bernie hadn't swum a lap in years. Her arms and legs cramped with fear, and the darkness swelled and throbbed in her brain. She tasted the remnants of dinner as acid.

Dixie leaped. Lourdes followed an instant later. She stumbled, and she belly flopped. Water gushed over the rails and the boat was a stone headed for the bottom. Bernie held her nose and jumped—the frigid water slammed her kidneys like a fist. She gasped and kicked, thrashing as if through quicksand, and her clothes dragged, made, abruptly, of concrete. In those moments of hyperawareness, she had time to regret all of the cigarettes and booze, to lament spending her days off lying around the yard like a slug. The moon hung too low; it merged with the lake until water and sky reversed. She floundered, trying to orient herself in the great, dark space.

"Lourdes!" She swallowed water and it scorched her sinuses and throat. "Lourdes!" Her voice didn't project, and she began to cough. There was Dixie bobbing like a cork a few yards away, but no sign of her niece. The blaze of moonlight was eclipsed by red and black motes that shot from the corners of her eyes as she gulped air and dove.

On the first try, she found Lourdes in the freezing murk. The girl was feebly making for the surface. Bernice caught the girl's arm, began to tow her along. A distinct point of light flickered at her peripheral vision. It rose swiftly from blackness, so pale it shone as it tumbled toward her, rushed toward her, and gained size and substance. Bernice gazed upon the approaching form with abject wonder. Perhaps she'd fallen into the sky and was plunging toward the moon itself. Terror overcame her—she screamed and a gout of bubbles exploded from her mouth. She brought Lourdes to the surface in one convulsive heave, and then hands hooked beneath her arms and brought her away with them.

Later, in the fetal position upon the small, sharp rocks of the beach, and after Karla shoved the others aside and administered first aid until she spluttered and vomited and breathed on her own, Bernice tried to summon an image of the form she'd seen down there, to perfect its features, and couldn't. Even now, safely ashore and encircled by her comrades, the blurry figure was etched in her mind, and evoked a stark and abiding fear. It had come close, radiating a cold much sharper than the chill water. She squeezed her eyes shut, and rubbed them with her palms in a futile attempt to exorcise this image that had leaked from dreams into the physical world.

Dixie and Li-Hua implored her to go to the clinic. What if she was hypothermic? Bernice shrugged them off—after she regained her senses and hacked the water from her lungs, she felt fine. Weak and shivery, but fine. Lourdes was okay, too, probably better, insomuch as youth seemed to bounce back from anything short of bullet wounds. She huddled with Bernice, eager to relate her tale of near disaster. Her pants cuff had snagged on the rail and she banged her shoulder. Thank the stars for Aunt Bernice and Dixie!

"Guess I owe you one, too," Bernice said as Dixie wrapped her in a blanket and led her to the cabin.

"Not me," Dixie said. "No way I coulda dragged your carcass all the way in on my own. You should've seen Karla go—that old broad can *swim*!"

6.

Karla and Li-Hua suggested pulling stakes and heading home early in light of the traumatic events. Lourdes disappeared outside and Dixie lay in her bunk, inconsolable for cajoling her friends to accompany her on the rickety boat and then nearly getting them all drowned. "I really fouled up," she said. Her voice was rusty from crying into her pillow. "What a jerk I am."

"We should sue the pants off the lodge for owning such a damned leaky boat!" Karla had huffed and puffed her indignation for a good hour.

"We took the boat without asking, didn't we?" Li-Hua said.

"That's beside the point. It's outrageous to keep a death trap lying around. Somebody should give them what for."

Bernice forced herself to rise and go for a walk down to the beach where she smoked a cigarette and watched the sun rise while the moon yet glowed on the horizon. She stubbed the butt of her cigarette on the sole of her shoe. Her eyes were twitchy and dry and her hair was stiff. She shook her fist at the lake, and spat.

Lourdes stepped from the bushes screening the path and came to stand beside her. The girl's expression was different today, more sober; she'd aged five years overnight. The patronizing half smile was wiped from her face. "That is the coldest water I've ever jumped into," she said. "I dreamt about this before."

"You mean the boat sinking?" Bernice couldn't look at her.

"Kind of. Not the boat; other stuff. We were somewhere in the woods—here, I guess. Me, you, some other people, I don't remember. You kept telling the story about Dolly."

"Except I didn't tell the story. Dixie did. She's always been better at talking."

"I got it wrong. Dreams are funny like that. Mom thinks I'm a psychic. Maybe I'm only a partial psychic."

"Your psychic powers convince you to fly over here?"

Lourdes shrugged. "I didn't really analyze it. I just wanted to come see you. It may sound dumb, but on some level I was worried you might be in trouble if I didn't. Looks like I had it backwards, huh?"

Bernice didn't say anything for a while. She watched the water shift from black, to milk, to gold. "I've always had a bit of the sight, too," she said.

"Really?"

"Sometimes, when I was a child, I dreamed things before they happened. Nothing big. I sure couldn't pick lotto numbers or anything. It came and went. I don't get it so much these days."

"Wow. Thanks for telling me. Mom doesn't want to know anything. I confided in her once. Frank put his foot down."

They fell silent and lighted cigarettes. Bernice finished hers. She hesitated, then patted Lourdes's shoulder, turned and walked back to the cabin.

After breakfast at the Bigfish, their mood thawed, and by mid-afternoon everyone agreed to stay—anything less was an unreasonable waste of what promised to be fine weather and several as yet corked bottles of wine.

Indeed, the remainder of the visit was splendid. By day, they set up a badminton net and a crude horseshoe pit and played until dark. Karla and Li-Hua shot two memory cards of photos. Bernice taught Lourdes cribbage and gin rummy. She even managed to power through a book about dream symbolism by candlelight while her companions slept. The book wasn't particularly illuminating in regard to her specific experiences. Nonetheless, she slept with it clutched to her breast like a talisman.

On the final evening, Bernice went with Lourdes to the woodshed to fetch an armload of dry pine to bank the fire. They lingered a moment, saying nothing, listening to the crickets and the owls. From inside came the raucous cries and curses of the latest debate between Dixie and Karla.

Lourdes said, "I haven't thanked you. I was in trouble the other night."

Bernice laughed softly. "Don't worry about it. Nancy would've killed me herself if I'd let you sink. You have no idea how many years she spent freezing by the pool while I had my swim lessons when we were kids."

"That's Mom."

"Yes, well . . ." Bernice cleared her throat. "I think I was hallucinating. Lack of oxygen to the brain."

"Oh?"

"I've been meaning to ask. Did you happen to see anything odd in the water?"

"Besides you?"

"Watch your lips, kid." Bernice smiled, but her hand tightened on the frame of the shed. The pit of her stomach knotted. Last night she'd been under the lake again, and Nancy was with her, glimmering dead white, hands extended. Only, it wasn't Nancy. She'd simply given the figure a face. "No biggie. I sucked in a lot of water. I think a fish swam by. Panicked me a bit."

Darkness had stolen across the water and through the trees, and Lourdes was hidden mostly in shadow, except for where lantern light came from the windows and revealed her hair in halo, a piece of her shoulder, but nothing of her expression. She said, "I didn't see any fish." She was silent for a moment, and when she spoke again her tone was strange. "There was something wrong with that boat."

"I'll say. Probably rotted clean through."

"What I mean is, it wasn't right. It didn't belong here."

Bernice tried to think of a witty response. She wanted to scoff at what Lourdes was hinting. "Oh," she said. "The *Flying Dinghy* of Lake Crescent, eh?"

Lourdes didn't say anything.

7.

Three years passed before the Redfield Girls returned to Lake Crescent. This was Dixie's year to choose and she invited Lourdes, who agreed to join them. Bernice and Li-Hua declined to accompany their friends on the trip, a first since the women had established the yearly tradition. Bernice begged off because the week prior she'd fallen while cleaning her gutters and suffered a broken ankle. It was healing nicely, although it was wrapped in a cast and not fit for bearing any kind of weight. Li-Hua's excuse was that

Hung remained in China on a business trip and someone had to keep an eye on their rambunctious teenage sons, Jerrod and Jules.

Bernice knew better. While Dixie and Karla had quickly gotten over the close call with the rowboat, she and Li-Hua shared a profound antipathy toward the lake; its uncanny emanations repelled them. As for Lourdes, an invitation into the circle was irresistible to a girl of her youth and inexperience, albeit she expressed reluctance to abandon Bernice. In the end, they had a few glasses of wine and Bernice told her to go—no sense watching an old fuddy-duddy lie about all weekend listening to her bones knit.

Bernice spent the whole weekend at home, pruning rosebushes, and riding around on Elmer's sputtering mower. Sunday-morning news predicted a storm. She worked straight through lunch and finished putting away the tools and hosing cut grass stems from her ankle cast minutes before storm clouds blocked out the fading sun. Thunder cracked in the distance and it began to rain. She hobbled to the pantry, searching for flashlights and spare batteries. The power died a few minutes later, as it always did during storms, and she grimaced with smug satisfaction as she lighted a bunch of candles (some of the very same she'd purchased on Saturday!) in the kitchen and her bedroom. She boiled tea on the camp stove Elmer had always kept stashed in the garage, and retired to bed, intent upon reading a few chapters into a pictorial history of the Mima Mounds. The long, long afternoon of yard work put her under before she'd read two pages.

Bernice woke in complete darkness to the wind and rain falling heavily on the frame house. A lightning flash caused the shadows of the trees to stretch long, grasping fingers down the wall and across her blanket. Something thumped repeatedly. She grabbed the flashlight and crawled from bed and went into the living room, leaning on the cheap rubber-tipped cane she'd gotten at the hospital. The front door was wide open. The elements poured through, and all the papers she'd left stacked on the coffee table were flung across the floor. She put her shoulder against the door and forced it shut and threw the deadbolt for good measure.

She fell into an easy chair and waited with gritted teeth for the pain in her ankle to subside. While she recovered, the fact the door had been locked earlier began to weigh heavily on her mind. What was it that brought her awake? The noise of the door banging on the wall? She didn't think so. She'd heard someone call her name.

The storm shook the house and lightning sizzled, lighting the bay windows so fiercely she shielded her eyes. Sleep was impossible and she remained curled in her chair, waiting for dawn. Around two o'clock in the morning, someone knocked on the door. Three loud raps. She almost had a heart attack from the spike of fear that shot through her heart.

Without thinking, she cried, "Lourdes? Is that you?" There was no answer, and in an instant her thoughts veered toward visions of intruders bent on mischief and the spit dried in her mouth. Far too afraid to move, she waited, breath caught, straining to hear above the roar of the wind. The knocks weren't repeated.

8.

Bernice didn't fly to France for Lourdes's funeral. Nancy, mad with grief, wanted nothing to do with her sister. Why hadn't Bernice been there to protect Lourdes? She'd allowed their daughter to go off with a couple of people Nancy and Francois scarcely knew and now the girl was never coming back. As the weeks went by, Nancy and Bernice mended fences, although Francois still wouldn't speak to her, and the boys followed suit. Those were dark days.

She'd gone into a stupor when the authorities gave her the news; ate a few Valiums left over from when she put Elmer in the ground, and buried herself in blankets. She refused to leave the house, to answer the phone, scarcely remembered to eat or shower.

Li-Hua told her more about the accident when Bernice was finally weaned off the tranquilizers and showed signs of life once again.

The story went like this: Dixie had driven Karla and Lourdes to Joyce, a small town a few miles west of Lake Crescent. They ate at a tiny diner, bought some postcards at the general store, and started back for Olympia after dark. Nobody knew what went wrong, exactly. The best guess was Dixie's Subaru left the road and smashed through the guardrail at mile 38—Ambulance Point. Presumably the car went in and sank. Rescue divers came from Seattle and the area was dredged, but no car or bodies were found. There were mutters that maybe the crash happened elsewhere, or not at all, and conjectures regarding drift or muck at the bottom. Ultimately, it amounted to bald speculation. The more forthcoming authorities marked it down as another tragic mystery attributed to the Lake Crescent curse. There were further details that Bernice blocked out, refused to acknowledge. Details about her loved ones' last moments that she shoved into the cellar of her mind as a sanity-saving measure and soon forgot.

Bernice took a leave of absence from work that stretched into retirement. Going back simply wasn't an option; seeing new faces in Dixie and Karla's classrooms, how life went on without missing a beat, gutted her. Li-Hua remained in the counselor's office. She and Hung had come very late to professional life and neither could afford retirement. Nonetheless, everything was different after the accident. The remaining Redfield Girls drifted apart—a couple transferred, three more called it quits for teaching, and the others simply stopped calling. The parties and annual trips were finished. Everybody moved on.

One night that winter, Li-Hua phoned. "Look, there's something I need to tell you. About the girls."

Bernice was lying in bed looking at a crossword puzzle. Her hands trembled and she snapped the pencil. "Are you all right, Li?" Her friend had lost too much weight and she didn't smile anymore. It was obvious she carried a burden, a secret that she kept away from her friend. Bernice knew all along there was more to the story surrounding the accident and she'd pretended otherwise from pure cowardice. "Do you want me to come over?"

"No. Just listen. I've tried to tell you this before, but I couldn't. I was afraid of what you might do. I was *afraid,* Bernie." Li-Hua's voice broke. "Karla called me on the night it happened. None of it made sense; I was groggy and there was a lot of shouting. People sound different when they're scared, so it was a few seconds before I recognized her voice. Karla was panicked, talking very fast. She told me they'd lost control of the car and were in the water. I think the car was actually underwater. The doors wouldn't open. She begged me for help. The call only lasted a few seconds. All of them started screaming and it ended. I dialed 911 and told the operator where I thought they were. Then I tried the girls' cell phones. I just got recordings."

After they disconnected, Bernice lay staring into the glow of the dresser lamp. She slowly picked apart what Li-Hua had said, and as she did, something shifted deep within her. She removed the cordless phone from its cradle and began to cycle back through every recording stored since the previous summer, until she heard the mechanized voice report there was an unheard message dated 2 a.m. the morning of the accident. Since the power had been down, the call went straight to voice mail.

"My God. My God." She deleted it and dropped the phone as if it were electrified.

9.

Once her ankle healed, she packed some things and made a pilgrimage to the lake. The weather was cold. Brown and black leaves clogged the ditches. She parked on the high cliff above the water, the spot called Ambulance Point, and placed a wreath on the guard rail. She drank a couple of mini bottles of Shiraz and cried until the tears dried on her cheeks and her eyes puffed. She got back into the car and drove down to the public boat launch.

The season was over, so the launch was mostly deserted except for a flatbed truck and trailer in the lot, and a medium-sized motorboat moored at the dock. Bernice almost cruised by without stopping—intent upon renting a room at the Bigfish Lodge. What she intended to do at the lodge was a mystery even to herself. She noticed a diver surface near the boat. She idled in front of the empty ticket booth, and watched the diver paddle about, fiddling with settings on his or her mask, and finally clamber aboard the boat.

She sat with the windshield wipers going, a soft, sad unintelligible ballad on the radio. She began to shake, stricken by something deeper than mere sorrow or regret; an ancient, more primitive emotion. Her knuckles whitened. The light drained from the sky as she climbed out and crossed the distance to where the diver had removed helmet and fins. It was a younger man with golden hair and a thick golden beard that made his face seem extraordinarily pale. He slumped on the boat's bench seat and shrugged off his tanks. Bernice stood at the edge of the dock. They regarded each other for a while. The wind stiffened and the boat rocked between them.

He said, "You're here for someone?"

"Yeah. Friends."

"Those women who disappeared last summer. I'm real sorry." The flesh around his eyes and mouth was soft. She wondered if that was from being immersed or from weeping.

"Are you the man who comes here diving for clues?"

"There's a couple of other guys, too. And a company from Oregon. I think those dudes are treasure hunting, though."

"The men from the company."

He nodded.

She said, "I hate people sometimes. What about you? Aren't *you* treasure hunting? Looking for a story? I read about that."

"I like to think of it as seeking answers. This lake's a thief. You know, maybe if I find them, the lives that it stole, I can free them. Those souls don't belong here."

"I had a lot of bad dreams about this lake and my sister. I kept seeing her face. She was dead. Drowned. After the accident, I realized all along I'd been mistaken. It wasn't my sister I saw, but her daughter. Those two didn't have much of a resemblance, except the eyes and mouth. I got confused."

"That's a raw deal, miss. My brother was killed in a crash. Driving to Bellingham and a cement truck rear-ended him. Worst part is, and I apologize if this sounds cruel, you'll be stuck with this the rest of your life. It doesn't go away, ever."

"We're losing the light," she said.

Out in the reeds and the darkness, a loon screamed.

Afterword

The inspiration for "The Redfield Girls" originates from a particularly spooky bit of topography near my own neck of the woods in Olympia, Washington.

A popular tourist destination, Lake Crescent fills a glacial furrow at the foot of Mount Storm King on the Olympic Peninsula. It's a gorgeous locale, abutted by the Olympic National Forest, a region of immense evergreen trees and rugged mountains. One of the coldest and deepest lakes in North America, it is also allegedly cursed. Ancient legends of the

Klallam people have it that the depths are home to malign spirits eager to drag trespassers to their doom. In more recent times, a married couple vanished while driving along the cliffs near the water—some personal items were recovered, but neither they nor their car were ever found. The most famous tale concerns the 1937 murder of a local woman by her husband, who then sank her body in the lake. The corpse surfaced seven years later, preserved by the severe cold of the water as a kind of soap statue, and led to the husband's trial and murder conviction.

Ghosts, demons, mysterious disappearances, and assorted macabre tragedies—such is the dark side of Lake Crescent. "The Redfield Girls" is the first story I've set in this region, but I suspect it won't be the last.

PAT CADIGAN

Between Heaven and Hull

Pat Cadigan has twice won the Arthur C. Clarke Award—for her novels Syn-
ners *and* Fools*—and been nominated for just about every other science fiction and fantasy award. Although primarily known as a science fiction writer
(and as one of the original, and only female, cyberpunks), she also writes
fantasy and horror, which can be found in her collections* Patterns, Dirty
Work, *and* Home by the Sea. *The author of fifteen books, including two
nonfiction and one young adult novel, she currently has two new novels in
progress.*

As soon as the hitchhiker got into the Mondeo, he knew he'd made a mistake. That happened sometimes. After you'd spent several hours on foot, a car would finally, mercifully-thank-you-God swerve into the breakdown lane and stop. You'd approach with caution and when it didn't suddenly pull away in a tire-squealing display of so-called humor, you'd run toward it thinking that your luck must be on the upswing because it was a very nice car, maybe even brand new. The people who rolled down the window would smile at you with clean, friendly faces and ask where you were going, not sounding at all like they were going to give you a Coke spiked with roofies and leave you to wake up in the woods the next morning stripped of all your worldly possessions, including your clothes.

So you'd practically leap into the backseat and even as you were sighing with relief because it was now starting to rain, you'd suddenly realize that the music coming out of the expensive in-car stereo was a live recording of an untalented child's violin recital or Wagner's operas or country music's one hundred best-loved hymns. And as the rain pounded down and late afternoon turned to early evening, you'd have to decide which was more important: being dry or being sane.

In this case, the two women in the front seat were gigglers. They giggled like girls and they did it a lot. It wouldn't have bothered him quite so much if they'd actually been girls, but they were both far from it—early forties at the youngest, probably older. Hardly ancient but definitely too old for giggling.

Of course, he'd already known before he'd climbed in that this might not be the smoothest ride he'd ever taken. From where he'd been standing halfway up the entrance ramp, he'd had an unobstructed view of the car circling the roundabout in the wrong direction—a sure sign that one of his fellow Americans was behind the wheel. It wasn't the first time he'd seen an American do that, nor was it the most cringe-worthy. Sometimes he had been tempted to pretend he was Canadian.

But sweet God, he'd been standing on that damned entrance ramp for so long and it was starting to look like rain.

"Hi, I'm Doni," said the one in the driver's seat—no, that was the *passenger* seat. He kept mixing them up. "And that mad woman behind the wheel is Loretta."

"Hiya." The mad woman winked at him in the rearview mirror. The wind from the half-open window had blown her short, nearly platinum blond hair into a shapeless mess. The other woman had a mass of thick, curly dark hair caught up in a large plastic clip. They were such opposites he couldn't help thinking it had to be deliberate, as otherwise they seemed similar to him. Their giggling certainly was.

"Are you two sisters?" he asked, and winced as they giggled some more.

"Nope, just very old friends," the dark-haired one told him.

"Hey, who are *you* calling *old*?" the other woman demanded with feigned outrage.

"Friends of long standing, then. Is that more acceptable to you, madame?"

"Much better, thank you." The driver flicked another glance at him in the mirror. "So, where are you headed?"

"Aberdeen," he replied, watching big fat raindrops splatter on the windshield.

"We're going to Scarborough. Just might make it by nightfall, too, if we're lucky."

"Dunno, could be asking entirely too much of luck," said the dark-haired woman.

"My geography isn't what it should be," he said. "Is Scarborough that far away?"

"It is if it takes you forty-five minutes to get out of Heathrow after you pick up your rental car," said the blonde.

"Not used to driving here?" he asked.

"One way to put it. You know, Doni actually bet me that you wouldn't get in the car after seeing my little *oops* with the roundabout."

"Well, to be honest, I'm surprised you stopped for me," he replied. "Women almost never do."

"Since we're being honest, it was pure self-interest." The driver's giggle was sheepish. "I was actually hoping you were a Brit and I could get you to take over the driving." Another quick glance at him in the rearview mirror. "I don't suppose you're experienced driving in this country?"

"Sorry. Plus my license is expired. Forgot to renew it before I left."

The dark-haired woman frowned over her shoulder at him. "Jeez, you're just no damned good to anybody, are you?" She managed to keep a straight face just long enough to make him wonder if she were serious. Then both women giggled and he made himself laugh to show he was a good sport. Then all at once she frowned at him again, this time with concern. "You're not buckled up back there, are you? You really ought to be."

He found himself unexpectedly touched by her solicitude. Dutifully, he struggled with the belt, which kept jamming every time he pulled it out. Then, when he finally managed to get it the right length, he couldn't find the buckle.

"Probably wedged down between the cushions," she said. "Just dig in with your fingers."

He tried, hoping she wouldn't notice that he wasn't exactly making a big effort. He'd never liked being strapped to anything, even a car seat, safety or not. "Sorry," he said after a bit.

"Maybe we should pull over so I can try," she said. "My hands are smaller."

"Leave him be, worrywart," said the blonde. "If he were in the front seat, it would be different but the backseat is safer. Tell you what—if it looks like we're gonna crash, I'll sing out ahead of time so you can curl up on the floor. Deal?" She winked at him in the rearview mirror.

"Works for me," he said, making a small salute. Still more giggles, of course, although he didn't find that quite so annoying anymore. Apparently you really could get used to anything, he thought, and anyway, at least they weren't missionaries or opera fans. Not unattractive, either. He couldn't say that if he'd met them at a party or a bar, he wouldn't have been interested.

His gaze met the dark-haired woman's and he realized she had said something to him.

"Pardon? Sorry, I guess I zoned out for a minute there. I must be tireder than I thought."

She gave him a kindly smile. "I said, how long have you been on the road?"

"Quite a while, obviously." He laughed; they giggled.

"No, really. How long? I'm just curious."

"She means nosy," the blonde put in wryly.

"That's OK," he said, sitting back and stretching out. The blonde sat close to the dash, which left him quite a lot of leg room. "When I was in Gdansk, the weather was really good—sunny, very warm. Until you got right to the beach. Then the temperature dropped about twenty degrees. There was this long pier you had to pay to walk out on. That must have been . . . late June, early July, I guess."

"And I thought *I* lost track of time," the blonde chuckled.

"I've given up wearing a watch. I can't keep one longer than ten days, two weeks at most before I lose it or it breaks. I have bad watch karma." The giggles were actually kind of musical, he thought absently; like wind chimes.

"And before Gdansk, where were you?" prodded the dark-haired one.

He had to think about it for a few moments. "Ekaterinburg, in the Urals. It was beautiful but they had this unexpected heat wave and there was no air-conditioning anywhere. I got a ride from a couple who invited me to supper at their lakeside dacha."

"That must have been pretty far out in the country, away from Ekaterinburg."

"Do you know the city?" he asked.

"We've been up and down every street. But only on the Web," she added as he started to ask if she'd been inside any of the ornate Russian Orthodox cathedrals. "Amazing definition. At street level, you can see the texture of the stone buildings so clearly, you'd think you really were there."

"Sounds like pretty heavy surveillance," he said uneasily.

A few dark, curly tendrils fell loose as she shook her head. "Oh, hell, no. It's that company, what's-their-names. They've been sending vans with cameras all over the world to photograph all kinds of cities and then stitching the pictures together to make a virtual diorama."

"Shouldn't that be 'panorama'?" asked the driver.

"Tomayto, tomahto." The dark-haired woman waved a hand carelessly.

"So you went to Gdansk after Ekaterinburg. Didn't stop in Moscow on the way?"

"No," he said, thinking that it seemed kind of foolish now that he hadn't. At the time, however, it had seemed more important to get moving. He waited for them to ask him why he'd passed up the opportunity to see Red Square and the Kremlin but they didn't. In fact, they said very little except to prompt him when his recall turned spotty. They never commented on his memory, either, because they were too polite or they had actually traveled enough themselves to know how sometimes things could blur after a while.

Their interest surprised him as well. He'd have thought listening to him talk about where he'd been and what the weather had been like and what minor, uneventful things he'd done would have bored them to tears. Every so often, he would mention a city—Basel, Berlin, Calais—and they'd perk up as if he'd said a magic word. It was always because they had explored it the same way they had Ekaterinburg, via detailed, high-definition photos on the Web, uploaded by some corporation that was apparently determined to scan the entire world into a computer file.

"I know very little about computers and all that online stuff," he told them after a while. "Sometimes I go to an Internet café to check the news from home or watch a funny film clip but I can't sit still for very long. Fifteen, twenty minutes and I have to get moving."

"Now that's what I call restless," the driver said. No giggling, which seemed rather strange.

"I'm hopeless at remembering things like e-mail addresses and passwords anyway," he went on. "I tried opening an e-mail account once but then I couldn't even remember where I opened it. Forgetful-dot-com. Braindead-dot-com. Memory-like-a-sieve-dot-com—that's what I'd need."

"Well, let's just check if those domains are available," the dark-haired woman giggled. His polite laughter cut off when he saw she had a thin, shiny notebook on her lap.

"Oh, Christ, don't do *that*!" he said, alarmed without knowing why.

"Too late!" she sang. "But it's all moot anyway, those names are all taken."

The blonde gave a surprised laugh. "Seriously? Even memory-like-a-sieve-dot-com?"

"Even that one."

"How can you get on the Web from the car?" he asked, amazed.

"Wireless access," she said, as if that explained everything. "Wow, you really don't get online much do you?" she added, seeing his expression. "Ever thought about getting a BlackBerry—"

"Also known as a CrackBerry," the blonde chuckled.

"—or a netbook," the other woman went on, ignoring her. "Or even a PDA with sat nav."

"I prefer to travel as light as possible," he said.

"The new netbooks aren't even as heavy as a large bottle of water. And a PDA weighs even less."

"Must cost a fortune," he said.

"You'd be surprised."

"Well, it's a fortune if you don't have it to spare," he said, starting to feel slightly defensive. "And it'd just be one more thing for someone to steal. I try not to carry too much that anyone would want to hit me over the head for." He tried a good-natured grin on the dark-haired woman; she didn't smile back.

"Ever thought about not traveling so much?" she asked.

He blinked at her. "Pardon?"

"Just getting off the road, taking up residence at a fixed address?"

"Waking up in the same place every morning," added the blonde, her gray-green eyes twinkling at him in the rearview mirror. "Someplace with a door you keep the key to, so you can have nice things."

He sat back without answering.

"You've really never thought about that?" the dark-haired woman said incredulously.

"No. And it's not something I really want to discuss," he said, trying to keep his tone firm but pleasant.

The dark-haired woman started to say something else but the blonde talked over her. "OK, forget we said anything. Really."

"Thank you," he said with pointed formality. The dark-haired woman looked frustrated as she turned around to face forward. The small computer on her lap was still open but he couldn't see what was on the screen.

Abruptly, she turned back to him. "A PDA with sat nav would help you a lot, though. You'd always know where you are and how to get wherever you wanted to go. You could find the most direct route like that." She snapped her fingers.

"I'm not always big on the most direct route," he said, unconsciously digging his heels into the carpeting.

"Then you could find the least direct if you wanted."

"I'd rather be surprised," he said, politely obstinate. "You know, I've had people try to sell me on this stuff before. The virtues of high-tech hitchhiking, Goo-Goo maps or whatever it's called. I'm just not into it. Sat nav—what's that? Satellite navigation? You connect to *satellites* to find your way around one minute and the next you're worrying about how your privacy's being invaded? What's *that* about?"

Nobody said anything for a long moment. Then the driver cleared her throat. "The man's got a point."

"Guess I'll have that ID implant taken out of my arm," said the dark-haired woman.

He was horrified. "You have an ID implant in your arm?"

Both women burst into hearty giggles. "Omigod, *no!*" said the dark-haired woman when she could speak. "It's something that fancy exclusive clubs have been doing for super-VIP members."

"I don't believe you," he said. "No one would do that, not even the craziest crazy-rich. That's got to be some kind of urban legend."

"I don't think so," said the dark-haired woman, still laughing.

"Of course, if it were, it wouldn't be the first time you fell for one of those," said the blonde. She gave him another wink in the rearview mirror. Was he supposed to be in on some joke or did she just have a nervous tic? "Or the second or third. Or fourth—"

"All right, that's enough. You don't have to rub my nose in it."

"Which 'it'?" laughed the driver. "The tiny Mexican dog that turns out to be a rat or the cobras in the fur coat? Or—"

"I *said*, that's *enough!*" The dark-haired woman tried to sound stern but giggled instead. "I guess that's why I like the high-tech stuff so much. Hardware, hard data, hard facts."

"Hard ass," he added before he could think better of it. Immediately he tried to apologize but couldn't make himself heard over their giggles.

"This guy's definitely got *your* number, Doni," the blonde said when she had caught her breath.

"No shit." The dark-haired woman was still laughing. "And please, don't apologize," she added to him. "That was a good one."

His smile was more like a grimace. It wasn't *that* good, he thought. Maybe he had tapped into some subtext he was unaware of, some secret in-joke that colored everything for them. That would certainly account for all the giggling. Except in-jokes were never as funny to anyone on the outside. It might be time to get out of the car and go his own way, he thought uneasily.

As if catching the flavor of his thoughts, the blonde slowed down and pulled into the breakdown lane.

"Is something wrong?" he asked, bracing himself on the seat as she twisted around to look at him.

"Not at all," she said cheerfully. "It's just that there's an interchange coming up where our routes diverge. If you want to take a more direct route to Aberdeen then we should leave you off there so you can pick up another ride. *Or . . .* " She made a small flourish with one hand to punctuate her dramatic pause. "You can come with us and see the Humber Bridge."

Both women were looking at him with eager, expectant expressions. "Is there something special about the Humber Bridge?"

The women glanced at each other briefly. "You've never seen it," the dark-haired woman said to him.

"Otherwise you wouldn't have asked," the blonde added.

"It's *gorgeous,*" said the dark-haired woman.

"A gorgeous bridge?" he asked, skeptical.

"Absolutely," replied the blonde. "I know, it's hard to believe. I didn't believe it myself when Doni first told me the first time I came here. But then I saw it. If there are bridges in heaven, my man, this is what they look like."

He smiled, still doubtful. "How far is it from where we are now?"

She turned away to look at something on the dashboard. "Sat nav says only a few miles. It's not that far out of *our* way—crossing the bridge will take us to Hull and Scarborough's just north of that. But we can leave you off at a spot where you can pick up a ride going west, back toward Leeds."

"Shouldn't I just keep going north with you and try to get a ride out of Scarborough?"

"You'll probably end up going to Whitby and having to pick up yet another ride from there," the dark-haired woman advised him.

"Tomayto, tomahto," he said, making them giggle. "Like I said, I'm not all that big on taking the most direct route anywhere."

"Your choice," said the blonde. "But if you end up having to spend the night in Whitby, eat some garlic for supper so Dracula won't bite you."

"Dracula?" he asked, baffled.

"Yeah. That's where he came ashore after leaving Transylvania," said the dark-haired woman matter-of-factly. "You didn't know?"

"No, but that would have been about a hundred years ago, wouldn't it?" He chuckled, sitting back as the blonde pulled the car onto the road again.

"Yeah, but that doesn't matter with Dracula. He's undead."

"I thought he got staked and turned into ashes or smoke or something."

The dark-haired woman shook her head emphatically. "Dracula *always* comes back."

"Bela Lugosi's dead," he replied, unperturbed. "There's even a song about it."

"Bela, sure. But not Dracula."

He couldn't tell if she were really kidding around or not; she was keeping a straight face again but this time she showed no sign of breaking. He looked at the rearview mirror, waiting to see if the blonde would wink at him. When she finally did glance up, it was only for half a second and her eyes told him nothing.

What the hell, he thought; it was a strange world, made more so by the people in it. He'd ridden with atheists who believed in ghosts and people who thought astrology was another branch of astronomy. These probably weren't the only two otherwise sane people who thought *Dracula* was a documentary. He shifted so he could look between the seats at the road ahead and what he saw scared him a hell of a lot more than ghosts or vampires.

The road was far too narrow to accommodate their car and the one coming toward them going the other way, even if the latter had not been towing a trailer the size of an elephant. He opened his mouth to say as much but his voice wouldn't come. Before he could cower on the floor in the fetal position, the blonde slowed down and steered to the left.

"Inhale!" she sang out cheerfully. He obeyed without thinking and held his breath as he watched the other car and trailer cruise past with what looked like less than an inch to spare.

"Close one," said the dark-haired woman. "You sure we didn't scrape some paint off?"

"It looks closer than it was," said the blonde.

"No, it doesn't," he said shakily. "When did we leave the highway?"

"We didn't," the blonde told him. "If we were in the U.S., we'd be lost in the sticks. In rural England, this is a major artery."

"Warn me next time we're gonna do that, so I can curl up on the floor and pray." He tried to laugh with them and couldn't.

. . .

Fifteen minutes later, the blonde pulled the car onto the dirt shoulder. "Behold," she said. "The Humber Bridge."

He sat forward and gazed through the windshield, all but awestruck in spite of himself. "Suspension bridge" seemed too plain a term for the structure that spanned the water under the late-afternoon sun. Had the builders imagined it this way—a mile-long structure of metal, stone, and asphalt that would look somehow as elegant as a section of spiderweb? The suspension appeared almost delicate and yet strong enough to hold anything, even a piece of the world.

Abruptly, he shook off the sensation of dreaminess that had been creeping at the edges of his mind and rubbed his eyes hard. He looked at the bridge again; the clouds had bunched up again, cutting off the late-afternoon sunlight, and mist was beginning to build up.

"See? Amazing sight, isn't it."

He nodded silently, unsure which woman had spoken to him. The car was moving again and they were heading toward the bridge. As they got closer, he saw that it wasn't anywhere nearly as narrow as it looked from a distance. That was a relief; no danger that they'd go over the side and end up in the water trying to pass another car and trailer.

Before they were even halfway across, however, the mist had built up so thickly that the rest of the bridge ahead of them had disappeared. He was about to suggest that the blonde should put on the headlights when, to his horror, she brought the car to a complete stop.

"What are you doing?" he asked, his voice rising with fear as she put on the emergency brake.

"This is where you get off," she said as the dark-haired woman opened her door and climbed out. She pushed the back of her seat forward and leaned in to look at him.

"Come on, you heard Loretta," she said.

"Are you two crazy? You want me to get out in the middle of—"

"The sat nav's never wrong," the blonde said. "Now hurry up. You've got less than a minute."

"Till what—I get hit by a car in the fog?"

The dark-haired woman leaned in and grabbed hold of the front of his shirt. He tried to draw back and discovered that she was a hell of a lot stronger than she looked. She dragged him out of the car and shoved him against the rail that divided the road from the pedestrian walkway, tossing his backpack at him so hard he nearly fell.

"What are you *doing*?" he demanded.

The dark-haired woman paid no attention, looking up into the mist. Abruptly, she grabbed his arm and pulled him closer to her. "Just shut up and stand there," she snapped.

He reached for her but she drew back and his hand closed on empty air. Angry, he took a step toward her, reaching for her again. The next thing he knew, he was falling, rolling over and over down a cold, muddy incline covered with wet leaves. He came to rest flat on his back, looking up at the night sky. Somewhere nearby, a truck rumbled by doing seventy, air-horn fading as the pitch dropped.

Stunned, he pushed himself to his feet and struggled up the incline. Another truck blew past as he reached the side of the road. Route 2A—he knew it immediately. He knew every inch of it; it was still the best place to catch a ride with one of the many long-haul truckers avoiding the newer interstate so as not to get weighed. Or someone traveling on business in a company car who preferred the old highway for the quality of the roadside cafés.

He brushed himself off as best he could, shrugged on his backpack, and stuck out his thumb, thinking he must have been pretty tired to fall asleep in a ditch.

.   .   .

"All gone," said Doni, climbing back into the passenger seat and slamming the door.

"I just wish he'd stay gone," Loretta grumbled. She released the emergency brake and inched the car forward cautiously, watching the side-view mirror for anything coming up behind her before she pulled all the way onto the lane again.

"Never mind that now," Doni said. "As soon as we get off the bridge, we're in Hull and I for one would like to find the road out of it this time instead of driving around and around in circles for an hour."

"Hey, it could be worse," said Loretta good-naturedly. "At least I know how to find reverse gear on this thing now."

"Shut up and drive already."

ʃ Afterword ʃ

If there's anything I love other than chocolate, a wild party, and the love of a good cat (to name but a few things I cherish), it's an urban legend, especially if there's a possible supernatural angle to it. Great stories to tell after dark and into the night, when you're too tired to be much of a hard-headed realist, and the shadows are long and deep enough so that you think you might have seen something moving out of the corner of your eye.

Or you can tell them right out in the light of day on a long car trip. Especially if the long car trip is exceptionally long, much longer than it should be.

In 1993, Ellen Datlow and I took a long car trip from London to Scarborough. We had no idea how long it would be, although the fact that it took me forty-five minutes to find my way out of Heathrow Airport with the rental car should have given us some idea. We did not reach Scarborough for another eight hours (the last forty-five minutes of which we spent trying to find the parking lot for our hotel). In between, we had An Adventure.

In a perfect world, it would have been this one. A Phantom Hitchhiker, after all, would have no trouble hitching all around the world. If the Web can spread computer viruses, why can't GPS spread phantoms?

We did see a few hitchhikers. One of them did watch as we zoomed the wrong way around a roundabout (if you're going the wrong way, you'd better do it fast). Then, as we barreled up the entrance ramp where he was standing, he very deliberately pulled his thumb in, put his hand in his pocket, and averted his gaze. I doubt he was a phantom. But if he was, perhaps there are also two phantom American women in a phantom rented Ford Mondeo still driving around and around in a phantom Hull, desperately trying to find their way out.

P.S. When my license finally expired, I gave it a Viking's funeral.

RAMSEY CAMPBELL

Chucky Comes to Liverpool

Ramsey Campbell has been described as "Britain's most respected living horror writer," and he has been given more awards than any other writer in the field, including the Grand Master Award of the World Horror Convention, the Lifetime Achievement Award of the Horror Writers Association, and the Living Legend Award of the International Horror Guild. His most recent novels are The Darkest Part of the Woods, The Overnight, Secret Story, The Grin of the Dark, Thieving Fear, Creatures of the Pool, *and* The Seven Days of Cain. *His short fiction has been collected in* Waking Nightmares, Alone with the Horrors, Ghosts and Grisly Things, Told by the Dead, *and* Just Behind You, *and his nonfiction is collected as* Ramsey Campbell, Probably. *His novels* The Nameless *and* Pact of the Fathers *have been filmed in Spain. His regular columns appear in* All Hallows, Dead Reckonings, *and* Video Watchdog. *He is the president of the British Fantasy Society and of the Society of Fantastic Films.*

Ramsey Campbell lives on Merseyside with his wife, Jenny. His pleasures include classical music, good food and wine, and whatever's in that pipe. His website is www.ramseycampbell.com.

Campbell is a writer whose work has been consistently excellent, despite its quantity. His influence has been felt over the several decades since he started publishing (originally perhaps overinfluenced by Lovecraft when very young), and his current output hasn't faltered. Most of his short fiction takes place in England.

As Robbie watched his mother he felt ten years old, but it wasn't unwelcome for once. She looked as she used to when they played board games together; her eyes would calm down while her face hid its lines until she seemed no older than she was, hardly twice the age he'd racked up now. She'd been happy to concentrate on just one thing, and it included him. He was buoyed up by the memory until she glanced away from the computer screen in the front room and saw him.

Did she think he was spying on her through the window, the way his father had after they'd split up? Her head jerked back as if her frown had pinched her face hard, and Robbie hurried to let himself into the house. Her bicycle and rucksack had narrowed the already narrow hall. As he dumped his schoolbag on the stairs she was snatching pages from the printer, so hastily that one sailed out of her grasp. "Leave it, Robbie," she said.

"I'm only getting it for you."

It was a cinema poster headed **CHUCK IN THE DOCK**. Most of it consisted of a doll's wickedly gleeful round young face, which was held together with stitches that looked bloody even in black and white. Whatever it was advertising would be shown over the weekend at the Merseyscreen multiplex as part of the Liberating Liverpool arts festival, which was all Robbie had time to learn before his mother reached for the sheet. "Well, now you've had a good look after you were told not to," she said.

"What's all that for?"

"Something you mustn't see."

"I just did."

"That isn't clever. That's nothing but sly." Once she'd finished giving him a disappointed look she said "It's about films I don't want you ever to watch."

There were so many of those he'd lost count, if he was counting—any with fights or guns or knives, which could make him behave like boys did, or bombs, though mostly grownups used those, or language, which didn't seem to leave him much. "More of them," he said.

"I won't have you turning into a man like your father. Too many of you think it's your right to bully women and do a lot worse to them." Before Robbie dared to ask what she was leaving unsaid, which was very little where his father was concerned, she added "I'm not saying you're like that yet. Just don't be ever."

"Why did you print all that out? What's it for?"

"It's time we took more of a stand." He guessed she meant Mothers Against Mayhem as she said "They're evil films that should never be shown. They were supposed to be banned everywhere in Liverpool. They get inside children and make them act like that."

"Like what?"

"Like that thing," she said and poked the pages she'd laid facedown on the table. "Now that's all. You're bullying me." She gazed harder at him while she said "Promise me you'll never watch any of those films."

"Promise."

"Let's see your hands."

He felt younger again, accused of being unclean. While he hadn't crossed his fingers behind his back, he didn't think he had quite promised either. Eventually she said "You'd better put dinner on. We've a meeting at Midge's."

Midge was the tutor on her assertiveness course and the founder of Mothers Against Mayhem. Robbie sidled past the bicycle to the kitchen, which was even smaller than the front room, and switched on the oven. He still felt proud of learning to cook, though he would never have said so at school. He only wished his mother wouldn't keep reminding him that his father was unable or unwilling even to boil an egg. He watched bubbles pop on the surface of the casserole of scouse, a spectacle that put him in mind of a monster in another sort of film he wasn't meant to view. Gloves too fat for a killer in a film to wear helped him transfer the casserole to the stained mat the table always sported. "Mmm," his mother said and "Yum," despite eating less and faster than Robbie. "Enough for dinner tomorrow," she declared. "Have you got plenty of homework?"

"A bit. A lot really."

"Give it all you've got." She was already shrugging her rucksack on. "I don't know how late I'll be," she said as she wheeled her bicycle to the front door. "If I'm not here you know when to go to bed."

He left the stagnant casserole squatting on its mat while he washed up the dinner items before making for the front room. Like the television, the computer was inhibited by all the parental locks his mother could find. He logged on to find an essay about Liverpool poets, and changed words as he copied it into his English homework book. He was altering the last paragraph when his mobile rang.

It no longer had a Star Wars ringtone since his mother decided that was about war. Robbie didn't give peace much of a chance—he silenced the chorus before they had time to chant all they were saying. "Is that Duncan Donuts?" he said.

"If that's Robin Banks."

His father had named Robbie for a Liverpool footballer, but now his mother told people he was called after a singer. "My mam's with your mam," Duncan said. "All mams together."

"The midge got them."

"More like the minge did."

This went too far for Robbie's tastes. "What are you doing tonight?"

"What do you think? I'm in the park."

"Just finishing my homework."

"Wha?" Duncan improved on this by adding "Doing your housework?"

"Homework," Robbie said, not without resentment. "I'm on the last lap."

"Whose?" Duncan didn't wait for an answer. "Hurry up or I'll of smoked it all."

Robbie found some words to change as he transcribed the paragraph. Shutting the computer down, he hurried out of the house. Across the road Laburnum Place was just a pair of stubby terraces of houses almost as compressed as his, but the next street—Waterworks Street—led to the park. A wind urged clouds across the black October sky while another brought a thick stink up from the grain silos at the Seaforth docks. Robbie heard explosions and saw violent glares along the cross streets, but war hadn't broken out yet; they were premature fireworks, and the huge prolonged crash behind him wasn't the work of a bomb—it was another delivery of scrap at the yard beyond the Strand shopping mall.

A pedestrian crossing guarded by nervous amber beacons ended at the park gates. Shadows of bushes sprawled across the concrete path leading to a disused bandstand. Sleepy pigeons fluttered on the cupola as if waiting to compete for a position on the birdless weather vane. There was no sign of Duncan inside the railings that encircled the bandstand, but Robbie located him by the smell of skunk.

The other thirteen-year-old was sitting on the balustrade at the top of a wide flight of steps that climbed beside a bowling green. Above him a noseless whitish statue on a pedestal brandished the stump of a wrist like the victim of a maniac with a cleaver. Behind the statue a deserted basketball court was overlooked by houses at least twice the size of Robbie's. Duncan must have watched him search around the bandstand, since the vantage point commanded a view in every direction. Robbie ran up the steps two at a time as leaves slithered underfoot, crunching like a baby's bones. "Give us some," he said.

Though Duncan hadn't finished the fat joint, perhaps he had already smoked one. He took a drag before passing Robbie the remains. "It's fucking special, that," he gasped as he laboured to contain the smoke.

Robbie inhaled as much as he could and held it until he had to let some of it out through his nose. More emerged in a series of belches while Duncan had another toke. "You're right," Robbie said, or someone using his voice did.

"Wha?"

"It's special."

"Fucking special."

"Fucking," Robbie had to agree as, with a rumble, the world started to collapse. It was another crash of scrap down by the river, but he could barely hold on to that sense of it. The statue pointed the gun barrel of its arm at a silhouetted tree, bits of which swelled up to flap across the park. Fallen leaves cawed as a tree took them back, and he was afraid he'd smoked too much too soon. In a bid to recover control of the teeming interior of his skull he said "Do you know what they're talking about?"

"The crows? They's saying they's black. Respect, man," Duncan called to them.

"Not them." Robbie laughed, but it didn't help much. "The mams," he said. "Can't hear them. Can you?"

"Course I can't," Robbie said, hoping their voices wouldn't invade the cavern above his eyes. "I know what they're disgusting, though."

He wasn't sure if he'd intended to use the wrong word. "Wha?" Duncan said.

"The most evilest film anyone's ever made anywhere ever."

Duncan passed him the smouldering roach. As the tip reddened like a warning light he said "Bet I know which."

Robbie exhaled the token toke as if he were anxious to discover "Which?"

"Chucky. One of his."

The idea lit Duncan's face up. It glared pale as plastic, and lines like stitches pinched his red eyes narrow while his teeth gleamed unnaturally white. The jagged lines were shadows of twigs cast by a firework in the sky, however much they lingered, and Robbie tried to erase them by asking "How did you know that?"

"Give us that if you're not having it." Duncan sucked the roach down to his fingertips and doused it on his tongue and threw his head back to swallow it. At last he said "I know everything, that's why. You turn into a puppet if you watch those films."

"Films can't do that. They're just films."

"Those ones can. It started round here."

Robbie had a notion that he already knew all this, and yet he had to ask "What did?"

"Two kids killed a littler one like Chucky does. It was up the road when my mam was living with my real dad before they had me. And then some bigger kids tortured some girl and they were listening to Chucky when they did. A man that had a shop with Chucky videos by the Strand, someone smashed the window and stabbed him with the glass. Chucky does that to people, and a kid in Liverpool stabbed his mam's friend and said Chucky made him. And there was a Paki shop up the road they set fire to because he had magazines with Chucky in them."

Robbie was distracted by a sense of being spied upon. The watchful face was on a screen. He glanced toward it and saw curtains bring the film to an end—no, fall shut at the window of a house beyond the basketball court. "Want to see him?" Duncan said.

Robbie saw shadows clawing their way up through the concrete paths. Pigeons shivered as they strutted across the dim stage of the bandstand like the opening act of a show whose star performer was about to appear. Surely their feathers were only trembling in the wind. "Where?" he risked asking.

"At mine next time they have a meeting."

"You've never got those films."

"I can get them whenever I want them, and lots of others she doesn't like too."

"Why don't we get some of those? Can you get—"

"You're not scared of Chucky, are you?" Duncan's grin widened as if stitches were about to split his cheeks. "Godzillions of kids have watched him and they haven't done anything. Even girls," he said and let his grin drop. "If we smoke enough we'll be too stoned for him to make us." His gaze strayed past Robbie, and he slipped down from the balustrade. "Time we went," he said.

Robbie twisted around to see red and blue fireworks in the gateway beyond the basketball court. They were the roof lights of a police car, and Duncan had already dodged behind the cleaver victim's plinth. "Don't go that way," Robbie had to whisper in case the crows raised the alarm. "Some-one in those houses called the police."

"I'm not going. I'm gone," Duncan said and crouched lower. "You go somewhere else."

Robbie was sure that if he encountered the police his face would betray him, grinning too much while he struggled not to grin. He retreated down the steps and showed Duncan his severed head. "Catch you at school. Me, not the police."

"They won't bother much about kids having a smoke. Wait till they've gone and we'll skin up again."

"You can," Robbie said and ran down the steps, desperate to leave behind the swarms of beetles that crunched underfoot. The police might hear that, or the applause his sprint past the bandstand earned from his pigeon audience. He skidded to a halt at the gates that framed the pedestrian crossing, where the beacons were trying to measure his pulse, and then he dashed across the road. Lights flared down the cross streets, but they were fireworks, not police speeding to cut him off. Nobody grabbed him from behind as his key scrabbled to let him into the house.

How long did he have to spend at perfecting the use of the toothbrush on the teeth a face was baring in the mirror? Only the fear that his mother would see that he'd changed sent him to bed. The bed was a boat in which he was floating away from explosions on a beach, and then he was brought home by the soundtrack—the thud of the front door, the trundling of the bicycle along the hall, the thump of the dropped rucksack. Other noises followed—some that he was embarrassed to overhear—but the impact of the rucksack left an echo in his skull. It brought him out of his room once he believed his mother was asleep.

A streetlamp lowered its bulbous head to watch him through the window over the front door. Suppose his mother had left the pages with Midge? They were in the rucksack, and he took them into the front room. Since he couldn't risk switching the light on, he tiptoed to the window and unfolded the crumpled wad in the glare from the street. Except for the poster for a showing of all five Chucky films and a talk about them, the sheets were copies of newspaper reports. Fifteen years ago but less than a mile away, two boys not even his age had tortured a toddler to death. Several newspapers blamed a Chucky film, and one said **For the sake of ALL our kids . . . BURN YOUR VIDEO NASTY.** The bold letters seemed to glisten like the stitches on Chucky's face. He wasn't so easily destroyed, even if the cinemas in Liverpool had banned him. He'd made some young kidnappers use his voice while they were torturing a girl, and it had been Chucky's idea for a seven-year-old Liverpool boy to stab his mother's friend twenty-one times with a kitchen knife. Newspapers had tried to have him stopped, but two more films had been made about him, though they hadn't been shown in Liverpool. Now he was getting his way there too. No wonder he was grinning, and as Robbie stared into the gleeful eyes the expression tugged at his own mouth.

It must be all right to watch the films when you were old enough—otherwise the dockland cinema wouldn't be allowed to show them. The showing was for adults only, but videos didn't need to be. If Duncan could watch them, Robbie could; he wasn't going to let his mother make his friend despise him. He was years older than any of the boys Chucky had manipulated. Maybe they'd all been young enough to play with dolls and believe in them along with Christmas and fathers and the other things that went away as you grew up. Being frightened of films must do, and it was time it did.

Robbie folded the pages and stowed them in the rucksack and took his grin to bed.

He always felt dull the morning after he'd had a smoke, but his mother brightened him. "Good job we've got that dinner," she said over breakfast. "We're at Midge's again. They have to be stopped, those films."

She was on her way to work at Frugo in the mall by the time he left the house. He joined the parade of boys and girls in black and white, which seemed to lead to a funeral for the past—a Liverpool history lesson where most of his classmates were silent as mourners. He didn't have a chance to speak to Duncan until the morning break. As they emerged into the corridor Duncan said "I've got them."

"Chucky."

As Duncan's grin confirmed this, a girl they didn't even know demanded "What about him?"

"We're going to see him," Robbie said.

"My mother says nobody should out of respect."

"That's what crows get," said Duncan.

She and her friend blinked blankly in unison. "They'll bring him back," the other girl said with an extravagant shudder.

"Who will?" Robbie protested in case he was being accused.

"Anyone that watches him."

"Anyone that does when they know they shouldn't," said her friend. "That's like trying to call him up."

"It's like calling up a demon so you'll get possessed," the first girl said.

"These won't, though."

Their scorn provoked Robbie to blurt "Why won't we?"

"They'll never let you in to see those films."

"We don't care. We—"

"We'll get in anyway," Duncan interrupted. "Chucky'll let us in so we can see him."

He mustn't want the girls to know about the viewing session at his house. He wasn't quite as reckless as he liked Robbie to think. The girls scoffed at him and ran into the schoolyard as Duncan muttered "I've got two for tonight. I'll text you when."

For the rest of the day Robbie was dry-mouthed and brittle-skulled and barely able to sit still. He had to at dinner so that his mother wouldn't notice. "Lots of homework again?" she said.

"Like last night."

This was cleverer than usual, because she didn't realise. He must be growing up. "Never mind, you've got all evening," she told him.

He was altering an article about the slums of Victorian Liverpool when his mobile took a message. *shes gon cum ruond*, it said.

Comming, Robbie responded. His head tingled and throbbed while he searched for words to change so that he could leave the house. Televisions relayed images from room to room all the way along the street to the Jawbone Tavern. Duncan and his mother lived in a house as small as Robbie's almost opposite the pub. His friend and a smell of skunk met Robbie at the front door. "Better be ready for this," Duncan said.

Robbie hesitated, only to see several men emerging from the pub for presumably another kind of smoke. Duncan raised two fingers, displaying the joint and gesturing at the men. "Get some of that. Last night's was for wimps."

"Not out here. Someone might see."

"I don't want her smelling it in the house." With a protracted red-eyed look Duncan said "Go out the back."

He needn't make it seem as if Robbie's caution were the problem. Robbie followed him along the hall, which at least was free of bicycles, and through a kitchen cluttered with furniture into the yard. He had a manly toke that made him thoroughly aware of the spectators—upstairs windows, all of them lifeless except for the wailing of a child somewhere he couldn't locate. Before he and Duncan finished the joint he'd had enough of the windowless cell above which fireworks clawed at the sky on his behalf. "Where's Chucky, then?" he said.

"Waiting for you."

Duncan meant for both of them, of course. He led Robbie to the front room, where a plump couch and two undernourished chairs were miming patience at a blank television. The chair that had been on less of a diet was occupied by a romance of the Liverpool slums, while a woman's orange cardigan sprawled across half of the couch. Duncan slipped a disk into the player and lounged beside the cardigan. "Chuck that," he said.

Robbie laid the rumpled paperback on the carpet and propped his spine—more especially the cumbersome head it was sprouting—against the chair as *Child's Play* started on the screen. That was the name of the film and, he supposed, what you called the mischief that the Chucky doll got up to once a killer's spirit hid inside it. Why did everyone blame the boy who owned the doll? Why couldn't they see that the doll was pretending to be him? They even took him to a psychiatrist for the doll to kill. At last the boy's mother caught Chucky misbehaving and the boy helped throw him on a fire, burning him for the sake of all the kids as the paper said you should, though the mother still had to blow him to bits with a gun. Robbie was relieved she'd seen the truth at last. As he let go of the bony arms of the chair, which had apparently been bruising his hands for some time, Duncan said "Wimp."

"Who is?"

"Him, going crying to his mam. Hope the other one's better."

How could the doll come back? It had grown its stitches now, but this wasn't even its second film, and so Robbie couldn't tell what had revived it. It killed a woman who used to go with the killer, and then it put her inside a girl doll. As that one began to speak, a noise crept into the room—giggling that ballooned into shrieks. "What's so funny?" Robbie was panicked into asking.

"It's Marge out of the Simpsons."

At once Robbie recognised the croaky female voice from his mother's favourite cartoon show. He felt isolated with the sight of Marge Simpson disguised as a doll that helped Chucky kill people. Eventually she was burned alive, which didn't finish her off, and Chucky was exhaustively shot once again despite shouting "I'll be back." Didn't someone else say that? How many films had Chucky and his partner taken over? A baby or a bloody doll popped out of her to end the film. Duncan ejected the disk and set about searching the cable channels, which fluttered past like slides snatching at the chance to move until Robbie cried "He's there."

Duncan jumped up, and the cardigan cowered away from him, flailing an armless arm. "Who?" he snarled, dashing to the window.

"Chucky. Not out there."

Duncan shut the curtains and glared at Robbie, whether for unnerving him or because he hadn't pointed out that passersby could see what they were watching. "That's not him."

"It's one of him," Robbie protested, but as the grinning doll sprang from under a boy's bed Duncan poked the information button to reveal it was a Spielberg film. It was meant to be about a poltergeist, which didn't reassure Robbie. "I'd better get home before she does," he said.

Duncan grinned like Chucky. "You're never scared of your mam."

"I'm not scared of any fucker or any fucking thing."

"Better believe I'm not. My dad tried to make me scared of stupid fucking Chucky. Not my real dad, the one I got for my birthday when I was four."

"What did he do?"

"Never mind what he done." Having stared at Robbie, Duncan added "Said Chucky would get me if I was bad. That's what they used to tell kids."

Had someone once told Robbie that? It seemed uneasily familiar. "They didn't know what they were on about," Duncan said. "That's not how Chucky works."

He meant in the films, of course—he couldn't mean anything else. "See you at school," Robbie said.

"Shut it on your way out. I'm going to watch him give the doctor shocks again."

The street was deserted. Lamps patched the pavements with light, which mouldered on the roofs of parked cars. If Robbie were a girl or in a film he might be daunted by the gaps between the vehicles, where a small jerky figure could dart out as its victim reached one of the stretches of pavement the lamps didn't entirely illuminate. The only place he had to look for Chucky was on all the televisions, and he was lingering outside a window to see that no doll attacked the young couple in bed on the screen when a woman in an armchair caught sight of him. As she sprang to her feet he fled home. She didn't chase him, but did she know where he lived? Suppose she told his mother? She couldn't say he'd been looking for Chucky; nobody knew that, not even Duncan. Chucky was safe in his head where nobody would notice him.

The house was unlit, which meant that Robbie's mother wouldn't see him until he had a chance to sleep off any guilt that might escape onto his face. It didn't look guilty in the bathroom mirror, where it foamed at the mouth while the toothbrush polished its grin. He was in bed well before his mother came home, though he couldn't sleep. If he'd been allowed a computer in his room he would have played on it, but the games might have been too violent for his mother's taste; she'd decided even board games were ag-gressive. He slept once the grinning doll subsided inside the jack-in-the-box of his head.

He thought he was behaving normally at breakfast, however dull his head felt, until his mother said "What's the matter, Robbie? Why are you looking like that?"

"I'm not looking like anything."

"Your eyes are. Aren't you sleeping?"

"It's all the stuff you've been saying about Chucky."

"I won't again. Don't worry, we'll be getting rid of him." As a further comfort she said "My turn to make dinner."

So there wasn't a meeting. Perhaps that was why Duncan didn't seek him out but only gave him a grin across the classroom. He joined him at the morning break, when the girl who'd accosted them yesterday caught up with them in the schoolyard. "Hope you're happy now," she said.

Robbie grinned, though it felt inadvertent if not meaningless. "Why?" Duncan demanded.

"Someone's brought your Chucky back."

"We haven't lost him," Robbie blurted as Duncan said louder "Who's brought what where?"

"They've got him in a shop down by the Strand, in the window where everyone can see him."

"They've got no respect," her friend said.

"Nobody can stop him. He'll get everywhere," Duncan said, baring his teeth.

He kept the grin up until the girls left them alone. If he seemed to find it hard to abandon, that was just a joke. He made the face at any girls who looked at him and Robbie as they slouched around the yard, and the trick amused Robbie so much that he couldn't help joining in, even if it felt as though strings were attached to the corners of his mouth. His lips had grown weary by the time the bell herded everyone into the school.

The history mistress wanted to hear stories of the past that people's families had told them. One boy said how the government had hated Liver-pool so much they'd tried to take all the jobs down south, and a girl retorted that the unions hadn't let her dad or anybody do their jobs. "I think those are legends more than they're history," Mrs Picton said, and Robbie took the cue. "What about Chucky?" he said.

"What about . . ."

"He's a story mams and dads tell, isn't he? How it all started when those kids watched that film."

Before Mrs Picton could respond, Robbie's classmates did. Someone used to dream Chucky was under the bed after she'd read about him in the paper. Someone knew a girl who'd set her dolls on fire in case any of them might be Chucky. Someone else had heard of a boy who'd attacked his sister because he thought Chucky was inside her. Several people confirmed this, but Duncan said nothing at all. "It's only a film," Mrs Picton said, which sounded somehow familiar. "That doesn't mean any of you should watch anything like that at your age."

"Didn't those boys really kill anyone, then?" Robbie said.

"Of course they did. It's history, and now please leave it alone."

Why should he feel accused? He didn't speak for the rest of the lesson, despite the doubtful glances she kept giving him. When the bell jerked him to his feet at last she said "Will you wait, please, Robbie."

He stood like a doll at his desk until she took him to the headmistress. If someone had reported him for being Chucky in the yard, why wasn't Duncan with him? It should be Duncan who was being stared at and whispered girlishly about as he was escorted along the corridor like a killer to the execution chamber. Robbie and his guard were almost at Mrs Todd's office when he realised they couldn't do this to him; his mother had to be there. But she was in the office.

She looked even more disappointed than the other women did, and he turned on Mrs Picton. "You said it was only a film."

"What have you been watching?" his mother said.

"I didn't see them all. Dunk saw more. They haven't done anything to us. Like she says, it's just a legend. Just some wimpy films."

"Have you been too busy watching films," Mrs Todd enquired, "to do your homework?"

"I did it all. Who says I haven't?"

"The school does," Robbie's mother said sadly. "Your teacher found it on the Internet."

Robbie's skull felt close to cracking like plastic. "That's only like looking it up in a book."

"It was practically word for word," said Mrs Picton. "You'd think you wanted to be caught."

"What have you been filling your head with instead?" his mother clearly didn't care to know.

"Try devoting your imagination to your schoolwork. That's what it's for," Mrs Todd said. "I'm letting you off with a warning this time, but I'll treat any further offence much more seriously. Please remember you're letting yourself and your mother down as well as the school."

"And I'll want to see that work from you done properly," Mrs Picton said.

His mother played his silent jailer as far as the schoolyard. She was hardly out of the gate when Duncan came to him. "What did they want?"

"Just about my homework."

"Was it bad?"

Robbie had to imitate his grin, because he didn't know if Duncan meant the homework or the interview. "It was evil."

This widened Duncan's grin, which aggravated Robbie's. It was starting to feel like a contest when a girl said "What do you two think you look like?"

"Chucky," the boys said in chorus, which made them grin until Robbie's cheeks felt in danger of splitting like plastic.

He couldn't keep it up all afternoon, though his lips stirred if any of the teachers even glanced at him. Though the lessons felt interminable, they ended far too soon. Where could he go except home? He wasn't about to be scared of his mother when he wasn't scared of Chucky, especially since she was. Her nagging would just leave his head duller still—and then he thought of somewhere to go on the way home.

The metal benches outside the shopping precinct were crammed with quartets of pensioners, warily eyeing his schoolmates while they fought at bus stops or flung litter at each other. Robbie felt watched by them as he caught sight of the face across the road, in a small shop on the side street opposite a corner of the precinct. He sprinted in front of a bus stuffed with children and gave the driver his best grin, encouraged by the face in the shop window full of skulls and hairy visages and greenish corpse heads. Though the eyeless round rubbery mask was decorated with stitches, Robbie wasn't sure whether they were all where they should be. The longer he gazed at it, the more secretive the grin seemed to grow. He thought of wearing the mask while his mother lectured him, but she wouldn't let him own it, any more than he could buy even one of the fireworks lined up at the foot of the window. Suppose she didn't know? He could wear it when he went out at night while she was with Midge. He hadn't enough money on him, but there was more in his room, and that was why he hurried home.

His mother came into the hall as he shut the front door. "What have you been doing now?"

"Nothing. Coming home."

"Can't I trust you any more? Whose idea was it to do exactly what I told you not to?"

"Both of ours." Robbie dropped his schoolbag on the stairs, only to feel that it was blocking his way as she and her bicycle were. "You won't tell his mam what I said about him, will you? You don't have to. Please don't, please."

"Why, are you frightened how he'll behave now you've watched those films?"

"Course not. That's stupid. Why do you want to stop people seeing them? They aren't that scary, and they only make little kids be bad."

"I wouldn't grin about it. Is that really what you think? You'd better look at this." Grabbing her rucksack, she extracted the crumpled pages and flapped one at him. "What do you call them?" she said.

She was brandishing the report about the girl who'd been tortured in Manchester. Robbie thought he was expected to say that her tormentors were monsters or just men until he saw what he'd overlooked: the people who'd listened to Chucky's voice had been years older than he was now. He would have liked to have the Chucky mask to hide his face. All he could find to say was "Some of them were girls."

"That shows how bad those films are. That's why they have to be stopped, and now I can't leave you on your own."

"Why can't you?"

"I almost wish we had your father back. Are you going to turn into something else for me to worry about? Aren't you ever going to do anything to make me proud?"

Robbie ducked to his schoolbag so that she wouldn't see his face. "My homework," he muttered.

While he was no more eager to do it than usual, rewriting the history essay distracted him intermittently from his fears—that the English teacher would notice he'd copied from the Internet, that Duncan would discover Robbie had told on him, that they weren't as immune to the films as they'd thought, because they weren't old enough after all. His nerves kept jabbing the dull lump of his mind, and he was glad when his mother called him to dinner.

Perhaps she looked reproachful because she'd made turkey burgers, his favourite. Whenever their eyes met he thought it best to grin. The meal ended some time after he'd stopped enjoying it. As she returned the chutney to the refrigerator his mother said "Now look what you've made me do."

She was craning inside, her neck between the doorframe and the edge of the door, as she held the refrigerator open with one hand. "What?" Robbie said.

"I forgot to buy orange and now there's none for breakfast."

As the legs of his chair and the linoleum collaborated on a squeal that a maniac's victim might have been proud of, Robbie said "I'll go."

"Just hurry there and hurry back."

He ran upstairs and made sure she heard him go into the bathroom, and then he dodged into his room. Now his footfalls felt as light as plastic. The money was the only secret in his room, not that it was much of one; less than half was change he'd kept the last time she'd sent him to the shops. Dust squeaked beneath his fingernails as he groped behind the wardrobe for the coins. He flushed the toilet and sprinted downstairs, to be met by his mother. "Remember what I said," she told him.

As he hurried to the shop he felt as if his face was shaping itself so that the mask would fit. What would the mask allow him to do? He thought of peering in the windows at the televisions inside which Chucky might be hiding, and his grin expanded, only to sag when he reached the street that led down to the Strand. The shop with the masks in was dark.

The door didn't budge, and nobody answered however hard Robbie clattered the letter box. "What are you grinning at?" he demanded, but the mask didn't seem to hear. It looked entertained by his plight, unless it was amused by its secret thoughts. Suppose he smashed the window and set Chucky free that way? He glanced about to make sure the street was deserted and in search of something he could use. Then, with a shock that turned his mouth so dry it felt raw with skunk, he realised what he was planning to do.

Had the mask put the idea into his mind? What else might Chucky have sneaked in? Robbie remembered wishing he could wear the mask so that he could deal with his mother, and all at once he saw her neck in the guillotine of the refrigerator. Lightning widened the empty eyes as if the mask had been enlivened by the memory. The flash was the explosion of a firework above the houses, and it sent Robbie away from the window, to the grocery around the corner.

Had the flash been an omen too? There were fireworks under the glass counter, and he used the carton of juice to point. "One of them as well."

He thought the shopkeeper was about to refuse, but she must have been waiting for politeness. As she shook her head and laid the firework on the counter Robbie said "And some matches."

She didn't take the second chance to say no. Robbie paid and hurried back to the intersection. If there was anybody in the other street he wouldn't be able to carry out his plan—but the street was deserted even by traffic. He wandered over to the shop as if he were bound somewhere else entirely, and then he lit the firework.

The stitched mask seemed to watch him askance as he inserted the long cardboard barrel through the letter box and gave it a violent sideways shove. The firework landed inside the window. In a few seconds it spouted fire, and moments later several fireworks were ablaze. Even if Chucky never stayed burned in the films, mightn't this destroy his face? The mask appeared to writhe in fear as detonations shook the window. The glass held, but the masks slithered down it to fall on top of the outbursts of flame. Gouts of fire spurted from Chucky's eyes, which grew larger and blacker and emptier, and then the helpless upturned face began to split apart as if the stitches had torn open. When the pieces started curling up and bubbling like slugs, Robbie dashed home.

He felt both reckless and justified. His mother should be proud of him, but could he risk telling her? As he inserted the unnecessarily shaky key into the lock he was trying to decide how much he might hint. He'd eased the door shut when he heard a voice croaking somewhere in the house.

It was Chucky's mate. Before Robbie could begin to deal with this, his mother darted like a killer out of the front room. "Where have you been this time? How long does it take to buy juice?"

He was distracted by the film she'd been watching—the Simpsons film. "There was a shop on fire," he said.

"I suppose I can't blame you for that."

Robbie didn't grin until he was heading for the kitchen, and managed to suppress the expression on his way back. Once he joined in watching the film he had no idea how to look. He tried only laughing if his mother did, but this was almost always when Marge Simpson spoke in that unnatural voice. He peered at the film as if it might show him what else he could do, and then his mobile clanged. As he brought up the message his mother leaned over to read it. *chuckies burnd shop down,* Duncan wanted him to know. "What does he mean?" Robbie's mother demanded.

Robbie thought it wisest just to shrug, and she was rediscovering how to laugh with Marge when the ringtone interrupted. "Is that Duncan again?" Robbie's mother said and silenced the television. "Put him on the loudspeaker."

Robbie was unnerved by the sight of her dubbing Marge's dialogue. Poking the loudspeaker key seemed to bring an audience into the room. "That shop those girls said about, it's on fire," Duncan shouted over the sounds of the crowd. "You want to come and see."

"I saw."

"Did you see Chucky? He's gone now. Maybe he done it and went."

"No he didn't." Since Robbie's fervour apparently impressed his mother, he added "He's just in his films."

"Till someone lets him out."

"I've got to go now," Robbie said and cut the call off.

He still had to face his mother. "Was he trying to tell you he'd started the fire?" she said.

"It wasn't him."

"How do you know?"

"There was a Chucky mask he'd have wanted. It's all burned up."

Far too many seconds passed before her gaze relented. "Just please don't ever watch any of those films again."

"I won't."

"Don't go anywhere near them."

At once, having realised what else he could do, Robbie was afraid she meant to extract the promise. She picked up the remote control, however, and restored the doll's voice. He kept hearing it and Chucky's even once the film was over, but now he knew how to stop them. When his mother started watching a programme about refuges for women he used it as an excuse to go to bed. "You get your sleep. You've plenty to do tomorrow," she said.

She had no idea. He wasn't sure himself. As he lay in bed he saw Chucky's face bubble and blacken while it struggled to crawl out of the flames. It didn't let him sleep much; he kept jerking awake like a puppet someone was testing. He was afraid his mother might interrogate him at breakfast, but perhaps she was used to his red eyes or too preoccupied to notice. He tried not to grin every time she looked at him, and eventually he was able to stay out of her sight by taking his homework into the front room.

For English he had to write about a film. He was tempted to discuss Chucky but didn't know what he might say. He wrote about the Simpsons film, although the need to avoid mentioning the truth about Marge's voice felt like wearing a mask. As he strove to keep his mind on the essay, the phone in the hall went off like an alarm.

Had someone seen him set fire to the shop? Would the police believe why he'd had to do it? He heard his mother take the receiver to the kitchen, but he couldn't distinguish her words or even her tone. He wrote very few words while he listened for her footsteps in the hall. At last she came back and opened the door. "Midge wants us to picket the films tonight," she said. "What am I going to do with you?"

He was searching for an answer when his mobile tried to crawl across the table. *what you doeing tonit,* Duncan wanted to know. Robbie couldn't say, and he felt his skull grow thin as plastic as he waited for his mother to decide. Neither of them had spoken by the time Duncan rang. "Let me hear," Robbie's mother said.

As Robbie amplified the sound Duncan said "Where have you fucked off to now?"

"Doing my homework."

"Hope it's evil." When Robbie didn't respond Duncan said "My mam's got me picketing Chucky tonight. Should be a laugh. Want to come?"

Robbie's mother shook her head as hard as she was gazing at him. "Can't," he said.

"Why, what'll you be doing?"

"Homework," Robbie said, the only safe answer he could think of. "I've got to do some of it again."

"All right," his mother said as he ended the call, "I'm going to trust you. You don't need to come with me tonight."

She was making sure he wouldn't be with Duncan. Robbie felt as if he were in a film where whatever the plot required was bound to happen. Nothing else had to for the rest of the day, and he stayed in the front room when he wasn't helping his mother shop. He wondered if he was grinning too often over dinner, but she left him to clear up. He waited to be certain she was well on her way to Midge's, and then he left the house.

He might have borrowed the bicycle if she hadn't locked it. As he hurried to the bus stops, the smell from the grain silos hovered in the cold dark air like the stench of melted plastic. Burning claws reared up to sear black prints on the sky or on his eyes, and he heard the mound of Chucky's grave collapse as the doll fumbled its way out, but that was scrap being dumped beside the river. A bus took him into Liverpool, where he alighted just short of the dockland multiplex.

People were converging on it—students, older couples, solitary characters carrying *Gorehound* magazine with Chucky's face on it. All of them were met outside the cinema by pickets waving placards—**CHILDREN NOT CHUCKY, HORROR ISN'T HEALTHY, CARE FOR KIDS INSTEAD OF FILMS, SAVE OUR BABES FROM SADISM** . . . Whichever Robbie's mother might be wielding, he ran behind an apartment block without locating her.

The luxury block was guarded by an electrified fence, the outside of which led him parallel to the river. He didn't think anyone saw him sprint from the corner of the fence to the rear of the multiplex, where the plot he was enacting seemed to abandon him. All the back doors of the cinemas were locked, and the side doors were just as immovable. As he faltered in the recess of the exit closest to the pickets, they began to chant "Chuck Chucky out" and drum the staves of their placards on the concrete. Somebody was remonstrating with them, and when Robbie peeked around the corner he saw it was the manager, supported by quite a few of the cinema personnel. Among the pickets growing louder in response were Duncan's and Robbie's mothers, but nobody appeared to see him dodge through the nearest front door into the multiplex.

Nearly all the staff must be confronting the pickets, and the girls in the box office were dealing with a queue. There wasn't even anyone to take tickets at the entrance to the screens. While the staff at the popcorn counter might have, they were serving customers. Robbie walked not too quickly or too surreptitiously past them into a corridor where posters indicated which door led to which film. He hadn't found the poster he was looking for when he heard Chucky's voice.

It was beyond a door marked STAFF ONLY. Robbie glanced around to see that the corridor was deserted. He hauled the door open and slipped past as it began to close behind him. He felt as if he were not merely in a film but in a dream he'd had, unless he was having it now. He was where he would have hoped to be—in a projection room.

The projectionist was elsewhere. Six projectors—half the number of screens—were casting images through dwarfish windows on the far side of the room. The mocking gleeful voice led Robbie to the second machine from the left. A window next to the one the projector was using showed him Chucky's face swollen larger than any of the audience beneath it in the darkened auditorium. They were watching a documentary about the films, all five of which were stacked in cans beside the projector.

Robbie lifted both fire extinguishers out of their cradles on the walls and laid them alongside the projector. A film magazine was lying on a table by the door, and he tore it up to pile the pages between the extinguishers. Prising the lid off the topmost can of film, he tipped out the contents, which unwound across the heap of paper. The chant of the pickets and the drumming of sticks urged him on. By the time he'd emptied all the cans his fingernails twinged from opening the lids, and his arms ached with his efforts. None of this mattered, because the extinguishers had prevented the tangle of celluloid from burying all the paper. Perhaps Chucky wanted to be caught—to be stopped. Robbie took out the matchbox and struck a match.

The paper flamed at once, blazing up beneath the pile of film. In a moment the celluloid was on fire. Chucky was still ranting in the shaky darkness, but he wouldn't be for long. Robbie would have liked to see the flames reach the film in the projector, except that the fire or the projectionist might trap him. As the room began to fill with a plastic stench he retreated into the corridor. He was loitering outside the toilets near an exit—he would look as if he were waiting for someone if anybody noticed him—when a man appeared at the far end of the corridor and made for the projection room.

For just an instant Robbie wanted to warn him, and then he realised that the projectionist must have watched Chucky while checking all the films. Robbie observed him as he pulled the door open and uttered a syllable and lurched into the room. The door shut behind him, puffing out thick smoke, and then there was silence apart from the noise of the pickets. Robbie was at the side exit when a figure covered with flames and partly composed of them staggered into the corridor.

Was it a doll? Bits of plastic were peeling away from it, unless they were pieces of film. It wasn't making much noise; a clogged rising groan was the best it could do for a scream. Perhaps its face was melting. As it pranced away it looked more than ever like a puppet, growing smaller while its hands clutched at and flinched away from its blazing skull. It had almost reached the far end of the corridor when a woman and her children came out of a cinema to scream on its behalf. Robbie had to cover his grin with a hand as if he was overcome by their emotion; he might have been putting on a mask. As the family retreated screaming into the cinema and the puppet fell on any face it had left, he let himself out of the multiplex.

The pickets were still chanting and thumping their sticks. He would have told them there was no longer any need, but however necessary his actions had been, suppose he was misunderstood? He sprinted behind another apartment block while fireworks in the sky celebrated his success. The top deck of a bus from the stop beyond the multiplex gave him a view of people streaming out of all the exits, and just a few signs sprouting from the crowd. A placard sank out of sight as he watched, and he thought it was acknowledging him.

He had to shut a smell of melted plastic out of the house. He felt hollow, but in the best way—emptied of the need to intervene. He drowsed in bed until he heard his mother come home, and then he fell asleep. He didn't dream or waken, even when a church started ringing its bells. Perhaps they were for Chucky's funeral, but there must have been a phone as well, because Robbie opened his eyes at last to see his mother in the doorway of his room. "You had a long one," she said. "My nan used to say you only sleep well if you've been good."

Could he tell her how good he'd been? As he tested the mechanism of his lips she said "You missed it all."

His lips parted, but she headed off whatever he might have said. "It's a good job you weren't there, though."

"Why?"

"There was a fire at the cinema. The police think it was deliberate. They want to talk to us."

Would they understand? She ought to hear before they did, and Robbie was about to tell his secret when she said "One of the staff was in the fire. Midge just called to say he died. We're all going over to hers for a while. I've left your breakfast."

So she hadn't meant the police were after him. He should have seen how normal she wanted life to be. She looked sad for the projectionist, and perhaps he hadn't deserved to be burned, but he'd had to be. All at once she looked sadder. "I forgot your juice again."

"I can get some."

"You're a good boy really. Stay like that," she said and hurried downstairs.

As soon as the bicycle trundled out of the house Robbie headed for the bathroom. He still had work to do. Perhaps he could be sad about it, if you needed to be sad about people who'd turned into dolls. He didn't look sad in the mirror; he could see no expression at all—his ordinary face was the only mask he needed. He was contemplating it when his phone struck up its slogan.

There wouldn't be peace yet, but there might be soon. "You should of been there last night," Duncan told him.

"What happened?"

"My mam and yours nearly got in a fight with the cinema. And somebody started a fire and half of it's burned down, and a feller was in it. I'll tell you all about it when I see you. I've got some stuff that'll do your head in."

Watching so much Chucky had done that to Duncan, Robbie thought. "Where?" he said.

"In the park. I found somewhere nobody'll know we're there. Are you coming now?"

"I've got to go to the shop first."

"Being your mam's good boy again, are you?"

"You'll see." Robbie knew Duncan was grinning, and imagined how they both would when they met. His grin wouldn't be the same as Duncan's; it was a mask, because he was the opposite of Chucky. "I won't be long," he said. "I'll be back."

🐲 Afterword 🐲

Chucky and his films have indeed become Liverpool legends of the darkest kind. The media ascribed the murder of James Bulger in 1991 by two Merseyside ten-year-olds to the influence of *Child's Play 3*, although the film had been seen by neither of them and was never mentioned in evidence. (In fact the film that the murder resembles is the PG-rated *Home Alone*, in which the ten-year-old Macauley Culkin amuses the audience by submitting burglars to some of the violence James Bulger was to suffer three years later.) Subsequent Chucky films were never shown in Liverpool, and the newspaper reports quoted in my story are real. Footage of the abduction of James Bulger can be seen on YouTube accompanied by a pop song.

JOE R. LANSDALE

The Folding Man

Joe R. Lansdale has been a freelance writer since 1973, and a full-time writer since 1981. He is the author of thirty novels and eighteen short story collections and has received The Edgar Award, seven Bram Stoker Awards, The British Fantasy Award, and Italy's Grinzani Prize for Literature, among others.

"Bubba Hotep," his award-nominated novella, was filmed by Don Cos-carelli and is now considered a cult classic, and his story "Incident On and Off a Mountain Road" was filmed for Showtime's Masters of Horror.

He has written for film, television, comics, and is the author of numerous essays and columns. His most recent work is the collection from the University of Texas Press, Sanctified and Chicken Fried, The Portable Lansdale, The Best of Joe R. Lansdale, *and* Vanilla Ride, *his latest in the Hap Collins, Leonard Pine series. All of the series have recently been released in paperback from Vintage Books.*

They had come from a Halloween party, having long shed the masks they'd worn. No one but Harold had been drinking, and he wasn't driving, and he wasn't so drunk he was blind. Just drunk enough he couldn't sit up straight and was lying on the backseat, trying, for some unknown reason, to recite the Pledge of Allegiance, which he didn't accurately recall. He was mixing in verses from the "Star-Spangled Banner" and the Boy Scout oath, which he vaguely remembered from his time in the organization before they drove him out for setting fires.

Even though William, who was driving, and Jim who was riding shotgun, were sober as Baptists claimed to be, they were fired up and happy and yelling and hooting, and Jim pulled down his pants and literally mooned a black bug of a car carrying a load of nuns.

The car wasn't something that looked as if it had come off the lot. Didn't have the look of any carmaker Jim could identify. It had a cobbled look. It reminded him of something in old movies, the ones with gangsters who were always squealing their tires around corners. Only it seemed bigger, with broader windows through which he could see the nuns, or at least glimpse them in their habits; it was a regular penguin convention inside that car.

Way it happened was, when they came up on the nuns, Jim said to William at the wheel, "Man, move over close, I'm gonna show them some butt."

"They're nuns, man."

"That's what makes it funny," Jim said.

William eased the wheel to the right, and Harold in the back said, "Grand Canyon. Grand Canyon. Show them the Grand Canyon . . . Oh, say can you see . . ."

Jim got his pants down, swiveled on his knees in the seat, twisted so that his ass was against the glass, and just as they passed the nuns, William hit the electric window switch and slid the glass down. Jim's ass jumped out at the night, like a vibrating moon.

"They lookin'?" Jim asked.

"Oh, yeah," William said, "and they are not amused."

Jim jerked his pants up, shifted in the seat, and turned for a look, and sure enough, they were not amused. Then a funny thing happened, one of the nuns shot him the finger, and then others followed. Jim said, "Man, those nuns are rowdy."

And now he got a good look at them, because there was enough light from the headlights as they passed for him to see faces hard as wardens and ugly as death warmed over. The driver was especially homely, face like that could stop a clock and run it backwards or make shit crawl uphill.

"Did you see that, they shot me the finger?" Jim said.

"I did see it," William said.

Harold had finally gotten the "Star-Spangled Banner" straight, and he kept singing it over and over.

"For Christ sake," William said. "Shut up, Harold."

"You know what," Jim said, studying the rearview mirror, "I think they're speeding up. They're trying to catch us. Oh hell. What if they got the license plate? Maybe they already have. They call the law, my dad will have my mooning ass."

"Well, if they haven't got the plate," William said, "they won't. This baby can get on up and get on out."

He put his foot on the gas. The car hummed as if it had just had an orgasm, and seemed to leap. Harold was flung off the backseat, onto the floorboard. "Hey, goddamnit," he said.

"Put on your seat belt, jackass," Jim said.

William's car was eating up the road. It jumped over a hill and dove down the other side like a porpoise negotiating a wave, and Jim thought: Good-bye, penguins, and then he looked back. At the top of the hill were the lights from the nun's car, and the car was gaining speed and it moved in a jerky manner, as if it were stealing space between blinks of the eye.

"Damn," William said. "They got some juice in that thing, and the driver has her foot down."

"What kind of car is that?" Jim said.

"Black," William said.

"Ha! Mr. Detroit."

"Then you name it."

Jim couldn't. He turned to look back. The nun's car had already caught up; the big automotive beast was cruising in tight as a coat of varnish, the headlights making the interior of William's machine bright as a Vegas act.

"What the hell they got under the hood?" William said. "Hyperdrive?"

"These nuns," Jim said, "they mean business."

"I can't believe it, they're riding my bumper."

"Slam on your brakes. That'll show them."

"Not this close," William said. "Do that, what it'll show them is the inside of our butts."

"Do nuns do this?"

"These do."

"Oh," Jim said. "I get it. Halloween. They aren't real nuns."

"Then we give them hell," Harold said, and just as the nuns were passing on the right, he crawled out of the floorboard and onto his seat and rolled the window down. The back window of the nun's car went down and Jim turned to get a look, and the nun, well, she was ugly all right, but uglier than he had first imagined. She looked like something dead, and the nun's outfit she wore was not actually black and white, but purple and white, or so it appeared in the light from high beams and moonlight. The nun's lips pulled back from her teeth and the teeth were long and brown, as if tobacco-stained. One of her eyes looked like a spoiled meatball, and her nostrils flared like a pig's.

Jim said, "That ain't no mask."

Harold leaned way out of the window and flailed his hands and said, "You are so goddamn ugly you have to creep up on your underwear."

Harold kept on with this kind of thing, some of it almost making sense, and then one of the nuns in the back, one closest to the window, bent over in the seat and came up and leaned out of the window, a two-by-four in her hands. Jim noted that her arms, where the nun outfit had fallen back to the elbows, were as thin as sticks and white as the underbelly of a fish and the elbows were knotty, and bent in the wrong direction.

"Get back in," Jim said to Harold.

Harold waved his arms and made another crack, and then the nun swung the two-by-four, the oddness of her elbows causing it to arrive at a weird angle, and the board made a crack of its own, or rather Harold's skull did, and he fell forward, the lower half of his body hanging from the window, bouncing against the door, his knuckles losing meat on the highway, his ass hanging inside, one foot on the floorboard, the other waggling in the air.

"The nun hit him," Jim said. "With a board."

"What?" William said.

"You deaf, she hit him."

Jim snapped loose his seat belt and leaned over and grabbed Harold by the back of the shirt and yanked him inside. Harold's head looked like it had been in a vice. There was blood everywhere. Jim said, "Oh, man, I think he's dead."

BLAM!

The noise made Jim jump. He slid back in his seat and looked toward the nuns. They were riding close enough to slam the two-by-four into William's car; the driver was pressing that black monster toward them.

Another swing of the board and the side mirror shattered.

William tried to gun forward, but the nun's car was even with him, pushing him to the left. They went across the highway and into a ditch and the car did an acrobatic twist and tumbled down an embankment and rolled into the woods tossing up mud and leaves and pine straw.

• • •

Jim found himself outside the car, and when he moved, everything seemed to whirl for a moment, then gathered up slowly and became solid. He had been thrown free, and so had William, who was lying nearby. The car was a wreck, lying on its roof, spinning still, steam easing out from under the hood in little cotton-white clouds. Gradually, the car quit spinning, like an old-time watch that had wound down. The windshield was gone and three of the four doors lay scattered about.

The nuns were parked up on the road, and the car doors opened and the nuns got out. Four of them. They were unusually tall, and when they walked, like their elbows, their knees bent in the wrong direction. It was impossible to tell this for sure, because of the robes they wore, but it certainly looked that way, and considering the elbows, it fit. There in the moonlight, they were as white and pasty as pot stickers, their jaws seeming to have grown longer than when Jim had last looked at them, their noses witchlike, except for those pig-flare nostrils, their backs bent like long bows. One of them still held the two-by-four.

Jim slid over to William, who was trying to sit up.

"You okay?" Jim asked.

"I think so," William said, patting his fingers at a blood spot on his forehead. "Just before they hit, I stupidly unsnapped my seat belt. I don't know why. I just wanted out I guess. Brain not working right."

"Look up there," Jim said.

They both looked up the hill. One of the nuns was moving down from the highway, toward the wrecked car.

"If you can move," Jim said, "I think we oughta."

William worked himself to his feet. Jim grabbed his arm and half pulled him into the woods where they leaned against a tree. William said. "Everything's spinning."

"It stops soon enough," Jim said.

"I got to chill, I'm about to faint."

"A moment," Jim said.

The nun who had gone down by herself, bent down out of sight behind William's car, then they saw her going back up the hill, dragging Harold by his ankle, his body flopping about as if all the bones were broken.

"My God, see that?" William said. "We got to help."

"He's dead," Jim said. "They crushed his head with a board."

"Oh, hell, man. That can't be. They're nuns."

"I don't think they are," Jim said. "Least not the kind of nuns you're thinking."

The nun dragged Harold up the hill and dropped his leg when she reached the big black car. Another of the nuns opened the trunk and reached in and got hold of something. It looked like some kind of folded-up lawn chair, only more awkward in shape. The nun jerked it out and dropped it on the ground and gave it a swift kick. The folded-up thing began to unfold with a clatter and a squeak. A perfectly round head rose up from it, and the head spun on what appeared to be a silver hinge. When it quit whirling, it was upright and in place, though cocked slightly to the left. The eyes and mouth and nostrils were merely holes. Moonlight could be seen through them. The head rose as coatrack-style shoulders pushed it up and a cage of a chest rose under that. The chest looked almost like an old frame on which dresses were placed to be sewn, or perhaps a cage designed to contain something you wouldn't want to get out. With more squeaks and clatters, skeletal hips appeared, and beneath that, long, bony legs with bent back knees and big metal-framed feet. Sticklike arms swung below its knees, clattering against its legs like tree limbs bumping against a windowpane. It stood at least seven feet tall. Like the nuns, its knees and elbows fit backwards.

The nun by the car trunk reached inside and pulled out something fairly large that beat its wings against the night air. She held it in one hand by its clawed feet, and its beak snapped wildly, looking for something to peck. Using her free hand, she opened up the folding man's chest by use of a hinge, and when the cage flung open, she put the black, winged thing inside. It fluttered about like a heart shot full of adrenaline. The holes that were the folding man's eyes filled with a red glow and the mouth hole grew wormy lips, and a tongue, long as a garden snake, dark as dirt, licked out at the night, and there was a loud sniff as its nostrils sucked air. One of the nuns reached down and grabbed up a handful of clay, and pressed it against the folding man's arms; the clay spread fast as a lie, went all over, filling the thing with flesh of the earth until the entire folding man's body was covered. The nun, who had taken the folding man out of the car, picked Harold up by the ankle, and as if he were nothing more than a blow-up doll, swung him over her head and slammed him into the darkness of the trunk, shut the lid, and looked out where Jim and William stood recovering by the tree.

The nun said something, a noise between a word and a cough, and the folding man began to move down the hill at a stumble. As he moved his joints made an unoiled hinge sound, and the rest of him made a clatter like lug bolts being knocked together, accompanied by a noise akin to wire hangers being twisted by strong hands.

"Run," Jim said.

· · ·

Jim began to feel pain, knew he was more banged up than he thought. His neck hurt. His back hurt. One of his legs really hurt. He must have jammed his knee against something. William, who ran alongside him, dodging trees, said, "My ribs. I think they're cracked."

Jim looked back. In the distance, just entering the trees, framed in the moonlight behind him, was the folding man. He moved in strange leaps, as if there were springs inside him, and he was making good time.

Jim said, "We can't stop. It's coming."

. . .

It was low down in the woods and water had gathered there and the leaves had mucked up with it, and as they ran, they sloshed and splashed, and be- hind them, they could hear it, the folding man, coming, cracking limbs, squeaking hinges, splashing his way after them. When they had the nerve to look back, they could see him darting between the trees like a bit of the for- est itself, and he, or it, was coming quite briskly for a thing its size until it reached the lower-down parts of the bottomland. There its big feet slowed it some as they buried deep in the mud and were pulled free again with a sound like the universe sucking wind. Within moments, however, the thing got its stride, its movements becoming more fluid and its pace faster.

Finally Jim and William came to a tree-thickened rise in the land, and were able to get out of the muck and move more freely, even though there was something of a climb ahead, and they had to use trees growing out from the side of the rise to pull themselves upward. When they reached the top of the climb, they were surprised when they looked back to see they had actually gained some space on the thing. It was some distance away, speck- led by the moonlight, negotiating its way through the ever-thickening trees and undergrowth. But still it came, ever onward, never tiring. Jim and William bent over and put their hands on their knees and took some deep breaths.

"There's an old graveyard on the far side of this stretch," Jim said. "Near the wrecking yard."

"Where you worked last summer."

"Yeah, that's the one. It gets clearer in the graveyard, and we can make good time. Get to the wrecking yard, Old Man Gordon lives there. He al- ways has a gun and he has that dog, Chomps. It knows me. It will eat that thing up."

"What about me?"

"You'll be all right. You're with me. Come on. I kinda of know where we are now. Used to play in the graveyard, and in this end of the woods. Got to move."

.   .   .

They moved along more swiftly as Jim became more and more familiar with the terrain. It was close to where he had lived when he was a kid, and he had spent a lot of time out here. They came to a place where there was a clearing in the woods, a place where lightning had made a fire. The ground was black, and there were no trees, and in that spot silver moonlight was falling down into it, like mercury filling a cup.

In the center of the clearing they stopped and got their breath again, and William said, "My head feels like it's going to explode. . . . Hey, I don't hear it now."

"It's there. Whatever it is, I don't think it gives up."

"Oh, Jesus," William said, and gasped deep once. "I don't know how much I got left in me."

"You got plenty. We got to have plenty."

"What can it be, Jimbo? What in the hell can it be?"

Jim shook his head. "You know that old story about the black car?"

William shook his head.

"My grandmother used to tell me about a black car that roams the highways and the back roads of the South. It isn't in one area all the time, but it's out there somewhere all the time. Halloween is its peak night. It's always after somebody for whatever reason."

"Bullshit."

Jim, hands still on his knees, lifted his head. "You go down there and tell that clatter-clap thing it's all bullshit. See where that gets you."

"It just doesn't make sense."

"Grandma said before it was a black car, it was a black buggy, and before that a figure dressed in black on a black horse, and that before that, it was just a shadow that clicked and clacked and squeaked. There's people go missing, she said, and it's the black car, the black buggy, the thing on the horse, or the walkin' shadow that gets them. But it's all the same thing, just a different appearance."

"The nuns? What about them?"

Jim shook his head, stood up, tested his ability to breathe. "Those weren't nuns. They were like . . . I don't know . . . antinuns. This thing, if Grandma was right, can take a lot of different forms. Come on. We can't stay here anymore."

"Just another moment, I'm so tired. And I think we've lost it. I don't hear it anymore."

As if on cue, there came a clanking and a squeaking and cracking of limbs. William glanced at Jim, and without a word, they moved across the lightning-made clearing and into the trees. Jim looked back, and there it was, crossing the clearing, silver-flooded in the moonlight, still coming, not tiring.

They ran. White stones rose up in front of them. Most of the stones were heaved to the side, or completely pushed out of the ground by growing trees and expanding roots. It was the old graveyard, and Jim knew that meant the wrecking yard was nearby, and so was Gordon's shotgun, and so was one mean dog.

Again the land sloped upward, and this time William fell forward on his hands and knees, throwing up a mess of blackness. "Oh, God. Don't leave me, Jim. . . . I'm tuckered . . . Can hardly . . . breathe."

Jim had moved slightly ahead of William. He turned back to help. As he grabbed William's arm to pull him up, the folding man squeaked and clattered forward and grabbed William's ankle, jerked him back, out of Jim's grasp.

The folding man swung William around easily, slammed his body against a tree, then the thing whirled, and as if William were a bullwhip, snapped him so hard his neck popped and an eyeball flew out of his skull. The folding man brought William whipping down across a standing grave-stone. There was a cracking sound, like someone had dropped a glass coffee cup, then the folding man whirled and slung William from one tree to an-other, hitting the trees so hard bark flew off of them and clothes and meat flew off William.

Jim bolted. He ran faster than he had ever run, finally he broke free of the woods and came to a stretch of ground that was rough with gravel. Behind him, breaking free of the woods, was the folding man, making good time with great strides, dragging William's much-abused body behind it by the ankle.

. . .

Jim could dimly see the wrecking yard from where he was, and he thought he could make it. Still, there was the aluminum fence all the way around the yard, seven feet high. No little barrier. Then he remembered the sycamore tree on the edge of the fence, on the right side. Old Man Gordon was always talking about cutting it because he thought someone could use it to climb over and into the yard, steal one of his precious car parts, though if they did, they had Gordon's shotgun waiting along with the sizable teeth of his dog. It had been six months since he had seen the old man, and he hoped he hadn't gotten ambitious, that the tree was still there.

Running closer, Jim could see the sycamore tree remained, tight against the long run of shiny wrecking yard fence. Looking over his shoulder, Jim saw the folding man was springing forward, like some kind of electronic rabbit, William's body being pulled along by the ankle, bouncing on the ground as the thing came ever onward. At this rate, it would be only a few seconds before the thing caught up with him.

Jim felt a pain like a knife in his side, and it seemed as if his heart was going to explode. He reached down deep for everything he had, hoping like hell he didn't stumble.

He made the fence and the tree, went up it like a squirrel, dropped over on the roof of an old car, sprang off of that and ran toward a dim light shining in the small window of a wood and aluminum shack nestled in the midst of old cars and piles of junk.

As he neared the shack, Chomps, part pit bull, part just plain big ole dog, came loping out toward him, growling. It was a hard thing to do, but Jim forced himself to stop, bent down, stuck out his hand, and called the dog's name.

"Chomps. Hey, buddy. It's me."

The dog slowed and lowered its head and wagged its tail.

"That's right. Your pal, Jim."

The dog came close and Jim gave it a pat. "Good, boy."

Jim looked over his shoulder. Nothing.

"Come on, Chomps."

Jim moved quickly toward the shack and hammered on the door. A moment later the door flew open, and standing there in overalls, one strap dangling from a naked arm, was Mr. Gordon. He was old and near toothless, squat and greasy as the insides of the cars in the yard.

"Jim? What the hell you doing in here? You look like hell."

"Something's after me."

"Something?"

"It's outside the fence. It killed two of my friends . . ."

"What?"

"It killed two of my friends."

"It? Some kind of animal?"

"No . . . It."

"We'll call some law."

Jim shook his head. "No use calling the law now, time they arrive it'll be too late."

Gordon leaned inside the shack and pulled a twelve-gauge into view, pumped it once. He stepped outside and looked around.

"You sure?"

"Oh, yeah. Yes, sir. I'm sure."

"Then I guess you and me and Pump Twelve will check it out."

Gordon moved out into the yard, looking left and right. Jim stayed close to Gordon's left elbow. Chomps trotted nearby. They walked about a bit. They stopped between a row of wrecked cars, looked around. Other than the moon-shimmering fence at either end of the row where they stood, there was nothing to see.

"Maybe whatever, or whoever it is, is gone," Gordon said. "Otherwise, Chomps would be all over it."

"I don't think it smells like humans or animals."

"Are you joshin' an old man? Is this a Halloween prank?"

"No, sir. Two of my friends are dead. This thing killed them. It's real."

"What the hell is it then?"

As if in answer, there was the sound like a huge can opener going to work, and then the long, thin arm of the folding man poked through the fence and there was more ripping as the arm slid upward, tearing at the metal. A big chunk of the fence was torn away, revealing the thing, bathed in moonlight, still holding what was left of William's ragged body by the ankle.

Jim and Gordon both stood locked in amazement.

"Sonofabitch," Gordon said.

Chomps growled, ran toward it.

"Chomps will fix him," Gordon said.

The folding man dropped William's ankle and bent forward, and just as the dog leaped, caught it and twisted it and ran its long arm down the snapping dog's throat, and began to pull its insides out. It flung dog's parts in all directions, like someone pulling confetti from a sack. Then it turned the dog inside out.

When the sack was empty, the folding man bent down and fastened the dead, deflated dog to a hook on the back of what passed for its ankle.

"My God," Gordon said.

The thing picked up William by the ankle, stepped forward a step, and paused.

Gordon lifted the shotgun. "Come and get you some, asshole."

The thing cocked its head as if to consider the suggestion, and then it began to lope toward them, bringing along its clanks and squeaks; the dead dog flopped at the folding man's heel. For the first time, its mouth, which had been nothing but a hole with wormy lips, twisted into the shape of a smile.

Gordon said, "You run, boy. I got this."

Jim didn't hesitate. He turned and darted between a row of cars and found a gap between a couple of Fords with grass grown up around their flattened tires, ducked down behind one, and hid. He lay down on his belly to see if he could see anything. There was a little bit of space down there, and he could look under the car, and under several others, and he could see Gordon's feet. They had shifted into a firm stance, and Jim could imagine the old man pulling the shotgun to his shoulder.

And even as he imagined, the gun boomed, and then it boomed again. Silence, followed by a noise like someone ripping a piece of thick cardboard in half, and then there were screams and more rips. Jim felt light-headed, realized he hadn't been breathing. He gasped for air, feared that he had gasped too loudly.

Oh, my God, he thought. I ran and left it to Mr. Gordon, and now . . . He was uncertain. Maybe the screams had come from . . . It, the folding man? But so far it hadn't so much as made breathing sounds, let alone anything that might be thought of as a vocalization.

Crawling like a soldier under fire, Jim worked his way to the edge of the car, and took a look. Stalking down the row between the cars was the folding man, and he was dragging behind him by one ankle what was left of William's body. In his other hand, if you could call it a hand, he had Mr. Gordon, who looked thin now because so much had been pulled out of him. Chomps's body was still fastened to the wire hook at the back of the thing's foot. As the folding man came forward, Chomps dragged in the dirt.

Jim pushed back between the cars, and kept pushing, crawling backwards. When he was far enough back, he raised to a squat and started between narrower rows that he thought would be harder for the folding man to navigate; they were just spaces really, not rows, and if he could go where it couldn't go, then—

There was a large creaking sound, and Jim, still at a squat, turned to discover its source. The folding man was looking at him. It had grabbed an old car and lifted it up by the front and was holding it so that the back end rested on the ground. Being as close as he was now, Jim realized the folding man was bigger than he had thought, and he saw too that just below where the monster's thick torso ended there were springs, huge springs, silver in the moonlight, vibrating. He had stretched to accommodate the lifting of the car, and where his knees bent backwards, springs could be seen as well; he was a garage sale collection of parts and pieces.

For a moment, Jim froze. The folding man opened his mouth wide, wider than Jim had seen before, and inside he could glimpse a turning of gears and a smattering of sparks. Jim broke suddenly, running between cars, leaping on hoods, scrambling across roofs, and behind him came the folding man, picking up cars and flipping them aside as easily as if they had been toys.

Jim could see the fence at the back, and he made for that, and when he got close to it, he thought he had it figured. He could see a Chevy parked next to the fence, and he felt certain he could climb onto the roof, spring off of it, grab the top of the fence, and scramble over. That wouldn't stop the thing behind him, but it would perhaps give him a few moments to gain ground.

The squeaking and clanking behind him was growing louder.

There was a row of cars ahead, he had to leap onto the hood of the first, then spring from hood to hood, drop off, turn slightly right, and go for the Chevy by the fence.

He was knocked forward, hard, and his breath leaped out of him.

He was hit again, painfully in the chest.

It took a moment to process, but he was lying between two cars, and there, standing above him, was the folding man, snapping at him with the two dead bodies like they were wet towels. That's what had hit him, the bodies, used like whips.

Jim found strength he didn't know he had, made it to his feet as Mr. Gordon's body slammed the ground near him. Then, as William's body snapped by his ear, just missing him, he was once more at a run.

The Chevy loomed before him. He made its hood by scrambling up on hands and knees, and then he jumped to the roof. He felt something tug at him, but he jerked loose, didn't stop moving. He sprang off the car top, grabbed at the fence, latching his arms over it. The fence cut into the undersides of his arms, but he couldn't let that stop him, so he kept pulling himself forward, and the next thing he knew, he was over the fence, dropping to the ground.

It seemed as if a bullet had gone up through his right foot, which he now realized was bare, and that the tug he had felt was the folding man grabbing at his foot, only to come away with a shoe. But of more immediate concern was his foot, the pain. There hadn't been any bullet. He had landed crooked coming over the fence, and his foot had broken. It felt like hell, but he moved on it anyway, and within a few steps he had a limp, a bad limp.

He could see the highway ahead, and he could hear the fence coming down behind him, and he knew it was over, all over, because he was out of gas and had blown a tire and his engine was about to blow too. His breath came in chops and blood was pounding in his skull like a thug wanting out.

He saw lights. They were moving very quickly down the highway. A big truck, a Mac, was balling the jack in his direction. If he could get it to stop, maybe there would be help, maybe.

Jim stumbled to the middle of the highway, directly into the lights, waved his arms, glanced to his left—

—and there it was. The folding man. It was only six feet away.

The truck was only a little farther away, but moving faster, and then the folding man was reaching for him, and the truck was a sure hit, and Jim, pushing off his good foot, leaped sideways and there was a sound like a box of dishes falling downstairs.

.   .   .

Jim felt the wind from the truck, but he had moved just in time. The folding man had not. As Jim had leaped aside, his body turned, through no plan of his own, and he saw the folding man take the hit.

Wood and springs and hinges went everywhere.

The truck bumped right over the folding man and started sliding as the driver tried to put on brakes that weren't designed for fast stops. Tires smoked, brakes squealed, the truck fishtailed.

Jim fell to the side of the highway, got up and limped into the brush there, and tripped on something and went down. He rolled on his back. His butt was in a ditch and his back was against one side of it, and he could see above it on the other side, and through some little bushes that grew there. The highway had a few lights on either side of it, so it was lit up good, and Jim could see the folding man lying in the highway, or rather he could see parts of it everywhere. It looked like a dirty hardware store had come to pieces. William, Gordon, and Chomps, lay in the middle of the highway.

The folding man's big torso, which had somehow survived the impact of the truck, vibrated and burst open, and Jim saw the birdlike thing rise up with a squawk. It snatched up the body of Mr. Gordon and William, one in either claw, used its beak to nab the dog, and ignoring the fact that its size was not enough to lift all that weight, it did just that, took hold of them and went up into the night sky, abruptly became one with the dark.

Jim turned his head. He could see down the highway, could see the driver of the truck getting out, walking briskly toward the scene of the accident. He walked faster as he got closer, and when he arrived, he bent over the pieces of the folding man. He picked up a spring, examined it, tossed it aside. He looked out where Jim lay in the ditch, but Jim figured, lying as he was, brush in front of him, he couldn't be seen.

He was about to call out to the driver when the truck driver yelled, "You nearly got me killed. You nearly got you killed. Maybe you are killed. I catch you, might as well be, you stupid shit. I'll beat the hell out of you."

Jim didn't move.

"Come on out so I can finish you off."

Great, Jim thought, first the folding man, and now a truck driver wants to kill me. To hell with him, to hell with everything, and he laid his head back against the ditch and closed his eyes and went to sleep.

.   .   .

The truck driver didn't come out and find him, and when he awoke the truck was gone and the sky was starting to lighten. His ankle hurt like hell. He bent over and looked at it. He couldn't tell much in the dark, but it looked as big as a sewer pipe. He thought when he got some strength back, he might be able to limp, or crawl out to the edge of the highway, flag down some help. Surely, someone would stop. But for the moment, he was too weak. He lay back again, and was about to close his eyes, when he heard a humming sound.

Looking out at the highway, he saw lights coming from the direction the trucker had come from. Fear crawled up his back like a spider. It was the black car.

The car pulled to the side of the road and stopped. The nuns got out. They sniffed and extended long tongues and licked at the fading night. With speed and agility that seemed impossible, they gathered up the parts of the folding man and put them in a sack they placed in the middle of the highway.

When the sack was full of parts, one nun stuck a long leg into the sack and stomped about, then jerked her leg out, pulled the sack together at the top and swung it over her head and slammed it on the road a few times, then she dropped the sack and moved back and one of the nuns kicked it. Another nun opened up and reached inside the sack and took out the folding man. Jim lost a breath. It appeared to be put back together and folded. The nun didn't unfold the folding man. She opened the trunk of the car and flung it inside.

And then she turned and looked in his direction, held out one arm and waited. The bird-thing came flapping out of the last of the dark and landed on her arm. The bodies of William and Gordon were still in its talons, the dog in its beak, the three of them hanging as if they were nothing heavier than rags. The nun took hold of the bird's legs and tossed it and what it held into the trunk as well. She closed the lid of the trunk. She looked directly where Jim lay. She looked up at the sky, turned to face the rising sun. She turned quickly back in Jim's direction and stuck out her long arm, the robe folding back from it. She pointed a sticklike finger right at him, leaned slightly forward. She held that pose until the others joined her and pointed in Jim's direction.

My God, Jim thought, they know I'm here. They see me. Or smell me. Or sense me. But they know I'm here.

The sky brightened and outlined them like that for a moment and they stopped pointing.

They got quickly in the car. The last of the darkness seemed to seep into the ground and give way to a rising pink; Halloween night had ended. The car gunned and went away fast. Jim watched it go a few feet, and then it wasn't there anymore. It faded like fog. All that was left now was the sunrise and the day turning bright.

Afterword

When I was growing up in the sixties, I began to hear about the black van, or sometimes the black car. I think it became a van because a lot of folks were scared them there hippies was gonna come get us. But the story goes back farther, and was not only a car, but a buggy, and sometimes a stranger on a horse, and sometimes just a shadow that walked, or so my grandmother told me in some old tales when she was in the mood. I heard it from other people, too, usually the black car part. I got to wondering. All right, let's say there is something bad in that car. What is it? The imagination took over.

About the Editors

Ellen Datlow has been an editor of short science fiction, fantasy, and horror for almost thirty years and has won multiple awards for her editing, including the World Fantasy Award, Locus Award, Hugo Award, International Horror Guild Award, the Shirley Jackson Award, and the Bram Stoker Award. She was named recipient of the 2007 Karl Edward Wagner Award, given at the British Fantasy Convention for "outstanding contribution to the genre." She lives in New York. For more information, check out her website: www.datlow.com.

Nick Mamatas is the author of two novels, *Under My Roof* and *Move Under Ground,* and over fifty short stories, many of which were collected in *You Might Sleep. . . .* His work has been nominated for both the Bram Stoker and International Horror Guild Awards. He does not believe in ghosts.